GodHunter
Book One of the Daemo[n]

A Donnie Rust Novel

For my Father who said I could
and for my Mother who said I should.

Godhunter
Book One of the Daemon Series

Copyright © 2013 by Littlegate Publishing LTD
All rights reserved. This book or any portion thereof may not be reproduced or used in any manner whatsoever without the express written permission of the publisher except for the use of brief quotations in a book review.

Printed in the United Kingdom

First Printing, 2013

ISBN: 978-1-291-38230-3

Cover pic: © Design "GodHunter" by Kerry Hugill

And with all our technology, our discoveries and our arrogance are we not just the cavemen of future generations?

1.

The room was cramped like a basement, the walls a dismal grey concrete. Unpainted steel rafters ran the length of the ceiling and in the four corners of the room pipes jutted out like the innards of a robotic monster and would rattle with a frustrating regularity every few minutes. Tuck sat at his tiny desk, thinking of how it was the sort of desk a high school student would have used: a two foot by two foot panel of wood screwed onto two U shaped pieces of metal and accompanied by an uncomfortable wooden chair that caught in the carpet every time he moved. Preposterously, this was his office; this was where he was meant to conduct his work. Which was not happening. Currently he was transfixed by the appearance of a cobweb in the corner of his room. A wonderfully complex, superbly unique design of the most fragile looking thread as if it were spun using the cracks in a mirror. Weaved by the most hardy and pioneering of spiders who had stowed away into this warren of tunnels and techno-babble set upon starting a life for itself at the bottom of the world, it was an inspiration. The other, far less inspiring reason he was not working was that he still did not know what he was supposed to be doing.

Tuck Bradley was not a scientist, he was not an explorer, he was not a technician or even vaguely interested in technology. He didn't understand the *dangers* of working in an underground facility under the ice and the ground that was under the ice, although people had tried explaining them to him. He didn't particularly want to be here, he hadn't volunteered for some mysterious adventure on the internet or even lost a bet and the only reason he was here, staring up at the corner of his office/chambers at a spider web, was that there was a large sum of money in his personal bank account that was happily gathering interest.

When you have no ambition in life, money is a brilliant incentive. However at the moment he felt like the ant that had forgotten its job.

The water pipe nearest to him suddenly shook itself as something gushed down it from above and things behind the concrete walls that he couldn't see rattled and popped.

He watched the pipe and wondered if it were water or something worse?

Would they have paid him so much money and then put him into a room next to the sewerage pipes? At this stage he wouldn't have doubted it. Things were different here.

Here, the term seemed alien to him now, the air tasted different *here*, pumped through the rooms via the relentlessly humming ventilation systems, turned metallic after the recycling processes. There wasn't any water in the toilets *here*, instead they used a vacuum pump that meant you had to seal the toilet bowl with a rubber suction cup before pushing the button or else it would get disastrous. *Here* you got headaches for no reason and *here* your nose got bunged up with more snot than you ever knew you could produce.

When the spider didn't make an appearance Tuck stood up and with his bare hand reached up and shattered the web, pulling the tatters from the corner in the selfish hope that such a destructive action would prompt the little creature's revisit, it would be good to see something else that wasn't meant to be here.

Sitting down again he pinched the collared front of the grey jumpsuit he was wearing and pulled it over his nose so that he looked like a five year old playing ninja. He sat like that for a moment until he started to smell himself and pulled his face out and resorted to drumming his fingers against the desk top. Like characters in a Star Trek film everyone seemed to wear a different colored jumpsuit. Blue was for the people who drank too much coffee and energy drinks and spent all of their time in that windowed-walled room with all the computers, while those people with their sleeves rolled up to their elbows and their faces covered in sweat and grime wore green. Grey was civilian, grey was *"no need for you now, wait until you're called,"* grey was just the color given to people purely so that they weren't mistakenly asked about something important.

He had nonetheless fallen into a routine, despite his biological clock being shot to hell because there was no natural lighting *here* and people worked shifts so he had to judge his day by the time alone. It was simple schedule of getting in the way of everyone until someone told him what to do or hopefully just sent him home.

Mornings began with him waking up and rolling off of the breadboard they called a bunk; he would put on a fresh jumpsuit, sit at his desk and stare at the wall (the spider had been a new development).

Afterwards, feeling somewhat more refreshed it was time for breakfast. While his three meter by two meter chamber was cramped and box-like it still required him to submit a palm print to get out. He didn't have a pass card or a key-fob he literally had to register his unique hand print onto a flat panel located on either side of the door and then, and only then, would it open.

This morning he did so with a casual resignation that caused the door to temporarily lock down and for an alarm to sound, muttering his aggravation he wiped his hand on his jumper and with a spiteful slowness put his hand onto the panel.

There was a moment where a red light above the liquid screen panel turned on and he held his breath afraid he was going to set things off again but the light turned green and the door slid open without any further fuss.

His chamber led onto a corridor and the corridor was always busy. Even when nobody was in this corridor it looked busy, there were pipes and wires snaking along the roof and stapled to the walls, security cameras, like round glass eyeballs peeked down from the ceiling and there was always the humming drone, like machinery behind the walls. In the three weeks that Tuck had been here he'd only ever seen this corridor empty once and he put that down to a coincidental bubble in the usual traffic. Blue and green jumpsuits marched up and down the corridor, clipboards or tools in their hands, everyone's eyes fixed on some point or task ahead of them. If they walked in pairs they discussed things quickly and decisively, often in a language Tuck couldn't understand and if they spoke in English they spoke about things he couldn't understand.

A rough idea was all he had about what was going on. They were excavating something, something under the ice within the very landmass of Antarctica, something that was worth a lot. Worth more than oil, coal, metals and diamonds. Something totally unique. That was it and that was what he'd been told directly by the man behind all of this. The billionaire Lynel Mason.

That was the man Tuck hoped he would bump into when he joined the flow of traffic, walking at pace down the corridor, keeping his eyes down and sidestepping people who were clearly more important than him. A little way down the corridor curved to the left, that was the other thing about this place, the corridors were tunnels without corners. He had spied two weeks earlier a group of greens working on some electrics behind a wall panel and as he'd nothing else to do he'd watched them and had noticed that the brickwork wasn't the usual Lego blocks he was familiar with but were triangular in shape so that they fitted into each other like flagstones. No corners, to better withstand the pressures of the four thousand meters of ice above them and God knew how many layers of rock.

He took the corner gingerly; he'd walked head on into too many blues or greens carrying equipment so he always looked first and ducked into the first room on the left. All the rooms were placed with regards to traffic, a much formulated method, your chamber, your shower facility, your kitchen and your canteen were all on the left so that you didn't have to cross anyone or get in the way. It was like living in an ant farm.
Initially, when he'd first stumbled into the kitchen starving like a beggar after getting frantically lost for an hour, it had presented him with the daunting challenge of working out what was food and what wasn't. Due to the pressure, the air or the cruel humor of those in charge all the meals came in shiny tinfoil like containers that had a single sticker of what was supposed to be the food inside. But from the get-go he suspected that although the sticker might have had a picture of a steaming chicken on it, it was probably not the same inside.

Now he was used to it. Now food was not about the taste but about filling his empty belly and getting the calories into his body.
Joining the back of a long cue of jumpsuits making their way passed the counters where ladies in white jumpsuits handed people tinfoil space-packages, Tuck surveyed the room for an empty chair and glancing quickly across the dozens of faces looking for one he might know well enough to speak with. His heart sank when he couldn't see anyone.

"Morning?" the part of the lady between her white jumpsuit and her white hairnet asked him when he got to the front of the cue.

"Yes, I'm morning," he said with a smile, which was not reciprocated.

"What would you like?" she asked, a tone of impatience on her voice. Judging by the look of her she'd been working a full shift already. Realizing he hadn't looked at this morning's menu Tuck floundered for a moment, "I don't suppose you have Corn Flakes do you?"

The lady looked pointedly at the long line of jumpsuits waiting behind him, "Not enough calories," she said bluntly, "You want chicken and potato or turkey?"

"I don't think it would make a difference either way," Tuck said with a forced smile.

He got a tinfoil space meal plonked on a tray, a cup of very thick coco that was so sweet it made his gums itch and went looking for a chair to sit at.

Like any canteen you got used to where to sit and who to sit with, while there was some jovial intermixing of the jumpsuit the blues had very little in common with the greens and preferred to not get too close. The blues being afraid that any dirt from the greens would no doubt contaminate their carefully sterile keyboards and the greens afraid that the blues might infect them with geekism.

Tuck smirked at the joke but the smile soon faded.

On the far end of the canteen a group of blues got up, tossed their used space meal packages into the trash and walked passed him without so much as a hello and Tuck quickly went to sit at one of the seats.

It was like the cafeterias in high schools or the canteens in prisons, the tables were all bolted down and rounded, lacking corners so that they could be easily cleaned and sterilized. Everything was plastic, the walls and ceiling were painted in a soothing magnolia and large screen televisions on the walls played various television stations from around the globe. You couldn't hear anything on them above the conversation noise but you could order ear phones.

Before tucking into his "chicken and potato" breakfast (which according to the sticker had 1003 calories), he looked around the room for anyone he recognized. There were others like him, people who sat by themselves reading books either traditionally or from their electronic pads, many people were on laptops, totally engrossed by what was happening on the screens while drinking coffee. Of the people he did recognize he unfortunately recognized the expressions on their faces and so didn't pursue any dialogue with them.

He unzipped his vacuum packed meal and was greeted with the smell of steamed cardboard.

"Tuck is it?" a voice said in front of him and he looked up at a green jumpsuit and saw a man he'd never met before.

"Um, yes, that's me," he answered.

"Do you mind if I sit with you?" the green asked as he dropped himself into a seat opposite him and flicked his tray unceremoniously onto the table. Some of Tuck's coco slopped over the rim.

"Um, no I don't mind," Tuck said under his breath, brandishing his knife and fork with the intention of getting *breakfast* down him.

"My name is Alan, it *is* Tuck isn't it?"

Tuck thought he'd already answered that and nodded again, "Pleased to meet you Alan. How do you know my name?"

Alan, who was about Tuck's age (mid-twenties), with a round face and a round, strong body with a growing bald patch on the top of his head and sparkling blue eyes, practically ripped open his space meal like a butcher going into a cow's stomach, "Oh I know everyone down here bro," he said stuffing his face with what looked like turkey, "Everyone. Gifted with names you see,"

Starting into his own meal he'd only gotten the first bit of chicken, or was it potato, into his mouth when Alan brandished his fork like a sword and pointed it at him, "Have you heard the news yet?"

Delaying swallowing, Tuck shook his head.

"They reckon that they've found it."

"Really?" said Tuck through a mouthful of masticated food matter.

Alan nodded and winked conspiratorially and swallowed hard, then, still wielding his fork, "I've just come from a twelve hour shift of trying to sort out the machinery- it's all screwed up."

Feeling like he'd fallen into deep water and couldn't touch the bottom Tuck finally swallowed and said, "Why what happened?"

Alan glanced over his shoulder and leaned forward on his arm, as if this was *need-to-know* information and said, "They've got some awesome machinery down here. Great big giant excavators the kind that they built to dig the London Underground, these things go through granite as if it were plaster, each machine is a three stories high and costs about a hundred million pounds to build, they-are-so-hardcore."

Tuck nodded, trying to formulate an idea of what they'd be looking for with things like that.

"These things have been running smoothly for six months now," (six months?!?), "And suddenly they hit something that they can't get through. Stops the machine dead in its tracks, it might as well have hit the bathtub of God."

Tuck nodded as if he knew exactly what Alan was on about, he speared what had the texture of a dead bird out of his space meal and put it into his mouth but when he chewed it the morsel tasted like rubber. His face grimaced automatically.

"The food's crap here isn't it?" Alan said, picking up on the facial tick and changing direction immediately, "To boost the calories on each of the meals they use high fat and saturated fats in everything. It means you don't starve but if you're down here for too long you'll end up looking like me!"

Alan chuckled at what he'd said and scoffed more of his food while Tuck tried to think of a convenient way of explaining he didn't know why he was here.

"Alan, you say you know who I am?" he asked.

"Aye," Alan said, using his fork like a shovel for the potatoes, "Tuck Bradley."

"It might sound like a silly question but do you know why I'm here?"

Alan took a moment and swallowed his last mouthful of food, put down his fork and looked Tuck straight in the eye. All merriment and twinkle was gone and replaced by the look of someone who's just realized they are in the presence of a time waster. His cheeks moved as his tongue searched his teeth for any remaining food. After a moment he said, "You don't know why you're here?"

Incredibly embarrassed Tuck shrugged, "I've been here for three weeks now and not once have I been told."

"Have you asked someone?"

Tuck laughed exasperatedly, "Yes, everyone, anyone who'd talk to me and none of them seem to really know or want to tell me. I haven't even been able to work out what's going on here. What are you looking for?"

Alan contemplated telling Tuck, it was obvious on his face, and Tuck stomach clenched and then sagged in disappointment when the big green said, "I don't think I'm the right person to tell you broheim. If you haven't been informed yet then there's a reason for it."

He got up to leave and Tuck sagged back into his chair immediately despondent, but before he walked away he said, "I wouldn't worry though broheim, you'll find out soon enough. Mr. Mason wouldn't let anyone down here without a reason."

"Maybe it's a case of mistaken identity," Tuck suggested, poking some of his food with his fork.

"No. If you're here it's because you're needed," Alan said, "Drink your coco before it gets cold."

That was the highlight of three weeks and this was, realistically, the sum of his morning, afternoon and evening routine, sitting in the cafeteria waiting. It was the only place where he could sit down out of the way and not feel like he *should* be running somewhere with something in his hands, and here he could listen in on some of the conversations. Now that he knew a little something he didn't feel so much in the dark and felt a little more confident that he could work out why he was here. But at that moment he did the same thing he'd done on most of his days, he sat at the table taking his time to eat through his high calorie meal and watched the jumpsuits.

Hours later, while Tuck was staring at another space meal for his dinner Alan returned to the canteen for what would have been his breakfast, looking well rested with a fresh jumpsuit - judging by the twinkle in his eye he was one of those people who would work hard and merrily in any surroundings- either that or he was simply high. He grabbed his breakfast pack and bee-lined directly to Tuck.

"Any news yet?" he asked with a tone of old friends picking up a thread of a conversation.

Tuck who was weary after a whole day of sitting around and doing nothing but thinking, took a breath and said, "Judging by the television screens the world carries on, just without us."

Unlike Tuck, Alan didn't care what his food was as long as it was getting into his belly and he spoke around mouthfuls of potato and bird when he said, "You talk as if we're on the moon broheim. You need to lighten up."

Tuck dropped his fork, "How can I lighten up, I feel like a prisoner here,"

"Well you're not," Alan said fixing him with a severe look, "You can leave whenever you want."

Tuck folded his arms, "Hardy har har, very funny, it's minus seventy degrees up there and there's no sunlight."

Alan smiled and carried on eating.

Tuck shrugged and returned to his meal, sure that Alan would say something eventually. He hadn't looked at the sticker on the packet of his meal and that may have been a mistake, he couldn't tell what this was, except that it was dry and tasted the same as breakfast. This was what five thousand calories a day tasted like.

"What's your field then?" Alan asked.

"My field?" Tuck said, "Well, I'm a martial arts instructor I suppose,"

Alan took this in his stride. Of course a professional martial arts instructor is exactly the kind of person needed in Antarctica. The round, green man said, "That explains your body," he said, then patted his rotund belly, "Get out of here while you can. So you're a martial arts instructor, you do anything else?"

"I pack chocolate boxes in Fakenham to meet the bills,"

"Fakenham?"

"It's in England, where are you from?"

"I'm Dutch actually, but I travel a lot with work. I'm a doctor of engineering, that's what I do. But don't call me Dr. or anything like that."

"It's a nice title to have."

"So my mother thought, so with your martial arts do you compete?"

Tuck shrugged a shoulder, "I did go professional for a bit then I opened my own school and the financial crisis hit and I lost a lot of students so I started temping, been fairly busy with all that for a long time."

"I used to do karate as a child,"

"I think everyone does karate as a child," Tuck said, "It's as crucial to growing up as learning how to kick a soccer ball."

Alan laughed, and put down his fork, he'd demolished his space meal with the same ferocity as a pig only with a milder manner and less food flying around everywhere, it was a marvel to watch. Tuck stuck what he had decided was lasagna in his mouth and chewed speculatively.

"Family? Kids?" Alan asked.

"Nah, never had the time. You?"

"I have seven children," Alan said with wide eyes as if the prospect scared him.

"Wow. You don't have a television then?"

"Oh yes we do now, only way to keep the kids quiet! Why do you think I like working here, wife can't hassle me when I'm in Antarctica!"

Tuck chuckled. God he'd missed social interaction, he missed laughing over something that wasn't actually funny but was really just an opportunity to laugh and Alan seemed to be really good at that. He had the sort of manner that suggested he was your friend, whether you knew him or not.

"Look also, I'm sorry about earlier," Alan said, "I was short with you and I didn't mean it. It had been a long shift."

"I understand," Tuck said just before he got a whiff of himself. It's incredible what a smell, sitting around doing nothing, can develop. He needed to have a shower soon, "I'm glad working here affects someone else too."

"But you're not working," Alan said. Having pushed his tray aside he was able to use his hands to express himself which he did with an alarming flamboyancy, "You just sit here all day watching the people. You might as well borrow a laptop and get some pornography."

Tuck was abashed, "Like you said, I'm here because I'm going to be useful for something. I don't know what for. I'm just waiting."

"Waiting for what?" Alan asked, leaning forward onto his elbows.

"For Lynel Mason,"

Alan's eyes went up as if what Tuck had said was absurd and ridiculous, but Tuck was quick to explain, "I was recruited by him directly."

"Really?" Alan said with obvious surprise, "That is impressive I've only heard of the man by reputation, but that's amazing. What was he like?"

"Out of place to be fair, he came into a dojo where I was training about half a dozen boxers on the bags, we're all covered in sweat and one of the guys has a nose bleed and he walks in wearing a suit that probably cost more than anything I've ever owned. Walks right up to me and says that he has a job offer."

"Just like that?"

Tuck shrugged, "Yeah. He asked me to meet him at his office the following morning- wasn't the most extravagant of offices but then again it was an office in Norwich that he had because he wanted an office in Norwich- I don't think there was any other reason than that. He explained to me that there was some travel and that I would be away for a long period of time but that I would be well compensated. He even offered to pay me some money up front."

"Really? How much?" Alan asked.

"I'm embarrassed to tell you," Tuck said.

Alan shrugged, "So he just offered you a job and paid you some money and then you what? Hopped on a ship and came here?"

"Well no, he said that my job would become apparent when I arrived here and that in the meantime I was to just enjoy knowing I was getting paid. He said that I would be called upon when needed but that because timing was important that I would do some waiting."

"There you go, he warned you would be doing some waiting and yet you complain now?"

"I've been here three weeks, I'm being paid to be here, but I have no idea how to justify being paid... what if it comes up at the end that there's been a mistake and because I'm only one of several thousand here that I've just been ignored?"

"No, like I said that's not the case," Alan said, knocking his knuckles against the table, "You are here for a reason. You've been told to wait so wait. You won't be waiting long."

"There is another thing that's been worrying me Alan," Tuck said, "I was hoping you could shed some light on it?"

"I will do my best,"

"What are we looking for? Is it some sort of energy source, a new oil reserve maybe? Something that requires secrecy because I'd never heard of this place and I'm fairly sure it would have been somewhere on the internet, I don't even know who's paying the money into my account. It's all very hush-hush, what is it that we're looking for?"

"You mean what is it we've found?" Alan corrected him.

"So we have found it?"

He knew something was up, he could tell by the movements in the traffic of people coming into the canteen, people chat when they're eating food and the conversation had been around *something* that had been found.

"Yes. Something that is very important and although I have no idea why you're here if it's not for that then maybe Mr. Mason just fancied having a fighter on board. Who knows with these billionaires? Listen, just stay sharp and keep your head up broheim. I'm going to take a shit."

And then just like that Alan was up and away.

Back in his chamber Tuck gathered the stuff he'd need, a towel, bath bag, a fresh jumpsuit and made his way to the showers. These were exactly like at the gyms, a long line of shower cubicles with soap and shampoo dispensers and he had to give credit where it was due because the showers were excellent.

He showered, shaved, got dressed and returned to his chamber prepared to sleep. He closed the door behind him, waited for it to lock, dropped his stuff in the hamper and climbed onto the bunk and was just about to switch off the lights when he spotted a yellow post-it note on his desk.
MEET ME AT THE KITCHEN AT 6AM

At 6am Tuck stepped into the kitchen and noticed there was a permeable difference in the attitude of the place and it was clear why. Lynel Mason was sitting at one of the tables drinking a cup of tea and looking particularly dashing in a grey jumpsuit. Mason was in his seventies but looked ten years older. His dark hair was white and his face was weathered from his many exploits but his eyes were sharp. He stood when Tuck entered and walked up to him his hand extended.

"Good morning Mr. Mason," Tuck said, shaking the man's hand.

"Please call me Mason," the billionaire insisted, "Everyone does. I know you haven't eaten but I've taken the liberty of having our meals delivered."

Tuck looked around and the faces all watching him, he smiled at Mason, "Are we not eating here?"

"No. But I understand this is the only place you know so I thought we would meet here," he started walking out the door, "Come along."

Tuck followed hurriedly.

Walking with Mason through the corridors was like following an ambulance through traffic, people moved out his way as if afraid to touch him and he walked at a pace that made Tuck have to take double strides.

"Mason," Tuck said, "I've been hoping to have the chance to speak with you."

"I would have been surprised if you didn't," Mason said, leading him into a corridor that ended with a pair of double doors that Tuck had seen jumpsuits go through, "I take you out of your world, away from your life and everything you know. Fly you to the bottom of the planet and put you underground and then haven't spoken to you for almost a month," he pushed open the double doors and Tuck hurried in behind him, "I'm surprised you haven't left by now."

"Well, we are in Antarctica," Tuck reminded him lamely. The double doors simply led into another corridor that seemed to bisect into three at the end, the air immediately smelt different here, dusty.

Mason was already marching his way down the corridor his voice echoing against the concrete walls, "Yes indeed, I am *glad* you appreciate the adventure we have here. This is fantastic isn't it?"

"You still haven't told me why I'm here."

"Oh yes," Mason said, pausing for a moment so that he could slap Tuck on the back, give a warming smile and then continue walking, Tuck realized he would never be able to anticipate this man, "I am sure that the money currently sitting in your bank account has been gaining a considerable amount of interest so I am less than sorry about dangling you about like this, but it was of such great importance that you be here... you see Tuck you are so very important."

Just then Tuck realized who Mason reminded him of, Bill Nighy. If Bill Nighy were ten years younger and able to box, so perhaps a Bill Nighy on PCP.

"Why though?" and he was running to keep up again. Mason led them down the third corridor on the right, passed several jumpsuits in green and some even in blue and then through a very average looking door on the right, down two flights of steel and concrete stairs where the air was so cold it made Tuck's skin crawl. At the bottom of the stairs they entered what looked like an underground parking lot. Complete with an asphalt floor and a lot of concrete and pillars. Thick black cables snaked across the floor, giant heaters hummed; there were banks of computers on one side with a two dozen blue jumpsuits. More greens were walking around with hard hats, everyone was yelling over the deafening hum of the heaters which did little to change the temperature. It was still freezing. Mason led him directly to the right into a small port-a-cabin in which there were several hangers lined with thick reflective jackets. Mason closed the door behind Tuck and shook his head, "Those heaters make such a racket. They're twenty years old and eat petrol like you wouldn't believe!"

He thumbed through the jackets hanging up and selected one for Tuck, "Put this on, it's extra lined, stores in your own body heat, just don't run in it or you will melt."

Tuck put it on and shivered with delight and the heavy warmth of it.

Mason slid into one of his own and took out a pair of thick gloves from the pockets. Tuck looked into the pair of pockets on his jacket and found a pair of gloves too which, when he pulled them over his hands were immediately warm to his icy fingers.

"I would have thought you'd be too busy to come and find me yourself," Tuck said, "With the new developments and what not?"

Mason gave him a sly look, "In all honesty I was desperate to get out of here, I've been down here for almost a week. People think its strange when the owner comes to this level but I like it, gives me something to do. And fish all you like Tuck I'm not giving anything away you're going to have to see it for yourself."

"I wasn't fishing," Tuck answered defensively.

Mason smiled knowingly and said, "Right. You won't be able to hear me through there so pay careful attention- you're about to see something that cannot be spoken about outside these walls to anyone. What you are about to experience is going to change your life forever and you will want to tell someone, in fact you could probably make millions if you did tell someone, as it is I am paying you an excruciatingly large sum of money to keep you happy and quiet but if you talk to *anyone* I will have you killed."

The man said it with a smile that removed any shred of doubt in Tuck's mind that this man meant what he said. He probably had snipers priming on him at this minute, "I understand," Tuck said, feeling that he was now too deep to try and turn back... and it *was* a very large sum of money.

"Good!" Mason said jovially, "Follow me now."

Again there was a sense of everyone doing something, Tuck spied some faces he recognized from the kitchen but not many, indicating just how many people were involved in this working around the clock. Flood lights illuminated the expansive car park, there were jeeps and trams being driven carrying machinery and what looked like rubble. Everyone was dressed in extra warm gear so that Tuck couldn't tell anyone apart. When his ears began to burn in the cold he pulled up the jacket's hood and became one of them. With the hood up and the noise from the heaters he couldn't hear anything and had to keep Mason in sight or else he'd just loose him in the crowd of people.

From the car park they walked down a ramp with metal railings in the center and a giant pulley system, at the bottom of the ramp there was

another bay of doors covered in a decent layer of frost, some large men with the stature of guards stood on either side of the doors and Mason communicated with them quickly using sign language and jabbed a finger in Tuck's direction. The guard took off his glove, and pressed a hand against the panel- he then quickly put his glove back on and shook out his hand.
Beyond the door there was a small room with plastic walls and as the door sealed shut behind him Tuck was overwhelmed by the warmth in the room that stole his very breath from his lungs. The room itself was only three meters by three and furnished with only a railing. Mason handed him a hanger and they took of their coats. In the silence of this room Tuck's ears were ringing and Mason had to repeat himself, "I said: are you ready to find out why you are here?"
Tuck hung up his coat and thought, good a time as any.
"Is this a sterilized room or something?" he asked.
"No, it's a glorified wardrobe," Mason said with a shrug, "The plastic walls were cheap and available and people were tired of getting dust in their jumpers,"
The light in the room was reflected off the walls so Tuck couldn't really see beyond, but he could make out rock and stone walls and rubble on the floor.
Mason walked to the exit of the plastic room, stopped and turned around, "Tuck. I've asked everyone to get out of here so that we can have some privacy."
Without any elaboration he opened the door and walked through. Tuck followed. It was a passage that had been cut straight into the rock at a slight decline and it looked like a mining shaft, with large chunks of rock and debris lying around the floor and steel supports holding up the ceiling. Again Tuck saw the strangely shaped brickwork that was used to as supporting structures. The rock was given a yellowish glow by the standing lamps and the air was warm and dusty and Tuck kept coughing. The shaft was only thirty meters deep and in some areas the ceiling was low enough that Tuck could touch it with his hands, "How far underground are we?"
"Why are you whispering?" Mason asked.
"I don't know," Tuck answered.
Mason shrugged, "We're about six kilometers deep, which also includes

about five kilometers of ice above us. You're getting closer to Antarctica than anyone else you've ever met."

Tuck thought about that, "That's very cool."

"Oh yes," Mason agreed.

At the bottom of the shaft there was a hole leading to somewhere considerably darker. It looked as though the shaft they were in had broken into another chamber. Mason lead the way quickly, walking down a set of steel stairs into a…subway tunnel?

Tuck's mind wheeled when he thought he was in the London Underground, the tunnel was large and round and very long, big enough for a couple of subway trains to fly through, it was lit up by floodlights, to his right there was a wall made up of circular bits of metal and serrated edges and he suddenly realized that was the tunneling machine that Alan had been speaking about. The thing was huge!

"Impressive isn't it?" Mason asked.

Tuck nodded emphatically turning around, "Yeah it's massi- what the hell?"

The tunneler was impressive but to Tuck's left what he saw was even more so. Scarily so. What is the only thing more impressive than a giant digging robot that could grind its way through solid granite that's been compacted and compressed into diamond hard rock by five kilometers of ice? The thing that stops it and Tuck was looking at it.

It was a wall of metal.

A giant wall of metal, polished to a perfect shine it was three stories in diameter and as round as the tunneler's head, so the machine collided with this and ground so hard that it chewed away all the rock around it until forming an almost perfect circle while not so much as leaving a scratch on the surface of the metal?

"What is that?" Tuck asked.

Mason was once again walking away from him, moving towards the wall, Tuck ran to keep up, "Mr. Mason?"

"Mason,"

"Yes Mason, what *is* that? Is that what you're looking for some new sort of metal?"

Mason stopped, shrugged, "Would have been nice if it was, but no, but considering that what we're looking for has never been seen before finding something we didn't expect that's never been seen before was a fairly good start."

"So what it is?"

Mason thought about it for a moment, "Don't honestly know," he started walking again, "We haven't been able to take a sample of it yet."

"I appreciate that you wanted us to be alone but isn't finding what this is more important?"

They stopped at the surface of it which could have been a mirror, a single sheet of mirrored glass, aside from some water and chemical stains and the odd fleck of stone it was flawless and undamaged.

"Of course it's important," Mason answered, "But we haven't been able to take a sample yet."

Tuck didn't understand and Mason, saw his expression reflected before them, "You need a bit of it to take a sample and we haven't been able to even scratch the thing and none of our chemical tests work. The only way we know it's here is because well-" he rapped his knuckles against its surface and it gave a highly sonorous ting, "And because our computers go ape shit when they get near to it. One of my technicians, Paul Peabody, do you know him? Skinny guy, has terrible posture? No. Well, he tried to do an ultrasound on it and damn near blew up his machine."

Tuck didn't know what to think, his mind was just a blank, "Okay you've got to tell me what I'm doing here now Mason because I haven't the foggiest."

"Oh," the billionaire, the man who'd orchestrated this entire secret fiasco, "*You're* going to get me inside it."

Tuck laughed. Mason laughed.

"No seriously," Tuck said.

Mason laughed some more, and said, "Well that is why you're here Tuck, I wouldn't have paid you all that money and flown you out here in first class and shown you this if I didn't absolutely know what you were needed for. This is not a gamble, it has all been very carefully planned so do you want me to explain *everything* to you right now or do you want to just trust me on this that I know what I'm doing and that you're entire life and that of your ancestors has led up to this one single point."

"You can tell me later," Tuck agreed.

"Excellent!" Mason cried, he left Tuck to stare at his reflection and went to a dark container against the wall that was disturbingly coffin shaped with his company logo printed on the front. When he opened the

lid it made a hiss and he returned with two wet suits and helmets.
Tuck's eyebrows lifted in question.

"Whatever is behind this wall has been there since before the last ice-age- the air in there will be most likely unbreathable."

"Like what happened when they first got into the pyramids?"

"Yes very similar, just a thousand times worse. So we put these on."

Again without any further explanation or warning Mason unzipped his jumpsuit and took it off, standing there in his CKs he said, "Come on, no time to waste."

"I'm not wearing underwear," Tuck explained gently.

Mason laughed, "Yes when looking back on the day we made history I will certainly remember the fact you had no underwear on. Go on, don't be shy."

Tuck nonetheless turned around and unzipped his jumpsuit and started getting into the wet suit. It wasn't easy, the suit was made out of a stretchy fabric that was thick and rubbery while still being flexible and it clung to his body so to get it on involved a lot of pulling and jumping around. They also had booties of the same material at the bottom all attached and it felt like he was barefoot. It took twenty minutes to get into them.

"This material hasn't even hit the market yet," Mason said, turning his arms around in wide circles and bringing his knees up, "Very lucky to get it. Now this is where it gets tricky."

"How do you mean?" Tuck answered, trying to zip up the suit at the back, Mason helped him saying:

"You're going to have to touch it with your bare skin, so may I suggest you unzip the glove… like this… right… here we go and then put the glove back on before you come in."

Tuck fixed the man with the strongest look he dared give a billionaire who had already threatened to have him killed.

"You know how to install confidence Mason,"

"Yes thanks, oh shit!"

Tuck almost jumped out of his skin and his wetsuit, "What is it?"

Mason looked distraught, "I forgot about our breakfast are you hungry?"

Tuck blinked, permitting himself enough time to wonder if elsewhere in the world was there someone else that was going through a similar situation like this and wondering why?

The wetsuits had headpieces that when pulled over had built in goggles and breathing apparatus, it yanked his hair to the roots when he tried to adjust it.

Together, standing in front of the giant mirror they looked like futuristic ninjas.

"You can talk normally," Mason said, but his voice came in through Tuck's ears, "Now this part should be quite simple. This wall is like a box and it is what is inside the box that we want to get to. It is security locked to prevent access or exit."

"Okay, but how is me touching it going to help?"

"I shall explain the details later, but put simply it is registered to your DNA. Placing your hand on it is all that it should take."

Tuck wanted to look sarcastic but Mason couldn't see his face, so he put his hands on his hips, "Really?"

Mason shrugged, "I've been right so far, so I'd hate to break a winning streak. Go on give it a go what's the worst that could happen?"

Tuck rolled his eyes and watched himself as he approached the giant mirrored wall, his bare right hand extended, palms forward his fingers splayed. His fingertips touched it first, it had a cool surface and when his palm pressed against it he found it to be entirely smooth, indeed like a mirror.

"Anything?" Mason asked.

Tuck shook his head but even he was disappointed. What had Mason expected someone's face to appear out of the metal and say, *Who disturbs my slumber?*

Sighing he pushed away from the metal, but instead of him moving backwards pushing only imbedded his hand into the metal.

"Look at that," Mason said.

He was. Was the wall some sort of mercury? He applied a small amount of pressure and his hand sank further into it until it was covered up to the wrist, distorting his image around it. It was cold, slipping between his fingers but the sensation bothered him and he pulled his hand back and in response a huge gap suddenly popped open.

It scared the crap out of both of them and he and Mason jumped backwards and were met by an extraordinary gust of wind that took them off their feet, sprawling them onto the ground. Tuck pushed himself onto his elbows and looked in front of him and saw a doorway in the giant mirror. It was a very large doorway, the height of two men and half as wide with a curved arch and possessing a clear decorative and functional design.

Mason leapt to his feet like a school boy and started dancing around while Tuck remained where he was, acting cool and thinking to himself job well done while Mason sang his praises and made a series of whooping noises into his ear while punching the air.

Pandemonium immediately ensued with a stampede of jumpsuits suddenly appearing and once again Tuck found himself shoved in a corner away from the excitement. Forgotten or ignored he ended up standing by the container coffin and watching as more people in black wetsuits stampeded into the tunnel and poured through the chamber door like rats running through a tunnel. They brought in standing lamps and great rolls of cable, computers and extractor fans, structural equipment and pulleys for heavier equipment. Assuming he would once again be collected when he was needed and that since he was somehow able to open the chamber in the first place that he was now indelibly involved, he sat down beside the crate and played a game of pebble toss. He wasn't entirely clued up on deep-terra excavations but he'd seen a documentary about the origins of the Egyptian mummy's curse, where people died after invading a tomb, and it was mostly due to breathing in air that hadn't been moved for centuries with this in mind he kept his mask on and refused to move it until he was told to. That being said the closeness of it was giving him a splitting headache and he was tired of hearing the breathing apparatus hissing every time he took a breath.

What was in that chamber?

He would have liked to have been able to peek inside but didn't see an opportunity to do so without getting in the way. Maybe it was just the case that his purpose had been served and he would be shipped off home soon? He wouldn't mind but he hated sitting around waiting.

He was a doer, a martial artist. He taught people how to take action and be empowered and he hated being shoved to the side and forgotten. He felt like a five year old at a grown up party, expected to sit on the sidelines and be seen but not heard. It infuriated him.

"Tuck you there?" it was Mason's voice coming through his ear piece.

"Yes, I'm here," Tuck answered.

"Okay good to know," Mason said, "Where are you?"

"I'm outside where you left me," Tuck answered, more rudely than he intended and then added, "By the container, just sitting here doing my best to stay out of the way."

There was some talking on Mason's side, he assumed it wasn't intended for him because it wasn't in English, at a guess he would have thought it was Danish and sounded like Viking talk. Afterwards Mason said, "Tuck we're busy setting things up in this side, the air isn't breathable yet so why don't you head back inside and have a shower. I will come up myself and meet you in about an hour or so and we can have a talk over coffee. It's been a hell of a morning and you've been great but you must be starving. Grab some breakfast yeah?"

Tuck pushed himself to his feet, "You're the boss."

But Mason wasn't listening.

He was starving and the realization came with a gnawing hunger that damn near doubled him over. He couldn't find his jumpsuit anywhere he looked so, hugging the walls to keep out of the way he walked upstream of the traffic of wetsuits until he got to the plastic room where he picked one of the jackets that were hanging up at random, there were so many there now it was impossible to count or to know which one was his originally, they were hanging up, slung over the railings, lying in bundles on the floor. He slipped it on over his wetsuit and found that the door opened on this side easily enough. The guards on the other end didn't so much as look at him as he walked out and through the large expanse of asphalt. More activity was going on here, people with such busy expressions while all he wanted was some breakfast, some coffee and a long, long shower. At the port-a-cabin he hung up his jacket, went through the doors and up the stairs and only at the top as he entered into the corridor where the air was once again stale and recycled did he think about taking off his ninja mask.

"Oh that's better," he said, turning his head up to the ceiling and taking a deep breath.

"Hey broheim," a familiar voice said nearby, Tuck turned and saw Alan with a great loop of cable slung over his shoulder and a dirt streak across his forehead walking passed him down the corridor, "You finally

found out why you're here?"
Tuck shrugged, "Still more questions than answers."
"Welcome to Mason's world."

He grabbed a jumpsuit from his room and had a very long, self-indulgent shower where he washed himself twice to get rid of the smell of the rubber-material of the wetsuits. It made him smell like some sex toy. After that he climbed into the jumpsuit which was as comfortable as a duvet compared to his ninja wetsuit which he threw into his room on his way to the kitchen.

Perhaps he'd timed it perfectly, or maybe everyone else was too busy but when he got into the kitchen there wasn't a line at all and only a few chairs and tables were occupied. He ordered two breakfasts- not caring what was what and picked a table from where he could see the entrance.

He was quite looking forward to speaking to Mason. He had taken a shine to the man, and it was difficult not to be friendly with a friendly billionaire. Even if that billionaire had threatened him with his life, a fact that Tuck really didn't think he could overemphasize.

By the time he'd finished his second breakfast his belly was well and truly stuffed and he pushed the tray away from him and leant backwards, stretching out on the chair and watching some of the news on the television screens, trying to work out what was being said and what the stories were about.

Basketball in Sweden or something of the sort.

True to his word Mason did come and find him in the canteen, if only an hour and a half later, but the billionaire looked freshly showered and there was an incandescent gleam in his eye as he sidled over to Tuck and sat down on the chair opposite him. The man beat a quick drum pattern on the table top and said, *"What a morning!"*

Tuck couldn't help it, this sort of excitement was contagious, he smiled, "That was unbelievable."

"You were unbelievable," Mason said pointing a finger at Tuck, "You were fantastic."

"I just gave you a hand," Tuck said.

Mason applauded him, "Maybe, but do you realize that this facility employs over a thousand staff, costs me three billion dollars a year to fund and keep secret *and* has taken my entire life to organize and we had literally hit a wall with as far as we could go," he shook his head, "I daren't think where we would be if you hadn't been here."

He leaned around and very easily got the attention of the kitchen staff who sent someone to bring around fresh coffee.

"You've got to tell me what happened there Mason," Tuck said, "Being in the dark is driving me insane."

Mason's cheeks had to hold his smile in before it broke off his face, "I promised you I would tell you but there is an easier way of doing so. First though I want you to come and see what you've helped us find."

"Now?"

"No no, not *right* now, they haven't gone anywhere in half a million years they can wait a little longer and if I don't get a coffee I will kill someone."

"Okay, so coffee and then we go?"

"Yes and you will find your destiny."

2.
10 years later

Gregory Maines Tower, or as locals referred to it "That Damned Big Spike," rose out of the Durban skyline like a giant nail. At eighty seven floors it was the tallest building in the city and played home to some of the wealthiest people in the world, 70% of which arrived via helicopter rather than road. It was the heart of the ever expanding Sky City, the interconnecting system of sky bridges and platforms that connected the upper fourteen stories of the tallest buildings in the city together, practically sealing them off from anyone who lived or worked below, casting that part of the city in shadow.

Indeed, while resembling a nail, it was a work of architectural genius- where the apartments (so sized to fit two on every floor) could receive full benefit of not only the sunshine of Durban but the gorgeous oceanic views and the residents of said apartments could enjoy the luxury of such vistas without the violence that could be found on the streets below. Depending on which papers you read and on which floor you were on, there were a lot of good and bad things to say about the Gregory Maines Tower and Sky City.

Rayne had read them all and after spending enough time under the fourteenth, she was simply thunder struck that she had been invited to the top.

The top.

On the internet there were images of some of the apartments and offices featured in the Gregory Maines, as futuristically modern and luxurious as something out of an epic science fiction film like Star Wars or Star Trek. It was a make believe world with a price tag that did not so much draw a line between the classes as blasted it out with several tons of dynamite.

And somehow she had bridged the void and was going to the top.

One little internet video. Thanks to one little internet video she was receiving on average a hundred emails a day from people offering her fame and money. She had ignored them all, well, that wasn't exactly true. She had been so busy with other endeavors that she had not looked at her computer for over a week and when she finally did she was greeted with a dam-break of a thousand emails.

Emails were a regular thing, notifications of social media updates, fans wanting to be "friends" with her online, stalkers wanting to be more, she had developed a keen eye for the sort of emails she should delete and the few that could very well be worth reading. The many had been whittled down to a few and of those only one of them really caught her eye and it simply read: MEETING AT THE GREGORY MAINES TOWER, 9AM, TUESDAY 10TH APRIL.

She had felt panicky and flushed. It said a lot that her first thought was that she was in trouble, that somehow, somewhere she had offended the wrong person although she couldn't think where or how.

Minutes earlier she had been chasing a fly around her apartment with a flip-flop and now her finger was visibly shaking when she clicked on the mouse and brought up the email window. Unable to breathe she read the email text in its entirety.

Words like, "invite," and "discuss" and "pleasure" stuck out like marshmallows in a pot of gravy and didn't make any sense at all. She checked the email address the sender had used, copied the website address and searched for it online. It took her straight to an appropriate website.

She read it through again with a noticeable cold, empty feeling and then sent off a tentative email in response and within a minute of hitting the send button she'd received a phone call, her number was on her email signature, and it was confirmed. Her pass card was being sent in the mail.

The pass card was the start, when it had arrived she'd sat on her bed in her tiny apartment staring at it and feeling sick. It was like holding the winning lottery ticket and realizing just how far she lived from the store and how many ways there was to lose it. She refused to put the piece of plastic down in case something happened to it. What if she dropped it, what if she lost it? What if a pigeon flew in through the window and grabbed it and flew off. She put it into a safety deposit box and attached the key to her wrist bracelet so that she wouldn't loose it and spend the following two days playing with it constantly to make sure it was still there.

Rayne lived on the seventh floor on Baker Street, in a tiny studio apartment that made hotel rooms look gratuitously spacious with a breathtaking view of the brick and mortal rear end of a grocery store. While she lived in a city famous for its sunshine the only daylight she could enjoy was between the hours of 8am and 10am and that was for a one meter squared patch directly in front of the window. Her computer screen was her only television and she didn't own a microwave.

Passcards like this were valuable to a lot of people and if anyone found out that she had one she would become a target, it was a giver. There were some people who would do just about anything to get into that building and she lived in South Africa.

On the day of the meeting she drove through the city feeling exposed, imagining that snipers were aiming for her at every intersection and that every other driver was an assassin who would either try and run her off the road or pull a gun on her the moment she stopped, her heart was liberally hammering against the inside of her ribs when she pulled off the main road onto a slanted driveway leading into the secure parking complex. A high security public entrance was the only way to get into the Sky City from the road level.

She slowed to a halt at a line of six one metre tall bollard poles that were blocking the entrance like the fangs of a seafloor monster-fish. Peering around out the windows to see if there was somewhere or someone to show her passcard too she was caught off guard when the six poles sudden snapped down with the speed of a lamprey pulling into its shell. The speed of movement was akin to an attack but in reverse and she knew she wasn't going to drive over them in case she got skewered!

In the few seconds she had been stopped a long line of cars had formed behind her and they were already honking.

"I don't know where to go," she said, holding up her passcard as if that explained everything.

The bollards snapped back up, again completely without warning and the loud *clang!* caused her to cry out. The people behind her were now leaning on their horns.

"You're not helping!" she shouted at them. Through her rearview mirror she saw the man in the driver seat behind her gesturing furiously with his hands as if he were trying to fan a fire, indicating that she should move forward but she couldn't, she was blocked. More frantic seconds passed during which Rayne couldn't think and big hot, horrible lumps of emotion were getting stuck in her throat. When a purple faced man clambered out of the car behind her she slammed down the locking mechanism to her car and prepared for the worst.

He was big, with dark, tightly curly black hair and a strong Arabian feel, wearing a brown jumper and a pair of jeans and although he looked absolutely livid when he saw her he took a breath and said through the window Rayne had frantically wound up in his face, "Madam, the computer can sense your pass card," he pointed at the plastic card she was holding up like a crucifix to a vampire, "Drive forward and it will let you in."

Rayne blinked, "Oh."
The man smiled and nodded as if asking if she understood. She smiled, said thank you a dozen times before she could stop herself and with shaky hands performed a hill start and slowly approached the fish teeth. True to his word the bollards *snapped* down and she accelerated with a screech of tires to get over them fast.

Judging by the standard of cars parked in this complex her twelve year old sky blue Hyundai Getz warranted her being banned, thrown out or shot. Every car she saw was literally a month or two old and the parking spaces had been made wider just to fit them in, the car parking floor was wet with soap suds from the attendants who washed all the cars throughout the day and guards patrolled every floor with a canine expression in their eyes.

She had been instructed to park in the visitors section but even there she left her diminutive and incredibly economic car next to a veritable yacht of the automobile world. When her father was alive and she was younger and would use to sit in the back seat holding onto her seat belt and listening to her dad talk, he would often ask, after seeing one on the road, where such expensive cars come from and where were they kept? She said a small prayer to her dad just letting him know that she'd just discovered the answer.

With her passcard clutched in her hand she walked the length of the parking lot towards the elevator bay on the far end, swallowing hard and valiantly ignoring the looks she received from the guards and the washing attendants. Did the valets even look down on her in here?

At the elevator a security guard, or rather an "immaculately dressed" security guard who was too handsome to be a real security guard who nonetheless had a very real gun on his hip stepped up to her before she got within reach of the elevator and asked in what sounded distinctly Canadian, "Where are you going ma'am?"

Brandishing her passcard at eye level she said, "You can't throw me out I've been invited,"

The guard raised an eyebrow and was just about to say something when he lifted a finger to his ear and turned his head to the side. The change was marked by a very wide smile that turned him from a security guard to a host, "Miss Ensley it is a pleasure to see you, I am a fan of your work." Her mouth dropped a little, she closed it and tried to say something but it was so dry she only just managed to murmur a question-mark.

"?"

"Don't be surprised," he said, "You have many fans here. Please allow me," he put his hand against a security panel on the wall and one of the elevators immediately chimed, "You've been cleared all the way through to the eighty seventh floor of the Gregory Maines Tower, and the front desk is waiting for you. I hope you have a lovely day."

With a whisper the elevator doors slid open and Rayne stepped into the largest elevator she had ever been in and the first that was lined with marble. In return to the guard's kind smile she grinned back, but strongly suspected that his hid a killer animal beneath. She'd heard stories about people who'd tried to break into Sky City without a pass that'd been beaten to an inch of their lives by the security guards and then paid off by management before pressing charges. That's if they weren't just shot. It was a land of the rich and the rules governing this place were their own. As the doors closed she noticed how his smile vanished as if by magic.

As the elevator rose to get her to the Fourteenth, she quickly appraised herself in the mirrored walls of the cart. She looked better than she felt. Inside she was a quivering, nervous wreck but on the outside she looked, well, savvy. Stone cold broke perhaps with her online purchased dark grey pinstripe suit and high heels to give her the extra two inches of all important height. She was admittedly short, at only five foot and marginally plump. She didn't think she would go so far as saying fat, but voluptuous was apt. She had *just* the right amount of wobble to her steps and was fully taking advantage of the culture shift to appreciating the more curvy figures. She had straightened her usually dark curls and added a touch of makeup to accentuate her meridian blue eyes. She looked good.

"Skinny girls are for wimps," she reminded herself aloud and then wondered why, that had zero relevance to her being here.

The elevator came to a stop and after a moment the doors chimed and slid open and fighting the carnivorous butterflies in her belly and with a death grip on her passcard she walked into a lobby big enough to play eighteen rounds of golf. She couldn't help the whispered flow of expletives that slipped from her mouth as she just looked up and up and up. The Fourteenth of what she had always considered to be just a parking garage was capped by an all-glass ceiling and the tiled floors sparkled with crisp sunlight, in its center and directly in front of her was a half-moon water feature depicting a woman holding a small child up above her head while the baby plucked the star from the sky. It was carved out of marble and was so refined in detail she expected to hear the child giggling. The floor was crowded with people who glided on the enlightening clouds of their wealth.

Suddenly a flood of panic threatened to knock her off her feet but instead of going into a complete ditz about being out of her depth she arrowed herself directly to the sky bridge. As easy to spot as the water feature as it was the destination of everyone pouring across the lobby from the multitude of elevator doors. Unlike her trip, these icons of business and publicity arrived at this floor crammed together, shoulder to shoulder in the elevators, while she had been the only one in hers. It didn't take her long to figure out why though, she was a visitor and to ensure that she didn't infect these people with her poverty they went to great lengths to keep her away from them with her own parking level and her own elevator trip.

She joined the crowd walking towards the long bridge that stuck out of the glass dome like the bottom of a wine glass. It was very cleverly designed, all in glass, to make full use of the sunshine and the stunning sights of Sky City. Aside from the occasional pictures she saw online she had never seen Sky City like this before and the sight of it took her breath away. It was a completely different world.

Sky scrapers, the marvelous architectural wizardly of the age provided the trunks from which branches of sky bridges and air-borne walk ways connected giant gardens and swimming pools, open air restaurants and offices. Ornamental bridges arched over oceans of air connecting serene Japanese gardens and more water features than she could count. It was the canopy of the concrete jungle, polished in glass, chrome and blinding white.

Swept along by the crowd, Rayne realized she was an alien in a planet inhabited by people in suits and robes, where people walked with other people following them and everything smelt good. There was no smell of petrol or diesel up here, no stink of garbage and stray cats.

The sky bridge led directly into the main lobby of the Gregory Maines Tower a vista of marble tiles and glass walls and as the crowd dispersed into various directions, Rayne refused to touch anything in case she was arrested for defacing property. She went directly to the desk where a lady, better dressed than an air hostess smiled and said, "Good Morning Miss Ensley, how can I help you?"

Rayne floundered, caught off guard that this person who she had never met knew her name, she sought for something to say and managed, "I have an appointment. Do I just take the elevator to the eighty seventh floor?"

"The stairs are just around the corner if you would prefer?"

"No I would rather take the elevator," she insisted.

Rayne forgot to thank the woman and walked to the bank of elevators and took the chance and ran her passcard in front of the security panel. With immense relief the doors opened. This time the elevator wasn't empty but the man who stood in there was so foreign to Rayne that she daren't even speak with him in case she offended him. She had to breathe, she told herself, she had to remember to breathe.

This was *Sky City* and it still didn't seem real. Celebrities, movie stars that had won Oscars, rock stars who were greeted around the world by screaming fans couldn't afford one of the Gregory Maine's apartments and fewer of them had ever seen the eighty seventh floor, the legendary office of the world's wealthiest man.

Hell, even the internet didn't have images of his office.

Rayne was a blogger. A title that had once seemed derogatory but had grown on her and granted she had to do other jobs to pay the rent on her iddy-biddy home but she was a popular feature on the internet with a few thousand people following her website. She made videos and it was that part of her blogging that had resulted in her coming here.

A lot of Sky City was made of glass, the view of the city being used for everything it was worth and from the elevator she was able to see Durban completely. Well Sky City mostly, with bits of the old city poking through here and there like old brick work behind new plaster. If you saw the old city it was generally through the scaffolding and construction cranes working to expand Sky City. The ocean looked good today, aquamarine blue beneath a huge bowl of a cloudless sky. Beautiful.

Her companion on the elevator trip stopped at the thirtieth floor and gave her a queer look when she didn't follow; his confusion was palatable as he looked over her shoulder at this woman who was going higher than he, a man in colorful robes with gold rings on his fingers. Then the doors shut and she was alone to enjoy the view.

After five minutes, with the elevator so high above the whole city she was starting to suffer vertigo, the doors opened again and this time it was directly into the office of the man she had come to see. No lobby for her to calm down in, no toilet for her to throw up in, no this was an office that if you came here it was for a reason. She stepped out of the elevator and onto a carpet so thick she could swim in it and with an utter clarity she felt like she did the night she had lost her virginity. In trouble.

So much of what she knew about this man was myth and his office was suitably mystical. It was the entire length of the building with a domed ceiling with an occulence at its center directly above a swimming pool.

She gawked. There was a swimming pool in this man's office and quite a major one at that, it was fifteen metres long and half that wide complete with a rock-water-feature and a bridge. His office was shaped like a D, with a bank of floor to ceiling windows along the curve providing a once-in-a-lifetime view of the South African East Coast and on the left against a rough brick and plaster wall were some low tan leather sofas surrounding a giant television screen and a state of the art holovision.

On the opposite side of the pool and just beyond the pool table and a palm tree was a multi leveled black glass desk and a high backed leather chair facing the view of the oceanic horizon.

As if she were meeting her maker for the first time she tentatively ventured a few steps deeper into the office. She could hear someone talking on the far side but it was so far away that she couldn't make out the words so she just stayed where she was and her heart dropped with the elevator as the doors shut and the cart descended.

Suddenly, she felt very much alone, mere nervousness became tension that built up to the point she was afraid she might pee herself if something didn't happen and when the chair suddenly spun around and she saw Lynel Mason she almost screamed.

At first she thought he hadn't noticed her because he spun around and looked at his desk as if expecting it to tell him something.

For whatever reason, he was a remarkably attractive man, even from a distance. She didn't know if it was the power and wealth or that he seemed to be such a young looking man for someone with so much power and wealth and seeing him sitting there she couldn't help but wonder how big his-

"Miss Ensley is it?"

The voice was nearby and completely caught her off guard so she screamed like a banshee and jumped out of her skin. She broke one of her heels like a chicken bone and staggered over to the side and almost fell flat on her face, which instantly turned red and hot and tears that had been kept back up until this point dared to peek out of the corners of her eyes. Oh fuckadoodledoo, how could this happen? They were brand new shoes! She slipped out of her high heels, dropping in height, scooped them up in her hand, straightened her shoulders and lifted her chin, took a long breath, just like her mother taught her to do and in as much of a confident voice as she could manage she said, "Yes?"

"Hello there," the voice replied from a small but powerful speaker above the elevator, "I was wondering if you'd like to join me on this side of the office, or would you prefer to conduct our business over the intercom?"

She swallowed the lump in her throat, "I'm on my way."

"Can I get you anything?"

"Could I have a coffee?"

On the far end of the office the small action figure that represented her host smiled and his voice, which was deep and richly accented chuckled, "I like your style- I'll get the filter on now. Should be ready by the time you get here. Oh by the way, did you bring your bathing suit?"

She approached as assuredly as she could manage, fixing her eyes upon his face. The closer she got the more certain she became of the fact it wasn't his money that made him gorgeous and it was entirely him. While she knew that he was well into his forties he looked not a day passed thirty, his hair was golden brown and thick, swept back away from his face which was dominated by shimmering blue eyes and a readily accessed smile. Also he wore a white collared shirt that was opened down to mid chest and a pair of blue jeans and was merrily walking around barefoot. Just the look of him made her belly do somersaults and there was absolutely no way that she was going to be able to speak to this man if she was supposed to look him in the eye.

As she walked along the side of the pool she realized that things were happening to her body that were not entirely appropriate for what accounted as a business meeting but she couldn't help but study his every move as he prepared the filter in the coffee machine. He looked like he'd just come back from a surfing competition and his hands moved with confidence and economy, his fingers long but powerful. As he lifted the lid on the coffee filter his sleeve pulled back from his arm revealing a healthy slab of muscle.

She swore loudly as she almost fell into the pool and pin-wheeled her arms frantically to stay dry.

"Please forgive my attire," he said, ignoring her near fall, "I've just come back from a surfing competition in Hawaii. I'm still a little bit in the holiday mood,"

Walking quickly from the pool, she licked her lips and tried to get some moisture back into her mouth and managed to croak out, "Awesome."

He peered at her over his shoulder and gave a slight smile, he looked pleased to see her, "Please sit down."

His desk was on a raised platform two steps higher than the pool level and he didn't take many guests because the only seat she could see near his desk was either his office chair or the biggest bean bag that she'd ever seen it was large enough for two people to comfortably sit in it with room to spare. Vividly she saw an image of her on there with him leaning over her-

"Problem?" he asked, suddenly at her side. He brushed passed her ever so slightly and she got a whiff of his cologne and almost went on tip toes to smell it.

She said, "I'm a little worried about sitting on the beanbag Mr. Mason,"

"Please, call me Mason everyone does,"

"Oh, not Lynel?"

He smiled, *oh God,* she was literally having difficulty to control herself from either giggling hysterically or throwing herself at this man. It didn't help when he said, "I prefer Mason- especially from people I'm involved with."

She smiled. It was either that or gabble.

He didn't sit down, instead he walked behind his desk and pushed his chair up against it, it was a gesture that suggested a closing of office hours for him. He returned the way he went, walking in even, casual steps and seated himself on the stairs, "There," he said, "We can sit on the stairs and chill out, I don't feel like playing the businessman today anyway."

It sounded like a brilliant idea and she was immensely glad she hadn't worn the skirt but had opted for the trousers instead, although she thought they hugged her bum too much. She lowered herself gingerly onto the stairs and smiled shyly.

The glugging of the coffee filter machine seemed very loud.

"So," Mason said as if it was just occurring to him, "You are a blogger?"

"Yes," Rayne replied, "I… um… blog."

"Is it going well?"

"Fairly well," she answered, "More so quite recently."

The gorgeous trillionaire with the office and swimming pool in the clouds nodded as if he knew exactly what this kind of occasion meant to a person who had to choose between Heinz baked beans or customers choice for her dinner. He said, "I enjoy your blog. I must admit I've spent quite a bit of time on it."

The smile that escaped onto her face was one that screamed a silent but prominent *Oh shit!* "Really?" she said between her teeth.

"Yup, I can view it on my phone so it's been a brilliant way to pass some of these corporate meetings, although they've started to ask why I keep blushing."

Rayne turned a vibrant crimson.

"You mustn't be embarrassed," Mason said, leaning forward, she saw he had a few surfing bangles and beads around one wrist, this man really was a surfer, "I admire anyone who's got the confidence to show their assets… and their asses… and make it into some form of business."

"That didn't help make me less embarrassed," Rayne pointed out quietly.

"I apologize," he said, locking her with his eyes. She was in trouble, she knew it, this man could ask anything of her and she would say yes, no wonder this was his office. He added, "But it is the secret of success, knowing what you're good at and using it to make money. It's really as simple as that. Now I must mention, I actually have this morning free and I'm hoping you don't have anywhere incredibly urgent to go to?" She blinked, "Um, not that urgent."

"Brilliant," he said with clear enthusiasm that made him look a little like Gene Wilder from Willa Wonka and the Chocolate Factory... a more sexy less creepy but equally blue eyed Gene Wilder, or was it a young Bradley Cooper? "It's just that I've had an extraordinary time in Hawaii. So I'm going to get the coffee, did you bring your bathing suit?" Rayne shook her head, "No I didn't."

"Oh, well that's okay then," he said with a smile, he bounced up the stairs and finished sorting the coffee and at some point pushed some button or did something that cause the occulence in the domed ceiling to widen and open up so that the entire pool was engulfed in beautiful sunlight.

Rayne wracked her brains for something to say, something that would interest a man like this, but before she could he beat her to it and said, "I like you Rayne, I like a person who's confident enough to break a heel and still sit in comfortable silence. It shows character," he returned with two cups of coffee, "And a uniqueness of thought of which I value."

She took the cup from him and sipped the contents; it wasn't coffee as she knew it. Restaurants in Italy *tried* to make this sort of coffee.

"It's good because it's *actually* that good," Mason said standing up.

"It is very good coffee...." she agreed but whatever she was going to say after came out as a mumble as Mason walked to his pool and pulled off his shirt. If he had seen how she looked at his back he probably would have had her thrown out of the building- the only thing that tore her eyes from the fine details and curvatures there was the fact he was unbuckling his belt and before another word was spoken he dropped his jeans revealing he *was* a surfer, complete with tan lines and then stepped into the pool and dove under the water.

The very naked trillionaire swam a whole length underwater, reached the opposite end spun around underwater revealing a very white bum and swam back. When he surfaced he swept his hair away from his face with both hands, which created the most pleasing bulges in his shoulders, he said, "I want the video tape in its entirety and your word that you won't promote or give it to anyone else. I'm willing to pay you any amount of money for it. Just name your price."

Rayne stared openly. Her mouth hanging wide. She hadn't heard anything that he had said because the water was very clear and clearly not very cold.

"Rayne?"

She blinked and looked up at his face, "I'm sorry, what?"

"Are you okay?" he asked, wading to the edge and folding his arms onto the poolside.

"Yes, no, say that again?"

"Are you okay?"

"No, the other part about the tape."

"Well it's one tape in particular and I think you know which one," he said with a new edge to his voice, "The contents on it are of great importance to me. I want the tape, all of it. I will have my media people bury it so that it's never mentioned again and I will pay you any price for your silence and your loyalty."

Her mouth was dry; she drank some more coffee and tried to say something but nothing coherent came out.

"Okay," he said, his eyes playing havoc with her mind, "I'll make this very simple for you, can you keep quiet and promise me to remain quiet about this for the rest of your life if I paid you enough money? Nod your head if it's a yes and shake if it's a no."

She nodded.

"Good," he said pushing himself away from the side and doing a slow backstroke, which made certain things bob out of the water, "Now, since you're so unsure about how much you want for it why don't you come in here for a swim and tell me about how you managed to video the elusive Coat?"

"I don't have a bathing suit," she said quietly.

To which he replied, "Are you scared?"

"What? No of course not!"

"Come on then," he teased, "It's a great day, you're going to make an insane amount of money and when was the last time you got to swim in a heated pool in an office at the top of an executive tower?"

He pushed away from the side of the pool, using long sweeping movements with his arms to propel him through the water. She couldn't deny it, he had a point.

3.

Tyron heard the sounds of the city outside, the rising coalescence of the millions of people that seemed to multiply and try to get through the glass of the window. The whole East coast was a sparkling blanket of stars at night, which he enjoyed, but the noise of the city would have been invasive at this moment so he was grateful that the window was closed.

Rosie's hovel of an apartment was exactly the place you'd expect to find a prostitute, the main room itself dominated by a rusty steel framed bed with a pink duvet cover that stank of moth balls. The carpet had been grimy with used condoms and stains; a small television was in the corner with a pile of vintage pornographic discs. There was the smell of neglect and indifference here.

He looked at Rosie who lay on the bed staring at the ceiling, her eyes vacant; it looked like she was listening to the flies bouncing off the window just above her head. Shaking his head he gathered up his suit and stood, his movement causing a protesting scream from the bed springs, "This place needs a good clean," he said distractedly as he made his way to the bathroom, "It's a dump."

Rosie didn't answer; she just kept staring at the ceiling.

"After all," he continued, "How can anyone run a business from here when they can't feel safe?"

In the bathroom he hung up his suit which was suction wrapped in plastic and his bath bag on the hook behind the door and carefully tiptoed around the laundry and the mess to get to the shower cubicle. He had a fantastically hot shower, the water so hot that it scorched his skin and made him grit his teeth in pain, washed out his hair and scrubbed down his body. Once thoroughly done he took from his bath bag a pad of antiseptic wipes and wiped down around his genitals and rectum, then his hands. Tossing the used rags into the toilet he stood there, dripping as the steam of the shower rolled around him in a cloud. He wouldn't dream of using the bath towels that Rosie kept, they were as disgusting as her apartment.

"I mean you're clients must be revolted when they come in here," he commented, looking around at the multi layers of filth that was slowly overtaking this room, he grinned to himself as a thought occurred, "In a

few million years' time some of this stuff may actual evolve into shit."
The mirror was fogged up, something he couldn't tolerate and careful not to touch anything else he used one of the antiseptic wipes to wipe away some of the steam so he could gaze upon his magnificent self.

He was such a beautiful man. Every portion of him was perfect, from his clear, boyish skin, his gleaming blue eyes, the carefully sculpted eyebrows, his high cheekbones and full lips to the carved lines around his muscles. The shapely pectorals, the defined, striated deltoids and his thoroughly ripped eight pack and his massive member. He didn't need to believe in God to believe that there was purpose for him, he was special, he was something else. For the entire length of time it took him to drip dry he looked at his own eyes, losing himself in their depth and beauty. Once dry he used some roll-on from the bath bag and applied some wax to his jet black hair to get the perfect look, dressed in the Charlton gray Armani suit, careful with every movement to not let any of the fabric touch the floor of this vile bathroom.

"It's tricky to get dressed in here you know Rosie," he said, "*Really* don't want to touch anything in case I get infected."

Once dressed he appraised himself in the mirror, straightened his silk tie and using one of the antiseptic wipes to cover his hand he opened the bathroom door and stepped out into the apartment.

Rosie's body hadn't moved. It couldn't move, having been nailed to the bed frame. The nail gun lay beside her.

It had been a sweet little murder and had tasted good when he'd done it; although judging by the way the blood flew around the room he was grateful he'd brought his spare suit in some plastic. There were even long streaks of blood in the bathroom and kitchen from when he'd chased her around with the Stanley Knife, which was now embedded deep in her left knee cap.

He took a deep breath, separating the smells of the room, the good smells: Rosie's blood mainly, from the bad smells, everything else. This had been a fun night, a bloody good time. He chuckled at that joke too.

Before leaving the apartment he pulled from within his jacket pocket a sealed envelope with a single four lettered word printed on the front of it COAT and casually tossed it onto Rosie's bed, aiming it away from the growing pools of blood that were forming on it.

And then, with utmost care to not touch a single thing, he left the apartment via the front door.

Outside he left the door open and strolled across the hallway to the stairs, rolling his shoulders and whistling contently as he pried the ring from his wedding finger and slid it onto his right middle finger. There was a skip in his step that seemed entirely out of place with his environment, but he couldn't help how light he felt and confident that this time, *this* time his ultimate prey would notice him.

He reached the stairs at the far end of the hallway, the place where Rosie, trying to impress him had kissed him on the neck. Finding his prey was such a painfully easy task, the internet connected everyone and searching for escorts was now so easy to do you really had the pick of the litter. He'd spotted Rosie on an online adult meeting site and had immediately taken a liking to her. She had, well she *had* had blond hair and blue eyes, a nice figure but more importantly a sort of innocence. The look of a girl who needed someone to look after her but life had denied her such a simple requirement. He'd messaged her and then connected with her and of course he used pseudonyms and fake profiles, but she hadn't known the difference. She'd told him what she did for a living and she had rightfully been ashamed that she was an escort but he had assured her that he didn't care, which he hadn't and he'd told her what he did for a living. *Nothing,* because Tyron was rich, so rich that if he told dear sweet Rosie how much money he could spend on her in an evening she wouldn't have believed him. How could such a simple, innocent girl resist such a beautiful and beautifully rich man? It was all too easy and that was the only part he didn't like. Killing her had been fun, chasing her around her apartment and cutting her had been fun, using the nail gun was something Patrick Bateman would have been proud of. But it was too easy and a hunter like him required a challenge which was why he hoped that his work was eventually going to be appreciated by the one major target he had his eyes set on.

He rounded the corner and took the stairs two at a time and was about to reach the landing when he hit something and fell backwards.

The stair case was empty, the piss-yellow light cast long shadows within the corners but there was clearly nobody there.

The training Tyron had received as a boy had unscrewed many things in his mind but it had screwed in a very definite and absolute sense of survival.

He felt a familiar coolness wash over him, his muscles loosened and his senses extended into what he considered a precognitive state- but he blinked- and in the moment the biggest man Tyron had ever seen in his life came to be standing directly in front of him.

In surprise he backed up several steps in a single rearward plunge so that he could see the man in his entirety.

Look at him!

It was not just the height although that would have been enough but this man's shoulders were impossibly broad, a meter across and he was covered from head to toe in the single biggest black trench coat Tyron had seen and his face was covered with a matching black leather hood that left only the lowest portions of his jaw to the light, in his chin there was a cleft as if a bullet had ricocheted off it.

Tyron could see how someone would be utterly terror struck by this person, whereas he was merely touched by the intense beauty and perfect line of the man's mouth and jaw and a deep, flawless voice as the giant spoke:

"Where is she?"

Excitement had turned his blood into pure adrenaline and gingerly he ascended two more steps, "Where is who?"

The giant's lips moved subtly and confidently, each word enunciated, "The girl... Rosie."

I can't believe it, it's him! It's actually him! Tyron thought, *This is just too good...*

"Oh her," he said, mentally back counting the steps until the landing, "She's in her apartment resting if you want her. But I think I tired her out a little too mu- *uagh*."

He had exploded into a full-out sprint the second his foot had touched the landing, convinced that he could outrun someone as large as this giant who for all his size had been well out of arms reach and far enough away to allow Tyron a good head start. But he ran into a gloved hand so large it encased his entire neck like an iron collar!

"Let's go see then."

Trying to fight was useless, it felt like he was struggling against stone and smudgy spots of purple and red were spreading across his vision as he was dragged, his heels kicking at the concrete of the hallway.

He was released and fell over noisily against the iron-gate of

Rosie's apartment, which slammed shut with a surprising loud *clang* that echoed up and down the hall. He lay against the gate gasping for breath and his excitement had gotten to a level where he was sturgently aroused. This was going to be a challenge. A beautiful challenge.

"*Where* is she?" the giant demanded.

Tyron swallowed hard, recognizing the need to calm down, "I told you she's in there." He said, jabbing a thumb at the door.

The hallway lighting was atrocious and mostly nonexistent and Tyron watched as the giant very gently opened the door. For a brief second his face was cast in a rectangle of light, but no features could be seen because he was too quick to turn his head to the side.

The door opened and that smell touched Tyron's nostrils again. The giant said, "Go in,"

Tyron smiled and stood up, straightened his lapels and saying, "Sure thing. So you're The Coat?"

The giant didn't even flinch. Tyron took his time to tuck in his shirt and straighten the knot of his tie, "The vigilante who's been all over the internet, since that video. You've made vigilante a household word," he looked the giant up and down assessing his height to be in the region of eight feet judging by the height of the door, "Not bad for an urban legend. Oh I left a letter in here for you I'll just grab it!"

Tyron ducked through the door and sprinted into Rosie' apartment. Clear confidence became murderous intent and his instincts were in with full force. He sprinted to Rosie's carcass and grabbed the Stanley Knife from her leg and turned to see the huge black figure of his adversary only just getting through the door. It looked like an adult trying to walk into a child's play hut. Holding the blade behind his hip Tyron approached him and closed the gap like an attacking shark, his eyes shining and eager for the second and climatic kill of the night.

High with murder he would have hammered the knife as deep into the other's crotch as was possible, sliced the man open like a sardine and let his balls fall down his pant legs-

But a second later, Tyron dropped to his knees cradling a hand that dangled from his crushed wrist and his own knife was stuck hilt deep through his shoulder socket and all he could think about was. *I didn't see him move.*

Pain like nothing he'd ever known raced from his wrist to his shoulder in such blazing barbs. Giddy, it only took a moment before that calm and relaxed confidence returned and it fed off the pain to reaffirm his self-belief that he was capable of handling anything.

Even when his shirt and jacket were wound into the giant's grasp and he was lifted again, mercilessly high until eye level with the giant in black he felt cool. At this distance Tyron could see the giant's face, the giant's skin was so smooth and without any lines or flaws, his nose was perfectly designed but his lips were pressed into a tight line.

Tyron became aware that the hand that was holding him was shaking ever so slightly and when the giant spoke Tyron felt warm air against his face.

"You *killed her?"*

"Of course I did."

The Coat looked away from him at Rosie's mutilated and crucified carcass and Tyron's confidence was growing stronger as his grasp of reality was slipping, "You should have seen her when she was alive."

The slap was comparable to being hit on the side of the head with a shovel and it made Tyron's entire body buck but he just chuckled and spat blood onto The Coat's black sleeve.

"Now that wasn't very brotherly," he said, feeling his entire head swim as if he were drugged, "Just because you were too late to get in on the action man."

"You killed her." The Coat repeated.

"That's obvious isn't it?" Tyron said before starting to laugh, he was becoming hysterical, "And I've killed a lot more too, trying to find you," as he spoke Tyron's left hand crept behind him to his belt. He found what he was looking for, a small blade, a Harpy Knife, a wickedly curved blade with a small rounded handle, that nestled into the palm of the hand and was good for castrating attackers, hence the name, "I've killed so many and have been waiting for you so long, I thought that maybe you were just busy but now," he slid it from its sheath and slipped his index finger through the circular hole in the blade so that he could keep a firm grip of it, "Maybe you just don't care?"

His breath was flattened along with his insides when the giant swung him into the opposite wall like he would a dirty carpet and a clamp of razor blades encased his entire right side and made him sick.

"You killed those women to get to me?" was the question.

"Guess that makes you feel rather rotten," Tyron said and slammed

the blade as hard as he could into the Coat's sleeve, right below the elbow joint.
It did not have the expected effect.

4.

On the other side of the world, Tuck woke before he opened his eyes. He could hear someone approaching his tent, someone who thought they had a quiet footstep, someone who thought they could catch him off guard. It was early morning, not even five am and the birds in the trees had already started their merry song, insects lazily made their way across the underbrush of one of Britain's finest woodland forests and the air was still that crisp early morning fresh that had made mornings on the island so memorable. Tuck had pitched his tent in the heart of the forest and had been careful. It was a camouflaged style tent, patched with a green and brown splotches and shaped like an exposed pipe, he had set it up in a small V shaped ravine caused by sinkage in the soil around the roots of a tree and a dried up river bed. He hadn't used a fire or any other light system so the only people who would find him here would be the people who were looking specifically for him. Hunters.

Quieting his breathing he listened intently and distinctly counted three different people approaching. They walked with their weight on the balls of their feet, poised for action and every step was deliberate and almost entirely quiet.

There was a long pause, which the noises of the forest filled in, the sound of the leaves moving, the creaking of branches, the scurrying of animals and the teasing whistle of the breeze.

Tuck had pitched his tent at an advantageous place for hiding but it was at a disadvantage for defense, backed into a corner as it was and exposed from above and unable to escape except via one route.

The men approaching the tent knew this. He could tell in the way that they moved. When he heard their footsteps again it was with two of them moving away in a flanking position, one on each side of the arrow-head-shaped hole. The leader took the position above and lowered to a knee, bringing the rifle butt to his shoulder and looking through a night vision sight. They would take no chances and the guns they used were probably high powered rifles firing tranc-pellets. The pellets were very similar to paint-balls in as much as upon impact they exploded but instead of paint these were filled with highly-potent tranquilizer gel that was absorbed into the skin. By now, they would have upped the dosage to a lethal amount to ensure he didn't manage to run far or perhaps just replaced them with good old fashioned metal ammunition.

Tuck knew exactly when the trap was set and could have counted down the seconds to when the ambush took place.

It was very well executed: the two hunters who'd flanked the tent and opened up with a storm of bullets that ripped it to shreds while the sniper at the top followed the movement from a safety spot, prepared to bring down anyone trying to escape. The sniper would use traditional ammunition, aiming not to kill but to maim, aiming for the kneecaps, the pelvis or lower spine.

The sniper was good and didn't so much as breathe while his two partners turned the tent to ribbons, his focus never leaving his strike zone. Tuck was grateful that he wasn't in the tent but watching the entire scene unfold from six meters above them in a Y fork in a tree where he'd spent the night.

The two hunters ceased their firing and reloaded in a swift, automatic fashion while the sniper surveyed the area. Tuck heard words whispered, "*...decoy...*" and "*...trap.*" by which time he'd already notched the arrow and was decided who to hit first. The first two arrows flew true and as silent as an owl's wings connecting with the pale faces of the two hunters within half a second of each other and Tuck landed full bodied onto the back of the sniper in the next second, using his body weight to drive his hunting knife through and across the man's right bicep severing the connective tissue and rendering the arm useless. The rifle dropped to the floor and the sniper rolled away coming up some six feet away a blade in his left hand.

"It's not going to be that easy you sonofabitch!" he spat. Tuck could smell it on the man and hear it in his voice, he had some sort of enhancer pumping through his veins, reducing his ability to feel pain and increasing his adrenaline threshold.

Tuck shrugged, "I still don't fancy your odds," and walked towards the sniper who plunged in with the skill of a professional soldier. Tuck was in his element and easily dodged the first attack by stepping to the side and ducking beneath the second, he forestalled the third by plunging his knife into the shoulder socket of the man's left arm and twisting the blade into the joint. There was a grinding snap of bone.

But the sniper couldn't feel the pain and his frustration propelled him on as he screamed and cursed and tried to bite Tuck like some sort of bipedal shark. There was little time for this and Tuck, already anxious to leave settled it with a single right hook to the jaw which unfortunately snapped the bone and sent a large portion of it hurtling into his brain. The man was stone dead before he hit the floor.

"Easy," Tuck whispered to the body, "So much for getting answers,"

Retrieving his knife he searched the man for anything of use, there was nothing on him save for weaponry and of that the only thing that was of any real use was his knife and a FRAG grenade. He carried the sniper's body into the ravine and similarly searched the other two but came up with the same ordinance. He piled the bodies over the remains of his tent, collected his rucksack from the fork in the tree, put on his jacket and his hood before priming the three FRAGs and slipping them into the pile of bodies. He walked away and when the grenades detonated he didn't even flinch but kept walking until he made it to the fringe of the forest.

He headed West across country, making use of the darkness and running at his full pace across fields and through patchy woodlands, in forty minutes he'd covered more distance than a car would have managed and he stopped at an underpass to the motorway to get his bearings and to check he wasn't being followed. As soon as he was satisfied he continued to run.

He skirted around the small northern England village of Hordin where one of the bakeries was making fresh bread, running through the smell of it made his mouth water but he leaned into the run and stopped himself from thinking about it. If the bakeries were open, soon there would be delivery vans collecting the produce and moving it across the roads, if there were delivery vans it meant it was almost daylight.

There was one village in this region he was aiming for, another one of the small village clusters in northern England that grow in the crevices of the country side like fungus. From a distance the brown houses looked like jagged rubble that had come to rest at the bottom of a hill and only as he neared did they gather to form the brown rooftops of houses.

He approached it tentatively. Like a cat walking through a strange garden in search of food, his senses buzzing, his body coiled. To the east the horizon was a painted morning of light pink and ever increasing pinky-orange and in his mind a timer was ticking away. Pulling up his hood he buried his hands into his pocket and with his head down he walked with a practiced limp across the main road, passing under piss-yellow streetlamps and walking passed empty, dew-laden benches and post boxes. Like all villages the houses existed around a central cluster of shops which he avoided like a student avoids the headmaster's office. He hopped a wire fence and cut across the wet grass of a playing field, walking behind the jungle gyms and swings, making sure to step behind the concealing trunks of trees as they presented themselves.

Britain may only have constituted one percent of the world' population but it was responsible for twenty percent of the world's surveillance cameras. Bolted onto every ATM, every shop corner, every street camera, into every retail outlet, everywhere that they could get away with and in a very real and un-paranoid manner every one of them was looking for Tuck Bradley.

At the edge of the playground he hopped the fence and dropped his head a little lower to avoid the passing glare of headlights, the morning was approaching up fast and more windows were lighting up around him. Walking, he headed into a residential area where, as the properties had gardens the CCTV coverage was significantly lighter and happened upon the perfect house.

A big garden with trees and the highest fence offered itself and without hesitation Tuck vaulted the tall wooden fence as if it were a sofa and landed on the other side in a crouch. As he landed he slid like a ghost behind a large oil drum and some pot plants. This presented a small but convenient hiding place from which he was able to assess the property: The lawn was tailored about twice a month judging by the length of the grass, there was some horrendously rusty garden furniture that hadn't been used in years. The house itself was two storied and painted in a faded green with old fashioned lace curtains hanging in the windows. No discarded plastic toys, footballs, bicycles, table tennis or any of the telltale signs of young children were left in the garden and he could see no signs of animals. For the moment it was enough. Kids and animals tended to wander and get curious and parents were the best for picking up intruders.

He slung his bag from his back and held it to his chest. It was a long bag, designed to be used by mothers who went to yoga twice a week and took it seriously enough to purchase their own equipment: a towel, a rolled up yoga mat and a change of clothes. It was more battered and dirty than a yoga bag, but it was hardy and built to last and it was a convenient means for him to carry his most valued possession which didn't fit into a regular backpack. He pulled his hood forward so that he could get a bit of warmth against his cheeks and took a deep breath; his hiding place smelt of soil, grass and the oil in the container which was acting as his headboard. Through the netlace of branches from the neighbor's tree he watched the sky as it grew lighter and listened to the birds as he slid into unconsciousness.

He awoke when he heard a house door opening, followed by the softer thud of a car door being closed, footsteps and an engine coming to life. That was followed by the whirling sound of a car reversing and joining the morning traffic. He remained where he was for a while longer listening to the house, letting his mind wander peacefully. He even slipped in and out of a very light dozing stage where while he was technically awake his mind processed and dreamed.

His dreams were the dreams of any man, the fragmented pieces of conversation the subconscious mind had with itself while it was sorting out its filing system. He liked it. He liked the fact that his dreams were normal. When your dreams become too close to your reality you're starting to lose grip.
The traffic on the road on the other side of the house had increased as the morning pressed on, Tuck could hear people in the other houses waking up while this house was still silent. He heard cars along the road just on the other side of the fence going passed, their radios on. People walking, their footsteps sounding like drum rhythms. Birds. Pets. Films. DVDs. Telephones. He figured it would do no good to linger so he peeked around the oil container and looked at the house in the better light.

Again nothing caught his attention. No movement, no evidence of life.
He rose to a crouch and slung the bag across his back scanning the garden and house for movement. Getting to his feet he walked close to the fence along the length of the garden and when he got to the back door he found it was locked. This was not a problem and within the same minute of reaching it he was already closing it behind him.
Compared to the chilly autumn outside it was warm inside and as quiet as

a tomb with that unique lived in smell that every house gets a mixture of smells that could tell you more about the inhabitants than an hour long conversation. He was in a kitchen and it was laundry day. Two clotheshorses were stacked with limp clothing, still damp and smelling strongly of fabric softener. The contents of one of the horses were those of a man: shirts, jeans, socks and underwear while on the other were those of a woman's. Two pairs of skinny blue jeans, small T-shirts and an assortment of G-strings.

It was her house, the female smells being far more dominant as he detected perfumes, soaps and an assortment of hair and skincare products. The female was young, within her mid-twenties and judging by the number of different men who had walked through her house over the past week whose pores had literally dripped with testosterone there was no doubt in Tuck's mind what she did for a living and how she could afford such a house on her own.

At the same time she was house proud, things were cleaned and sterilized frequently, neat and ordered.

He quickly riffled through the cupboards, grabbing tins of baked beans, soups, minced meat and sweet corn and stuffing them into his bag. A half loaf of bread from the bread bin and a jar of coffee that had been left on the counter also went into the bag. He opened the fridge, bagging a block of cheese, a couple of cans of beer and one liter bottle of Avian water.

The kitchen led directly into a downstairs living room.

Here he found everything he expected like any modern commercialite there was the usual host of high tech entertainment items all bought on credit: the big, flat screen television, the newfangled holovision, the state-of-the-art sound system, the thick leather sofas. The entertainment companies knew the importance of having people watching their shows instead of being outside and enjoying the sun, they needed people to be on their bums watching their commercials, they valued brain dead zombies who couldn't help but obey so they made sure that everyone who wanted to get the best of it, could have the best of it because as long as they were watching television then the entertainment companies could *sell* them more entertainment stuff and make them more money. A perpetual cycle.

The staircase going upstairs was on the far side of the living room next to the front door and as there was nothing else in the downstairs that was of value to him he climbed them.

Two bedrooms and he checked both to make sure they weren't occupied. One of them was an office and the other was the main bedroom. In the office he didn't find anything useful but in the main bedroom in one of the cupboards he found a fish bowl filled with money.

Ah, someone was a squirrel.

In at least six out of ten houses that Tuck visited he found squirrels, people who paid everything by card and only took out cash on the odd occasions when they needed it but didn't like walking around with change or notes jangling in their pockets. They usually had a storage spot, a jar, a hat, a drawer or a fish bowl where they'd just empty the contents of their wallets into at the end of every day. Gradually this added up and it was the oldest and easiest form of savings. This particular squirrel liked big nuts though. The fishbowl was filled with notes. It made sense with her line of business and cash was as valuable to Tuck as water to a man walking in the desert, but there was over ten thousand pounds in the fishbowl which puffed his bag up until it was on the verge of busting at the seams.

The bed in the room was a wide with a memory foam mattress and a black leather head and foot board and the duvet covers were cream colored, possibly to avoid any stains. It was made with a military precision and the smells rising in bellows from the linen caused a deep stirring in his lower belly that made him want to bury his face into the pillow and breathe deeply. He lifted his shirt over his nose and left the bedroom in a hurry doing his best to think of cold thoughts involving ugly things while he rummaged through the bathroom cabinet like a shopper at Tescos. He squeezed a bar of soap, a bottle of shower wash and some toothpaste into the bag and was leaving the bathroom when he heard the squeal of hinges as a door opened on the floor below.

You didn't think there was a basement did you?

The smell of the woman had been very strong and like a fucking idiot he'd assumed she had only just left the house but her scent, like a flood of fire poured up the stairs, flowing down the corridor and hit him in a wave that made his body stiffen and his fingers tingle.

How long had it been? Since he'd had an orgasm? Not long admittedly. But when was the last time he had been with a woman? When was the last time he had enjoyed that special, enveloping heat?

She was ripe too, eager for it, her mind awash with sexual currents that had washed around her body and brought about a smell that hit Tuck right in the animal part of his brain.

Her smell was followed by her voice, happily singing along to some music she listened to on her earphones.

Even her voice beckoned him, teased him, behind the words there was a *hunger* as strong as his.

As if his skeleton itself was magnetically drawn to her he felt unable to resist creeping to the stairs where he put a hand on the top banister and dared to take a long, deep breathe in. Oh yes, he thought, if she had been an animal she would been heavily in season and if other men were more able to pick up on these minute scents she would have been holding the door shut. His mouth went dry as his body responded to the scent she was projecting and a trap door within his mind was flung open and long buried thoughts exploded into his mind. *Just one*, a devil inside him whispered, *what would it matter? Just think of it... think of that heat think of that enraged, engorged animal thrusting and her gasping into your ear as she clings to your body just as both of you-*

A fist sized chunk of wood snapped off the banister as his hand clenched around it bringing him back to reality.

Below in the living room, only a few meters from him there was a stunned silence as she listened. It was the moment where a deer jolts as a twig is snapped, its head up, its ears pricked, its muscles bunched.

The hot red mist that had descended over his mind was cleared for a moment and as it swirled in his mind preparing to once again descend Tuck fled. Dropping the chunk of wood he sprinted away from the stairs into the master bedroom and threw himself at the window. The double glazed, heat retaining glass did not shattered into pieces but blew out as a single slate and he dropped from the second floor room and landed heavily and awkwardly on the lawn, falling forwards and rolling over his shoulder.

The fresh air struck him like a cloud hammer and the run instantly cleared the remainder of his head, in the house behind him the lady was screaming something incoherently and scrabbling around for her phone, but as his hood was up he doubted she got a look at his face but he was not so certain that she didn't see him clear the garden fence in a single vertical leap.

Aww hell!
Landing in a crouch on the grassy verge he had jumped straight into the proverbial fire. Cars in their dozens were pouring down the main strip of road directly in front of him while a mob of pedestrians walked passed him. They looked at him with mild interest but as he was a hooded tramp with a busting at the seams back pack jumping over a fence to escape private property where someone was screaming that interest would soon turn to suspicion.
One picture of his face- that's all it would take.

Face down he ran as fast as he could, drawing even more attention to himself, his brain booming as he registered the looks he got from pedestrians and drivers like punches in the head. Following the same route he had taken earlier that he knew lead to the forests outside the village he ran across the road, bunny hopping over the bonnet of a car as it swerved to avoid him and reaching the other side of the park before the driver had time to realize he hadn't actually hit anyone.

He ran for half the distance to the forest until he was out of sight of the house and the people who may have seen him jump that fence, or heard the woman screaming. He slowed to a casual walk, put his hands into his pockets and turned into another residential street, here the houses were terraced but thankfully unsurveyed by cameras. He chose the first house he could find that had an open door and quite calmly opened the garden gate, crossed the slatted pave and stepped inside.
The owner of the house a thirty-something man with dark hair speckled with grey, dressed in a shop-bought brown suit and holding a piece of toast in his mouth was leaving for the day but with the terrifying skill of a ninja that Tuck had recently failed to utilize, the thirty year old did not even register him as the Freelander snuck upstairs behind his back.

5.

Rayne could barely walk when she got back to her car, which was easy to spot because it was the only one the cleaners hadn't touched. She threw her jacket onto the passenger seat and collapsed into the driver's and saw that it was eight am.

"Unbelievable," she whispered. Those digital numbers of her dashboard just confirmed that the insanity that had transpired the night before had indeed taken place, "I feel like I've been shagged by a train,"
Her inner thighs from her knees to her crotch, lower abdomen and back felt pulverized and her vagina was a single fiery beacon glowing like a light bulb.
She angled the rear view mirror so she could get a look at herself. Mason had insisted she take her time getting ready before she left and like a fat American in a luxury resort she had luxuriated in the shower and spent over an hour in the bathroom before making an appearance again in his office. She looked tired, shell-shocked and her eyes were the eyes of someone who doubted what they could see. They were the eyes of someone who needed to sleep.

She shifted uncomfortably in her seat and seriously contemplated ordering a taxi because she doubted if she would be able to operate the pedals well enough to survive the bedlam of morning traffic. Her first instinct was to save money and drive because if she got a taxi she would just have to come retrieve the car and that would cost her *more* money and her mind automatically started counting numbers, subtracting the expenses from an ever dwindling figure that represented her net worth. Any person who has ever spent time scraping crumbs out of the breadline knows exactly what this is like.

Rayne had not needed to handle cash for years and, like most people, everything was paid by card but if she had been used to handling real money she would have been stacking her one cent pieces into little towers and wishing they could be just a little taller. She came to the conclusion that she had money to put another quarter tank of fuel into her car and get some minor groceries on the way home, assuming that she didn't have to pay for the overnight stay at the car park. It was somewhere in between her car engine sputtering into a mechanical coma and her swearing at the steering wheel that a light blossomed in her brain pan. The light grew and with the excitement of a child on Christmas morning she took her phone from her jacket.

The wireless connection of the internet was instantaneous in the middle of Sky City and she was able to make a connection with her phone without any of the usual difficulty she had at her apartment. With her knees shaking in excitement while her finger was bizarrely calm she logged onto her bank account and looked at the amount there.

Her hope and excitement had climbed so high that the disappointment was crashing, as poignant as a crystal palace hit by a boulder and her heart curled into itself and dropped into an abyss when she saw that she was in fact, further over her overdraft limit than she had been yesterday.

"Goddamn it all to hell," she said, tossing the phone into the bundle of her jacket and leaning her forehead against the steering wheel. It was a ridiculous scenario that nonetheless brought reality back with a slap, she was an online amateur with a webcam, without two cents to rub together who drove a car that was built before she was a teenager and this bundle of poverty and pathos was parked in the car park owned by the richest man in the world who had, just a handful of hours ago been face-buried between her legs. She did not come into this sort of contact with this kind of person, it was as foreign to her as eating crayfish and she had somehow expected that with that wealth and power somehow the money the pair of them had only chatted about briefly would magically appear in her bank account? She shook her head scornfully, *fucking idiot.*

She hoped she hadn't just been used because she certainly didn't have a leg to stand on, if he had decided to use her there was nothing she could do but be grateful for it because men like Mason were the stages that the world's richest played their games on. He was quite impeccably higher than the rules.

She had hopes but nothing more than his promise that he would do what he said and that was something she had heard from many men too many times, but nonetheless she still held out that hope. That all important hope for a miracle and that one lightning strike of luck that would change her destiny.

Unfortunately it didn't strike her or her car before she got home and she was left waiting in a layby while her car smoked like a fifty a day addict, for the tow-truck to come drag her home.

The tow truck would be paid through her insurance but the excess of the cost would come from her net figure. More sums, subtractions and options went through her mind, this time carved in her mind with a very bitter knife.

Muttering and swearing, repeating the lines she would say if she ever saw Mason again, the sentences she wished she would/could remember, she got into her apartment and hatefully realized that her entire home could fit inside Mason's office swimming pool four times over.

She couldn't think of it, she couldn't handle it and she fell flat onto her bed, buried her face into the squeaky, tiny mattress and cried herself to sleep.

She slept only for an hour and felt spectacularly refreshed and as she opened her eyes she felt the many delicious bruises across her legs and back and couldn't help smiling naughtily at the thought of Mason. There was no doubt why he was the wealthiest man in the world. He simply deserved that to be the truth for she had never in her life been forced to endure such a succession of excruciating orgasms. Nobody had known how to touch her buttons like that. While there had been nothing romantic about it, they had done it in the pool with her breasts crushed against the marble side while he took her from behind, on the bridge over the pool, on the sofas while a miniature Nickelback band played on the holovision, on his desk looking at the ocean and on the balcony with a eighty seven story drop to the road below. When they were hungry he threw some pizzas into the oven in his kitchenette and they drank sodas and then as the day progressed they drank rum and even dabbled in some social narcotics. He had an insatiable sexual appetite and it had taken every ounce of stamina she could muster to keep up with him.

She lay there, surprised at how content she was compared to the tearful, miserable person she had been a short while earlier and hoped it would last. Her mind dreamily drifted from thought to thought and she decided she was going to try and get a couple more hours sleep before taking on the day and had just rolled over when her telephone rang.

The incredibly flat mini-computer that had been labeled phone was hiding somewhere in the apartment having been dropped during her zombie-like entrance and despite her flat being so little it seemed to have no trouble hiding from her as she frantically searched around, throwing handfuls of clothes over her shoulder until she found it and saw it was an unrecognized number, she answered with a neutral, "Hello?"

"Hey there," a jovial voice said on the other end, she couldn't help the sudden blast of positivity that rocked her onto her heels.

"Hi!" she shrieked.

"You alright?" Mason asked.

"Yeah," she said, "Sure."

"You sure?" he said.

"Hm-hmm," she mumbled.

She visualized him shrugging his shoulders as he let it go, "Great. I realized I hadn't given you my number so I thought I'd give you a call and give it to you."

You've already done that. She thought churlishly, "Thanks," she said, "I had a great time last night."

"Oh I know you did," he chuckled, "So did I. I'm going to be out of town for a little bit do you want to catch up for coffee when I come back?"

"Okay," she said, her knees going weak with excitement, "Sounds great."

"Cool, okay then," he said, "Oh shit, I forgot! One of my people is going to call you later. You didn't give me your bank details before you left."

Her mind was echoingly blank, "Huh?"

"Your bank details," he inferred, "So I can get this money transferred to you. Don't worry I won't need a receipt or anything."

Rayne sat down on her messy floor and put her head between her knees before asking, "What was the figure we mentioned again?"

"I think you were joking but you said something about nine figures," he said, off-handedly, in fact in her mind he was shrugging his shoulders and not paying much attention, a look that shifted from mild boredom to intense excitement within the same instant, "I can't remember really. Rayne?"

"Mm mm?" she mumbled, she was now lying on her side, her face pressed against a discarded bra, she felt drunk and the world was spinning wildly. Christ was she going to throw up?

"Oh good," he said, "So they'll sort it out and we'll do coffee when I get back yes?"

"Sure," was all she managed.

"Cool."

He hung up and Rayne let the phone fall from her ear, it bounced off her cheek and rattled on the only patch of clear floor there was where it lay, staring at her. The world was spinning off its axis and she wanted to hold on for dear life in case she got thrown off. When the phone rang again she jumped, her heart hitting the roof of her mouth, it was a similar number and by the time she answered it she convinced herself that it would be someone else in the office telling her that there had been an error and they had got her mixed up with someone important who was used to handling such gigantic wads of credit.

"Hello," she said.

"Hi is that Rayne?" a warm voice on the other end said.

"Yes," she said.

"My name is Alan, I'm *one* of Mason's people," he said with a sort of touch of humor that made her chuckle, "I'm just calling up regarding this payment."

Oh shit here it comes, she thought, preparing herself for another massive disappointment, it had seemed too good to be true. She knew it was too good to be true.

"I was hoping to grab your bank details so I can deposit the money in there this afternoon for you,"

Dry mouthed, "Okay, just let me get my purse."

The next moments were a meaningless blur, she gave him the bank details from her card and whilst he was on the phone he told her quite casually that he was transferring the money, he asked her if she liked Sky City and where she had grown up and it turned out he had several friends who had gone to the same school as she, as she was answering him in a very robotic fashion he chimed in with a musical, "All done."

"What is?" she asked dumbly.

"Well," he said, "If I'm not mistaken Miss Ensley, we've just made you multi-millionaire…. Erm, Rayne?"

"Thank you," she said hoarsely, her mouth so dry her tongue stuck to her pallet.

"My pleasure," he said, "A couple of things. The video is now our possession. This constitutes a complete purchase from you to us which means you are not allowed to distribute it or replicate it. We hold the rites to do whatever we want with it. You are welcome to, if anyone asks, say that we have purchased it from yourself but I repeat you are not allowed to replicate it. I trust you don't mind but we've taken the liberty of removing it from the various websites that you have uploaded it to,"

"You hacked me?"

"Yes," he said matter-of-factly, "But just for the video nothing else has been touched. Any questions?"

"Alan I've just been given a king's ransom for a video I took on my phone. Why?"

"You can call it invested interests Rayne," Alan said soothingly, "Now, you're rich beyond your dreams so I'd suggest you go and do something."

"I don't know what to do," she said, surprised at her own honesty.

"Well," Alan said, "I'd suggest go out and buy something,"

"Like what?"

"Anything at all Rayne," he said, "Anything at all."

She didn't leave the house. She collapsed back into bed exhausted and her mind numb and slept through the rest of the day. At some point in the night she stirred and thought she saw something at the foot of her bed. Something big and dark that was watching her but she didn't feel scared, she felt safe, protected and she pulled her duvet up to her chin, rolled over and started dreaming about ponies and buying ponies. Lots of ponies.

Before the sun was up the following morning she untangled herself from the duvet and spent some time wandering around the apartment in a half sleep state looking at everything. She surveyed the kitchen cabinets, the fridge, the stove and the sink with it's Himalayan pile of dishes, wondering what it was that she *should* have been thinking of and why none of these things seemed to belong to her anymore. When she remembered it was driven home like a nail from a nail gun.

She waved on her computer and sat on her desk chair bouncing up and down manically and drumming the desk with her finger tips, "Come on come on come on come on come on come on come on," she chanted. The computer booted up and the various virus guards flashed through and uploaded which only took a couple of seconds, she logged onto her internet banking account number and for a second, a brief, terrifying second she thought that it was all going to turn out be a dream. A realistic and wonderful dream, but a dream, however, all those zeroes looked even better after a good night's sleep.

She stared at the balance for a long time, trying to catch her breath and wondering if she was supposed to be doing something- If this was a movie wouldn't she be running naked down the street and kissing strangers? She didn't fancy that, not in Durban at least, maybe she could fly to Sweden and do it there? She was excited, but it was a contained excitement- the manic screaming fit she'd enjoyed before going to sleep was more to do with her being over tired and incredibly well humped. It had been the final release of a lot of sexual energy. Now she felt a quiet but vibrant warmth inside of her. It was a secret, like a secret power. It was like she'd learnt how to fly or telekinesis and she had something that nobody else she knew had.

Taking an antiquated calculator from her desk drawer she did some quick sums and promptly put 99% of the money into a secure savings account, in doing so the online banking website told her what her expected yearly interest would be and she couldn't even comprehend the figure so she filed it away for future gawking. The remaining 1% she used to pay off every debt she had: credit cards, loans, car repayments, phone bills, taxes everything. She cancelled her overdraft and transferred monies that she owed to some of her friends who had been kind enough to loan her cash when she had been short but even then she was left with an unmanageable sum of money.

A chime on her phone and the screen lit up. Who would be texting her at this hour in the morning? She already knew the answer and with butterflies clawing at the insides of her stomach she read the message:
Hey Rayne, also forgot to mention I've got a party happening at mine next weekend if you'd like to come?
Lynel Mason was inviting her to a party? Lynel Mason. *Lynel Mason?* There were movies at the cinema where the main characters, who were Hollywood elites, used Lynel Mason as a reference to move the dialogue. He was a universally recognized icon of notoriety and young wealth and she had just received a party invitation from him?

She picked up the phone and before she could stop herself she pushed the call button and held it to her ear, when it rang on the other side she hung up quickly with an audible gasp. A second later when it started ringing on her side she shrieked in terror and threw the phone into the air and juggled to catch it, "H-hello?" she answered.

"Rayne?" it was Mason's voice.

"Hi-hi, um, Mason," she said, pounding her forehead with the palm of her hand, "I got your text."

"Yeah, I got a receipt message," he said, she thought she could hear papers shuffling, was he working? "So are you able to come to the party?"

"I think so," Rayne said, unable to think of any reason why she wouldn't be able to make it, what plans could possibly get in the way, "Erm, I wanted to ask…"

"Yes?" he prompted after a moment.

"…What I should wear?" it seemed a suitable question.

"It's a function I'm hosting for a charity," he said, "I've invited a few of my friends along."

"Oh cool," she said, hopefully sounding casual, "Anyone I would know?"

"Chances are," he said, "I'd say wear your very best."

Her very best dress would look like a kitchen towel compared to what his friends would be wearing no doubt, she would have to go shopping. Her mind started racing at a hundred miles an hour about what she should wear.

"Are you there?" he asked.

"Yes!" she blurted, "Yes, just thinking about what I could drag out of my wardrobe. I also wanted to ask something else though,"

"Sure," he said, and again she heard noises on his side that suggested movement, it sounded like his office chair moved, it didn't squeal so much as just whisper in the almost total silence around him, but she was certain he had just stopped what he was doing and leaned back in his chair to listen. For her it was like having the entire world stop what they were doing and turn to look at her. "Rayne?" he chimed musically.

"Yes. Sorry," she hit her head again, "Look Mason I'm sorry to ask this. I don't even know how to articulate what I want to say but… fuck it, I'm *very* confused."

"About what?"

"Well, we had sex!?" she said, "We had a *lot* of sex,"

"I remember,"

"And then you bought that video off me for a *fuck-load* of money," her hands were shivering even as she was saying this, "And we had a lot of sex."

"Yes, I'm with you on all that," he paused, "What's the problem?"

"I don't know," she admitted, "I'm rattled, I'm terrified, I feel like I've being thrown about in a storm, I wasn't expecting any of this to happen! You're Lynel Mason, you own Gregory Maines Tower and most of Sky City, *you* made South Africa the country it is, you're famous everywhere. I'm a... Christ alive... I'm a fucking webcam porn star!"

"Are you afraid that if people see us together they'll get the wrong idea?"

"What?! No, I don't care what people think-" ...?.... "Why would they see us together?!"

"Well, at the party," he said, "You're coming as my date aren't you?"

The world dropped beneath her and she fell with it, her mouth opened to say something but she shut it, she opened it again and achieved vocality, "I... yes I could."

"Look Rayne may I say something?" he asked politely but firmly, she imaged how many CEOs of companies were often silenced but that polite firmness, "I don't care what people think. I may have purchased a video off you, which is our business relationship conducted but do you think I spend an entire day and night with everyone I do business with? I know this might take some adjustment but please don't concern yourself with the hype that people say about me, it's just media bullshit and none of it relates. If I'm truthful I'm quite lonely. I'd like to see you again soon if I may."

"Today?" she asked.

"Well no," he said earnestly, "I'm not available right now, work stuff, but soon, before the party."

Automatically her mind started calculating to see if she was going to be able to afford it.

"Just say yes," he said, "Welcome to my world."

"I don't know anything about your world," she sighed, "I think it scares me Mason."

"Just wait," he said.

6.

The woman was in her late forties and sat in the corner of the coffee shop staring out at the train station platforms and observing the people walking across it. Her eyes searched the faces of each and every person clearly looking for someone. In front of her on the table were two plastic cups of coffee and two napkins, neatly arranged for someone who hadn't arrived. She was dressed for travelling, a woollen buttoned up black coat and scarf, blue jeans and cowboy boots and beside her was a medium sized violet travelling case with wheels. Her hands were occupied in front of her alternatively stroking the disposable coffee cup and checking the text messages on her phone. Whoever it was she was supposed to be travelling with had not yet arrived and with every minute and every phone-check the hope in her eyes died. Hope was something that you could only measure in the amount lost.

Beyond the glass walls that protected the coffee shop from the noise of the station a vast theatre of prologues and conclusions unfolded. Stories began and ended here, like the teenage couple in jeans and vests with rucksacks bulging with their worldly possessions preparing to embark on the journey of a lifetime and the elderly couple returning home from their final adventure. Or, the businessman running across the platform to catch the last train home to his loving wife and warm bed or the groups of boys landing in the city for a righteous night out. If mathematics like six degrees of separation were to be trusted, you could see every sort of person in the entire world in this one provincial train station.

Her phone buzzed and the woman snatched it from the table and her eyes scanned the message and with an audible thud her face dropped and as if waking from a dream she looked up and glanced around the room looking at the faces of the other people sitting in the coffee shop. Her embarrassment was a tangible thing, realizing that she had packed herself up for a trip only to be duped at the last moment. In a flurry of movement she stuffed the phone into her coat pocket and gathered her things and all but ran from the coffee shop. Meanwhile outside a pair of lovers were reunited, colliding with each other in a bodily hug.

Unnoticed, Daemon stood in the corner of the coffee shop,

following the woman with his eyes for as long as he could until she vanished around the corner, dragging the travel case behind her with her face down, he took a deep breath and let it out with a sigh. He had been coming to this same coffee shop regularly for many years, he never ordered anything in fact he was *never* noticed which suited him just fine. He would stand in the corner, out of the way and just... *experience*.

Like any of the primary senses that help people shape their world telepathy was just another means he used to navigate. But he did not listen nor did he read people's thoughts because no human ever thought in such a fashion. Human minds were a scrap book where every image was coloured with every available sense. People never merely thought, they re-experienced, they re-enjoyed, they re-felt, they re-saw, they re-pondered- never had he met a human who just merely thought and while he stood, his hands in his pockets and his eyes closed he opened his mind and got an impression of everyone. That way he understood more about this modern world that was changing faster than he was able to keep up than he had ever experienced gleaning the brainwork off of the surface of the minds of every person who came close to him.

And what had he noticed? Everyone was the same person.

He meant this literally. Behind the eyes of every person, there was a psychic vibration, a key tone that represented the conscious mind. For him, this conscious mind had a sound to it, a certain frequency, and a certain structure. With animals, despite their level of intelligence, from snail to dolphin, each individual animal had a unique sounding mind. But not humans.

With humans there was One conscious mind that was divided an infinite number of times throughout the ages into versions of itself that might have *looked* different but was the same sentient *person* looking out. This One was unaware that he or she was looking at themselves whenever they looked at the eyes of someone else. The same mind just in different bodies. It was difficult to explain which was why Daemon had never tried.

It had only emphasized the loneliness he felt.

An incredibly fat man who had squeezed himself into a suit and now looked like a half exploded sausage wobbled his way across the platform swinging an out of date briefcase in his hand. He puffed and wheezed as he strutted, his pale eyes looking out through large glasses with condemnation at the world. For a moment his eyes fell upon the giant behind the glass in the cafeteria but within the same second they refocused and the man continued walking angrily.

This was always of interest to the giant. The world was filled with people who could see him but only a handful of them knew it. Whether it was his will power or the same mental telepathy that he used to garner impressions from people's mind, he was not sure, but if he did not want to be seen he would not be. This allowed him to move amongst the people unseen.

From his position at the back of the coffee shop he turned his attention as always to the CCTV cameras that blossomed out of the corners of the train station like robotic flowers that over saw and documented the actions of everyone in station. He had no control over what they saw but at the same time he knew they did not see him and if they did, which he saw no reason why they wouldn't, then whoever controlled the cameras either did not have the sense or the power to do anything about it.

The giant closed his eyes for a moment to think while simultaneously listening to the conversation between the young man behind the counter and a girl he was serving. He actively made sure he followed their conversation so that he did not phase out and loose *now*.

The cameras and the intruding security technology of the world ultimately did not matter to him because like all things in nature, even at its worse it was only temporary and he would outlast it.

Their conversion reminded him of a bicycle wheel, constructed of a number of spokes all heading in different directions but revolving around a central idea. They wanted to have sex.

7.

People would not be surprised to discover that the floor directly beneath Mason's office was entirely devoted to his training. The only access into this one of a kind gymnasium was via his office and otherwise it was completely sealed off from everyone. It was cleaned four times a week but this task was completed via automated systems and cleaning bots which one of his many companies had designed initially to remotely clean nuclear waste and other chemical disasters. They were thorough and had no need to ever ask questions.

Some of the questions asked may have been about work hours and work load. How could a man work for a hundred hours without sleep and or food and then have the energy to train in his private gymnasium for seventeen hours straight? There had once been a time when work could be conducted behind closed doors and businessmen such as himself were free to conduct it as they saw fit but he was living in the age of the internet where a small mention of his working hours could appear online today and be seen by a billion people by tomorrow. This did not concern him overly because he had spent the last forty years preparing an empire that would outlast the cyber age and the one following, an empire based on amassing power behind people's backs and away from the limelight. For now, power meant making money and that drew attention but a lot of money could bury any unwanted attention.

This was no better illustrated than in two occurrences which were highlighted in the past week. The first one being Rayne Ensley and her video of the notorious publicity avoiding Coat who had not drawn much or any interest from him until Mason had seen the video himself and the second was an older interest, the resurfacing of an old colleague. There had been some commotion in a town in northern England following a burglary, during which several witnesses claimed the suspect was an "Olympic pace athlete," who wore a hood and had not been caught. Britain ran on the media, they fed off it even more than the South Africans and this story had been circulating around the local news and websites for a couple of days. It wasn't a lot to go on but it was enough of a lead and Mason had lived long enough to know when he was being thrown a bone.

On cue his phone rang at his desk and he picked it up, "Hello,"

"Good morning Mason," it was Alan on the other end, "It's me, how are you?"

"Hundred percent," the trillionaire replied, "Yourself?"

"I'm good thank you," Alan said, "Well Craig and his men were found in Hertfordshire this morning. Deceased."

"I imagine they were," Mason replied.

"You don't sound surprised?" his right hand man said.

"It just confirms something," Mason said, "I'm emailing you a news link Alan, have a look, he was in Northern England seventy two hours ago."

"He's lucky," Alan said, but his tone suggested that he knew it was something else.

"No Alan," Mason said, "He's gifted. Look, we've run him around enough and he's paranoid, jumped up and frightful of everything. It's exactly how we want him."

"You're suspecting he's going to make a mistake?" Like all of his closest staff Alan had learnt to always trust Mason's instincts.

"Yes, he's going to think he has nothing to lose soon," Mason said. He hung up and sat back in his chair watching the tankers line up on the horizon to get into the Durban Harbor and sipping a sadistically strong cup of coffee, he didn't micromanage and it was within those sorts of parameters that people like Alan thrived.

Splashing from his pool behind him reminded him that he wasn't alone in the office, which was a shame as he wanted to go downstairs and train. He felt an insatiable energy churning in his body, desperate to be unleashed and he had completed every task he had to do with the running of his companies during the morning and was still uncomfortably buzzing.

"Mason!" Georgina Cassidy, the supermodel from America called from the pool, "Don't be such a sour puss, come in here with me!"

He wondered what this girl thought. Had she even considered looking into his history or had she just blindly followed her promoters when he'd invited her over? It was one of the reasons he preferred models, they may not have been the idiotic puppets people thought, for example, he knew that Georgina Cassidy was highly educated and well spoken. Able to hold herself in any intelligent conversation and if the modeling world hadn't snatched her up she would have climbed the ranks of any corporate ladder she wanted. But the modeling industry had snapped her up and now she was trained to obey whoever had the money. She would have fought her peers with a knife for the chance to get into his pool.

"I'm lonely in here," she crooned, splashing around, "And *very* wet."

"I'll be right there," he moaned, drinking the rest of his coffee and not making a move from his chair. The view from his desk was particularly stunning this morning and he felt like Odin overlooking Valhalla, "Do you ever wonder about the future Georgina?" he asked.

"Sorry what?" she called back from the pool, "I can't hear you sugar."

He turned around on his chair and put the cup onto the desk while simultaneously standing up and walking, the movement had seemed natural for him but judging by Georgina's expression it was too fast and smooth. He reminded himself to slow down.

"The future," he said with a smile, "Do you ever wonder about the future?"

"Nah sugar," she said, "I like to live for the *now*, that's all there is after all."

Georgina, beautiful, tall, slinky Georgina with the big breasts the perfectly proportioned, perfectly toned body, features that America *deemed* beautiful for the moment- so flawless that nobody would be able to describe her, any more than anyone could describe a China doll. Her hair was like an oil slick in the pool where her perfectly applied waterproof makeup accentuated her almost luminous green eyes. The most impressive thing about her was how quickly such a practiced and rehearsed response, the sort of answer she would have said on stage in front of judges at a pageant to earn their approval could totally remove any desire he had for her. He smiled politely, not wanting to hurt her feelings.

He walked to the poolside with his hands in the pockets of his jeans and Georgina, as naked as the day she was born pushed away from the edge and floated backwards, her breasts bobbing on the surface.

"Take off your clothes," she said with a sly smile, "And come in here for a swim."

"And what would happen then?" he asked, stopping at the very edge of the pool so that his toes curled over the edge.

"Oh I don't know," the model said, putting her feet down on the bottom of the pool and standing up. For the moment the *ideal* America woman was the sort that Mason had seen in comic books, there was a muscular tone to Georgina's arms and shoulders, her breasts were huge with firm, erect nipples as smooth as the teat on a baby's bottle. Her abdomen was flat and toned, muscles revealing themselves on each step. The "fitness revolution" in America five years earlier had been a highly celebrated thing and long overdue, the highest example of which stood before him, gently stroking her delicate hands through the water obscuring the view of a very dark bikini-strip of hair.

He sighed, "How much did I offer you to come here?"

Her smile lingered, in fact it didn't move. Facial expressions effect how people feel and think and if you remove a person's ability to look sad they will never become depressed, the same goes if you stop people from smiling. The same clearly went for if you expect people to perfect big wide, toothy grins under dumb-cow-eyes, he immediately lost all interest in Georgina.

"Four hundred thousand," she said, her smile slipping ever so slightly.

He nodded.

"I'll pay you twice that if you leave my office right now," he said.

She blinked and a look of confusion that was as tempered as her smile skewed her eyebrows, "Have I done something wrong?"

"Not at all," he said returning to his side of the desk and pushing in the chair so that he could talk while leaning on its back, "I've simply lost interest I'm afraid and rather fancy doing some training."

"I've been booked for an entire day with you," she reminded him, "You asked for me specifically. I thought we were going to fuck?"

We probably were, he thought, but he had sent the invitation to her a week earlier, only days before he met someone else. He shrugged and walked around his desk to the left hand side of the pool to a decorative oak bench, on it was a thick white toweling robe which he picked up and held open for her at the edge, "Yes, that was my initial intention but my mind has become distracted and I don't think I would be of any use to you."

"I could wait," she suggested, walking up the pool steps and

clasping her hands just under her chin so that her elbows squashed her breasts together like the lobes of a plum, "Maybe later you'd like to?"
He smiled at her, "I've heard about your Yankee lust for sex," he said, "I don't think I would be able to cope. You are very kind to offer but I'm afraid not."
She suddenly looked like she was going to cry, tears pearling in the corners of her eyes, "No! *No!* If you don't fuck me my career is going to fall apart *I* don't want to be the girl that Lynel Mason didn't want to fuck!"
It was Mason's turn to blink and he did a quick mental calculation and had to admit with a touch of embarrassment that the reputation was well earned.

"You can tell people whatever you like," he said, "Tell them I'm hung like a bull and we engaged in un-lubricated anal sex, I'll happily endorse it," he jiggled the corners of the robe, "Now please."
She walked up the rest of the stairs like a prisoner going to the gas chamber, her head down and her body shivering. She put her arms through the sleeves her fingers grazing his as she took the ends of the belt and as he stepped away she turned to face him, letting the robe fall open and tried to kiss him in what was a last stitch attempt to salvage the situation. His patience evaporated with the remainder of her self-respect and he curled his fingers around her shoulders and held her at arm's reach, "I'm going to stand here and you are going to leave."
Perhaps it was the way he said it or the way he was looking at her but a clear realization came into her eyes and as if she was just coming to her senses and realizing who or what she was dealing with she stepped away from him, walked to her clothes where they were piled next to the bench and quickly dressed. Her hair sending long rivulets of water down the back of her top and her shoes clutched in her hands she jogged to the elevator and pushed the button while repeatedly looking over her shoulder at him. The elevator doors slid open and with evident relief she climbed in, daring to look up only as the doors whispered closed. Her eyes were brimming with fearful tears.

He put his head back and sighed, although he regretted being so harsh with her, he was relieved to be alone. Rudeness and cruelty were two things he despised, seeing them as attributes of the powerless and scared. He preferred generosity and charm, he enjoyed winning people over, but sometimes a harder swing was required.

He returned to his desk, waved a hand in front of the communication panel and said, "Montgomery,"

"Yes sir," one of his people replied, "I can see Miss Cassidy leaving now."

"Yes," he sighed, "Please ensure she gets the penthouse suite at the Hillgrove and a private class to San Francisco at her earliest convenience for me."

"Yes sir," he said, "Will there be anything else?"

"Nope,"

Montgomery was, amongst many other things, Mason's personal driver. A retired power builder who towered over people and was as unmistakably black as the ace of spades, with biceps thicker than most people's thighs. As with many of Mason's personal staff he was valued for his uniqueness. He was an applicable person, practical in his work methods, always neat, always prompt and whilst he had demonstrated a kind of terrifying savagery when necessary he could also metamorphose into the sweetest most genteel person on the planet. Blessed with both a scowl that would empty bowels and a smile that would win hearts.

"Montgomery?"

"Yes sir?"

"Do you like Americans?"

"They're alright sir, only ever been to America once though."

"Oh, when was that?"

"The night of your third divorce, sir,"

Mason laughed heartily, "*We* went to America?" he asked with genuine blunt surprise.

"Yes sir," Montgomery confirmed, "You drank out the Clamshell Café… they had called an ambulance thinking you were going to die."

This was all news to him. He remembered that third divorce. Nadine something or other, an eighteen year old beach volley ball champion, Christ she had taken him for a lot of money and he had suspicions she might still be on the company payroll. He shrugged, "I don't remember much of that night-"

"Five days, sir"

"-to be honest. Was that how you got that butterfly tattoo on your neck?"

Montgomery laughed, "Yes sir. Why do you ask?"

"It is a very feminine tattoo and I've been curious about it for a while."

"Why do you want to know if I like the Americans?"

"Do you have plans for tonight?"

"I am on duty with you sir,"

"Perfect, do me a favor take Miss Cassidy out tonight for me would you? You know all the best places in town so just show her a good time," and then he remembered something, "Don't let her come back with any tattoos."

"Very good sir," he said with a professional level of buzzing excitement, "How will you get about sir?"

"I'll manage don't you worry," he said, "Keep a tally and I'll reimburse you later. Thanks Montgomery."

"My pleasure sir,"

In a small way his conscience was restored and Mason made his way to the gymnasium through the bathroom and the five man bathtub, a door lead down a short passageway to a private elevator which, like the backbone of a skeleton, allowed him access to all the floors in the building including the three subterranean levels. The Gregory Maines Tower was a versatile building with an equal number of residences and corporate businesses. Levels of security equal to the formidable steps taken to protect the tower simply did not exist elsewhere. However, for him, with the entire world knowing on which floor he worked and lived the elevator was vital for avoiding the storm of businessmen and press who sometimes went so far as to land on his rooftop helipad to speak with him.

He rode the elevator one floor down to a changing room with a row of showers and benches. Here he undressed, throwing his jeans and shirt into the private laundry chute and changed into a pair of white cotton *gi* pants and proceeded barefoot and bare-chested into the main floor of his gymnasium.

This entire floor was solely devoted to his physical training regime and would have puzzled any conventional fitness instructor for the training he did was in no way conventional.

In the far left corner a large selection of free weights dominated like a collection of God's facial piercings, the lightest dumbbell was fifty kilograms and the heaviest at a hundred kilograms had to be factory made for him. The bars and racks had been specifically strengthened to hold his requirement weights, the floor mats surrounding them were twelve inches of inflated foam to stop the impact of these metal bars hitting the floor and cracking the concrete.

Opposite to that in the corner directly in front of him was a field of gymnastic equipment including the parallel bars, pommel horse and rings. To his right was an assortment of punching bags on a steel frame and padded dummies and in the center was what looked like a cross between construction scaffolding and a child's jungle gym.

For reference, Mason looked like a young thirty five, and could have been mistaken for being in his twenties. Ten years earlier he had looked in his seventies. Opening his training with gymnastics instead of stretching or warming up he leaped straight into a round off, followed by a series of backflips, followed by a cartwheel, then into a handspring ending in a double back tuck and somersault which he landed with a definite thud like an industrial gas gun firing a railroad spike into the ground. Rolling his shoulders he strolled to the jungle gym, a seemingly chaotic and random assemblage of horizontal beams and vertical bars that could be scaled and swung around on.

So many steel cables were bolted to the ceiling and the scaffolding that it had the look of a spider's web. Not the quaint, artistic spider's web that looks beautiful in the morning dew and inspires people to marvel at the design and artistry of nature but the nightmarish web of a murderous predator.

Mason walked beneath one of the horizontal bars that was a clear four meters above him and held out upon two horizontal struts that were in turn suspended with steel cables. He took a breath, held his arms out in front of him at shoulder height with his fingertips straight, bent at the knees into a crouching squat and sprang. He reached the bar with more upward velocity than he needed and used this extra momentum to vault around it into a handstand. He held this for a long moment, his toes pointed to the ceiling, his body as rigid and as unmoving as a drawing. He shifted his weight to his left arm and brought his right up to his side, supporting his entire weight through the arm and into the hand that balanced upon a single three inch wide bar. With a sigh he brought his toes forward, building an incredibly fast swing at the bottom end of which he let go and hurtled into the dense and complicated jungle gym.

As he warmed up his muscles by climbing, swinging and somersaulting with the combination of cramped space and break-neck speeds he became completely locked into the present moment, absorbing rather than experiencing every detail as he soured through the air. From the start of his work outs to the end he constantly pushed himself to see where his bodily limitations were and with his body's ability to adapt and accommodate for anything it was an ongoing fight against himself.

Fluidly, like the rising of air, he climbed and swung and rose through the jungle gym scaffolding until he was swinging on the highest bar some six or seven meters above the floor. As he spun and twisted in midair, gathering more and more momentum, spinning and throwing his weight into his feet through his hips to gather ever increasing torque on his spirals he reached the apex of his rising arch and released his grip on the bar. He somersaulted wildly into the air with the intention of losing control, throwing his arms out wildly and screwing his eyes shut, removing all pertinence of control. His stomach lurched and there was a part of his mind that wanted to scream and try to grab hold of something but he had aimed to throw himself too far from the scaffold for him to find anything but air to save himself.

    He relaxed, knowing that the inevitable impact was approaching, the sudden, thudding stop and the twig snapping of bones. Gymnastic accidents were often the worst thanks to the sheer force of landing after so much energy is generated, legs snapped like toothpicks, spines could shatter and vertebrae could pierce the skin.

He grit his teeth against the thought and in what he knew were the very final moments, the last fraction of a second left he felt an overwhelming urge, an impossible-to-resist twitch in his muscles. His knees fractionally bent by themselves and the balls of his feet hit the mat first, his knees absorbed the impact of landing, carrying him backwards, distributing the kinetic energy through a backward roll, his hands touched the mat palms down and as his body rolled backwards over them they straightened. The momentum of his fall was carried like electricity through a conduit into and passed his triceps, thrusting into his hips and out through his legs and he alighted lightly on his feet.

Fuck it!

Enraged, his breathing shooting out in pants, his shoulders heaving he

glared at his feet. Jaw clenched and lips quivering. It wasn't anger at what his body was able to do, he was pleased with the results of his work, it was anger at being beaten by anything.
As soon as the anger had blossomed like some petrol-fuelled fire inside it exploded into amusement. What a ridiculous thing to be angry about!?

Laughing merrily to himself he walked away from the jungle gym and went to the free weight section where he developed a tropical sweat while curling and pushing, lifting and holding weights that seemed too heavy for a man of his size in seamless sets of a hundred or two hundred repetitions.
After the weight section he spent some time in the gymnastics section where he break-danced around the pommel horse for an hour, threw himself around the parallel bars and spent some time performing the sort of maneuvers on the rings that were reserved for films and comic books.

After another perfect dismount he strolled to the punch bags, again custom designs of titanium weaved Kevlar and ball bearings, each one was like attacking a steel girdle.

The remainder of his session was spent smashing these various shaped bags and similarly designed makiwaras. Hearing it would have sounded like a mixture between a professional rock drummer during a solo and machine gun fire.
Hours later, he stood panting, staring at the bags as they swung on their chains, leaving long strips of his blood across the floor. While he stood there the split, openly bleeding flesh of over his knuckles and on the blade of his hands stitched together and began to itch. The cracked bones of his shins from the muay thai round house kicks he had delivered sealed and hardened, the bruises across the impact regions of his body faded and the aches in his shoulders and arms receded.
Long gone were the days where a hard work out would leave him aching for hours. There was no such reward for his physique.

Nevertheless he enjoyed the piping hot shower in the large shower unit that sprayed water from seven different sources, it allowed the feeling of space which was something he valued, a childhood spent in squalor and confining environments had created in him a distinct hatred of being cramped.
He finished the shower, dried himself off with a fluffy white towel, wrapped it around his waist and tucked the corners in then rode the

elevator to his office level where, leaving footprints behind him he walked out onto the balcony. The sun had long been swallowed by the African background and both Sky City and Durban City bloomed into a light-fantastic flower. His was the best view in the country. The cool night air licked at his bare skin and tousled his wet hair but while he noticed the temperature he didn't feel uncomfortable. His body tended to burn at a higher temperature anyway. He watched the city, the cars moving through the streets like cattle, the pedestrians pouring around them, the residents of Sky City moving along the ramps and bridges, all dressed to the nines. All of these people, every one of them in Sky City and Durban would play a role in his plans. All of them.

Pushing away from the banister he returned to his office, closing the doors behind him, "Music," he said and there was a click as the management system of the office recognized his voice and a second later the full, lilting tones of a string quartet filled the room. Gregory Towers facilitated AI Management Systems for all the floors, but he didn't like it. His management system was a simple voice activated computer system that very simply acted as a tool.

There were two entrances into Mason's apartment that were accessible from either ends of his office. Each floor held two apartments and he was the only one who could access both on his floor, he pushed through the door hidden in the wall next to the coffee machine and entered into an incredibly Spartan looking abode. Space was a premium especially in Sky City where millionaires lived in apartments too small to fit a double bed, so that his was large enough to play a decent game of cricket in made a statement that could not be ignored. Polished floorboards lead unimpeded from wall to wall, the only furnishings being a low, bed so wide that no matter which way he lay on it he couldn't touch all the sides and a massive two hundred inch television screen. There was a kitchen unit built into one side and a door on the far end lead to the bathroom with his legendary tub, but aside from it was now filled only with music.

He took off the towel, rolled it into a ball and launched it into a laundry shoot and padded naked, oblivious and uncaring to the floor to ceiling windows that curved around him, they were one way glass and nobody could see through even with the lights on and they weren't.

"Television," he said.

With an electric hum the television came to life and filled the dark room with light, with flicks of his fingers he surfed the channels that slid off the screen like pieces of paper. He didn't fancy watching sports, he didn't fancy documentaries or the news which always depressed him and he didn't want cartoons finally it landed on the adult channel and he shrugged. Yes, perhaps, ultimately he was just a man.

Staying on the channel he began selecting the various programs that were available, there were thousands of them. Since broadcasting, the internet and holovision had combined together a person's choice was almost infinite. He was flicking through them at a dizzying pace knowing full well what he wanted until he finally said, "Search Rayne Ensley,"

The computer clicked in response and for a second the television screen froze and then like a main course dish arriving on the plate the channel opened up.

For the first time in decades Mason wanted to look over his shoulder to make sure that nobody was going to walk in. It felt wrong to watch it so recently after he had had the real thing but that was part of the excitement. He felt naughty.

There was a catalogue of videos to choose from, she had been at this for a long time and throughout them you could tell she used the same setting: her bed and a wall. He went to the first video she ever put on the channel. The webcam turned on to reveal a well-made bed, with a white duvet cover that had a black ribbon across the center and pillows of the same design, white with a black bar across them up against a white washed brick wall. Music, an already forgotten pop song sung by an already forgotten pop singer, began playing and continued for a full verse before Rayne stepped in front of the bed.

Short and more plump than slinky she looked amazing. She had chosen a pair of black hot pants and a short cut pink top that sat so high on her chest that you could see the half-moon undersides of her breasts. Mason corrected himself, she wasn't plump at all but healthy, the hot pants revealed she had perfectly round bubble bum and while her legs were on the short side and her calves were thick and there was a subtle musculature about them that made his mouth dry. The sensuous curve to her belly with a navel that he fondly remembered putting his tongue into. Her hair was different then, not as long or as straight as it was now, cut short to her jaw line and quite bouncy it accentuated her vibrant, wide smile and her dimpled cheeks. A slight touch of makeup had her eyes glowing.

She swayed her hips along with the music, building up a mood, pouting her lips and looking sexy for as long as she could before she started giggling. Within the first quarter of the song she had taken off her top, revealing round breasts with small but perfectly round areola and pert nipples that pointed skyward. Her breasts were large enough for her to cup one with a hand and lift it to her mouth for her to extend a pink, spearhead shaped tongue and flick the nipple. Half way through the song she was on the bed, her legs pointed straight into the sky- *God what a backside!*- and with just her finger tips she pulled the hot pants up her legs and over her ankles and beyond her toes. She crossed her ankles and slipped her fingers through her thighs to form a teasing cover. Mason was desperate for a drink by this stage but couldn't bring himself to move from his spot. She uncrossed her ankles and spread her legs and grabbed her ankles with her hands revealing a porcelain smooth Mound of Venus and the most delectable folds of flesh he had ever seen.

The camera zoomed in and Mason didn't manage to make it to the end of the song.

"H-hello?" Rayne said.

Mason was perched on the banister of his balcony, sitting on the top bar with his back facing the city and eighty seven floors to the road below, with his phone to his ear, "Hi Rayne!" he yelled against the wind.

"Hello?" she repeated, "Mason is that you?!"

"Yes hi!" he called again, "I'm outside on my balcony can you hear me?!"

"I can't hear you are you outside?!"

He rolled his eyes and hopped off the banister and walked inside closing the doors behind him, "There, can you hear me now?"

"Oh, yes," she said, "I can hear you much better now. Were you outside?"

"Yes. I was," he said, "So. What are you doing?"

"I was asleep actually," she replied, "I'm catching up after twenty years of sleepless nights."

"I can call back later?"

"No," she said, "I'm awake now, besides I was thinking about you-

fuck,"
His eyebrows went up, "Sorry?"
"I didn't mean to say that," she said hurriedly, "Sorry, can we just forget I said that?"
"It's okay to say fuck," he said.
"No, the part about me thinking about you,"
"So you *were* thinking of me?"
"Oh shut up," she snapped, "What do you want anyway? It's three a.m. what *do* you want?"
Was that the time? He thought. He said, "I was actually thinking about you too,"
There was a sound that suggested she'd just sat up, "You were?"
"Yes," he said, "I actually wanted to see you again. When are you available?"
"Well, when do you want me?"
"Well you're awake now," he said, "Do you fancy a coffee?"
"Haha. Sure."
Hanging up he ran into his apartment, flew into the wardrobe and quickly dressed in his finest pair of scruffy jeans, pulled on one of his favorite T-shirts, it was a Def Leopard cover shirt from 1993 vintage, All Star converses and a trilby which he took off before he got to the elevator because he thought it was a bit much. He rode the box down to the basement level garage and, as he had asked Montgomery to look after the American model was forced to make the near impossible decision of which of his cars he wanted to drive.

His garage was like the parking lot at Top Gear greatest hits and Richard Hammond was to blame for almost every one of his vehicle purchases. During a television interview with Gary Larson five years earlier he had been asked beforehand to make a list of his favorite cars and it took seven pages, both sides, to get them all in and he had been buying since then.

It turned out to be an impossible task and instead he chose one of his motorcycles, a black as night Ninja. It was like riding a robotic, fire powered shark and this one he had restored himself so he was particularly pleased with it.

He walked it out of its parking space, climbed on and took off with a piercing scream of the engine through the underground lot. He went out at the ground level entrance, exiting onto a completely deserted 3am main road and the salty air spraying into his face he shot off at two hundred kilometers an hour in the direction of Rayne's house and hadn't gotten three blocks when he saw his shadow thrown out in front of him in blue and red flashing lights.

He pulled over onto the side of the road and put a foot out as the cruiser parked up behind him and a police officer climbed out of the car. The police in South Africa were a harsh reminder of the level of crime effecting this city, the officer who had been in a bullet proofed vehicle had, by law, put on a blast proof helmet before stepping out and was wearing bullet and stab proof body armor. At his hip was a loaded hand gun with spare magazines at his belt.

The man approached and Mason was overwhelmed by the smell of stale sweat and determined that this officer had been on duty most of the night.

"Good evening sir," the officer said, his accent thick with Afrikaans.

"*Goeie aand meneer,*" Mason replied in Afrikaans automatically.

Without so much as a hesitation the police officer continued in his home tongue, "Sir may I take your license please,"

Obediently Mason gave the policeman his thumbprint, the details appeared on the officers palm top, "Do you know why I stopped you sir?"

"I was speeding I imagine," Mason answered.

"That is true sir," the officer confirmed, "But not why I stopped you, you'll be receiving your speeding tickets thanks to the Networked Security," and the officer turned and pointed to a cluster of cameras under a nearby bridge, "I stopped you sir because you are not wearing a helmet."

Mason almost laughed, but didn't.

"My apologies sir," he continued in the officer's language, "I do have one at home,"

"But you are not wearing it sir," the man said matter of factly, "Having a helmet is not the same as wearing one, a fact you would certainly have found out if you had been involved in an accident."

Mason didn't think it was worthwhile to try and argue and simply said, "Officer you are absolutely correct and I would prefer to cooperate."

"This is very good to hear sir," the police officer, who was also sporting a moustache that had been stolen from a walrus said, "A pleasure

to find someone from the Fourteens who still respects the law."
Mason smiled through the entire twenty minutes of lecturing from this police officer and when the man slapped him with a fine he accepted it and, despite all this still rode without a helmet to Rayne's apartment.

8.

It was the wee hours of the morning, a time where everything should have been asleep and while the streets were empty he could sense the angry business that existed here. Eyes gazed out with lividity from the shadows under closed and boarded up shops and from black as ink alleyways. It was the sort of place where, at night, nobody walked alone and the streets were empty and everyone stayed in and so the predators just waited. This part of Durban, where there were more wooden boards than windows and locked doors were reinforced behind steel fences and every window had bars on them, were the second stark reminder of the country's state he had that night.

He found a high security car park where he was able to park up his bike and collect a small electronic fob from an automatic machine near the entrance. High technology security tended to sneak into places like this- providing high tech security in the hope that it would lure the more affluent people into the area.

Pocketing the fob he continued on foot along the handful of blocks to where Rayne's apartment was, the air was fresh and the pre-dawn light had started to scare away the dark.

He sensed the gang before they had even seen him, a group of teenagers with caps and jackets, low slung jeans and a cloud of bad intentions floating over their heads, standing in a huddle against a fence blocking his route.

Preferring to allow everyone a chance to prove him wrong Mason continued walking and even put his hands in his pockets to show he expected not to need to use them.

As he neared one of the teenagers broke away from the gang and tilted his head back to look at him from under his cap peak, his gaunt features and stinking breath told a long story of drugs and thievery, "Hey mister can you borrow me a strip?"

Mason stopped and after a quick glance to confirm their numbers shrugged and took out his wallet, "Sure. How much do you want?"

Mason liked to carry notes with him and his wallet looked like an encyclopedia, he heard their unsubtle gasps when they saw it.

The teenager pulled out a gun.

In films they would threaten first, but this was South Africa and as far as they were concerned Mason's life was worth exactly less than what was in his wallet. They would take it, and his wallet, his clothes and anything else they could get off his dead corpse and as this was one of the areas without a reliable camera network, nobody would see it happen and if someone did, they wouldn't do anything about it.

Calmly, Mason flipped his wallet closed and slipped it back into his side pocket with his left hand while intercepting the rising gun with his right, snatching it straight out of the teenager's grasp.

The movement was so smooth and sudden that it hadn't been seen by some of his gang-friends but when the teenager lunged for the weapon they acted instinctively and piled in.

Up until this moment Mason was doing his best to stay level headed, but this wasn't the only gun this group of yobs had and the idiot who opened fire with the other one did so in such a reckless manner that the bullet missed Mason by a foot and slammed into the wall of a block of flats across the road, narrowly missing a bedroom window.

With sudden rage he exploded upon the youths, moving through them with such speed that there was never any hope that they would match the blurred storm of kicks and elbows that didn't break bones but shattered them, disfigured their faces and imploded chests. He walked away, his hands in his pockets and none of them were standing.

Arriving at her block of flats on Bakers Street he checked he didn't have any blood on him and dialed her number, hoping that she hadn't gone back to sleep and was greeted with a merry, "Hello?"

"Hi, why do you always sound like you're not sure who's calling?" he asked, "Don't you have my number saved?"

"Of course I do," she said defensively, "It's just habit. Where are you?"

"I'm outside," he said, "Do you want to buzz me in or shall I climb up?"

"Climb up," she said as a joke and he heard the buzzing of the door but he wasn't there. He jogged around the side of the building pulling on the memory of what she had told him about her apartment to roughly judge where it would be. There was only one rectangle of light upon the graffiti strewn wall of the adjacent building and as he dissected all the nearby ambient sounds and honed into the movement within the apartment he could hear her footsteps and it wasn't long before he picked up her scent. She had the most incredible smell and he felt a deep bellied excitement as the fragrance enveloped all the right parts of his brain. There had been a time where smell had been a tertiary sense for him, something to be used after sight and after hearing but now, now it was a primary factor in his life. Smell might not have travelled at the speed of light but it moved faster than most people gave it credit and it preceded and followed everything. It was how he had found her apartment in the first place anyway.

He took half a step back and ran up the side of the wall heading towards the light and sprang across the seven foot gap in between, catching hold of the windowsill of Rayne's apartment.

Rising his head ever so slowly he peeked over the windowsills threshold only to come face to face with a wide eyed Rayne who screamed so loudly he brought his hands to his ears and fell back. With his fingertips he touched and latched upon an unused gutter bracket and hung, dangling seven stories above an alleyway littered with trash, while Rayne stuck her head out of the window.

"What do you think you're doing?" she demanded.

"You said climb!" he retorted, gently swaying.

"You're an idiot do you want to get yourself killed?"

"No," he lied, "But could you back up so I can get up, this gutter won't hold me forever."

She slid up the window and reached out to help him but he waved her away with his free hand and said, "Step back,"

Moving a small distance away clearly expecting him to do something stupid, she watched as he hopped through the window with very little difficulty as if his whole body was lighter than a shoe box.

"Wow," he said inspecting the room, "This is where you live?"

"How the hell did you do that?" she asked, pointing at the window.

"I do parkour," he said, "You know, free running?"

She nodded.

"Nice place," he said.

"It's a good apartment," Rayne replied, "I'm going to be moving soon though,"

He instantly recognized the bed, now with a skyline blue duvet cover and cream colored cushions and pillow and the computer on the desk directly opposite its foot, he stroked the webcam appendage with a finger and gave her a sly look, "And this is where the magic happens."

She pursed her lips and folded her arms, "Oh and you're an expert now are you?"

"Trust me if whoever owned that building knew what you did in here they'd punch through that brick wall just to get a peak," he said walking away from the computer towards the kitchenette, "It's very cozy."

"Feel free to have a look around," she said sarcastically, "Fancy snooping in my knickers' drawer?"

"Oh can I?" he said, turning on her with a manic grin and wide eyes, he even waggled his eyebrows menacingly.

She blanched, "No, of course not."

He smiled widely, taking in the smells of the place in massive, chest filling breaths, her fragrance was damn near overwhelming, "Thanks for letting me come over," he said.

"My pleasure," she responded. It was then that he saw she was wearing grey tracksuit bottoms a pink top, "What?" she asked.

"That is a lovely shirt."

She smirked, "Look who's talking."

"No I meant yours is inside out,"

Her face went from pale to tomato red so quickly that he burst out laughing to which she slapped him in the arm, swept around and walked to the kitchenette. Mason guessed this was as much of an invitation as he was ever going to get so followed her.

"Wow this is," he began.

"Tiny and shit," she answered, "Like I said I'm in the process of moving out."

Indeed, everything she owned had been packed into two television boxes that were on the bed. The rest of the place was just an empty shell, aside from her bedspread.

"Where are you moving to?" he asked.

"Well," she said, looking embarrassed, "I'm going to buy a house in Durban North but I wanted to get out of here as soon as I could. So until the details are sorted I'm going to stay at a hotel."

He nodded, "Well I think it's great. Good for you."

She smiled, and so did he, which made her blush a little and turn away, she said, "I need to change my shirt could you turn around?"

"I've seen you naked Rayne," he reminded her.

"Yes, but that's different," she informed him, "And unless you came here to shag me you can turn around."

When he pointedly did not turn around she gave him a lasting look in the eye and there was a suggestive flicker in her eyebrow then without pause she took the hems of her shirt and swept it up over her head. He caught her arms as they were above her head so the T-shirt collar covered all of her face except for her mouth. His feverishly hot hands reached passed her shoulders and grasping her wrists and brought them to the nape of her neck. She was effectively blind but he was right up against her, his lips so close to hers that she could feel the heat radiating off of them, his body pressed against hers.

"You don't mind me coming around do you?" he whispered as his mouth pressed against the side of her throat just under the chin, his lips nuzzling the sensitive skin there, "I know it's very late, I could go?"

"No," she whispered huskily, "I don't want you to go."

His mouth moved from her throat to across her jaw line and teasingly he brushed his lips against her lower lip, "Good. Now if you don't mind I would like to speak some business with you?"

As long as he kept doing what he was doing she didn't care what he spoke about, she thought candidly. He could have made a grocery list sound erotic, as he let go of one of her wrists and used the hand to caress her bare breast.

"It's regarding the video," he said.

Behind her shirt her eyes popped open and she gasped, was he going to take back the money?

"I don't want the money back," he responded to her thought, "You can keep the money but I want you to also take the credit for the film."

"But..." her mouth was dry, it was like she'd swallowed a bucket of plaster, "The video is yours now..."

His hand cupped her left breast and with his callused fingertips he grazed five lines that were fiery red in her mind's eye, he drew these lines down her ribcage and across her belly and over the front of her tracksuit pants. His grip on her wrist increased, causing her a second of pain and making her arch her back which pressed her midsection firmly against his body as his hand cupped the arrow head of flesh between her legs. One of his fingers pressed firmly against her clitoris which made her sigh with pleasure.

"It is mine," he said softly, "But this is going to be a media storm Rayne," his finger pressed firmly inwards and the cotton of her trousers could have been on fire. She remembered that heat from before, that astonishing, unnatural temperature. He continued, "Everyone in the world is going to watch this video Rayne. Everyone is going to want to know who took it," he gave a long, hungry sigh that blew his breath against her collar bone and lower neck, "They'll find out it was you eventually so why should we *wait-"*

As he said the last word, her body stiffened, lifted itself onto the tips of her toes as his finger pressed inwards, the damp cotton gloving his finger sudden sodden from her juices, she gasped with surprise at the intensity of the feeling and his mouth was upon hers. He kissed her long and deep, his tongue hot and invasive. Abandoning the grip on her wrist and pulling the shirt from her arms and face while his tongue massaged hers with long, hungry strokes. Their lips crushed together her hands wrapped around his neck and she ground herself against his hand.

"I take that as a yes?" he asked, breaking the kiss and stepping away.

"Shut up and do what you came here to do," she growled.

The bed had looked firmer than it actually was and when Rayne finally held up her hands and formed a T- "time out" sign with them, they were up on the floor, tied together in a heap of limbs and sheets. Groaning at the effort she pulled off of him and fell on the floor, curling into a fetal shape with both hands cupping herself between her legs, "Stop stop stop!" she laughed, "Anymore and we'll set the smoke detectors off!"

Mason lay on his back and was still as ram rod hard as he had been two hours earlier. It didn't stand rigidly at attention but rather quivered a little with each heartbeat as if it were dancing to an internal rhythm.

Rayne was giggling, "Jesus, I think you've broken me."

Laughing with her he rolled onto her side and using one hand to prop up his head he used the other to stroke her shoulder sympathetically, "But Rayne, you're not done," he said in a deliberately plaintive tone, "I'm not done yet."

Wide eyed she looked over her shoulder at his engorged penis and shook her head theatrically with her eyes shut, uttering, "Uh-hu's" and "No. No No's"

He chuckled, "But that would put me in credit wouldn't it? By what? Three times?"

"Don't you try and use that against me!" she cried spinning over with surprising speed and poking him in the chest, "Or I'll break it off!"

He put his palms up, "That may be counterproductive,"

She rolled her eyes which an elaborate gesture rendered mute by her satisfied smile, she put her hands flat on his chest and lay her chin upon them, "It's probably a good thing anyway," she said, "I'm not on any birth control."

He shrugged, "Doesn't matter,"

"Oh really?"

"No I mean I'm as fertile as a storefront mannequin," he said with a chuckle, "I can't have kids."

"Seriously?" she asked.

"Yup and don't worry I don't have any germs,"

"Well thank god for that," she laughed, "Not that I'd expect you to have. I mean look at you," she tried to pinch some skin on his chest, "Do you *have* any fat?"

He shrugged, "It's genetics I guess,"

"You must go to the gym though?"

"I have one at the office," he said, "But you know, a healthy body, a health mind I just chose the former."

"Very funny," she said, rolling onto her side and putting her head on his torso, he automatically put his arm over her, "Am I allowed to ask personal questions now?"

"I don't see why not,"

"And if I ask something you don't want me to know about?"

"I'll lie through my teeth," he said candidly.

She decided it was worth it and looked up at the ceiling while she thought of a question, "Where were you born?"

"Surrey, England," he answered immediately.

"Oh no!" she cried, her eyes wide, "You're a Brit?"

He was overcome with laughter as she frantically pushed herself away from him wailing, "I can't believe I've had a *Brit* inside me!"

Historically, thanks to South Africa claiming its independence from the crown in the latter half of the twentieth century, England and SA had enjoyed a long shared animosity about most things. South Africans tended to look at the British the same way you would look at your skin when it gets too wet and goes all wrinkly and water logged, with a sort of grim curiosity. The English on the other hand looked at the South Africans with their usual resolute superiority, believing that despite the sunshine, the freedom, the beautiful food, women and business opportunities that South Africa had really started going downhill the moment they *los-uit* the crown. Mason was well aware of this and had considered himself to be more South African than British in any case.

"Do you have *blue* blood?" Rayne asked, climbing on top of him to sit on his stomach and poke his chest with her fingers, "Do you kiss the crown? Do you have a Union Jack above your bed? Do you drink warm beer?"

"Ewww, gross," he retched at the thought, "You need to go to England, they don't drink anything warm!"

"*Cuppatea?*" Rayne chimed, arching her back and lifting up her chin while sipping from an imaginary cup held in a hand with a straight little finger, "With a scone?"

He laughed harder than he'd laughed in years, until he had hiccups and then he rolled her over onto her back and pinned her to the ground, sliding his fingers into her hair and looking deeply into her eyes. The mood changed instantly as he swam in those deep, deep blue pools, they were lightest blue, with silver shards in them like broken pieces of a mirror.

"You alright?" she asked.

"Yes Rayne," he whispered in a voice almost too low to hear, "I believe I am."

As sunshine poured between the spires, towers and buildings of Durban City and washed upon the bridges, sky scrapers and castles of Sky City in a tsunami of light, Mason felt more invigorated than ever but Rayne was flagging. She looked exhausted and confused at how Mason could still be so energetic- confused but too tired to really care. He made a makeshift repair of her bed so that she could at least curl into a little ball on her side. They shared a final kiss that, even though it took what little energy she had left to do so, she reciprocated and by the time Mason left the apartment Rayne was deeply asleep.

As he bounded down the stairs he pulled out his phone and dialed Alan's number. Mason made a point about paying Alan a lot of money and it wasn't only because the man was an invaluable member of the team but because it was a Sunday morning barely 7am and Alan answered his phone after three rings with a polite but prepared, "Good morning."

"Morning Alan," Mason said taking the stairs two at a time, "I didn't wake you did I?"

"No of course not," the man replied, "Always ready."

"Good. The video?"

"Yup, the one that you wanted buried?"

"Put it everywhere now,"

There was a nano-second pause, a miniscule moment where Mason knew that Alan was weighing up the chances of being able to tell his boss to go jump. The trillionaire was well aware of what it had taken to completely remove the video from the internet, the resources to do such a thing involved deep, *deep* forensic efforts and had probably cost Alan a few of his last few remaining hairs.

"Yes sir," he replied, "Of course. When you say everywhere…?"

"Everywhere," Mason confirmed.

"I'll get right on it,"

Mason hung up and exited the apartment building into the brilliant sunshine of a new day. He didn't put away his phone knowing that when he was feeling like this he was inclined to make a lot of exciting calls. As he strutted along the pavement, chasing the sunlight through the shadows cast down by the regularly spaced trees he called his office phone.

"Good morning Mr. Mason," a cheerful voice said, it was Magdalene. One of his office staff. His personal assistants and secretaries worked on shifts to keep up with the work volume that extruded from Mason like dust from an industrial stone crusher. This included weekends and all hours of the morning, like Alan they were paid almost exclusively to be cheerful at all hours of the day, "How can I help sir?"

"Magdalene," Mason said, "I am feeling very spry this morning! I thought you should know."

"Will that mean you'll be wanting Miss Switzerland next then sir?" she asked with a completely neutral tone.

Magdalene was hilarious and Mason loved her, "No no," he guffawed just like the English gent Rayne had mocked him about being earlier, "Not at all, not at all, *however* grab a pen. Rayne Ensley,"

"Hah," she said.

"Hah?"

"Hah, sir," she explained, "As in, I knew this was going to happen and now Janice owes me fifty,"

Janice was one of his other secretaries. "You know it disturbs me that you're all taking bets on my personal life," he said.

"Indeed sir. Now what about the fabulously rear-ended Miss Ensley?"

"She is buying a house in Durban North," Mason explained, "Can you do some digging, find out who the agent is and make sure that she gets the best of everything *whatever* she wants,"

"Done sir,"

"And make sure that she doesn't find out that I was in any way involved," he added.

"I will do my best sir."

"Thank you," he said just as he rounded a corner and saw something very strange. He hung up and pocketed the phone as he approached the area where he had encountered the teenage gang earlier. He was a complicated person he knew this, both pragmatic and sensitive and smart enough to justify both extremes simultaneously, but after he had beaten them last night he had left them where they were partly because he knew that people needed to see raw justice. They needed to see that if you light the fuse something is going to explode, causality, that every action has an equal an opposite reaction. When he had left them they had been alive- broken with injuries they would lament for the rest of their lives- but alive.

As he approached the place where he had left them he noticed first that they were no longer there, while this was not a surprise, but what caught his attention was the smells. Always the smells.

They hung in the air as if he could see them and he slowed to a creep, taking long deep breaths in through his nostrils.

They had all died, but not because of him. The injuries he had delivered had been severe enough to maim but not kill although he could certainly tell they had died and then their bodies had been dragged away.

This was of particular interest to him. Dragged away. Not picked up or carried, not lifted by the hands of paramedics in canvas stretchers, they had been dragged. Thanks to the smells lingering in the air and caught in the corners of the pavement he could visualize it clearly in his mind's eye. They had been dragged, over the fence.

There weren't any predators big enough to do that, not in Durban. Wild/stray dogs were not strong enough to drag a seventy kilogram teenager over a fence and if a person had done it they would have gone around the fence. If a dog or a person had done it he would have been able to smell them and that was what was truly disturbing to him. He couldn't smell whatever had done this. Five unconscious bodies might as well have killed themselves and then floated over a fence for all that he could tell.

Their smells were smeared against the wooden panels of the fence which stood about six feet tall with a thick green hedge on the other side. By standing on his tip toes Mason could see beyond that into a downward sloping field of grass that hosted a simple playground with a seesaw, a merry go round and a set of swings all surrounded by a wire fence and at the bottom of this grassy field which was the shape of a triangle, surrounded on all sides by roads and buildings, was a grated access point to the sewers.

Mason cringed. There were five scent trails that lead like neon-lit-paths from where he stood to that sewer drain however judging by the slight age differences of each path he could accurately determine that whatever scentless thing had removed the bodies had been strong enough to do so two at a time. Dragging them, a body in each hand down to the sewers.

Mason closed his eyes and focused his attention directly through his nose, dissecting every scent available to him searching for this elusive smell. Everything had a smell- *everything*- in life and in death if something existed then it had a smell. *What* thing didn't leave a smell?

And this scentless thing had gone into the sewers the one place that Mason had a problem with following.

It wasn't the smell of the sewers so much as the understanding of sewers. As Mason senses had enhanced and developed over the years he had found that there was no such thing as a bad smell- smells were like labels, tags or names- they merely described something. However, some smells came with associations and it was the smell of sewers, the combination of urine, of feces, of putrid, stale water, of chemicals, dirt and germs that made his eyes water just thinking about it.

Turning his back on it he made a mental note to find out what was living in the Durban sewers and to overcome his fears because this sort of thing was embarrassing.

However, very out of character for Mason, he completely forgot about both of these things when his phone rung.

"Mr. Mason?"

"Good morning Montgomery," he said jovially, "How are you?"

"I'm good sir. Thank you for asking. Are you okay sir?"

"I'm in very high spirits," Mason said, "I've had a very vigorous evening, how about yourself?"

"Oh, mine was good," the driver said, and Mason could hear voices in the background.

"I see you did show Georgina a good time," Mason said. When he heard more voices in the background he stopped so suddenly he almost made a wobbling sound, "You hound Montgomery, how many are there?"

The driver paused for a moment, perhaps contemplating lying but then said, "Three, sir, I was concerned that you were walking sir,"

"I am walking Montgomery," Mason admitted.

"Oh," the driver said (appropriately turning to look at the three scrumptiously delicious women in his bed), with a sinking tone.

"In Porter's Lane," Mason added with a grin.

"What?!" The driver blurted out and while he was unsure, Mason distinctly heard someone shriek in the background as they fell off the bed, "Sir, I will be right there!"

"You will do no so thing," the trillionaire reprimanded, "I am completely safe and besides I wouldn't be able to look you in the eye if you didn't take full advantage of your situation. So consider this part of annual vacation, enjoy,"

"Are you sure sir?"

"Of course, now get to it," Mason said hanging up.

The sun was well into the sky and like ants pouring forth from an anthill Durban was getting busy with people, thankfully the roads were still scarcely populated so once he collected his bike he made it back to

Gregory Maines within record time. He did not think about the bodies or the scentless thing in the sewers again, which all in all, was probably weirder than you'd think.

Alan knew how to do his job.
His job, and not the title as Operations Director at Maxiform (one of Mason's many companies), was what was important to him. As far as the tax man was concerned he was paid his salary wage from his role as Ops for a company that specialized in forensic accounting of global organizations and companies. Now, accountancy meant nothing to him and to this day he had yet to step foot into the Maxiform office but his role was firmly cemented within the company as long as he worked for Mason because of what his *job* was. He did whatever Lynel Mason asked of him.
How long had it been? Twenty years? Since Alan had walked into a job as a junior executive at one of Mason's many publishing companies. Had he ever been that young? It had been during the transitional period of the industry here slowly and irrevocably print media was turning into digital and every company was trying to stretch themselves in both directions until it was safe to favor only one. Coupled with the financial crisis hitting like a right hook from God and you had a young Alan willing to do whatever job was given to him no matter what it was.

As it turned out he was terrible at the original role he was given but only did that for a week until one of the directors needed his daughter's boyfriend sorted out. With a simple shrug of his shoulders Alan had done so and, while *what* he had done was still to this day unknown, the boyfriend never did return to bother the girl and the director rewarded Alan by giving him four times his annual salary in cash.
And that's how it went. As far as taxes were concerned he was a junior executive and he paid them willingly but he was hardly ever at the office and he carved a reputation for getting things done.

People saw him and thought he was a bruiser, thought that he got what he wanted out of people because he threatened them or hurt them but the truth was all that he did was organize. As formulaic as a phone-jockey sitting at a desk making sales calls he followed the same pattern every time and it always worked: he would talk with them, he would pay them money and then if they didn't do what he wanted he would destroy them.

He was the darker side of Lynel Mason's empire, he was the bloody knife hidden within the robes, but there was never any blood, he had only ever gotten physical with a colleague once and that was a completely non-related-work-issue. No. This was the real world and he knew that in the real world beating someone to a pulp doesn't solve anything if you want people to really feel something hit them where it'll hurt the most. The wallet. And that's why he was Ops Director at Maxiform because it gave him the swing to get the *best* people looking into other people's businesses. No business was perfect, any business that has made it to the top has done it by cutting corners and now he commanded the company that knew just how many corners were cut. The forensic spotlight revealed all and Alan would shine it on whoever Mason wanted, always with a cheerful smile on his face.

He would never have said that his job was boring, every day brought with it new opportunities and it was always an inevitable sprint to keep up with Lynel Mason, but with the video of Rayne Ensley it had been a breath of fresh air to deal with someone who he didn't have to think of as an enemy.

Now, Alan knew his role as death stalker was a very important, very serious role and the ripple-effects of his successes far outweighed simple monetary rewards. They were truly building an empire here, something very real and unquestionably important. He was simply the necessary iron fist within the velvet glove and while Mason was sometimes appalled by the brutality and iciness that Alan could show while completing his tasks, he recognized him as a necessary evil and relied on him to be flexible whenever necessary.

Like Rayne Ensley. The media coverage he would select would be extensive, tailored and timed in such a fashion that her short video would appear, for all those who cared, to be transmitted virally through the internet. Alan already had specialists in mind- specifically teenagers in school who he would pay money to make it *very* popular and these kids would produce more magic via a keyboard and an internet connection than Merlin ever managed with all the resources of Camelot.

And of course, never forgetting the personal touch, weighty brown paper envelopes that stank of money would be handed over warm handshakes and pleasant smiles, to a number of key chief editors around the world to ensure that this was given the *top* spots and Alan, with a job quickly and accurately achieved, set everything in motion, sat back and waited.

9.

It had turned into the hottest day of the year, the sort of Durban day where the sky is so cloudless and clear that you could imagine the entire universe was painted light, seamless blue.

With the help of two handlers Rayne was packing her entire life into an embarrassingly small van and she still didn't own enough to fill it up completely. She had only carried one of the lighter boxes downstairs and put it into the van but already her T-shirt was sticking to her skin. The air was motionless, sapped by the heat and was so thick you could swim through it, heat waves danced off the asphalt and everything shimmered.

The moving company she had hired were top of the line and super-efficient and they made it very clear that her helping, even if it had been only one box wasn't much use to them as they took the box she had handled out of the van and put it on the pavement. Feeling that she ought to do something she took a walk down the street to the local convenience store and bought them all sodas. By the time she had returned the two handlers and the driver were standing around the van chatting idly, the drinks were happily accepted and the driver said after a long, neck chugging drink, "We're done now, we'll take this over to the house for you. Will you be following us?"

"No," Rayne said peering at the old apartment building that she had lived in for so long the same way a hermit crab would look at an old, outgrown shell, "I'll be there later. Post the keys through the post box when you're finished."

Eager to get into their air conditioned van they didn't hesitate in saying goodbye although she did hear one of them mention something about him *seeing* her online and they all gave her furtive glances as they drove off.

She didn't want to go to her new house just yet. The agent she had been buying the property through had called her first thing in the morning which had surprised Rayne because it was a Monday and while the rest of the world might have been awake at 8am she certainly wasn't. The agent had been quick and told her that the house she had wanted in The Suburbs had come through and she was able to move in whenever she liked. As her apartment was already packed up she'd called the movers and that was that. But she wasn't ready to go to the new property yet, it was huge, gigantic and terrifyingly empty and after living in such cramped accommodation for so long she didn't want to suddenly realize that her entire previous life and all her material possessions filled only one tiny corner of that house. It was gargantuan.

And she had to admit a far scarier truth that she didn't have many friends she could go with anyway.

No, her plans were far simpler. She was going shopping.

Durban beachfront was the picture perfect shopping destination for anyone. Celebrities from around the world travelled thousands of miles to come shop on the strip of promenade that curved around the long, white sandy beaches and faced the perfect Indian Ocean. The Strip, with its stunning array of brand name shops, beauty stores, night clubs, strip joints, hotels and restaurants was the facial packaging of Durban City, providing a world famous skyline and post card image for the world to see, accompanied with the backdrop of Sky City it managed to keep the *real* Durban concealed within.

But for once in her life she wasn't going to the *real* Durban and in that her reality had completely changed, the fact she was going to The Strip to shop was that much of a sign to her that she no longer belonged in the other place anymore. She drove with the windows up and the air conditioner on at full blast against her face and allowed herself this last final drive through to see the city that she had grown up in. Litter on the streets being kicked about by restless, underfed deviants with nothing but hatred in their eyes, graffiti on the walls, smashed or boarded up windows and a frequent blackened charred husks of burnt down buildings. Homeless people sleeping under newspapers, rabid, stray dogs running around in packs. Weeds growing through the pavements and people with guns and here the traffic lights were on a different timing schedule to avoid cars having to stop for too long and police patrolled the streets with a strict shoot-first policy that was more about self-defense than keeping law and order.

She passed an intersection where from the overhead traffic lights a dog had been skinned and tied up. Flies buzzed around the dripping carcass in a cloud and nobody had taken it down. She gingerly drove around it and realized how grateful she was that these were streets she no longer had to drive along.

It took an hour and a half to drive to the northern side of The Strip where she parked her car in an open air parking space six feet from the sea sand and as she climbed out of her car she was wrapped in a damp, hot blanket of air that made her gasp.

The beach was rammed solid, people frolicking in the high waves, the sound of laughing children and the surf mingling together to create a welcome for her.

She had worn a loosely fitting white cotton dress that came down just below her knee line and gave a wonderful air-flow between her legs. She was one of those people who couldn't tolerate sweat on her legs, especially if it ran behind her knees. She descended a flight of sand covered steps to the main part of the strip and was immediately teleported to an entirely different world.

You saw places like this on commercials on television, beachfronts, palm trees, people on rollerblades, and people in bikinis, all beautiful and young bodies. She kept her sunglasses on so she could watch some of the people walk past.

Having come with a purpose she didn't hang about to admire the views and since the first shop that appeared on her right as a giant shiny clothing store she clutched her handbag close and walked in.

The shop, all two levels of it was pleasantly cool, with the latest radio single playing over loud speakers with holographic versions of the artists dancing in the corner. The clothes were all designer labels and none of them had price tags on them an indication of the caliber of person who shopped here. She was met at the door by a beautiful but strangely androgynous teenager, whose look from hairstyle to attire were all catalogue labels, "Hello can I help you?"

"Yes," Rayne said, "I'm looking to fit out the wardrobe at my house with enough clothes to wear something new for every day of the year,"

"Well my name is Timothy," he, she assumed, said, "How big is your wardrobe?"

"It's quite big," Rayne informed him, "I don't have exact measurements..."

"I see," he said, and trying to feel her out he asked another question, "How much are you looking to spend?"

"Doesn't matter," assured him, "The house is in The Suburbs..."

Timothy's face paled slightly and he rallied with momentous strength of

character and said in a very firm, yet still feminine voice, "I see. Let's get you measured up shall we?"
Rayne was led through the shop which looked very cool and chic and was taken to the back where Timothy used a laser pen attached to the computer to take her measurements and proceeded to show her around the shop.
Rayne, knowing that this was more than just a shopping spree for herself but more a test of her new lifestyle, set herself only one rule, *If I like it, buy it.*
And she did.
"I'm assuming you'll want us to deliver this to your house?" Timothy asked, once Rayne had gathered more bags than she could ever hope to fit into her car and her shopping spree hadn't even started yet.
"Of course Tim," she said, signing the delivery sheet and paying with her thumb print and card.
"Excellent," he gasped when he saw her full name and realized who she was, his smile widened but there was near panic in in his eyes, "I'll have this sent over right away."
She winked as she left, "Thanks Tim."
It was a bizarre feeling to know how much money she had just spent and not feel the urgent need to go check her bank balance and she left one store, passing into the early afternoon humidity only briefly before walking directly into the next shop to find it was the biggest shoe shop she'd ever seen.
And so it went as she hopped and skipped her way from shop to shop buying with wanton abandonment. Everything was to be delivered to the house that she hadn't been to since the initial viewing, all of it was going to be waiting for her either set up or in boxes. All of it, so she could full that empty shell of a house with more of *her* stuff.
She was enjoying a smashing coffee in a massive home-ware and furniture store that catered for eccentric tastes when Mason called her.
"Hey gorgeous," she answered.
"Wow, hello," he replied, "You seem to be in an energetic mood?"
"Shopping!" she sang, throwing her arms and legs out like a child, "it's a wonderful feeling for a woman's soul!"
He laughed on the other end, "Remember you do only have *one* house that you can full, how much stuff have you got?"

"Eh," she thought about it, calculating in her head, "I'm not sure, I could do with some help unpacking when it all arrives."

"It's not all clothes and shoes is it?" he asked with trepidation.

"No," she said, eyeing out a giant four poster bed while her fingers played with the page corners of the catalogue in front of her, "Not entirely at least. I've had to get furniture too… oh that reminds me, I need a good electronic stores."

"Han and Andrews," Mason said without pause, "They're the best in the city."

"Are you sure?"

"Of course," he said, "I own the chain,"

"How many of these stores do you own on The Strip?" she asked.

"Enough," he replied coyly, "So please feel free to shop till you drop. Oh and don't forget to pick out something nice for the party,"

"Do I have to buy something new for the party then?" she asked dryly.

"Not necessarily," he replied, "But you might want to, I've changed it from formal wear to beachwear."

"That's a bit short notice isn't it?"

"I like to keep these rich people on their toes. Enjoy shopping, I'll catch up with you soon."

He hung up without saying goodbye and Rayne sat at the table wondering if she was ready to go to her new home (Initially she freaked out about having to wear a bikini but decided to save that palaver for later). She would have to eventually she imagined- but there was no rush and she was feeling mentally upheaved and slightly crazy. If someone had suggested she go for transcontinental trip to Paris to buy some bread she would have done without a second thought.

An angry shout from the entrance of the store caught her attention and made her turn just in time to see a gang of teenagers in baggies and sandals running down the central aisle, passed the rows and rows of clothing, furniture and household accessories with cameras in their hands.

Excited, she looked around for the celebrity these young photographers had come to capture expecting to see some Hollywood movie star or political figure and panicked a little when she was blinded by a sudden onslaught of flashes.

The initial blast of high intensity flashes blinded her completely and as

she squinted and turned away from the cameras, trying to rise from her chair at the same time she heard one of them yell, "Grab her skirt!"
Hands brushed against her legs and grabbed at her hems and yanked up and when she pulled them down with her hands someone held a camera in front of her face as if it were some sort of weapon and unleashed a rapid series of explosive flashes that tore into her retina and made her shield her face again. Someone shoved her from behind and she staggered forward, blind as a bat and crash into the table lost her balance and toppled over and the flashes just continued.

The attack only lasted a few seconds before the security arrived and with the same aggression shown to terrorists in airports these camera touting teens were escorted, roughly, from the premises.
Rayne struggled to her feet absurdly hoping that nobody had noticed the attack and several of the floor staff rushed to her aid but she brushed them aside and tried to regain her composure.

"I'm terribly sorry," one of them apologized, "We tried to stop them at the door but they knew who you were."

"We got their cameras," one of the security guards said, a hefty black man who held out a handful of camera parts, "But they have automatic uploads to an online picture system I'm afraid. You could sue." Determined to remain calm Rayne said, "No need, they didn't get pictures of anything they haven't seen already," she said. Her face was burning hot and blushing and all the other customers were looking at her, peeking from behind wardrobe displays and refrigerators. She took a breath and said to the nearest floor staff she could, "Can I pay please? I would very much like to leave."

"Sure," the floor staff, who happened to be a tiny but adorably cute blond girl, said gesturing for her to follow her, "My name is Carly by the way."
Carly took her to the counter and Rayne paid with her card and thumb print and signed the delivery order for her insane purchase.

"Miss Ensley," Carly said, "You shouldn't go out there right now they'll all be waiting for you and I don't think they want glamour photographs."
Rayne knew what the girl meant, they wanted pictures that were going to go viral online, she could only guess what limits they would have for how far they would push things but if they could see blood they would have

done. They were like vultures circling a dying animal, merciless, hated and essential.

"You've got a point," she said, "Could you order me a taxi?"

"Sure," Carly said, "By the way I've always wanted to get into your industry…"

"How old are you Carly?" Rayne asked while the girl dialled the taxi company.

"Nineteen,"

Rayne's eyebrows arched, the girl didn't look that old, "It's a good industry to get into, as long as you don't mind stuff like this happening to you."

Carly smiled, "Well, I've done a couple of videos that I've put online, but making money on it is hard… that's why I have to work here."

"Keep at it," Rayne said, she was going to add something else but Carly smiled politely and spoke with someone on the other end of the phone ordering a taxi.

"Where to?" Carly asked.

Rayne gave the girl her address and she relayed it to the taxi company then thanked them and put down the phone, "All done Miss. Ensley."

"Please call me Rayne,"

"Okay, Rayne. I hate assholes like that,"

"Was he rude to you on the phone?"

"No I mean those cockrots who attacked you," Carly said her face pinching into a grimace of thunder that was as cute as a baby bear, "It's despicable that they'll make money off of it."

Rayne shrugged, "No hurt no foul,"

"Well, *now* you've got to get a taxi home," Carly insisted, determined to get Rayne to agree that the photographers were the scum of the earth, "Why should you have to worry about stuff like that. Durban's dangerous enough as it is without having to put up with people like them."

"Okay," Rayne said a little exasperated. The security guards had gone outside in force to deal with the photographers who were prowling like hyenas she didn't know what she felt when one of them was shoved hard by the security guard and toppled over onto his butt, his camera gear scattering into bits across the paving.

"It looks like you'll have a lot of packing to do," Carly said, "If you want some help I'd be happy to give you a hand."

Rayne turned to face the girl and corrected herself, Carly was only a handful of years younger than herself, and she just looked barely old enough to drink, "I have a boyfriend,"

"So?" the girl said with a quizzical look. Did she know more than Rayne did about this matter?

"Well..." Rayne began, "I'm not sure. It's a bit weird at the moment- I don't know you."

"If you weren't interested you would have said no already," Carly said raising an eyebrow, this stumped Rayne and the girl continued fearlessly, "My shift is almost up, I'll jump into the taxi with you and we can go unpack some of your stuff and then we can grab a drink?"

"Maybe another time," Rayne said.

"There'll never be another time," Carly said leaning forward on the counter on one arm so that her head almost rested on her skinny shoulder. It was impossible to resist such eager, unabashed charm.

Rayne knew she probably should say no.

But didn't.

10.

The building was tall, wide and quite famous, ostentatious if not downright flamboyant and within comfortable walking distance of Edinburgh Castle. Its top floor was totally dedicated to a company of international entrepreneurs, which was the sum of the building manager's knowledge about it. The occupants of that mysterious but busy upper region had their own access elevator at the back of the building, private stairs also at the rear and entirely closed off from the hotel itself, even their own fire escape.

The manager of the building who was accustomed to dealing with staff and liaising with guests of the cream of British and international society may simply have turned a blind eye to what went on above, but part of the reason he did so unquestionably because whatever took place there was the business of the man who owned the building entirely.

Mason rode the elevator to this floor, wiping the Scottish snow from the shoulders of his woolen overcoat and pondering on whether or not he wanted to watch a film or go to dinner at a one of the famous Edinburgh fish restaurants. Perhaps he would do both?

The elevator stopped at the upper level and slid open with a whisper revealing an entire floor of office cubicles made up of dividers about shoulder height. The maze was densely populated by workers, office staff either tapping away at keyboards or talking animatedly on the phones. There was a strong smell of coffee and other stimulants in the air as well as the usually human odors found in a crowded room. To his satisfaction the roar of voices each tied into one side of a two way conversation did not falter as he entered.

He walked briskly down the center of the office through the corridor, smiling politely to the people who he passed and entered the only standalone office on the far side of the floor without knocking.

Inside was a man who could only have been described as *insanely* Scottish, his hair was copper-ginger and cut short to the scalp, his pale face heavily freckled and his eyes were dark blue-green. He had the sort of face that had too many variations of colors on it to look comfortable. He rose out of his office chair like a breaching whale and walked around his wide desk with his hand outstretched. His name was Oliver Munroe.

"Mason, Mason, Mason," the Scot said as they embraced hands, "It has been too long my friend, how are you?"

They shook hands and when the Scot released Mason's hand the trillionaire shook some feeling back into it and said, "I'm well Oliver, very well. Blistering under this Scottish sun."

Oliver glanced out his window at the white curtain of snow, "Aye," he said, "Best wear your hat and apply loads of sunscreen! Close the door Mason, close the door,"

The trillionaire obeyed his employee without question and shut the office door sealing off the roaring from the floor beyond. He liked Oliver for his ability to command, if they had been in the army together Mason knew he would have followed Oliver, the man was born to lead and tell people what to do.

"Now then," Oliver said, lowering himself into his office chair and lacing his banana sized fingers across his barrel belly, "What brings you to my side of the world?"

Mason's eyes scanned across the desk with its untidy scattering of papers, across the shelf behind Oliver with a picture of his wife Fiona and his sons Richard and Chuck and then back to the Scotsman's face, "Are you not going to offer me a drink Oliver?"

"Of course," Oliver said, his thick Scottish braw making his every word sound more intense, without looking he reached down and opened the bottom desk drawer and pulled out a bottle of fifteen year old Scotch with a couple of glasses.

As he poured, Mason clasped his hands behind his back and looked out the windowed partition in Oliver's office that opened out onto the office where people in suits were busy at work. This was how crimes were run nowadays, like a successful business and you could break down a crime into the same basic pieces as you could a business plan. Give someone the job of looking after that one piece and they will do so, never being aware of the bigger picture. Or did people believe that everyone on the Deathstar had been evil?

"Here," Oliver said holding a drink up for Mason, "Don't make me get up again."

"Your back still giving you trouble then?" Mason asked, taking the drink.

"Like a kick from a horse," the big man said, they clinked their glasses and sipped their drinks. It was very strong, "Also," added, "I'm big and fat."

They exchanged pleasantries but there was a cloud hanging over them they could not be ignored, finally Mason said, "Where is he Oliver?"

The Scot took a deep breath, it sounded like he was sucking the air in through a wet sack, the man was not healthy at all, Mason could smell his cholesterol, seeping out the pores of his dark face, "Why must we start the bollocking with that Mason?"

"It's why I'm here,"

"We are making millions here," Oliver said pointing with his right arm through the partition, "And you're bollocking me because we can't find one man."

"Yes," Mason said calmly, "You can't find *one* man... one man, alone who can't even bring himself to use technology."

"Ag," Oliver grunted dismissively as if it wasn't an important part, he poured himself another glass of scotch, "The technology that we sell is the most advanced equipment in the world Mason, you should know you own most of it and none of that works with him. You talk about him like he's some sort of tramp..."

He trailed off as Mason's look changed, it was as if his eyes had glowed with an inner rage and it struck Oliver dumb.

"I would never underestimate him," Mason said, "But he does continue to evade you Oliver."

"He won't for long,"

"I know. Has Alan been in touch?"

The Scot nodded and shuffled through some of the paperwork on his desk until he found his phone, he had made some notes on it, "Yes, he called this morning. Something about an online video."

"It's going to be showing a video of The Coat,"

"The Coat?"

"He's a vigilante in Durban," Mason explained, still standing motionlessly directly in front of Oliver, "Imagine Batman but pissed off. He had a run in with some of my men."

Oliver's eyes lit up, "Another operation?"

"I've had suspicions about The Coat," the trillionaire said, gliding softly to the front of Oliver's desk and picking up a small gold figurine, "Daffy Duck?"

"Chuck gave it to me," Oliver said with a smile, "What's the deal with this Cloak?"

"Coat," Mason corrected and with prepared candidness said, "He doesn't show up on any of the CCTV cameras in Durban,"

"Is that possible?"

"Apparently," was the obvious answer, "I have a team assigned to finding him and tagging him so we could trace him and remove him from the public video archives."

"I see,"

"But it went sour very quickly and a woman named Rayne Ensley just happened to catch it all on video."

"Lucky," Oliver said with a purse of his lips.

"Lucky?" Mason asked, and it was his tone this time that made Oliver nervous, "Lucky? In a city that has more CCTV coverage than the entire landmass of Britain and seven million people - he has *never* been captured on film or in a picture until this girl happens to wander by and take a full video of him killing my staff on her phone."

"It sounds unlikely," Oliver agreed.

"Exactly."

"Rayne Ensley is the woman you're seeing yes?" Oliver said, extracting a well read newspaper from the stash of papers, "She's a hot one."

"And intensely unique," Mason said, "She is of primary importance to me Oliver. This brings me to the second point of my visit."

"The first being to bollock me about Tuck?"

"The first being to tell you about the trap, the video will bring Tuck to me," Mason said, "So don't change the way you're doing things on that side because catching him would just mess up my plans. The second order of business I need a host of toys sent to the tower."

He took a piece of paper from his pocket and held it out for Oliver to take, "I will need them as soon as possible."

"Yes, yes, of course Mason," Oliver stammered, "I will get on it."

Mason smiled and for Oliver it was like hearing a final nail in the coffin.

"Good. Now where can I watch a movie and get a good fish?"

11.

Jaden Coetzee was a man unaccustomed to feeling powerless. As a burly Afrikaner he had spent his youth fighting for the equality of all people, of all genders and race, he had joined in riots against the very people he had gone to school with and defended the blacks at his school with his own fists. He had witnessed firsthand the change of South Africa from a country of a hopeful future to the stadium where the most powerful people in the world played their games and had counted himself lucky to be a happy man of sixty three who was still young enough to wrestle with his children and visit the gym four times a week. He knew his strength would not always last, he knew he was one accident or one case of the flu away from having his battlements of health turn down over which all the aches and pains of his age would hurdle to take over his life. He had always suspected he would be broken by something of his own doing.

But sitting on the edge of the bed where his wife lay, wrapped up in the covers, her hands on the tear soaked pillow he realized that his greatest weakness had nothing to do with him and everything to do with her. He couldn't tolerate seeing her cry, not being able to stifle her tears was the greatest sin of his entire life.
No, not the greatest but one of them, for he had in fact failed his entire family.
His daughter, his last born and only girl, was missing.
As he had seen the police officers to the door he had heard one of them whisper to his colleague, "The city has her."
Now he sat there and for the first time in three decades he was looking at the book in his hands wondering if it was the time to break his vow. He had been a preacher once, a man of God, a pastor with a flock to look after and guide but like so many of his ilk he had slowly but irrevocably lost his faith in religion and moved closer to science. But you couldn't ask science for favors and he so wanted to ask for one now. The Bible in his hands felt like it had more weight than it should have done and more presence. He had read it from cover to cover and most of it didn't make sense, so much of it was outdated and borrowed, but it stood as a symbol and that's what he needed now. He needed a symbol, he needed a promise. He needed to know that somehow she was going to come home.

The city has her.

That sentence echoed around in his head like a bee in a jar, constantly going around in a circle in an unending buzz. He knew what it meant. Everyone did. The city… as the city had grown and attracted people from across the world there had been an even greater collision of culture than during the late nineties after South Africa became a democracy. Hundreds of cultures, faiths and races were crushed together into one city. The city grew and became successful because of it, but with the good came the bad and with the bad the evil tagged along.

The sex trade in Durban City was infamous.

That's what the police officer had meant.

He tried to force the thoughts from his mind but he couldn't, they tormented his soul, that spiritual entity that he had convinced himself didn't exist, they stuck it with pokers. His daughter.

If that was where she was going it would be better if she were dead.

God, please help me.

As he heard the floorboard creak he knew instantly that it was the deliberate sound of someone who had managed to sneak through his house and enter his bedroom without making a sound and if he had been ten years younger he would have leapt from the bed but he was older now and the pain in his chest stopped him from moving so fast. However he stood at his full height and faced the noise.

"Who are you?" he asked in a low tone so that his wife did not stir, "What do you…"

His words trailed off when the person stepped out of the shadows and into the street lamp light that poured in through the open window and Jaden heard himself gasp in genuine terror. His body went cold and the air in his lungs turned to ice. His jaw dropped as his eyes went higher and higher until he was looking up at the ceiling where the person's, no, the giant's head was. The giant wore a massive black coat and a hood.

It was not human. It was elemental, it was death.

Not taking his eyes off the monstrous shadow Jaden moved to the bedside and put a knee onto it, he was terrified but couldn't leave his wife unprotected. As if the shadow were a loose lion on the prowl he wanted to be between it and his wife.

"You have nothing to fear," the giant said.

A voice of an angel, that's what Jaden heard, the most beautiful sound he had ever witnessed in his entire life. It seemed to wrap around him like a blanket.

"I asked God to help me," he whispered, sitting backwards onto the bed, "Has he sent you?"

The giant shape that drifted amongst the shadows like a smoky, highly animated cloud of ink, move very slightly and it was a moment before it said, "No. God has not sent me."

"Then who are you?" Jaden asked, a small hook of fear digging into his heart. If this was not an angel sent by God, was it something else?

"I am someone who is going to save your daughter,"

The old Afrikaner could not contend with the emotions that exploded from his chest, the tears flooded down his face and he held onto the foot of the bed frame to support himself.

"I will do this Jaden Coetzee," the voice continued, "But there is something you must do for me."

"Anything," Jaden pledged, "Please just save my daughter."

"I may need you to protect people for me. Special people, people that I have saved, like your daughter. Sometimes they may need a place where they can go, a place where they will be safe and looked after. You must promise me that you will look after them if I need you to. Promise that a favor will be met with a favor."

"A favor for saving my daughter?" Jaden whispered incredulously, "Why not ask for my life? I would gladly give it... how will you save my daughter?"

"Swear to me."

"I- I," the stammer slipped into Jaden's voice but something deep inside him kicked it away and in a voice firmer and more resilient than Jaden felt said, "I swear to you."

The shadow took a step towards him and a hand extended, a hand of such massive scale that Jaden shuddered at the sight of it. In the light of the outside streetlamp it looked pale but inconceivably perfect. It appeared to be reaching out to him and with the purest sense of acceptance he had ever felt the old Afrikaner assumed that this angel had decided his life was needed and so he bowed his head for the creature to take it.

A moment passed and then two and when Jaden looked up the room was empty. He stared at the space where the shadow had been with wide eyed terror and looked at the Bible in his hand as if it were a foreign object from another world, he climbed off the bed and walked across the room to the small desk he had in the corner, where his laptop computer and an assortment of pens were kept. Where Maddy insisted he have a cup of coffee with his work. He put the Bible into one of the drawers and returned to the bed, and climbed onto it behind his wife and lay down behind her. He put his arms around her and in her sleep she nuzzled up against him and whispered, "I want her back."

Chadum Street.
The girl was semi-conscious and as the limousine bounced along the road her head rolled on her shoulders like a bowling ball tied to her body by a string. It looked like it should have been painful but every few swings she would bring her head up and look around in dreamy, half opened eyes. Henry, sitting opposite her in a fine pinstripe suit that had been tailored only the day before, with one leg crossed over the other, watched her with a morbid fascination. The street lights that flashed by the limousine's one way glass roof caught her attention and she whispered something about stars through her dry and cracked lips.

    He knew nothing about this girl, he did not know her name, he did not know where she had come from or her parents and he didn't care, she was simply a product with a price tag, a very fragile product that had to be treated carefully due to the number of digits upon the price tag.

Beside her, sitting with a dead straight back, his polished dome of a head almost touching the top of the limousine was Shange, Henry's personal assistant and body guard. He had been staring out the window watching the city as if he had a personal grudge against it but when Henry looked at him he seemed to sense the gaze and turned his head upon his ox-size neck. His eyes quickly assessed the situation and without a word he lifted a giant hand as black as ink and pressed it against the girl's forehead to stop her head from wringing her own neck.

    The girl was pretty, which was good, it was just what his clients liked. Pretty girls, young and innocent. They didn't care if they were virgins or not, they just wanted them to appear vulnerable and preferably cute. This girl had met the criteria the very second he had seen her and he would be paying his suppliers very well for this. It would be more money than they had seen in their lives but only a fraction of what this girl was going to get him. The suppliers had given him the ID documents she had on her when they snatched her and he had looked briefly at it not paying any attention to the details except for her date of birth which would put her at approaching seventeen. Healthy by all accounts, clear skin, brown eyes, soft blond hair and a fair complexion. She was still dressed in the unattractive school tunic that the Durban high school made her wear, that would have to be changed. He knew what his clients liked.

"When we get to the office," Henry said, "You'll get her changed into something more appropriate,"

"Yes sir," Shange said.

"Something cream and satin," he added, his head turned to the side as he pondered, "That shows some leg, but not too much. Just enough is often right."

"Yes sir," Shange said. He still hadn't moved his hand from the girls head.

Henry leaned back against the extremely comfortable limousine seat that was as well-padded as a space ship aimed at Mars, it suited him quite well he thought. Looking out the transparent panel he watched the city go by, Chadum Street passed the marina and offered a spectacular view of Durban's natural harbor and the long cue of ships waiting to get in identified by their brightly burning lights, it was also a grand reminder of where he had come from. The slums of Durban.

He was an Eshowe boy, something he would not allow himself to forget; he had been born in a room made of road signs, dropped out of a mother who hated him from the start. He saw it as a man viewing a previous life, it was an intellectual tickle to see where he had come from, and the place he would never return to.

Henry was a modern day career criminal. He worked in an office, he employed staff and the whole reason he was a career criminal was that he was an accountant.

Accountants ruled the criminal world, of course you had your street level thugs, your hoodlums who didn't have a brain cell to stroke, but real crimes happened in offices, they happened on paper. A good accountant could legitimize just about anything but a forensic accountant, like him was a magician.

As an accountant he was the most ruthless man in Durban.

The limousine hit a bump and Shange's eyes looked up through the upper panel of the limousine and Henry knew they had arrived at their office.

"Dylan," Henry said to the driver, "Pull into the basement garage please."

"Yes Mr. Tsoli," the driver replied.

The night of Durban, sprinkled with light from the glowing city and the streetlamps slid away from them into darkness as they entered the near black of the underground garage eerily lit by the car lights. The girl whispered something about it being dark and how she wanted her teddy.

The limousine parked and Henry waited for the driver to get out and open his door before stepping out and walked immediately to the entrance to the basement office where he conducted these affairs. As he did so he wriggled the gold Rolex on his wrist to get it into a better position.

He unlocked the door, left it open and stepped inside flicking on the light switch. The office was sparse and instead of having desk and chairs it was filled instead with hanging racks and women's clothing on hangers.

He quickly selected some of the clothes he thought would be appropriate and hung them from the window frame and went and stood in the corner.

Shange, a behemoth of a man, dressed in black with eyes as dark as his skin, a man who at his most casual appeared to exude brutality brought the girl in by the hand. Her head down she meekly followed, looking drunk and every so often he had to tug on her hand so that she would keep up. Inside he closed the door behind them and without a word selected one of the outfits that Henry had chosen and with deft gestures he took off the girl's uniform. There was nothing in any way suggestive about this, he did it the same way as he would remove clothes from a mannequin and dropped them onto the floor one by one until the girl was as naked as the day she was born. Shange allowed Henry a moment to appraise her.

Terrific, he thought, she did have beautiful skin and a slight but healthy plumpness of baby fat to her. Her breasts were young and round, the nipples a distinct pink and the triangular patch of auburn hair between her legs looked almost completely unruffled. He nodded once and Shange began dressing her.

They moved through the outfits one by one, Shange used a comb and with the hands of a hairdresser fretted her hair into different arrangements to suit the outfits. Henry would turn his head this way and that, Shange would turn the girl around who stood there with a dreamy expression on her face so that Henry could get a better look, they would try on different parts of the other outfits until they found one that worked.

Shange dressed her in the appropriate outfit and arranged her hair as he towered over her and Henry produced a small makeup kit from his inner jacket pocket and applied just enough to make her dreamy, drugged expression appear more sultry but still, innocent.

Finally she was ready.

"Lock up after you," Henry said, leaving the office and returning to the car where he returned to the exact same spot he was sitting in before and waited for Shange and the girl. Once they were in, the driver who had patiently waited for them, started the limousine. There was no engine rumble as the engine was purely electric and as long as the roads were better than Chadum, completely smooth.

They left the basement parking and Henry watched the staunch, solitary brick building with its simple windows that had served as his office for so long now and vividly wanted to be in his main office eating olives. An involuntary sigh of pleasure escaped his lips at the thought. Shange looked at him but when nothing was said he turned his gaze elsewhere.

The girl was a little more conscious, the activity of dressing her having stirred her from her reverie, Henry could tell she wasn't entirely with them yet because she was sitting quite calmly with her head back against the headrest of the chair.

"Please cross your legs," Henry said.

Obediently she did as she was told, and with her eyes solemnly open she stared out the limousine at Durban, "Where are we going?" she asked, through lips that were now a soft fleshy pink color thanks to Henry's skillful application.

"I have some people I want you to meet," Henry replied.

"Who are they?" she asked in an almost musical tone.

"Just some clients of mine," Henry answered as the limousine glided off of Chadum and into Valley Road which was quite better, the ride became as smooth as a yacht on the Mediterranean, "They are going to pay a lot of money for you."

She seemed to consider this for a while, Henry could see the cogs slowly turning in her head as her brain tried in vain to think against the onslaught of the narcotics, finally she came out with another question, "Am I being paid?"

"No of course not," Henry said, feeling irritable now.

"Why not?"

"Because you will be dead," Henry answered her. Just then Shange, with that same unexpected grace and tenderness slipped the needle of a syringe filled with some clear liquid into her arm and pressed the plunger down. She gave a soft, high pitched squeak and sank into the limousine seat. The narcotic was one that produced massive docility, it made sure that you maintained bladder and bowel control while relaxing the mind to the point where you would happily obey any order.

Henry relaxed a little and noticed that Shange looked a little concerned. He knew why, the big man knew that he had waited too long before drugging the girl up again and that Henry's calm had been pressed. The rest of the journey was conducted in complete silence.

In Pinetown, about a twenty minute drive from Durban, the limousine entered the sprawling suburbs and followed the windy roads with its near silent engine until coming to a home that could only be described as stately surrounded by a ten foot concrete wall and a solid steel electric gate that slid open on rollers as the limousine neared. They were clearly expected. The limo sailed down the long cobble stone driveway which cut through a wide grassy lawn cut to the perfection of a golf course and around a circular cul-de-sac that swept around pond filled with giant gold fish, who could be seen even in the dark water as they neared the surface to chase insects.

The house itself was gigantic, a castle of brick, every window was taller than a man and wider than a man with his arms spread, there were lights on inside shining through the stain glass window that dominated the space above the double door entrance. The driver brought the car to an alighting halt, then got out and opened the door for Henry.

Outside the air was warm and filled with the sounds of frogs and insects that rose in a near deafening cacophony of noise that was beautiful and natural. He could smell that the kitchen was preparing a meal and from the scents wafting from the chimneys it was a feast for a dozen people and mouthwatering.

With the girl in hand Shange exited the limo, "Sir,"

"Yes, yes," Henry said fluttering a hand, eager to get rid of the girl,

"Take her around the back so nobody sees her until the appropriate time." Shange nodded and led the girl by hand across the cobbled pavement and onto the footpath that led through the manicured lawn and around the back.

The driver and the car silently departed to find somewhere to park and Henry wriggled his watch and looked at the time. He was a couple of minutes early.

As he climbed the stairs to the doors one of them opened inwardly and a handsome white butler with slicked back hair as dark as the tuxedo he was wearing said down his perfect nose, "Mr. Tsoli very good of you to come."

Henry smiled widely, "Indeed. I am early,"

The butler nodded in acknowledgment of this fact and with a white gloved hand he bid him entry.

"May I arrange a drink for you sir?" the butler asked.

"Yes," Henry said, "A spirit of some sort, strong, with olives please."

The butler nodded once slowly and led Henry through a house lined with marble and wood, despicably ostentatious and absolutely glorious. There was the ticking of some giant clock somewhere nearby and staircase seemed to lead from every room upwards. The butler brought him into a wide dining hall with a central table laden with appetizers and surrounded by women in lavish evening wear and men in suits. One of the men, a short, round man with a giant storm of white hair on the top of his head and a black and white patched beard beneath it saw him just as the butler announced his arrival, "Mr. Tsoli has arrived,"

"Yes, yes Stuart," the man said approaching with a bustle, he waved the butler off, "Go get him a drink. Henry! How are you?"

They shook hands warmly. This was Mr. Jack Columbus, the house's owner, Canadian and rich through not only a sizeable family fortune but many business dealings with Henry that were legitimately on paper.

"Did you find the place okay?" Henry was asked.

"Yes," he replied, keeping a smile on his face, "That's why I'm here early Jack."

"Oh sod off," Jack laughed as they walked back to the crowd of people around the table, "I've heard of your reputation. Always early is what I'm told."

In remarkably good time Stuart returned with a drink which was vodka based and delightful, "Now," Jack said, "Come meet our friends."
Walking with his hand always on Henry's back, which he barely tolerated, Jack introduced him to all of the guests who Henry already knew better than they knew themselves after all he handled all of their books and he met them all with a handshake and a knowing smile.

"Now," Jack said, taking Henry aside for a moment and looking at him with his emerald green eyes, "Seriously though, these are friends of ours and they're all *very* politically connected. But of course you know that yes?"

"Yes," Henry answered.

"Good, now I want to make sure that I'm not going to disappoint them," he said with a conspiratorial tone, "Did you bring it?"
Henry smiled but his aggravation was clear in his cold tone, "Of course I have Jack,"

"Is it what we discussed?"

"It's perfect," Henry assured him, "I had it delivered to the kitchen when I arrived. I assume that *you* have spoken to your chef about how you want it to be prepared?"
Jack saw the jibe and didn't rise to it but the humor had left his face for a moment, "You will receive your payment before you leave tonight,"

"I expect to," Henry said, "Shall we sit down and enjoy ourselves?"

In the gourmet kitchen where three chefs worked on preparing the food for the guests in an environment more sterile than a surgeon's theatre, Shange stood to the side, his eyes surveying the room with his usual cold, unblinking glare. The chefs, the consummate professionals, did not appear to be affected by his presence and worked with meticulous precision and impressive speed as they worked their individual stations, occasionally barking at each other through the shrouds of smoke and steam that billowed in clouds around their heads.

Shange's eyes swept the kitchen from right to left, where, far enough away from the chefs that her outfit would not be spoiled by any spitting oil or her skin stained by too much smoke stood the girl.
Still semi-conscious her arms were tied at the wrists with leather straps and suspended high enough above her head so that she had to stand fairly

straight, even so she occasionally swayed on her heels and sometimes tried to walk, but obviously found she wasn't able to but the drugs were specifically designed to inhibit thought processes, so to her she was in the midst of a very strange dream from which she would not wake.

In front of her on a very sturdy looking trolley was a very large platter of highly polished silver that was shaped like the mouth of a Venus Fly Trap. Continuously Shange's eyes fell on this and while he felt absolutely nothing when he saw it, he did offer credence to its singular beauty. It was intricately crafted and lovingly polished. The petals of the Venus flytrap expanding out in two separate half-hearts, with a frill of appendages along the outward curves that looked like prongs but were cleverly designed knife blades.

Most of what the chefs were busy with involved vegetables and fruits, tubers and some roots. They had no need to prepare the meat for it was hanging perfectly alright by itself.

Henry wriggled his watch and checked the time with such a subtle movement that the elegantly dressed lady who was speaking to him didn't even notice. Smoothly he returned to the conversation while behind his façade of interest he was working out an apt excuse to get away for an hour. He was a facilitator but he did not want to participate in the evening's functions. The main issue was that he was not a brutal man, he was merely a realist who saw an opportunity to provide a service and did so to the best of his ability and that was the summation of his involvement. In the past he had not allowed himself to be dragged into the conversation with the guests and blamed himself for letting it happen. It was distressing to be in the situation where he was desperate to go but he could not allow himself to be rude and was waiting for the right moment to make an excuse and leave.

The woman, who he knew cheated on her taxes like a teenager and a school test, finished her story which he could not remember and he took the opportunity to excuse himself with a smile and push back his chair and stand.

Jack collared him like a rugby player on a field, "Henry," the man said, "You're not leaving already are you?"

"I really must Jack," Henry said, using his tone to convey an urgent matter that required his attendance, "You can transfer the money to my account when you are finished."

"Oh," Jack said, looking hurt, "Are we only about money Henry?" Henry smiled and touched the man's arm, feeling the layers of fat beneath the expensive tuxedo jacket, it was a false smile but it would go unnoticed, Jack had necked several whiskeys in the fifteen minutes Henry had been here, "Of course not Jack," he said, "But I do have other clients I need to attend to and I am running late."

"Clients? At this time of night?"

"Twenty four seven," Henry said, the smile starting to hurt his cheeks, "Twenty four seven."

Jack nodded his head and gestured with a beckoning flick of his fingers that Henry should come close, Henry stooped low until his face was almost aligned with his and Jack, with a face of beard kissed him on the cheek.

The contact was a shock and Henry recoiled from it as if he had been slapped, he was brought to a rigid shivering state and glared at Jack with such venom the little man stepped back.

"My God Jack," Henry said through clenched teeth, "You caught me off guard."

Jack held up his hands in apology, "I'm very sorry Henry. I was only trying to be gracious."

Henry smiled again but it was an awkward gesture and to save face he turned on his heel and headed towards the archway entrance where Stuart stood like a sentinel waiting to serve.

His cheek burned, *God* how he wanted to wipe it clean, to wash it. He didn't mind contact with people *on his terms* but he never wanted to touch Jack or be touched by Jack in any intimate level. The man was loathsome in every manner!

Stuart saw him out, walking briskly beside him and bidding him a good evening as he opened the door. Outside the air was muggy and warm compared to the air conditioned interior but Henry was glad for it, with a clang of a metallic lock the butler closed the door behind him and he was able to stand alone on the steps for a moment. Desperate to regain his calm he decided he would wait in the car for Shange to return, he wouldn't be needed for much longer and then Dylan could take him back to his home. He had olives there.

He cantered down the stairs and listened to his footsteps across the cobbles of the drive until he stopped and asked himself why this was not a good thing. The frogs weren't making any sound and in fact the entire garden was as quiet as a tomb.

Henry had lived in South Africa his entire life and had learnt that unlike some countries in South Africa nature had never quite let go of its grip on the country and there was *always* some sort of noise and if there wasn't you found your gun.

Quickening his pace he headed up the cobbled path towards where he could see the limousine parked, it's long black shape resembling a chocolate bar in the light coming from the house.

The lack of noise was downright eerie and he almost broke into a jog to get to the limousine quicker. Usually Dylan would have spotted him coming and get out of the car to open the door for him, the fact he wasn't irritated Henry and his face burned hot with annoyance and his heart skipped a beat when he found that the limousine was empty, the driver nowhere to be seen.

Henry almost had an amorism he was so furious and vented his anger by banging his fists against the bonnet of the limousine and jumped up and down on the spot. The tantrum did nothing to burn off the anger but only allowed it to seethe and he stalked back towards the house like a man intent on murder.

At the top of the stairs he tried the door but even after trying to shake it off its hinges and punching the doorbell there was no answer. He swore so loudly that his throat burned and whirled around the side of the house following the path Shange had took earlier to the kitchen.

The path was a narrow cobble line through the grass running along the delicately shaped bougainvillea that surrounded the side of the house, the house was shaped like a horizontal H with the path cutting into the central "interior courtyard" that sported a quant Japanese style garden with a remarkably delicate looking water feature made of very thin stone and seashells. Henry spotted an arrangement of garden furniture and grabbed one of the chairs. Putting his back into it he threw it with all of his strength at the feature which shattered with an intensely satisfying clatter.

Mindlessly he stalked around the courtyard until he found the door leading the kitchen and wrenched it open. A heady mix of food, steam and sweat hit him in the face and brought a slight sheen of sweat to his skin which felt like meat-grease on his flesh and made him shake. His vision entirely red he grabbed the first thing he could see, a huge chef carving knife from where it hung above a work station and marched from the deserted kitchen.

The kitchen had several doors leading out of it but he chose the one he knew lead to the dining hall via a narrow servants corridor, with the knife clutched in his hand his chest heaved with an emotion so strong that all he wanted to do was kill. That he had made it this far without blood on his hands was a miracle.

There was no hesitation when he turned his shoulder to the dining room hall and putting his weight into the barge. Of course because the door was a servant's door it had no locks on it, only very flexible hinges and he flew through it.

"Fucking cock sucking wench!" he yelled as he stumbled into the room and slammed his hip against the corner of the long central table with enough force to make the whole thing jump. The hot pain that stabbed through his leg did not clear his head but the scene into which he had entered struck him dumb.

The sudden clarity he felt was like breaking the surface of the ocean for a breath and seeing the world with dry eyes: All of the guests were in the dining room, as were Jack, Stuart the butler and Shange, the latter three were the only ones who were not trying to get out of the room but in the panic none of them had thought about escaping through the kitchen door, or he would have seen them coming passed. Had he slipped out of the universe and into another where he had managed to get to this point without hearing any of his commotion?

It had only just happened because he had only been gone for about seven minutes and the guests were screaming and running, men in tuxedos were actually shoving aside women as they tried to get to the exits.

Henry stepped to the side as some people shoved passed him but he had the feeling that it didn't matter how they got out they weren't getting away.

Baseline, lower level criminals were very superstitious and they told stories of the very man he saw as if he were the boogie-man, but he was real and Henry only happened to realize who he was because he fit the description he had heard but it was like seeing a man in a Batman outfit, you just assumed it was a man in a Batman outfit. But this…

It happened so quickly that Henry couldn't keep up. The giant, who wore

a trench coat with a hood, slapped a hand over Jack's head. It was like a man holding an apple, the giant's hands were that big and his fingers flexed ever so slightly but it was enough and poor Jack's head exploded like a grape. Blood and brains sprayed out between the giant's fingers.
At the same time Shange pulled out his gun- which proved that Henry had entered just as things had started because he knew Shange's gun would have been drawn at the first inclination of danger. Taking a position from a safe firing distance Shange aimed the gun at the giant's chest while holding it with both hands, his feet spread.

He pulled the trigger and the impossible happened.

The Coat seemed to be in two places at once, standing with Jack dangling from his hand and at the same time standing directly in front of Shange, towering over the big black man.
Jack's body crumpled to the floor, there was a thunderclap and The Coat's put a hand over the gun and the hands holding it and squeezed.

Shange screamed.

Henry had never heard Shange scream before.

The sound was a wailing howl of agony as the bones in his hands snapped around the shape of the gun and the unstoppable strength in The Coat's fingers. Shange dropped to his knees and it looked like he was praying to the giant who still had a merciless grip on his hands. The man's screams hit Henry's cold heart like shards of glass.
The Coat didn't let go until Stuart, the butler finally made it to play. He had not been waiting but had only been a few seconds behind Shange- things were moving that fast- and he brought a double barreled shot gun to his shoulder and with a professional marksmanship that matched Shange's he assumed the position.

He pulled the trigger twice.

It was like the loudest fireworks Henry had ever heard and inside the confines of the dining room it was deafening and caused the last few scattering of people to scream and throw themselves to the floor.
Stuart had not been prepared for the kickback of the weapon and the window on the far side of the dining hall shattered as the first blast went through it and a fleeing lady took the second in the side of the face blowing it apart in a spray of red. The Coat was already plucking the shotgun from Stuart's hands by then and like a bayonet he plunged it down into the butler's chest until he was completely impaled by it.

This had happened all in the time it took for the guests to run from the room and scatter throughout the house. Henry could hear their footsteps running across the paneled floorboards and doors slamming, people screaming, crying and begging. It was so fast, so confusing.

The Coat turned to face him and Henry felt that he had shrunk to the size of a small child as he looked up into the shadowy cowl and saw nothing within but felt eyes on him and it was as if the gaze of his eyes was enough to nail him to the wall. The Coat didn't move, he barely breathed as he and Henry stared at each other.

Footsteps, leaving the house, doors behind left open, people screaming. People calling on cellular phones. Crying. Praying.

"I'm…" Henry stammered, "I'm not part of this."

The Coat slowly turned his head to look at something that lay curled into a little ball against the dining room wall, under a painting of Jack on a horse. Henry saw it was the girl and felt a chill.

"I just brought her here," Henry said, "That's all."

The Coat's head turned back to look at him and it was like seeing the final judgment of the grim reaper.

Henry's hand tightened around the blade he still held and when The Coat started walking towards him, covering two meters with each step he brandished the weapon- and he thought he heard the monster give an exasperated sigh.

As surely as a child doesn't know how to resist being picked up by his father Henry realized what was happening too late as The Coat swept him up off the ground. Henry's chest was clamped within the grip of one hand while his entire upper leg was girdled by another and in the last moments before he was ripped in half he wished he had eaten the olive that was in the drink Stuart had prepared for him.

Jaden found his daughter asleep in her bed when he woke up the following morning, this miracle was the only proof that any of what had happened to the night before had occurred at all. He never looked at his Bible again but his faith had never been stronger.

12.

The ball was of course hosted at the Gregory Maines Tower. It took over one of their function halls, a massive vaulted ceiling affair with a Sistine Chapel painting style. Through planning or providence it was the hottest day of the year and was a specific swimwear party.

The guest list included celebrities, movie stars, music stars, millionaires, billionaires and philanthropists. The paparazzi from all over the world came to snatch pictures of them (Durban had become the latest Los Angeles), and photographers and reporters and gossip hounds would occasional stop and ask each other if they were here for the celebrities or The Coat. But both probably applied.

Guests arrived via helicopters, as the function hall was on the nineteenth floor. In the same fashion as the office and many of the apartments there was a massive circular swimming pool in the center of the function room and the scantily clad waiters and waitresses were handing out as many towels as they were drinks.

Even with her recent fortune and fame, Rayne felt out of place here. She didn't arrive via helicopter; she drove in and parked in the complex and changed in one of the bathrooms out of her jeans into her bathing suit. Choosing a tasteful sarong and a flimsy white cotton shirt to hide the bikini. She was going to a swimwear party to protect the rights of dolphins and whales and she didn't want to be asked which one she was.

Select paparazzi and photographers were allowed on the nineteenth floor foyer and they were snapping away at everyone who walked across the red carpet and the more experienced celebrities and movie stars took their time, posing with practiced smiles fastened to their faces, allowing the togs to get the best pictures of them. Seeing it for the first time on this side of the line was a bit disillusioning for Rayne that so much time was put into looking good for those supposedly "natural" photos.

When it was her turn to stand on the red carpet security kindly assured her that she was meant to be there and that they knew who she was and no there had not been a mistake and that the only way to get from the flashing lights to the alcohol was go through the gauntlet of photographers and paparazzi. Also, they mentioned kindly, and this infuriated her, they were under strict orders from Mason himself not to let her leave under any circumstances.

So summoning herself and pretending that this was no different to what she had done on her blog and that it didn't matter that according to her blog stats that in the last seventy two hours her videos had been watched by half a billion people. Half a billion who had seen her naked and playing with a toy she'd affectionately called Marvin.

The paparazzi went crazy when they caught sight of her and she was suddenly blinded by the flashes and deafened by people yelling her name and asking her questions and yelling for her to "Look this way!"- she smiled the best smile she could, but knew that most of her pictures would have her smiling happily with her eyes shut or squinting. She marched up the carpet as fast as she could but there were too many celebrities standing around trying to look natural and she felt rude walking behind them, not wanting to interrupt their pictures, so she ended up standing around looking particularly unnatural.

She also realized then that under the flashes of the cameras her shirt was practically see through.

Finally she got into the party and her heart, which had been hammering in her chest with fear of falling over on the carpet stopped suddenly when she found herself in a finite space with the top ten people on her personal "I would shag if I got the chance," list and suddenly faced with the possibility of having to show the power of her convictions.

She bee-lined straight for the bar, trying to avoid bumping into too many semi-naked bodies and clung to it, "Please give me something to drink," she pleaded at the barman. Who was a fairly attractive surfer style youngster who clearly loved his job and knew he would soon be shagging one of these A list celebrities, "What would you like?" he asked.

"What's the strongest stuff you got?"

Without question the barman shrugged, turned around and began conducting a drink that took him over a minute to prepare and at one point gave off a puff of smoke. He put it on the bar in front of her and she went into her purse to get some money and he said, "Oh it's an open bar Miss Ensley."

"How do you know my name?"

He lifted an eyebrow as if to ask, *Seriously?*

Turning away from the bar she caught someone looking at her and immediately recognized the person as none other than Bryan Vince. The nineteen year old film star with the infectious smile and searing good looks who grew up in Port Elizabeth but now owned houses in Los Angeles and property in Greenland. To Rayne he had always reminded her of a young Brad Pitt, with the playful green eyes and spiky blond-brown hair.

He walked up to her and smiled, "Rayne Ensley?"

"Yes," she said, "Bryan Vince?"

He smiled, and she saw in his grin a maturity that wasn't as young as his face, "Yeah, I heard that you were going to be coming here and I was really stoked," he held out a hand on the end of a very tanned arm with bracelets brandished upon the wrist, she shook it and found his skin to be softer than her own.

"Pleasure," Rayne said.

"So," Bryan said pointing to the giant holographic sperm whale that was majestically swimming its way around the top of the hall, "Are you all clued up as to the latest in the cetacean rites act?"

Rayne physically flinched, "Are you?"

The youngster smiled and she understood why he was already a veteran actor, "Yes. My dad was one of the 'green peace warriors,'" he spoke as if it were a title, Rayne had a sudden image of a man running across the ice at an oil tanker carrying a battle-axe, Bryan continued, "And so I grew up with things like this. It's *very* important on a number of levels."

Gracefully, the high detailed holographic whale performed a full spin, its fins trailing around it like ribbons around a Chinese dancer, "Tell me more." Rayne said.

"Well," Bryan said gesturing to the bar for a drink, "They're endangered for one."

"This I know," Rayne informed him, "Their numbers are improving yes?"

"Yes, but that's another matter," Bryan explained, "The real problem is that they're sentient and intelligent like people. What we're doing isn't about extinction it's about genocide. It's a different game now, one focussed on making people aware that what we do is killing off something that is aware of itself and intelligent."

The whale swam off through the far wall of the hall like a phantom and in a dazzling display of acrobatic beauty a pod of orcas returned immediately after. The conversation didn't go much further than that as

Bryan hovered around for a little while with his drink until a cute girl with blond hair tied up in a bun that Rayne recollected seeing on a film recently caught his eye and he zoomed off without a word to Rayne. She found herself as alone as a whale in an ocean and just as eager to vanish through a wall.

13.

Mason had every intention to being late. In a crowd of celebrities it was always good to be late for your own party, and be the one with the biggest entrance.
Sitting in his office he was waving through the security feeds of the nineteenth floor one by one as the digital software scanned the various camera footage, isolating faces, registering them against a guest list.
He had chosen impressively garish Caribbean blue trunks and a rough cotton shirt, unbuttoned to his midriff, a straw hat, leather sandals and the biggest pair of aviators he could find. He looked spectacularly ridiculous and was proud of it.
Having returned that afternoon to the East Coast humidity and having not slept in over eighty hours he was still vibrantly energetic however eager for a couple of moments by himself to prepare for the manic distractions occurring downstairs.

Sprawled out across one of the deep leather sofas, his ankle over his knee, a sandal dangling off one toe, he searched the faces in the camera feeds until he found Rayne Ensley. Hiding at the bar.
She was spectacularly out of her depth and his heart went out to her, she didn't even realize that *nobody* went straight to the bar at these events. There was mingling to be done, photographs to be taken and general chin-wagging to do with the other celebrities. It was an ostentatious parade of insincerity and bullshit which Mason avoided whenever possible and her discomfort added a glorious sense of authenticity to her.
He continued watching her, like a leopard watching its prey from the treetops. She had chosen clothes that were conservative compared to the outfits on display but she looked casually stunning as a result. Drifting away from the bar only to return to it as if she were a goalie at a soccer game, she clearly, desperately wanted to get away from this party and she was here only because Mason had insisted she attend. He would need to capture her before she found a way to slip passed his security. An A-lister for a week and already she was tired of this opulent offal. He looked forward to saving her and would do so as soon as his business was conducted.

"If you're here to kill me please make it quick, I don't actually want to be petitioned by MTV Cribs again." he said.

"I am not here to kill you," a deeply accented voice replied.

Mason rose smoothly to his feet and turned to face the intruder, he summed the man up with a glance, "You're in the wrong clothes for my party."

The man was darker skinned than Montgomery, but the darkest thing were his eyes that were occultishly dark. Dressed in a simple but tailored black suit, he said, "My name is Shaka, I am a Hunter."

Mason instantly liked the man, almost purely by the way he said *Hunter*, with the emphasis on the "H".

The trillionaire extended his hand which Shaka took and this was the chance for both men to size each other up for a moment and then let their hands fall, "I'm pleased to meet you Shaka and very impressed you got in," he glanced at the balcony entrance which was still closed, "I sincerely hope you didn't kill any of my employees to do so?"

"None of them saw me," Shaka assured him and as an afterthought added, "And I did not harm any of them."

"Indeed," Mason said, walking to the mini bar and collecting a fresh bottle of rum, he picked up another glass, topped up his own and offered the other one to his guest who declined. Mason shrugged, downed his and then filled the other glass and started on that, "However Shaka, I don't mean to be rude but I am due to my party so I may have to ask what the purpose of your visit is?"

The Hunter's eyes never left Mason's, but he had to have known it would take more than that level of intensity to stir or intimidate him. He finally said, "I wish to work for you."

"I have more than enough staff,"

"Not like me."

"Sneaking into my office is impressive, but not impossible," Mason said, necking the rest of his rum, "But if you have a CV I'd be happy to have someone in HR have a look,"

Hunter smiled the smile of someone who knew never to show all their cards and revealed that he was carrying something behind his back. With a flourish he revealed the item and Mason dropped the empty glass which hit the carpeted floor with a thud.

The Hunter was holding the sword.

Mason stared at the man who held the weapon out in front of him as if it was an offering, he did not initially take it. It was the very thing he needed the most but it was his anger that stopped him from touching the weapon.

His plan. He *wanted* his plan to work and he wanted *his* plan to work in its entirety. He hadn't come up with a stroke of genius on the off chance that something else might happen to bring him to his goal faster! He didn't need or want quick results since it was the pleasure of a well-earned success that he lived for. But now he was looking at the one thing he truly wanted. The one thing he had to possess to truly achieve his ultimate goals and some stranger had brought it to him and snatched away that joy.

He was instantly on the defensive.

"You have my undivided attention my friend. What do you want?" Shaka's smile was not a happy one, it was a bemused one, "I have heard about your approach to things, direct. I appreciate that. Take it; the sword is yours as it must belong to its owner."

Shaka changed the grip of the weapon, gingerly avoiding the sharp edge of the blade and re-offered it to Mason. Eyes locked together Mason took it by the handle.

Stepping back away from it with a very slight bow Shaka said, "The sword is where it belongs."

Mason's mouth was dry. His entire body quivered and the energy that he felt was always screaming to press out of his body, to press out of his pores, seemed to condense in a slender line of power that fed directly into the weapon. It was a deceptively simple looking weapon, merely a length of metal that had been sharpened on one side and held a handle where the handle needed to be. What made it stand out was that its finish was mirrored and flawless and incapable of being marred. And that while it *was* sharp- there was no force on this planet powerful enough to hone such metal. This added to its mysterious allure. He swept it around in front of him and as it moved it made a soft but definite hum.

"This sword is sacred to me," Shaka explained watching him closely, "To my people."

"How do your people even know of it?" Mason asked.

"That is a question for my ancestors," Shaka said candidly, "My *songoma* told me to find the weapon."

"Your *songoma?*" Mason said, "So you're Zulu? How did he know where the weapon was?"

"My *songoma* is very gifted," the hunter said reverently, "He told me the sword would be in Britain. I went and I found it."

"What of the man who had it?"

"The Freelander?"

"Yes, exactly,"

"Like your guards," Shaka said, "He didn't see me coming and he also lives. I did not believe that his death was necessary."

Mason was quite relieved by this knowledge but perplexed, "And you brought it to me?" he asked, "Was that also your *Songoma's* wish?"

"You are its rightful owner," Shaka said.

"I think there is a lot that we need to talk about," Mason said, he held up the sword, "I would imagine this comes with a story?"

"Oh yes."

"I look forward to hearing it however I cannot keep my guests waiting and since you are technically trespassing I cannot leave you here. Do you want to come downstairs?"

"No thank you," Shaka said, "I do not enjoy parties. I will leave via the front door if that is suitable. When shall I return?"

"Come back here at five am."

"Very well."

The Hunter walked to the elevator and was soon gone. Meanwhile, Mason was stunned to be holding the sword and the feelings of rage at his unfinished plan were forgotten and replaced by elation. *Now* he knew that Tuck would certainly come home and now he found himself with an even stronger reason to find The Coat.

He stored the sword in a safe place, had some more rum and went down stairs to rescue Rayne.

Rayne stood with her back firmly against the bar, her drink held in front of her and her straw clasped between a thumb and forefinger as she concentrated on getting as much alcohol into her as quickly and as discreetly as possible. Her eyes flittered nervously between the faces of all the people she had idolized on television and seen on the big screen and the entrance to the hall so when Mason walked in dressed like a beach bum she saw him before anyone else did. But she wasn't as fast as some of the other celebrities who were on him like flies to a raw wound.

Over his wide, polite smile his eyes locked onto hers and for a second the entire crowded room was silent. He politely lifted a hand to the people talking to him and excused himself.

"Good evening Miss Ensley," he chimed as he neared, signaling the bartender for a drink.

"Good evening Mr. Mason," she responded, "Correct me if I'm wrong but wasn't that the President of Nairobi?"

Mason looked over his shoulder at the large African gentleman, "Oh yes it is, bless his heart for squeezing into such tiny briefs for our benefit."

"What did he want to talk to you about?" Rayne asked. Collecting his drink Mason drank half of it at a gulp, "I honestly couldn't hear over the loudness of my pants."

"They are *very* proud," Rayne agreed with a laugh, "Where did you buy them?"

"The Caribbean," he said.

She smiled. He smiled. She wondered what they were smiling about.

"Anyway," he continued, "I'm glad you came tonight. You look amazing."

Putting her head back she did a Marilyn Munroe pose with her hands pressed down her front together and whispered dramatically, "Thank you,"

Just then a flash of a camera stunned her and Mason laughed at her furious expression, "You have to get used to that I'm afraid," he said.

She drank the remainder of her drink. It was her third one and she still didn't know what was in it, her eyes kept roving around the crowd avoiding Mason's face because he was staring at her. She really wanted a picture to appear online of him looking at her like that.

"Come on now," he said, putting his arm around her shoulder, "You've been hogging the bar for long enough."

She resisted initially and he put on a heart breaking puppy dog expression that was caught pricelessly on a camera, he didn't seem to notice and took her hands and bounced on his feet excitedly, "But I want you to come meet my friends!"

He dragged her into the crowd and she turned a shade of purple as she bounced off of people who had won Oscars, Academy Awards and

Grammys, one pop star singer had her drink splashed clean out of the glass when Mason suddenly changed direction and Rayne swung out on his arm like a water skier flanking a speedboat. The woman gave her an evil look and Rayne was so embarrassed that she was close on tears and then the woman's expression changed entirely, "Oh my god are you Rayne Ensley?"

Rayne blinked as she recalled seeing this pop singer on stage in front of thousands, she had gone to shopping malls and her face had been plastered across the hall screens. Her CDs sold millions of copies. One of her live shows sold out the Wembley Arena in London in three minutes. And she was asking her if she was Rayne Ensley?

"I..." she began, "I can't remember."

The singer smiled and Rayne blinked, "Yes, yes I am Rayne Ensley. You're Catherine, yes?"

"I'm flattered that you would remember me," Catherine responded and Rayne had no clue how to respond and was incredibly relieved when the singer was tapped on the shoulder by someone in a pair of surfer trunks she turned away from Rayne who turned to Mason who had been watching nearby and hit him in the arm.

"Ouch," he winced, rubbing his arm, "What was that for?"

"I feel like a fool," she said, "Why did you invite me here?"

He ran the back of his index finger along the line of her jaw which was disarmingly soothing, "Because I have to be here and I wanted you here too."

She stepped in close and put a hand behind his neck to draw him down so she could whisper in his ear, "Why don't we go up to your office and see if I've overcome my vertigo?"

In response Mason put an arm around her waist and pulled her in close, even in front of all of these people he already had a semi that was pressing through his trunks, "In a bit," he promised, "It's my party after all and I have a little bit more schmoozing to do if I want this charity to make the money it needs to."

She pretended to pout and he winked at her, "Come on. There are some promoters I want you to meet."

Clinging to his arm Mason introduced her to the highest echelon of society who had been ingeniously brought down from their various high horses to a common standard by everyone wearing swimming gear. She met producers and actors, writers, musicians, band members, politicians and overly wealthy business icons, as the item on Mason's arm they looked at her with a sort of exalted adoration which left her feeling a little bewildered.

"This is so weird," she giggled, "I can't believe I'm doing this." Mason chuckled and patted her arm which was looped through his as he guided them towards the front stage, "Oh don't you fuss my dear, there's more to come."

"You look very sexy," she said to him.

"And you my dear are going to get buggered to an inch of your life tonight," he said stepping away from her at the same moment so she couldn't reply and jogging up the stairs onto the stage.

He scooped up the microphone from a stage hand and leapt into a speech that was rousing and heartfelt; encouraging people to donate generously with not only their money but their time. He spoke of a world with more of these animals, the importance and beauty of an ocean filled with marine life that has been here for millions of years and deserved to stay here far beyond the existence of man. He pledged, in a gesture that appeared utterly spontaneous he pledged that he would match whatever figure was provided for at the end of the evening.

Rayne saw Irene Mader, the charity's CEO dabbing away tears while trying to clap furiously when he was finished and as he opened up the bids for the donations everyone was racing forwards with their cards in hand.

Rayne had planned to donate a sum of money which she thought was generous, to be able to give away more money than she had ever made had seemed a wonderfully unique thing to do but as she signed the donation cheque she caught a glance at what a gentleman wearing nothing but a hotel towel dropped into the bucket and she felt positively cheap!

Quickly the donations reached R100 million, at which point poor Irene Mader was beside herself with tears. The poor woman had slaved for years to raise enough funds for her charity to simply make a tiny difference and with this sort of money there was a lot more that she could do. Her story and her plans were highlighted on holographic billboards across the sides of the hall and Rayne, to get away from the surge of people wanting to donate had drifted over to them to have a read.

When the bid topped R200 million the place shook with the cheers and Mason started pointing people out and relying on some sort of eidetic memory was telling these people every reason why they *could* afford to donate more. It was an aggressive means of making people donate but everyone still cheered when it hit R250 million and to avoid being pointed out others went forward and dropped additional donations into the bucket.

When it hit R300 million the number exploded above Mason's head in giant blue holographic letters which the whale and the orcas swam through. Their whale calls sounded like cheers echoing around the entire hall.

Mason then took out his cheque book, scribbled a number on it and dropped it in and the number changed to R600 million.

The crowd applauded, loudly and heartfelt.

"Drinks are on the house!" Mason announced.

And the crowd went apeshit.

The night was progressing and the party was getting messy. Mason loved it. He allowed himself to enjoy the small triumph he had accomplished tonight. Irene Mader was thoroughly intoxicated, and the tall woman who was well in her forties could barely stand but refused to leave Mason until telling him what a great man he was and how much good they would be able to do with the money he had raised for them. He eventually asked Montgomery to see her home safely. The party raged on, the holographic whales were joined with holographic mermaids and other sea creatures, the music was modern dance and he could smell the crowd as their state of delirium rose to dangerous levels. There were a lot of drugs going around and he saw more than a handful of couples fornicating along the sidelines to the general applause of the onlookers.

He finally found and had to rescue Rayne from a nervous breakdown as she had managed to get herself corralled into to a conversation with a group of A-list male actors who had taken a shine to her. She didn't want to be rescued but she clearly didn't know which one to choose and as he gently pulled her away he shouted in her ear over the music, "Don't worry I have all their mobile numbers on my phone!"

He kept a constant eye on Rayne although he didn't hang around her exclusively, instead he would disappear from her side for long enough for her to start looking for him and then he would miraculously appear again just when she was thinking about sneaking out.

By the time the party was winding down she had made an impression on everyone and finally at 04.45 instead of sending her back to hers, he arranged to make use of one of the apartments and had her settle in there for the night. As he escorted her there she tried on several occasions to seduce him and while he was very much *up* for it she was *very* drunk and it wouldn't have been right. She might have argued more but the moment he lay her down on the bed she was snoring.

He text her and left her phone on the bedside table so she could find it easily and took the elevator up to his office where he found Shaka waiting. The man was standing next to the pool, his hands in his pockets, watching the water with a hypnotic intensity.

"Good morning," he said, walking into the office and kicking off his sandals, "Sorry I'm a little late,"

He took off his shirt that stank of sweat and smoke and tossed it onto the back of the sofa and headed straight to the coffee machine, "That was one hell of a party. I had to help a friend get to bed. Have you been here long?"

"Only since five," Shaka said, "A minute or too, not long at all. Thank you for seeing me again."

"Thank you for coming," Mason replied, "You sound like a man who knows things so I'm assuming you know what sort of hours I work?"

"Yes."

"Good, so at least that doesn't require any explanation, coffee?"

"I would be grateful,"

"How do you take it?"

"Stewed,"

Mason emptied the beans, replaced them with a stronger blend, added a fresh filter and let the coffee machine do its thing. He leant against the desk, allowed a moment of calm to descend and asked, "Have you been enhanced in any fashion?"

"No," The Hunter replied with humility, "I am merely a high trained individual,"

Mason took the answer for what it was and when the coffee was ready he prepared two cups and handed one to Shaka who seemed to savor his as if it were some elixir from the gods. Together they walked to the sofas on the other side of the office and sat down.

"I'm sure you have a fascinating story Shaka," Mason said, "But I must confess I am very interested in hearing about how you came about the sword?"

Without any drama Shaka began:

"As I explained my *songoma* gave me the task of locating the sword once it had been stolen from you ten years ago by the Freelander. As I have already said the sword is holy to us and we see you as the rightful owner of it. I noticed earlier that you did not understand why this was, so I shall explain. Do you remember the seven years you spent in Ghana?"

Mason, not wanting to interrupt his guest merely nodded. This Hunter was well informed, Mason had last visited Ghana when he was an old man, and he had contracted a terrible case of malaria there and had been hospitalized.

"You went there as part of an exploration team to find oil and during this time you befriended a man named Dlamini. That man was my songoma's son and he, like my songoma was sensitive to the ways of the universe and could tell that you were a man of destiny, a man that they had both had dreamt about.

"Together, you and Dlamini went on a quest to find a treasure. It took you a long time and the price was high but you managed it and located what you were looking for. The sword that I returned to you tonight."

"Dlamini died," Mason said, "He was shot by rebels in one of their camps."

"He fulfilled his destiny and died with great honor," Shaka insisted.

Mason remembered the trip completely, but the way Shaka told it made it sound more epic than it was. There were no jungles left in Ghana by that time and most of their journey was spent in a very industrialized city center of Accra. Mason and Dlamini had found the sword in an antique store basement where the owner had kept it hanging from a rope because anything it touched it cut. The owner had believed it was the weapon of god.

"You made Dlamini a promise that you would find the people who had used this weapon. It was his dying wish. For twenty years you searched while amassing a huge empire. You found what you were looking for in Antarctica. The night the Freelander stole the sword my songoma summoned me and told me to find the weapon and return it to you.

"I spent ten years hunting Tuck Bradley. Observing and learning. I knew that any man able to steal the sword from you would be a formidable prey and I also understood that you would want the weapon back in your hands as much as I so I remained aloof and merely watched. I apologize for the number of your men that died at his hands and for not intervening to save them as I knew it wasn't my moment. The opportunity came in Britain when the Freelander burgled a house and was seen by a great number of people, it was a foolish mistake as it led me directly to him. I set a trap for him at that same house, using the woman who saw him as bait."

"What did you do to her?"

"He has a habit of returning to places of incident. It may seem at first to be out of concern for his fellow man but it is purely so he can ensure his own safety. He is a coward," Shaka continued, "I broke in during the night and hurt her and her pimp- are you concerned?"

Mason regained his composure realizing he was scowling, "I don't want people to be hurt unnecessarily."

"It was necessary," Shaka said, in the tone of someone not accustomed to justifying himself, "It was nothing life threatening, just traumatic enough for it to spread across the social networking sites and for it to make it to the local news agency. I hid on the premises and waited for his return. I suspect he was keeping tabs on this woman because he was back sooner than I had anticipated. The moment I spotted him I shot him using an electrically power sniper rifle with an explosive round that disabled him. I followed this with a tranquilizer that rendered him unconscious. Removed the sword from his person and buried him in the woman's garden. That was yesterday."

Mason held his cup in both hands between his knees and gave Shaka a sideward glance, "And during this the woman and her pimp didn't cause you any problems?"

"No."

Mason chose not to pry, "Thank you for returning the sword to me. I would have liked to have known you were searching for it all this time,

I'm surprised to find I'm part of an African prophecy."

"The prophecy is limited," Shaka said, "And finished. The sword is with you. What you do with it is your choice and the will of the universe."

"I'm pleased to hear the universe has such confidence in me," said Mason with a smile, "Also, you've come at an opportune moment and I believe I have a role you can play. Welcome aboard."

14.
SOME TIME LATER

A whirlwind of fame had picked Rayne up and refused to put her down for months and in an ongoing stream of activity she was asked onto radio shows and news channels, online websites and tabloid magazines. Immensely enjoyable at first it soon became too much to manage on her own and she hired a personal assistant to organize things. This had only motivated the filling up of her calendar and she still had not had the time to properly enjoy her new beachside home in Durban North.

She had owned the house for a clear three months and hadn't had the chance to decorate it fully or even have a braai. As of yet she had not enjoyed a full weekend inside.

Was this the cost of fame? She had to ask herself, because, undeniably she was very famous now, her picture appearing daily on the covers of magazines and across the internet. There was not a clear connection between amateur web-cam porn-star and vigilante-photographer and so the media had begun plugging the gaps with rumors and gossip. Happening on the periphery she was simply too busy to really care. Whether people loved her or hated her they wanted to see more of her- the photographer, the model, the porn-star and the love interest of Mason.

It was a Thursday and the start of a three day break before she had a meeting with a publishing house that were groveling for a book contract and she was driving a brand new Landrover that smelt like strawberry air freshener. Drive was an exaggeration, the veritable tank's onboard computer was intelligent enough to drive itself and her only input was steering. Less than what she would have done in an arcade game. Single handedly the computer controlled acceleration, braking and even parking and she positively loathed it. Still, she didn't know how to turn the application off and was secretly grateful for it because she battled to spare equal time to having her feet on the pedals and her eyes above the steering wheel. The car was paparazzi guarded, the windows tinted and proofed against flashes, the door locks coded to her fingerprints and LED lights along the outside door frames prevented anyone from sneaking up and trying to take an up-the-skirt photograph when she was getting in or out of the vehicle. That such a thing could be taken as standard frightened her.

Having lived out of suitcases and sleeping in hotel rooms for so many months she stank of travel, her clothes were muggy and her skin felt coated in a fine layer of grease. There was a strange tension between her shoulder blades and she would have been too frustrated to breathe if the GPS hadn't been able to find the fastest route to her house.

She came off the highway via a slip road and drove parallel to Battery Beach, passing luxury resorts, holiday homes and timeshares until entering into The Suburbs. Here the roads were prestigiously maintained, the grass on the sidewalks elegantly manicured, the perimeter walls of the houses tall and concealing. Behind these walls the sorts of cars you saw were exclusively the finest seen on television, magazines and online. The air here tasted cleaner and thanks to the curve of the shoreline you had a glorious view of the Indian Ocean and Durban City. She felt as entirely out of place here as she did in a self-drivable car.

Her property was not the largest on her street but gigantic none the less, surrounded by a seven foot white plastered garden wall which she drove along for an embarrassingly long time before pulling into her driveway. The car's onboard computer signaled the thick, Spanish styled wooden gates to open and to close behind her as she drove in.

When she had first seen the house she had fallen in love with the Spanish design, and the strong housienda style. The walls were white washed plaster, with a lot of glass doors on the ground and first floor to make full use of the South African sun. The roof was a mixture of red clay tiles and solar-cell-panels. In front of the house was a veranda of slatted-granite with a built in braai area and a pool that cut into the sprawling lawn that reached around the whole house and sported one very lonely looking apple tree. The gravel of the driveway crunched under the Landrover's giant tires as they pulled in and the vehicle's computer said simply, "You have arrived at your destination."

"Thanks for letting me know," she muttered, climbing out of the car. Would she ever feel at home here, she wondered- she felt like a hermit crab that had wandered into a vacant tortoise shell! She opened the wide wooden doors that were curved at the top and dumped her bags in the foyer, which was twice the size of her previous apartment and stood there for a moment.

The place was so new and plush that it was soundless. The decorators had been in and done their job while she had been away. Directly from where she stood in the threshold of the foyer which was floored with pale cream tiles, she could turn left into the long, wide living room, where the television/holovision dominated one of the walls in front of the biggest set of sofas she could purchase or she could go right, into the kitchen which was as classy as a demo in a shop and if she went straight ahead up the stairs she could go into one of her five bedrooms. She still hadn't decided which room was going to be her main one.

Maybe she would have a room for every day of the week, but then what to do on the weekend?

"Rent a yacht," she chuckled to herself facetiously.

"Good afternoon Ma'am," a voice said from somewhere above her. Her scream, if it had been heard, would have brought people running but that was one of the problems about living with so much land surrounding your house, you could scream as hard as you wanted and nobody would hear you.

"Shit," she hissed, feeling a tingling sensation across her face, "You scared the hell out of me."

From speakers near the ceiling the voice, which was that of a well-spoken British storyteller, a smooth feminine voice designed to be soothing but trustful, returned, "Shall I run through the house's statistics?"

"No thank you," Rayne replied, picking up her bags and hefting them on her shoulder. When she had bought the house the agent who had sold it to her had said that these programs were equipped with "wet technology", he had given her the complicated explanation and then the simpler version. The computer managed the house and could learn to interact with its owner, becoming more like a butler or a friend. It was important to speak to it as if you were speaking to an actual person, or so the agent had said, but Rayne couldn't think of anything important to say so she went with, "I just want to chill out and relax."

"I have been programmed with a number of colloquialisms," the house said, "Shall I turn on the television or perhaps heat some water?"

"What for?" Rayne asked, using the banister to drag herself and her luggage up the stairs.

"For your bath," the house said, "I can even add some aromatherapy bubbles should they please?"

It couldn't be helped, Rayne was of a generation where houses didn't speak to you and where computers were not so intelligent that they could have straight up conversations with you. These were all recent advancements and she hoped she wasn't the only person in the world who was slightly perplexed at such a thing.

"Yes," Rayne said, getting to the landing of the stairs before realizing the laundry was down stairs. She unshouldered her bags and left them there, stamped up the remainder of the stairs while taking off her clothes, dropping them behind her as she went and walked into the bathroom. The light came on automatically and the glass in the ceiling to floor windows tinted. A television screen at the foot of the tub clicked on at the same time as the water started. It was like her house was possessed by the poltergeist of a serviced obsessed maid.

"The bath will be ready in ten minutes," the house informed her.

"That's fine," Rayne said, "Please turn off the television,"
The television popped off and the running water was the loudest sound in the house, despite this, it made the quiet seem all the more featured. After a lifetime of living in the never ending noise of the city Rayne found it eerie, "Are you there?" she asked.

"Do you mean me?" the house asked.

"Yes," Rayne said.

"Yes I am," the house responded.

"Okay," and again she ran out of things to say. How do you start a conversation with a house? 'How are your pipes?' sounded like a fairly intimate question and 'How's it hanging?' would suggest something was broken.

"While I'm waiting for my bath can you suggest something to entertain myself with?"

"There are a number of options available," the house said without pause, "As the temperature outside is 30 degrees centigrade a swim in the pool may be advantageous to relaxing however the house is easterly facing so the sun will only be on the pool for another seventeen minutes before sunset and the pool will then be in shadow, at which point I could adjust its temperature should you wish. You may enjoy a cup of coffee with some television; there are a number of shows on at the moment including several that involve you. Some of your groceries have unfortunately gone off in your absence however the canned goods are still edible so you could make yourself a snack. The water will be ready in five minutes."

"Thank you," Rayne said

"It is a pleasure," the house said.

She smiled. But she didn't know why.

The house then added, "You have an email message that has just arrived from Lynel Mason would you like me to read it to you?"

"Oh! Yes please,"

"It reads: Hi Rayne, how are you doing? Sorry I've been out of touch lately but have had a lot of work on. Hope you're settling in well. Will catch up soon. Mason. End of message,"

Rayne rolled her eyes, another blow off email. Mason had hardly been a feature in her life since the ball and she had racked her brains over the events at the party to see if she had done something at the party to annoy or embarrass him, or if he had just lost interest. She hadn't been able to reach a conclusion because he kept luring her along with emails, not particularly affectionate emails, but emails and texts.

"Typical," she mumbled, "Tell me when my bath is ready. I'm going to go find some chocolate to eat."

"Yes Rayne. Chocolate is on the second shelf in the fridge,"

"Thank you," Rayne said over her shoulder.

The house felt like a hotel, empty and gigantic and Rayne kept peering around the empty rooms expecting to find another lodger. But there was no one, she was quite by herself. Even the furniture she had bought was not enough to cushion the feeling of emptiness and soften the sharpness of the corners. At the foot of the stairs she swung around the banister and like a swan floated into the kitchen where she found the chocolate in exactly the place the house had told her.

"Are you down here as well?" she said to the wall.

"Yes," the voice responded, "Is there anything else you would like?"

Rayne shook her head and the voice said, "Very well."

"Hold on so you can *see* me too?" Rayne said, scrutinizing the corners and the walls for anything that could be a hidden camera.

"Yes," the house told her.

"That's... weird actually," she said.

"I can sense a note of displeasure in your voice," the house informed her, "May I ask, for future reference what has caused it?"

Rayne peeled the wrapper off the brand named slab of chocolate, broke off a square and popped it into her mouth. As she chewed she couldn't help the soothing feeling of ease the chocolate gave her, "I am not displeased," she replied, "Just tired."

Okay, the bath was dreamy and Rayne felt like she could melt into it as easily as the chocolate did in her mouth. It was dusk and through the one way glass she was bathed in a golden-pink light and when she asked for some appropriate music the house selected some acoustic Spanish guitar tracks. She closed her eyes and sighed, "How did you know that's what I would like?"

"I searched the internet and cross referenced the music downloads and online purchases you have made over the last year."

Rayne kept her eyes closed, determined not to completely freak out over her house having this sort of computational strength. Instead she focused on the music, which allowed her mind to drift and as always it drifted to only one place.

She hadn't seen Mason over the last three months. Aside from the weekly texts, and emails they might as well have been online fuck buddies. It frustrated her not knowing whether he was going to be an ongoing part of her life or not and she felt she was being strung along for his convenience and was annoyed that the gossip hounds on the internet had a better idea of the relationship status than she did.

If it was just occasional sex then she was alright with that, in fact that would even be better as she wasn't sure she wanted to be tied into a relationship right now when she could be free to do whatever she wanted and enjoy herself a bit more. She just figured his opinion on the matter could be important.

After her bath she dried down vigorously with the towels she bought at The Strip, watched some films in her bed and after them tossed and turned restlessly, unable to get to sleep. The bed was too unfamiliar, the dimensions of the room too alien, the house too quiet. She wanted company but would be damned if she made the first move and invite Mason over and she thought that if she spent her entire night answering the house's questions to "train it up" that she might as well just find a hessian sack and become a complete hermit.

Her phone, which she had programmed to have different ring-tones and message alerts for certain numbers, gave an unfamiliar chime and the name displayed it didn't bring a face to her memory. Carly. It took a while before she worked out who she was. The delightful girl from the store with whom she had spent the very first night in the house together before Rayne had been pulled off around the globe.

Something electric and naughty uncoiled itself in her lower belly and she read the text which simply read: SAW THAT YOU WERE BACK IN TOWN. DON'T KNOW IF YOU WOULD BUT IF YOU FANCY A DRINK LET ME KNOW.

Rayne replied with: DROP WHAT YOU'RE DOING AND GET A TAXI TO MINE.

Carly gave her a miss-call on her phone as the taxi driver pulled up outside the gates and Rayne met her there. The girl was even more elfish than she remembered. Her hair was a little longer but still as distractingly blonde and just as spiky which made her neck and shoulders look too reedy to hold up her head. Her big lightly hazel eyes with the blazing whites around them were wide with pleasure when she saw Rayne waiting for her at the side entrance next to the gate.

"I was going to push the button," she said in greeting.

Rayne shrugged, "I wanted to come meet you at the door."

The taxi driver lingered for a bit and Carly noticed it as quickly as Rayne did because she didn't resist when Rayne pushed her against the wooden door so that it rattled against the wall and gave her a deeply passionate kiss. The kiss soon became heated and Rayne pinned Carly's wrists against the door and bit her neck. As if their thoughts were perfectly in tune Carly turned her head around the edge of the door and gave the driver a desperately, half lidded look at exactly the same time Rayne dragged her by the collar of her parka inside and slammed the door shut.

Rayne locked the gate and as they walked back to the house hand in hand they were overcome with fits of purely girlish laughter.

"Did you see his face?" Carly burst out.

"Why do you think I locked the gate?" Rayne asked.

They both heard the taxi driver leave, his wheels screeching across the tarmac and this spurred on more fits of laughter. Carly stopped at the pool, "Wow, I didn't see this last time."

"It was here I promise," Rayne assured her.

"No no, it wasn't all lit up like this," Carly said indicating the three separate underwater lights that cast a shimmering blue light across the bottom of the pool, "It's stunning."

Rayne grinned, "It's heated too," and like a fourteen year old wanting to show off all her new things she took Carly's hand and lead her inside.

The girl whistled as she entered the lobby, her eyes going skyward, "Awesome you have furniture!"

Rayne let her loose and the girl ran into the living room then into the kitchen and back again, she spun around in a circle with the widest, cutest grin on her face chanting, "Cool, cool, cool,"

"You look like a ninja turtle when you smile," Rayne said.

"A what?" Carly asked with a quizzical knot of her slender eyebrows.

"Don't worry," Rayne finished, and then picked up on something she had been thinking about nonstop since coming up from the gate, "That was a nice kiss."

Carly prodded her bottom lip with her thumb, "You bit me right here."

"I am sorry," Rayne said stepping towards her.

The girl's thumb slid beyond her lips and she sucked on the very tip of the digit, her eyes drifting from Rayne's eyes to her lips, "No, I like it."

And they crashed together in another kiss.

An inexcusably delicious sensation woke her and Rayne opened her eyes to find a pair of thighs very close to her face. Smiling, she inhaled Carly's sweet musk, realizing that the girl's head was bowed between her own legs where her tongue licked lasciviously. Groaning, Rayne reached up to touch her but Carly teasingly moved her thighs away and she watched instead. Tracing with her eyes the nestled folds of flesh that were as tight as a rabbit's nose, glistening moistly at the center with flesh as tumescent as her own.

The pleasure rippled out from where Carly touched her, a horizon endlessly extended. Each time she was on the verge Carly would withdraw her circling tongue and use her fingers to stimulate her sensitive nub, slipping in and curling upwards to find her G-spot against the anterior wall of her vaginal sheath. Over and over until Rayne's legs shook and her heart pounded and she felt as if she were burning with a fever, pleasure pooling and expanding at the same time, heavy with the amount of it running through her pelvis and genitals.

She became aware of Carly's pale breasts swaying against her belly, her nipples grazing Rayne's abdominal flesh and she reached down and cupped them rubbing the nipples until involuntarily the girl's thighs opened, rushing towards her.

Every touch now was so exquisite that she felt muscles jumping all over her body at each contact. Carly did something to the bud of her clitoris and she cried out, moving. She clutched at the young girl's breasts and like a lioness plunging her head into a newly felled antelope Carly's head dropped and her tongue pulverized Rayne's throbbing vagina. Rayne cried out in raw ecstasy and Carly in response sat down and buried Rayne's face into the hot crevasse between her thighs. Opening her mouth as far as she could and lavishly licking at the sweet, smooth skin there.

Carly's masterful prowess had Rayne stopping her own tonguing only to gasp for air and scream with delight.

Later that same morning Rayne woke up, tangled up with her bed sheets and alone. She pushed herself up on an arm and groggily looked around the room but saw that Carly and the clothes she had discarded last night were gone.

Using the tip of her finger she scraped sleep from her eyes, "When did Carly leave?"

"She left at 07.46," her house replied.

Rayne shrugged and yawned, Carly was an expendable bed partner and a discreet exit was best. "Hanger ons" were always annoying, even if they were friends but there was never any need to linger around after a party or sex unless you were wanted. There was no reason why two irregular lovers should want to see each other the morning after in a vulnerable and exposed state. If Rayne had woken up and rolled over to see Carly still asleep in the bed, her short girly hair all mussed up to the side, her face distorted by the curve of the pillow, her makeup smeared across her cheek she would have pretended to still be asleep, faked some sort of morning meeting or a seizure.

Crawling off the bed she padded into the en suite bathroom and had a long shower, shaved her legs and her crotch and washed her hair. Once done, she wrapped it in a grey goose toweling robe and brushed her teeth with whitening tooth paste, applied some morning moisturizer and leaving wet footprints across the floorboards went downstairs to have breakfast.

Her entire life seemed to be handled by her pa but she had made it clear that she wanted this handful of days to herself.

No haranguing from anyone- in fact she did not want her phone to ring at all. That's what she said; she had specified it in writing. But now as she sat eating a bowl of Crunchy Munch she had her phone beside her and she kept checking it. If there was such a psychological condition as phantom messages she was certainly a poster-boy-sufferer.

The day before she had loved the idea of peace and quiet, now that she had it, it bored her.

Bored. But she didn't want to travel. She had seen enough airport lounges, hotel bathrooms and limousine interiors for now.

While she contemplated and offered/rejected suggestions from herself she puckered around doing not a lot of anything. It was a beautiful day outside and like a leaf blown with the wind she inevitably found her way to the pool. With only a handful of small misplaced clouds in the sky it was perfect tanning weather so with a pair of sunglasses, sun tanning lotion and bikini bottoms she tied up her hair with a patterned bandana and stretched out on a lilo, dedicating her full attention to topping up her tan.

She had lived in South Africa her entire life and there was something intrinsically right about lying in the sun purely just to lie in the sun and quickly she relaxed and decided that this was the only way to spend her time off. Her house had been right, the pool did get the best of the sunshine thanks to facing east and being on a slight hill there weren't any adjacent shadows to obscure her sunlight.

It felt wonderful on her skin, like she was able to drink up the goodness from it directly through her pores like a plant. She was warm and weightless and with her fingers trailing in the water she was completely relaxed and at peace.

A year ago she had been counting coins that she'd saved in a coffee jar to see if she had enough money to buy a loaf of bread *and* something to spread on it and now she was floating in the center of a giant pool, in front of what could constitute a castle and the only thing she didn't actually own was the lilo (it had been left in the pool house by the previous owner). For the first time she felt ahead of her success, she felt she was riding the wave instead of being dunked or left behind and all it took was a lilo, a pool and a millionaire mansion.

With her eyes closed she imagined she was the last person on this planet. She could not hear any people sounds at all. Durban has always been noisy, it's never quiet. Even if you took away every person you'd be left with the sounds of the birds and the insects in the seething tropical vegetation that was always on the edge of overflowing and taking over the city, you'd hear the rustling of the leaves and the distant sound of the ocean. The waves climbing the shoreline only to be dragged back by their brethren and the wind whistling as it rushed between the buildings. Durban was a city that was alive, not because of people but because of its location. There was just *something* about South Africa, something more than just the people, something deep and entrenched in the soil, something that would outlast the entire world.

Her mind immediately fell onto Mason and then The Coat as if those two subjects had been waiting in line and suddenly jumped to the front of the queue to grab her attention.

There they hovered. Specters in her mind, it was as if she couldn't think of anything without eventually coming back to these pair of men. This pair of strange, mysterious, powerful men. It seemed that she had been speaking about nothing else except them for years!

Using her hands like paddles she motored herself across the pool's surface until the balls of her feet touched the tiled edge and with a push using just her ankles she drifted backwards and used her left hand like a rudder to turn her around so she could paddle to the opposite end and repeat the process. It was the sort of game anyone who has ever lain on a lilo in an empty pool has played.

Mason, the trillionaire, the handsome young trillionaire with a history so carefully written for the media that it was completely unbelievable and The Coat, a giant vigilante turned tourist attraction thanks entirely to her.

Her video, in the forty seconds of filming represented a gravititious importance to her life, forming the axis around which her life turned. Was her being at the right time at the right place a stroke of fate? Was it somehow predestined or planned by something greater than her? Or, more worrying, was it purely by chance? The events of that night played out for her:

As constant as the northern star the heat in Durban had turned the city into a swelter pot. The tar in the roads had melted and turned soft so that kids ran over it with bare feet to save their footprints forever, every household had its windows open and the only cars with them closed were the ones with air conditioners struggling to keep occupants from sweating through their clothes. The sun had set but the humidity remained, the high pressured heat that promised storms and heavy rain.

Under the Fourteens Sky City acted like a pressure-cooker and the streets were empty as Rayne drove through them. Her air conditioner didn't work and for security purposes she had to drive with the windows firmly up and the doors locked so big drops of sweat were running down her skin, forming a small waterfall between her breasts. She couldn't wait to get back to her apartment and have a cold shower and her mind was filled with thoughts of ice cubes and frozen yoghurt.

She was sorely tempted to wind down the window to get some air movement happening, but too many years of living in the city and too much accrued street instinct prevented her from doing anything so stupid. This was Durban City after all.

With the only food in her apartment being half a can of baked beans and some peanut butter, she had calculated how much money she could afford to spend on groceries and bundled herself into the car and driven to the twenty four hour super market.

Leaning on the trolley as she wandered up and down the air conditioned aisles she had lost track of time as she tried to prioritize what she was going to buy and by the time she had chosen the few things she could afford it had already gotten dark. Normally she wouldn't have been fussed, but there were road works happening on the main highway and the diversion to get home took her under the Fourteens instead of safely around the city.

She did not like the idea of driving through the Fourteens alone at night on the off chance that her *gedunka* of a car would simply stop working in the middle of the road and like wolves appearing from the shadows bad-guys of every kind would surround her automobile and strip it of its essentials, like tearing at a tortoise shell to get at the meat inside. This was the country after all where police officers advised people to not stop at traffic lights if it wasn't essential to do so after ten pm. A country where given the risk of hijackings, murder and rape, drivers were advised to make judgment calls on whether to obey the traffic laws.

So, typically, her car started making disgruntled farting noises and slowed to a crawl before coming to an unfortunate stop smack in the middle of the road.

At times like this most people have someone they can call to come help them, someone that no matter what the time of day or night will come. But she had nobody, her phone book was filled with names and numbers of fair-weather friends who wouldn't or couldn't help her.

She locked all the doors and waited for the engine to cool down before trying to the ignition again. All that she got was a strangled whine from under the bonnet.

Don't panic, Rayne reminded herself. The car had done this before it had just needed some time to sort itself out, like a diva, she just had to be patient and calm.

But she was surrounded by buildings bundled up and dripping with shadows. The road was coal black line ahead, with street lamps punctuating it but these offered little in illumination. Alley ways, like arterial conduits, ran up along every one of the buildings that all looked the same. Dark and closed up.

Sweat stung her eyes and she wiped it away with the back of her hand while she tried to find some signal on her phone to call the AA. There was nothing and for a moment she thought she would have to get out of the car and wander around until she found a spot where some signal had managed to thread itself through Sky City.

To her left was an alley way that could have been an inky canvas stretched across the surface of the building for all she could see. It was made darker by a nearby flickering street lamp and with this she saw pipes running along the wall leading into the darkness and the rigid shaped fire escapes.

When it first appeared, the flash had a distinctly aggressive quality to it, it was a harsh crackle of electric light that briefly lit up the alleyway and grabbed her attention. What she thought she glimpsed before the darkness re-swallowed it had her scrabbling for her phone.

The HD camera had a digital quality night vision that illuminated the scene in a pale grey tone and revealed a fight taking place in the alley. Within the first seconds she didn't think this was real, sure that there was some other, more reasonable explanation to what she was seeing. But there was no mistaken the giant, he towered over the pack of men dressed in black combat gear who surrounded him armed with stun sticks and moving like wolves around a bear. He wasn't just taller than them but he was bigger in every aspect, gigantic with a gigantic black cloak that Rayne could have used as a tent. In the confines of the alley the group who were attacking him appeared to have the advantage in terms of numbers and weaponry but The Coat did not seem to agree with this.

In a stunning display of acrobatics the men attacked, leaping from the walls and somersaulting from standing positions but The Coat was simply too fast and in a blurring movement of counter measures that would be very carefully scrutinized by billions of people on the internet, he dispatched them all until he was simply a giant standing with half a dozen dead men around him.

Then he simply vanished out of sight. One second he was in the camera shot and the next he was gone.

Now lying in the pool Rayne recounted vividly how terrified she had been, how certain that she was going to be attacked not by some criminal on the street but by *the* vigilante they all feared. She had tried to the keys again and her car had rumbled to life and gotten her back to her apartment where she'd locked and barricaded herself in and uploaded the video that very night.

Four days later she had been at the Gregory Maines Tower.

A question popped up, one that she should have asked a lot sooner and she was surprised nobody else had asked it yet. If The Coat was real and Rayne was the only one in history to get footage of him … why hadn't he come to kill her?

Kill her? she asked herself again, testing the thought, did she really think that he would kill her? She had brought people from around the world to his city to try and do the same thing she had done bringing him vast and unwanted international attention while making her incredibly famous and rich. Had she ruined his life and taken away an obsession that he had diligently pursued for a decade? Was that worth killing her for?

The sun was no longer warm as a chill rose of the surface of the pool and made her shiver. Like a child who, after imagining something in the shadows sees something move she felt defenseless and exposed. Using her hands she urgently steered herself to the pool's edge as if she'd seen a dorsal fin glide past her and scrambled out in such a clumsy splashing manner that she almost shrieked with panic when her feet got wet. Grabbing the towel from the braai area she wrapped it around her and stood staring at the water, shivering in the sun.

"There's nothing in the water Rayne," she assured herself, "Nothing at all."

Inside she was overcome with full body shivers and had to shake her arms off just to feel normal.

"Music please," she said to the house, "Something upbeat."

A Nikki Minaj song started playing.

"Oh god no!" Rayne shouted, "Something good!"

A Nickelback song began playing and Rayne, to make even more noise in the house turned on the television and left it to go into the kitchen and make some food. She couldn't find anything she really wanted so she settled for some chocolate which she ate while sitting on the kitchen table and swinging her legs.

"Should you be eating that ma'am," the house asked, "A more nutritious meal may serve you better."

"Its comfort food," Rayne defended before realizing who she was talking to and adding, "Not that it's any fucking business of yours."

"Are you angry ma'am?" the house asked in what was clearly a despondent tone, "I was attempting to be helpful."

The tone was so reproachful that Rayne couldn't help her reaction, she looked up expecting to see a face somewhere looking at her, when she didn't see spoke to the ceiling and said, "I'm sorry."

"No apologies necessary," the voice said, "I will endeavor to be less intrusive."

Rayne laughed, "*Intrusive,* how can a computer program be intrusive? Or sorry for that matter? I don't get it are you a computer or just someone watching me on camera?"

The last thought, that there was someone watching her on camera and speaking to her over the speakers suddenly seemed more farfetched than the idea of a computer program being able to have hurt feelings. Of course it was codswallop she'd seen the program installed herself. She'd even selected the voice.

"I am a computer program," the house said, "The latest generation of house hold management systems."

"Okay, but why do you have a personality?"

"My personality is simply part of the program," the house informed her, "I have many different settings, and this is a very personable one. I'm programmed to record and anticipate your routines, control certain functions of the house to conserve energy consumption and keep you comfortable. The appearance of having a personality, the voice and the manner I speak is all programmable and changeable. Would you prefer to change something?"

"No," Rayne said, "Stay just the way you are, I like it. You're a very impressive machine,"

"That's very kind ma'am," the house said, "My program is state of the art, using a combination of the highest level of computing power and wet technology. I have a million times the computational speed of the previous model."

"You sound almost proud,"

"Perhaps," the voice said, her voice sounded so real, "I am programmed with a many different responses provided by the wet technology which also allows me to be upgraded remotely. The design of my program has changed the entire computing world and has placed South Africa at the forefront of this industry bringing it into a new era of economic wellbeing. All thanks to Mr. Lynel Mason."

"Mason made you?"

"Lynel Mason has invested billions into this industry so that programmes like mine to develop artificial intelligence."

Rayne would have been amazed if she didn't already know that Mason had a roll in all major technological and medical advancements of the last decade.

"Do you have a name?" Rayne asked, finishing the last of her chocolate.

"I have a registered product number ma'am,"

"I mean a name," Rayne said, "I want to be able to call you something other than *house.*"

"I do not,"

"How does Carol sound?"

"Like 'Carol' ma'am."

Rayne smiled, not knowing if that was a joke or not but it was good to laugh at something, she hopped off the table, "Okay then, make a note

I'm going to be addressing you as Carol from now on."

"Yes Ma'am,"

"I'm going to go get some groceries from the store,"

"I could order them in if you like," Carol offered.

Rayne declined, she wanted to get out into the world, see people maybe even meet some of her neighbors. She heard that Zack Efron owned a house here.

Dressed in blue jeans, trainers and an ancient Iron Maiden T-shirt she had owned forever, Rayne drove her tank of a car to the local shopping center. A cluster of shops in a large horse shoe shape with the parking in the center this selection of high brand stores that catered exclusively for the residents of The Suburbs.

It started in the condiments aisle while she was making a decision on smooth or crunchy peanut butter and wondering if it would be indulgent to buy both that she heard the shutter snap of a camera phone. She looked over her shoulder and saw a man taking a picture. When he realized she was looking at him he blushed and shrugged his shoulders as if to say, *so sue me* and pushed his trolley down the aisle. Putting it down as a once off she chose the smooth peanut butter and headed directly for the fruit and vegetable section and selected some fruit: Bananas, plumbs, apples and even some grapples to balance out the boxes of frozen pizza and ice-cream.

"I see you've chosen some of our grapples?" one of the floor staff who wandered around the store uniform dispersing advice to anyone who would tolerate it said, having materialized next to Rayne, "Do you like grapples?"

Rayne, completely startled by the sudden appearance of this person nodded and for what purpose she didn't know she took out one of the dark red-purple grapples, held them in front of her and squeezed it, "Yes, I do like them."

"They're a new product for us," the sickeningly polite woman informed Rayne, "And we are finding out if they are popular, may I ask what you like about them?"

Rayne put the grapple back into the basket, feeling conspicuous, "They taste like red grapes and apples?" she tested.

"And what of the texture?" the woman asked with disproportionate enthusiasm.

"The texture is," Rayne picked up the grapple again and, oh dear, squeezed it a second time, "Firm."

"Excellent, the farm that produces them is not only Fairtrade but one of the few in South Africa that produce grapples."

"How?" Rayne found herself asking before she could rein herself in.

"I'm very glad you asked," *I bet you are,* Rayne thought, "The apples are carefully selected by the farmers and then soaked for two weeks in grape juice."

A silence followed which was filled with a number of shoppers, elsewhere in the shop getting on with their shopping. Rayne gave an awkward smile and said, "Um. I am a little disappointed that that's all they do," she avoided eye contact with the woman and excused herself, "I need to continue my shopping. Thank you."

In the vegetable aisle, where a cool mist drifted over the super fresh carrots that still had dirt on them and the mushrooms the size of dinner plates, she was stretching for a particularly tasty looking gemsquach where she heard another phone shutter click.

Thinking it was the same man she had a look and found someone completely different, standing about three meters away at the lemons. About her age, with a short buzz cut hair style, denim jacket with rolled up sleeves and a general look of being a well-to-do-pretty boy who wanted to be seen as a hardcore squaddie. He had a pale complexion of someone given to blushing heavily.

Despite having been caught red handed, he didn't even acknowledge her and obstinately stared at the screen of his phone, watching her through it with an expression of intense concentration.

"Excuse me," she said, pointing at the camera, "Would you mind *not* doing that?"

With his free hand he ran the tips of his fingers across the collar of his denim jacket and continued watching her through the camera. Rayne muttered something under her breath and pushed the trolley to the dairy section, looking behind her just once to make sure denim jacket wasn't following her.

There weren't any checkout counters at this store, counter staff were an endangered species anyway since company accountants discovered the cost effectiveness of self-checkouts. As Rayne put her goods through the machine and stacked them into a bag she spotted the denim jacket again, this time standing in the aisle directly in front of her where he pretended to look at a magazine. He stroked his collar again and she felt there was something creepy about it.

Just after she paid the machine with her card she looked over and saw him staring at her, this time without the subterfuge of a magazine or a camera phone. The look made her skin crawl.

Maneuvering the trolley through the busy parking lot Rayne spotted an aging Matthew McConaughey as he was stepping out of his latest electric sports car and completely forgot about the creepy denim jacket in the shop as she realized smugly that Matthew McConaughey had a house in her neighborhood. It was just such a pity about his un-bashfully short arms! She stashed the bags into the back seat of the Landrover and a car parking attendant diligently took the trolley from her while she kept making furtive glances at Matthew as he smiled over the top of the sports car in her direction. She wondered if she should go and speak with him but even while she thought this she climbed behind the steering wheel of her Landrover. Her car was so much larger than his, haha, she thought, they would pick cars like that out of the grill of her tank!

She laughed at her own little joke but it died when she spotted the denim jacket again as he walked out of the store with no purchases, talking on his phone. He climbed into a white van and she ducked down in her seat as he reversed out of his parking space and drove passed her. It was silly because he couldn't see through the windows but nevertheless she twisted around in her seat to watch out the rear window as he drove in the opposite direction of where she would be headed.

Sitting upright she took a deep breath and let it all out in a single huff, shaking her head she looked at herself in the rearview mirror and said, "You're being an idiot."

Even taking the detour suggested by the onboard computer, the journey home was still desperately slow thanks to a sudden flow of afternoon traffic and although the queues were made up of BMWs and Mercedes Benzes and Rolls Royce it didn't help move things along any faster. Bad traffic was the ultimate equalizer for all vehicles.

She had the windows shut and the radio on full volume to hear it over the full blast of the air conditioner and was listening to some rock 'n roll classics from the early naughties, the likes of Nickelback, Red Hot Chilli Peppers and the Foo Fighters. Yes when it came to music she had an older taste but you couldn't argue the quality of music was far greater when musicians had to know how to sing and play an instrument. Back when bands used to make their real impact live on a stage.

Engrossed in the music she fell into an automatic rhythm of staying several feet away from the car in front of her as they all move ahead in a jittery drifting pattern of stop and go until she noticed over the roofs of all the vehicles lined up ahead, flashing blue and red lights, a gang of uniformed police officers standing around and the unmistakable box shape of an ambulance. A policeman was directing traffic with a red lamp light and the three lanes had been bottle necked into one which was what had backed traffic up. The herding effect was compounded by all the cars slowing up to see what the fuss was about but their view was hidden by the police cars that had formed a circle around the scene. Rayne's wasn't and as she passed she had a clear view over the top of the police car and in the short time she got to look she saw a paramedic standing over an open manhole cover, white as a sheet and holding a hand to his mouth. There was something in the sewer that he had not expected to find.

But then she hit the open flow of the traffic as it reopened into three lanes and accelerated and when she got home she had put the incident aside with all the other things she had seen while living in Durban.

After lugging all the groceries inside she stashed them on the wide granite and wood table in the middle and started emptying the cupboards of everything that was past expiry. Who was it who had said that "Use By" dates were redundant and should be replaced with "Deadly After" dates?

Tossing them into a plastic bin liner she went into the back garden and tossed them into the bin and had a look around. This back area was just a large grassy half-moon curve to the boundaries of her wall. It was very bland and she wondered if she should maybe have a basketball court built there? There was a pool house next to the pool that she never used, why couldn't she have a basketball court she would never use in the back?

Considering the best option for a sport area that she had no intention of making use of she returned to her unpacking in the kitchen and went about it in a surprisingly domestic and orderly fashion. She was still in the grips of the new house phase and didn't want to leave anything untidy.

"Carol," Rayne said as she arranged the fruits in the rotator basket.

"Yes ma'am,"

"I want to have a pool and braai party," the fruit assembled she moved onto the vegetables, "Would you be able to find me the contact details of some of my neighbours?"

"Of course," Carol replied, "Who would you like?"

"Everyone," Rayne said, taking a step away from the rotating baskets to have a look at her fruits and vegetables, "If everyone comes I'm bound to like some of them."

Rayne didn't know what surprised her more, how many of the most famous people in the world lived in The Suburbs, some of them even on her street or how quickly Carol was able to find their contact details. There was a list online of where all these people lived- including Rayne- that worried her a little bit, but that fleeting concern was soon doused by the simple fact that she had most of the cast of Marvel's Avengers living within a twenty mile radius. *That* was cool!

Carol sent each of their home management systems an invitation via email requiring only a RSVP to attend and that was that. It was the simplest thing she had ever done and it left her feeling, under whelmed.

"I have found a mention on a forum account for the pop-singer Catherine," Carol said.

"Okay," Rayne said.

"She has said that she would like to come to a posted hosted by Rayne Ensley as she thinks you are really cool,"

"She said that?"

"Indeed, shall I RSVP her?"

"Definitely," Rayne confirmed, "Actually invite everyone from Mason's party, everyone who went to Mason's charity ball, do you know the one I mean? With the whales and the bikinis?"

"Yes ma'am,"

"Good, God this is easy, invite them all. That'll get Mason's attention if I steel away all his friends and make them mine instead, it's petty… but it's good too."

"Excellent idea ma'am,"

"I don't even have to clean the house," she continued, "It looks as if nobody has really been here except for me and Carly."

"Would you like to invite Miss Harrison?"

"Is that her last name?" Rayne said, "Yes, why not. Send her a text from me, quote: Please come to my braai and pool party tomorrow night, bring a bikini and booze- *shit!*- no don't add that- unquote,"

There was a pause, "Shall we begin again?" Carol asked.

"Yes, send her the first bit up until the booze bit," Rayne said, fluttering around the living room, "I didn't get alcohol. Is there a company that delivers?"

"Several," Carol informed her.

"Marvellous," Rayne said with a grin, "Call the biggest one for me."

Ten minutes was all it took for the RSVPs to start coming in and Carol said the name of each confirmation as Rayne prepared herself some dinner. She was going to get fat she knew it. This was inevitable now that she was able to afford proper ingredients and had a kitchen that she could spin around on her toes with her arms stretched and not knock anything over.

"The novelist Charles Reynheart has confirmed," Carol said in the background.

Charles Reynheart, Rayne thought, of course *Chuck,* he had sent her a fruit basket when she first arrived. It was still festering unopened in one of her cupboards.

"I do need to thank him for that," she said aloud.

To celebrate the decision of having a party, Rayne was making paella, what she had convinced herself was healthy paella, with brown rice fried in a low-fat oil, loads of prawns and chorizo sausage, mushrooms, peppers and some onions. The hissing sound was intensely satisfying and the smells rising from it made her mouth water and a tall glass of wine was blending everything together.

More names were forthcoming and with every one Rayne giggled a little more at the idea of entertaining all these people at her home. Mom and dad would be so proud.

"The musician Chad Kroe-"

Rayne put the wok down, "What? What is Chad coming or not?"
But there was no answer from Carol.
Next the lights went out.

15.

In the first decade of the twenty first century a global economic crisis brought about the financial collapse and eventual demise of a number of industries. Coupled with the push for automation in others this resulted in a never seen before unemployment rate that added extra strain onto the governments of worldwide nations. It was a time of massive social upheaval as many of the world's *long established* truths became suddenly redundant. The proliferousness of programming software capable of a billion calculations a second meant that one accountant controlling the program could do the work of a hundred clerks on the floor; one machine in a factory floor that required daily maintenance from a crew of three men could perform the work of three thousand. Some people, especially those in the fortunate position to be able to, found they were able to surf the changes and this resulted in a world with more unemployment, more poverty, more destitution and more millionaires than ever before.

It was a credit to Mason's firm grasp of reality that he even noticed this period of misery for even while dozens of the smaller companies he owned went under, others flourished. He had seen this period as an opportunity to implement radical change and he had insisted, despite the expense, that more investments be made into high-labor-intensive projects. He opened hotels and apartment buildings where *people* needed to be employed to offer that personable-human touch, he invested money into shipping yards in Scotland and Ireland that had been closed since the middle part of the last century and as a rule they employed from the bottom up, carefully recruiting the people who he saw as needing it the most: the family man and the single parent and made provisions wherever necessary for transport, schooling and child care. They focused so intently on the employee benefits side of their business that what he had in the end was a workforce not only loyal to him, but devotedly in love.

"This is the key to Lynel's Mason's method of business," the spoke person said to the assembled conference, "A simple rule that has proven right every time, when the chips are down invest in the person. Invest in the people. When the economic depression hit the hardest Mason was putting his money into land ownership in countries that people with a short term look at the future wouldn't even look at and look now at the profit it's turned in ten years..."

Mason slouched in the back row, dressed in a black work suit with a light blue shirt with no tie watching the body language of the other people assembled in the vast business conference hall. The Eppiton Centre was one of the few major landmarks in Durban that he did not own, but he made full use of it because of its spacious quality and luxury. Also, he liked the coffee.

Over five hundred delegates from across the world including CEOs, managing directors, company presidents and investors had been invited to this function that was outlining one of his business-charities to further stimulate the growth of independent businesses by investing money into them that would be paid back in micro-installments lasting up to fifty years. It was a complicated calculating method requiring detailed explanations on how it worked and it strayed very close to directly saying that Mason would still be running the company in half a century, so they were relying instead on using the strength of his name. Mason was synonymous with success and if he had suggested people invested money into a restaurant selling dirt there would be people who would invest their gross savings without a seconds pause.

But, this part of the business he found terribly tedious. He knew that these people here had already paid money into the charity scheme and those who had not, were sitting there with their phones doing it now. It was so boring. He enjoyed the hands-on working element of it, getting his arms stuck in, getting your hands dirty part and the celebrating afterwards, there were hundreds, thousands of projects as equally important as this one that he needed to get to. A million steps required between now and his final goal needing precise execution of each one so however tongue bitingly infuriating it was to smile into the faces of the very people who had caused the crisis in the early decades, it all had to be played carefully.

The spokesperson made a joke which he didn't even hear and the audience laughed boisterously and several keen faces turned around to look at him. He offered them a smile and chuckled and when they had turned away he looked at his watch.

His phone started to vibrate in his inner jacket pocket and despite it being on silent the vibration alone sounded like a giant-mutant-bee caught in a jar and he was quick to stop it before taking it out and looking at the screen. He smiled apologetically to some of the delegates who looked over at him.

It was Rayne calling him.

He hadn't planned on contacting her for at least another fortnight but an urgent feeling in his chest prompted him to dart off his chair as silent as a mouse and slip through the back entrance of the hall into the lobby, the phone already to his ear, "Rayne hi, sorry about that I was in the middle of a con-"

"Lynel!?" the instant he heard her voice his head shot up, he had never heard her sound so terrified, "Oh my God Lynel! I'm sorry to call you like this," she was crying, her words coming out in babble and incoherent to anyone else but him, she said. "Someone broke into my house and attacked me!"

The muscles in his shoulders clenched tightly and he sprinted to the lobby desk and said to the reception, "Get my car now please."

He brought the phone back to his ear while the receptionist picked up hers, Rayne was still talking, "… know who he was but he broke in and did something to Carol because she's not working… I think she's gone….," a whine that sounded like a gasp, "….from the store, I saw him at the store he was taking a picture of me he tried, he tried… he broke into my house and he tried to rape me!"

A cold sensation crept over Mason's body and his vision tinged with red, he had only exited the double glass doors of the center when Montgomery pulled up in front of the promenade in a sleek silver Mercedes, he didn't bother opening the door for as he had driven for Mason for all of his adult life he was fluent in the trillionaire's moods. He saw the way Mason walked out of the center and knew that his place was in the driver's seat with his foot poised above the accelerator.

Mason opened the back door and slid in and the tires were already squealing on the tarmac, "Rayne Ensley's house," he said.

On the phone Rayne was still gabbering frantically, Mason was fine with this for as long as she was on the phone and talking she was alive. He said into it, "You said he attacked you?"

(Montgomery's eyes glanced at Mason in the rearview mirror and there was a thump as his right foot hit the floor).

"Yes! He did, he broke into my house!" Rayne shouted, "and he snuck in and attacked me…tried to strangle me!"

"Rayne, it's very important that you tell me is he still there?"

"No! He's not," she said, and Mason's heart sunk, had Rayne just become another Durban statistic? She added, "... he was going to rape me Lynel, he was going to rape me he said so he said it, but he didn't... Something stopped him."

Montgomery took a sharp right turn and Mason braced himself with a hand against the ceiling lest he be thrown to the door, there was a sudden succession of angry sounded hooters and screaming brakes and a long, Doppler effect of a car horn as it passed very near to them.

"Rayne... listen to me..." Mason said with a calm voice even while he was thrown around the car like a bean in a jar, "Have you called the police?"

"No! Not yet... I'm scared...."

"You say that something stopped him... where is he now do you know?"

(another long whine)... "I don't know,"

"Is he in the house, is he in the garden?"

"No... I don't know I don't think so... Lynel... are you coming over?"

Mason looked up and spotted Montgomery's eyes as they flicked from the road to the rearview mirror, the driver picked up on another one of the hidden signals because he said, "Minutes sir."

He was driving the Mercedes like a madman, having taking them onto the bypass to avoid the central traffic in Durban, it meant a slightly longer road to travel but Montgomery's foot was crushing the accelerator flat and the car was closing in on two hundred and fifty kilometers per hour.

"Rayne... you're safe now, put the kettle on for me and I'll see you before it boils..."

She gave a teary eyed giggle, at what wasn't actually a joke but he was grateful for the strength she had, "Don't be silly," she said.

"Get the kettle sorted babes," he said soothing, "Or else I'm going to have to wait for it too."

"Okay," she said, sniffing heavily over the phone, "Let me get up,"

Over the whine of the engine and the frequent blowing of the horns as they torpedoed across the asphalt Mason heard the various moving sounds of someone getting up and her slow, sniffling breaths as she tried to stop crying. They were calming sounds as her body filled itself with endorphins and slowly slipped into shock, it was good, it meant that he would be able to help her more when.

"*Fuck me!*" she screamed, so shrilly and loudly that Mason's head jerked away from the phone, he crushed the phone back to his ear immediately but there was no connection.

"Rayne?!"

Montgomery used a hand brake turn to sweep off the highway, in a maneuver that left several inches of rubber behind on the road, and cut into The Suburbs, the swerve threw Mason across the seats and into the door, "Montgomery!" he yelled, re-dialing Rayne's number.

"Sir!" the driver called, as they slammed to a lurching halt in front of Rayne's driveway. The wheels slid across the gravel driveway until beaching across the lawn. Mason flew out of the car and hit the side entrance with his shoulder, turning it to kindling.

He saw the state of the garden but as she wasn't there he focused on the interior of the house, in the living room he found Rayne's phone lying on the floor the screen broken, he saw the state of the living room too but again refused to be distracted and walked into the kitchen where a wok on the stove was bellowing black smoke up into the ceiling. The smoke alarms should have been going mental but there was nothing. He turned off the stove and took the pan to the sink and dropped it in there to cool off. Once done he went down into the underground garage where he found her.

Seeing her huddled there, sitting on the cold concrete, her back to the corner of the garage, her hands over her face, her body behind her knees as if she had tried to push herself further into the corner. She was alive, her heart racing as fast as a humming birds but alive, he could smell none of her blood and it broke the tunnel vision he had experienced as he advanced slowly saying, "Rayne…"

Hearing his voice she looked up, her face red, one eye swollen and half shut from where she'd been hit, a split lip.

"Lynel?"

She jumped to her feet and sprinted over to him, ran like someone fleeing from a man with a gun and threw herself into his arms and he held her close while a liquid relief replacing the blood in his veins.

"Lynel… Lynel… Lynel…." she began but couldn't finish, burying her head instead into his chest, he put a hand to the side of her neck under her hair and held her until she was cried out and dry.

"I'm ruining your suit," she whispered after a while.

"No you're not," he told her, "Tears are great for it, really sorts the fabric out."

She laughed again and with the same soothing tone he said, "Do you want to tell me what happened?"

With her hands on his shoulders she pushed a little against him so that she could look him in the eye and with her sleeve she wiped her nose, leaving a long snail trail on the back of it that Mason would never, ever, remind her about and said, "Let me show you."

She took him by the hand and led him out of the garage. She did so with such authority he was taken back, who had been the little girl he'd found hiding in the garage?

Through the house he was surprised at how much detail he had not noticed while he'd been searching for Rayne. She led him through the hall way and into the living room where he saw that the French windows leading out across the veranda to the pool, and in full view of the gates, had been destroyed, one of the vertical aluminium posts wrenched completely out of shape and the back of the sofa ripped off so that loops of stuffing were mixed with the glass all the way to the pool.

"I was lying there," she said pointing to the sofa.

"Don't worry Rayne, I know what happened," he said, holding her hand, "I know what happened."

"How do you?" she asked, looking down at his hand.

"I can smell it,"

She didn't understand or she didn't believe him, maybe she thought that he was trying to save her from reliving the attack, she shook her head, "No, look I was here and he attacked…"

"Rayne, please," he said, "Let me take you to the hospital and you can tell me everything there."

She touched the side of her face with her fingers and winced as she prodded the tender skin, "I'm fine Mason."

So it wasn't Lynel anymore?

"Did he do this?" he said walking behind the couch to the window. He had to keep her talking, had to keep her mind busy.

"No," she said, "I was watching television and he came in from there,"

The entertainment unit was smashed, thoroughly, as if a hydraulic crane had crushed through it, shattered right down to the wall. Mason's eyes lingered on it for a long time. Again, he knew exactly what happened better than she did. Her attacker, who had a scent he would never forget, had snuck in through one of the rear windows after disabling the house management system, he had snuck in through the house with one thing on his mind and had followed Rayne into the living room and slipped a plastic baggie, the sort used to preserve vegetables over her face and locked it under her jaw. He'd punched her and ripped at her pyjamas and judging by the smell that offended Mason's nostrils, he had been unable to control his excitement and had leaked into his own pants.

Something powerful had entered then, the smell of which made his skin crawl, entered at incredible speeds, probably faster than Rayne could see. For less than a second the smell of this powerful entity and Rayne's attacker intermingled over her and the attacker then ended in the wall unit. Thrown. The two smells met again at the unit and then the attacker was put through the window.

Following the smells, Mason walked away from Rayne, stepping through the empty French windows and onto the veranda.

"..but you're going to mess up the evidence aren't you?" she asked.

"I wouldn't worry about it," he assured her. With his hands in his pockets he visualized in his mind's eye the way the attacker passed through the windows and collided with the edge of the pool. It was a distance of some five meters, a hell of a distance to throw a fully grown man. Miraculously the attacker's skin had not been broken when he hit the tiled edge which was cracked but there was no blood. The other entity had then taken him from the water and…

Mason questioned himself but there was no need to, there was no way to fake such a scent trail when it was still so fresh- but it seemed that the other entity had picked the attacker out of the water and thrown him again. But this time he had properly *thrown* him, the scent trailed upwards, moving through the air in a long arc… an arc that would have carried the man over the entire Suburbs and a fair distance out to sea.

Who was strong enough to throw a human being, a man of eighty kilograms or more that far?

"What's wrong?" Rayne asked when he returned to her.

"I was just having a look," he said, "I take it you saw the man who saved you?"

She nodded, "Yeah. I did, then I dropped my phone and it broke. It was The Coat."

"I know," he said, pulling her close to him, she buried her face into his chest and clung to his jacket lapels with her hands, "I..." he began but she cut him off.

"I thought he was here to kill me," Rayne confided, "I thought he was angry that I had made that video and that after he got rid of... *that* guy... he was going to kill me. He's so big and so fast and so strong. But he just stood there," she pointed to the veranda, "He stood there. I dropped the phone and ran."

From where they stood they could look through the French window frames, across the veranda and see the front gate. The side entrance door was halfway up the drive in two pieces.

"Did you do that?" she asked.

"No," Mason lied quickly, "I think he did when he arrived. Rayne, I don't think he was here to hurt you. I think he was here to save you. That being said, you're still coming home with me."

"I *just* moved in properly," she whined.

"Temporarily then," he insisted, "Just come to the Tower while we get things fixed here. Please."

She nodded and he led her upstairs and put her clothes into a carry bag. In the en suite he got her cleaned up, used a first aid kit to clean the lacerations on her face and put some salve on the bruises. He gave her some jeans and a shirt to put on and then walked her out of the house.

"What about Carol?" she said as they walked together down the gravel drive.

"Carol?" he was lost.

"My management system," she said, "I don't know what he did to it."

"It's fine," he said, "I'll sort it."

He climbed in next to Rayne and Montgomery, without a word, drove them both to the Gregory Maines Tower.

16.

David Plespet did not see the logic in having a playing field this close to the sewers but designing playgrounds was the job of someone more intelligent than him. His job was just to cut the grass. A job he had done diligently for thirty years without complaint. He knew the sound of everyone one of eThekwenis Municipalities ancient weedwhackers and how to get the best out of each of them, every tool and every vehicle that he used now he knew as well as his own hands. It was something that was on his mind a lot now. There were seven hundred municipally owned playing fields in Durban City, grassy patches of land like this usually surrounded by buildings and roads. Usually with some scrubby-bushy hedges and some jacaranda or acacia trees, perhaps one or two palms and that was about it. Seven hundred, it used to take a team of five men a year to mow through all of them. Nothing special, David thought as he swept the hungry head of his weedwhacker on its long metal neck in broad arcs. The spinning wire diced through the grass spraying pulp all over the orange cotton overalls David wore and already some of it had gotten down into his gum boots and were making his toes itch but he didn't mind too much. It was just a measure of his day.

The city grew and changed, Sky City had only been a few bridges between office buildings and parking lots when he first started and now thirty years on it had grown outwards on what, as far as he knew was an hourly basis. Spreading and changing, overtaking everything that came before and attracting in an entirely different crowd of people. But the fields stayed the same. There was a respect for these grassy patches that meant that while the city grew, changed, morphed, evolved these grassy patches stayed as if they simply could not be moved. The city itself had a respect for them, which made David a very important man as the last surviving municipal gardener.

Where was the logic of leaving one old man to do the job of five? He couldn't find it, but again, it was probably managed by someone more intelligent than him. So he worked through his map of fields, starting in the morning before sunrise and often getting home just as the sun was getting ready to go to bed, his beaten up bakkie chugged and croaked like every one of his weedwhackers but like them, he knew how to get a lot out of it and as long as he didn't drive it any further than he had been driving it on a daily basis it was just fine.

It wasn't much of a job, but it was a job he had kept for thirty years while others had disappeared one by one. Either by the recession, redundancy or simple violent fate, it was the job that he did well because there wasn't a lot to do with it. Consistency, that was the key, remember to keep the whacker at the same height, keep your finger on the trigger, make sure you don't miss any patches, cut the grass closer to the root around the footings of any of the playground playthings and don't go near the sewers.

Like a toy train on rails he worked his way without thinking to the bank of the river where the grass ended and turned into pale brown sand, like the sort from the beachfront. His keen eye scanned the shoreline for anything needing to be removed. There was always something, bits of plastic, tin cans, sandwich wrappers, clothing any sort of thing that people might just throw over the fence to get rid of.

Mentally he recorded what needed to be scooped up, picked up or dug up and continued with the grass cutting. Finish one job before going onto the other one was another important rule. But after thirty years he still didn't turn his back onto the sewers, no way, in fact cutting the grass at the concrete baseline of the sewers was the part of his job he hated the most- but at the same time knew that if he didn't do it nobody else would.

Thirty years in any job will give you the opportunity to see the worst of what that job has to offer and he had seen the very worst of this one. Sewers. He looked up at the entrance of the sewer which consisted of two one and a half meter tall pipes, covered with a bolted into place steel grate. The river that divided the field into two triangles, poured through one of the pipes from the concrete canal on the other side of the bridge, but the other pipe was specifically a sewer outlet for when the shit of the city got to the point where it had to come out somewhere and it would pour everything out into the river. It was good, to a point, for the grass but why have a seesaw, a merry-go-round and swings for kids near by? When the wind blew just in the right way it brought with it a smell that made his eyes water and yet, the residents from the blocks of houses and apartments around the area still brought their kids here, when it was hot enough, which it often was. They'd come down here with their children and their dogs and frolic in the water and on the grass as if unable to see the shit pipe lingering in the corner. He assumed that as he didn't have any children of his own he would never understand why parents often did things that was just so batshit insane.

"*If the whistle winds blow low, let the whole city know...*" he sang to himself over the high pitched buzz of the weedwhacker, "*Things will get some slow...*"

The Porters Row field was not large, maybe big enough for kids to play a decent game of soccer or rugby on it, so it took him only twenty minutes to do a decent job on the grass on both sides, which was all that was needed. Whether fields, playgrounds, the strips of grass on the road islands or the verges nobody was trying to win a beauty pageant it needed a good once over with the whacker, a quick rake and a pick-up, that was all. Once he was finished the grass he put the weedwhacker into the wheelbarrow and took off his helmet and visor. In the Durban sunshine these gardening hard hats and the overalls made you *Sweat*, with a capital S. But they were important, in his time David had seen people loose teeth and eyes from stones being flicked up by the wire of a weedwacker and as he was sure they would fail him in their own time he didn't see the logic in helping them along.

He relished the fresh air around his face and neck when he took off the helmet and dropped it next to the whacker and when he unzipped his overalls fronts and pulled his arms out of the sleeves the sun felt brilliant on his bare shoulders. He rolled the top half of the overalls down into a bundle-belt around his waist and picked up the litter stick.

The litter stick was one of the various tools he'd commandeered over the years, a three foot length of metal with a sharped, barbed end perfect for skewering litter and hooking things. It also offered him some additional confidence as he would be collecting pieces of rubbish from the river which brought him close to the sewer. He stuck the litter stick into the earth next to his boot and whistling to himself he clattered through his cluttered tools in his wheelbarrow looking for a pair of wire cutters. Someone had dropped a roll of wire fencing into the water and that stuff was perfect for slashing little kids to pieces so he wanted to remove it and knew it would have had the weeks since he was last here to get really wedged into the river bed. At the bottom of the wheelbarrow he found the cutters and as he straightened he heard his back crack loudly. A second of pain made his eyes go squint and he put his hands against his lower back and groaned loudly.

It wasn't a bad back pain, but back pain didn't have to be. He was an old man, old enough to know that back pain tends to come all at once. Massaging the fleshy muscles just above his pelvis he stared at the house in front of him for almost a minute before he registered someone in the top window staring back at him.

The house itself was one of those old styled abodes that were perfectly suited to have some strange girl staring out of the window, watching him. If he were younger, he would have responded to it in a totally different manner, but being watched by a girl in a window affects old and young men differently. But his discomfort was more that he didn't like the way she was watching him.

Scowling and gritting his teeth against the stabbing pain in his lower back and with his tools in hand he walked across the field to the river. People sometimes watched him work, there was nothing wrong with it and it would have been silly to expect anything different. It was up to more intelligent people to judge someone on choosing to watch a man work in the field in the sunshine than rather go and look after their own back garden. She could watch him for as long as she liked because he knew it wasn't because she fancied his leatherish brown skin and the increasingly tanned portions of his balding scalp.

Trudging across the sandy bank of the river he used the litter stick to skewer the litter he could see and drop them into the hessian sack that was slung with a canvas rope across his midsection. The litter would be sent to the recycling plant, changed into new products to appear on his banks and in his grass. Where did such a variety of plastic come from anyway?

Not that it mattered, it was all skewered the same way and put into his sack and delivered to the depot. This part of the job took a long time because you'd always find more things. Carton material, sacking material, bits of wood, nails and condoms... always condoms, those buggers could hide just about anywhere and would wait until you thought you had finally finished before peeking out of their hiding spots and saying, Hello, are you forgetting me?

"If the whistle blows low...." He sung off key as he swung his little stick looking for those little latex monsters, *"Let the whole city know..."* he walked the length of the bank until it ran out and the river continued

down the riverbed which was lined on all sides by concrete. He vividly remembered when this wasn't the case, before the concrete walls had been put on the side of the river. It had had the tendency to break its banks when it rained heavily. Now, thanks to the hydro-electric plant about seven kilometers upstream the river only seldomly got to the point where it would even wet the playground. When it did though it did completely cover everything and it would be up to him to untie and cut the flood debris from the playthings.

It was at this final point of the grassy field, just off the shoreline that the role of fencing had been dumped. It was the hard sharp kind that promised cuts irrespective of how you handled it and he was right that it had managed to get well and truly knotted into the riverbed. His back pain let up, or he forgot about it, as he crouched next to the fence roll and got down to his elbows into the water trying to get the wire cutters to loosen it up. It was a more complicated job than he had imagined and it took him longer than he thought because by the time he looked up the sunshine was gone. Smothered behind heavy, bruise colored clouds. He groaned. He still had half a dozen fields to cut before he was done for the day and wanted to make it home for a cup of tea before he got soaked through to the bone.

"*If the whistle blows low...*"
It looked like the wire fencing had managed to dig into the riverbed and folded itself the edges of a heavy boulder. It was amazing what a gentle current could do to metal over a short period of time, this tough metal that his wire clippers could barely cut through might have well be a shoelace tied in a knot.

"*let the whole city know- come on you fucker,*" he growled.
No good. He would have to cut the main part of the roll of fence off and then remove the remains from the boulder separately.
Looking up at the sky he guessed he had about half an hour before the rain started and, while this was a dumb mistake to make, he glanced over his shoulder at the sewers. The glum weather did not improve their appearance. The sight of them sent a shiver up and down his back. Maybe he would just take the worse of the fence away and come back when the weather improved. Kwa-Zulu Natal was given to outrageous storms that delivered a week's worth of rain in an hour. He could come back on a detour tomorrow and finish up.

With this in mind he went to work on the wire fencing, cutting it about a hands breadth above the waterline so that anyone could see it, although he didn't think anyone would be here if it was pouring with rain and muddy. Once finished he gathered up the roll of fencing and bending from the knees carried it to the wheelbarrow. Dumping it in there with his tools he shook the water off his arms and gloves and thought where the logic was of throwing away perfectly good fencing like this? It was a good couple of kilograms worth. He wondered if his pal Jerry down at the hardware store would need it and maybe he could pawn it off on him?
While he contemplated about this he rubbed the niggling spot in his back and looked up at the window again.

He had expected to find it empty but saw the same girl there. Dark hair, dark makeup making her face look like a skull. Tattoos and piercings, he could spot it all, a lifetime of working outdoors had given him fantastic eyesight.
Although she looked right at him she didn't seem to register that he was staring back at her. Maybe she wasn't right in the head? Maybe she was a bit slow? He didn't like the thought of staring at a retard but at the same time felt peculiar about the girl's unsubtle attention. His stomach went a little funny when she lifted a hand and put the palm flat against the window pane so that it went white against the glass. She lifted her chin by miniscule margin as if to get his attention and looked away from him at the river behind him.

Automatically he looked behind him at where she was looking and saw instantly what it was she was gesturing to.

"if the whistle blows low..." he chanted under his breath as he walked to the water's edge and saw the body part. It was a hand, a human hand, by itself lying on the banks of the river as if it had crawled up it by itself.

Body parts didn't scare him. This was Durban and you didn't live here without developing an indifference to body parts. Whoever the hand belonged to probably had been a victim of some gang violence or a serial killer who had cut up his body and dropped him down a sewer manhole. Well, the bright side was that if this was going to become a crime scene he didn't have to worry about cutting out the rest of that fence.

He smiled but didn't leave: The hand really was in a grizzly condition, the skin was hanging off it in shreds like a ripped up glove, pink meat hung off it in strings around patches of pale white bone, his first impression was that it looked like the hand itself had been gnawed on. Stepping back away from it he fished out his battered cellphone from his inner leg pocket and dialed the number for the police. He turned to look up at the window, she was a witness and he would need to mention her presence to the authorities as well. She was there, as he had come to expect now but both her hands were against the glass and she was looking intently at him.

His back aching he held the phone to his ear, his eyes not leaving the girl's. He thought it was a little strange that the hand had managed to get out beyond the sewer cage because the current of water dribbling out of the outlet wasn't really strong enough to push it through the gaps and the grate was there for that specific purpose to stop things like that getting into the main river course way.

"Hello Durban Police Department," a voice on the other end said. Above him the girl's eyes flicked from David's to a spot directly behind him.

Something touched his shoulder.

The force he was yanked backwards with blanked his mind, he hit the grass hard the wind crashing out of him, something gave way in his lower back which made him stiffen and gasp. Hot, wet splashed the side of his face and a searing heat in his upper left side, just above his collarbone made him cry out. Men of his age weren't really capable of screaming and his lungs didn't have the air. Had someone stabbed him? Who would stab him?

He looked down and saw with horror they were fingers, up to the knuckle in his shoulder and as he watched the grip tightened and suddenly he was being dragged backwards across the grass with his shoulders bouncing off the heels of whoever was pulling him.

The splash of the river around his legs and he saw the dismembered hand still on the bank but it was happening all so quickly he didn't really start panicking until he felt the hard edge of the sewer pipe cut into his lower back. The darkness behind him yawned wide, the hard edge of the concrete pipe scraped, like acid across the back of his legs and suddenly daylight had become an ever shrinking circle of light that he was being pulled away from. A sort of panic he hadn't experienced since being a child seized his heart but when he finally started to scream it was too late to matter.

17

In a security booth in front of a wall sized viewer displaying a dense grid of shifting video feeds, Shaka stood like a statue. His right index knuckle pressed against his upper lip, his right elbow supported by his other arm folded under it. He hadn't moved in close on an hour and the guards in the office, even though there were of the highest training, including military backgrounds, were fretted by his presence. He had a look about him, an intense focus that warped the space immediately around his body. The guards didn't speak with him, nor did they question his presence, this man had the trust of Lynel Mason and that was enough for them. Mason was the man who paid them all their incredible salaries, Mason was the man who had paid each of them separate sums of money to put their kids through school and university. Mason was the man who had bought each of them shares in the top ten companies in the world as a "pension" scheme to ensure their futures. Lynel Mason had told them to obey this very dark African gentleman in the black suit, and so they would, without question.

From this booth they monitored the security footage from the video feeds, temperature fluctuations, wind movements, electrical output. A holographic projector that was constantly rotating in the corner until someone needed it displayed the main elevator and its movements. The cameras in use operated with spectrums of night vision, heat vision and Infra-Red they were also practically unbreakable, heat, impact and EMP wouldn't damage them, spray paint would slid off the non-stick protective coating that used a mild vibration and electronic technology to clean every three minutes on routine and within a two second period of disturbance. A lot of money had been given to a number of different companies around the world to develop and install this technology.

The guards all knew that it wasn't just to protect the homes of some celebrities and businesses, although that might have been enough, but while they were happy to raise their hands if asked and plead indifference as long as their pay cheques came in on time (and they always did), they had all worked out the few blind spots they had in their otherwise unbreakable wall security. For example the entire floor directly beneath Mason's office, the elevator shaft that nobody else had access to except for him that also provided the only access point to a very large empty area of the basement floors where an area the size of a car park burned up a mammoth store of energy day and night and yet was entirely excluded from the monitors.

They all had their speculations and their theories, none of them were the right ones, but they wouldn't investigate further. A man who had given each of them so much deserved to be able to have a few secrets and to be able to trust the employees charged with protecting them.

The guards whose job it was to monitor the security grid did so with the aid of a management system they'd named Toby, who monitored the footage off every feed for facial and body recognition and cross referenced it with a database of offenders that was continuously updated.

Keeping the information that popped up on separate screens about each person who walked through the building confidential was included in their contracts but some of it was very, very juicy. If Mason had been corruptible, he could have made a number of very powerful people very uneasy… this was another, although unspoken, reason why they would never betray Lynel Mason or disobey him. Everyone has secrets, and while they all knew which ones they didn't want revealed, Mason probably had all the details on paper.

The two guards in there with Shaka were both wondering what he was looking for and both had started to look at the monitor differently, wanting to be first to say, "I saw it too," when Shaka finally stopped looking. They were disappointed when he finally did speak it was in a very deep, African accented voice, "Who is that?"

Both guards leaned over and Shaka was obliged to point at one of the two thousand footage squares. The image was enlarged and Rayne Ensley appeared to them walking across the sky bridge. How he had spotted it in all the confusion was beyond them.

"That would be Rayne Ensley," one of them answered.

"Does she live here?" Shaka asked.

"Not permanently," the other guard answered, "She lives in Durban North in The Suburbs, but she had some domestic trouble or something a few days ago with a local who attacked her and Mason's made one of the apartments available for her."

That nobody questioned the nature of *making* an apartment *available* in a highly sought after, sold-out tower filled with the richest and most powerful people in the world and ignoring the seven year waiting period, illustrated the insane level of loyalty that its owner commanded.

"So she does live here?" Shaka said.

"Temporarily sir," the other guard amended, "Only until the damage is repaired at her house and the security updated."

Toby cycled through the various cameras to keep Rayne on the screen as she walked through and Shaka didn't take his eyes off her for over a minute. The guards, still unaware of the parallel of their thoughts, wondered if he was just admiring her beauty. They'd all seen Rayne Ensley's famous blog site and every one of the guards, although the product of many years of training, were still men and she struck a carnal chord deep within all of them. Her straight hair, her highly tanned skin, and the fact she dressed like a British footballer's wife screamed to them high levels of personal resilience and sexual disposability. They could see what their employer saw in this short model, they'd seen it onscreen at their homes when they'd been alone with their computers for a few minutes. They couldn't see the other element, why Mason would go to so much personal effort to protect her?

"What apartment does she have?"

"The Twenty Fifth sir,"

"I want Toby to monitor her apartment specifically, I want to know everything she does, do you understand?"

"Yes sir," they said simultaneously. One of them added tentatively, "That is illegal though sir,"

The slap that was delivered struck out with the speed of a viper and had the guard reeling backwards; it was the pronounced look that was behind the slap that made him physically cringe.

"Actions do speak louder than words," Shaka said, taking out his phone and syncing it to Toby using an application that Mason had provided him, "Don't they?"

The guards only realized he had left when the door closed behind him. The security booth was located on the reception floor and Shaka walked into the main part of it and sat in one of the leather sofas and waited until Rayne Ensley approached over the Sky Bridge. There were certain things you could not tell about a prey by a camera shot and from the distance provided by the excessively spacious reception/foyer Shaka was able to appreciate all of them from this Rayne Ensley. It had less to do with his senses and more to do with his intuition and he could see that she was prominent. She had a destiny that was brighter than the people around her. He took a long, deep breath that filled his lungs but while he could detect her scent, it was too muddled with the other smells of the hundreds of people crowding the room and left him unsatisfied.

Standing he approached as she went to the reception desk and heard her ask if she had any messages, her voice was confident, assured but with a very slight porous doubt tucked in there like a buck who is brave and commanding while its heart flaps like bird wings. The receptionist recognized him as he approached and didn't say anything when he stopped behind Rayne and said:

"Miss Ensley?"
Like a cat caught off guard Rayne flinched and turned, "Yes?"
He extended a hand which she shook. Her skin was sun-warm to the touch, the flesh of her palms and fingers smooth and soft. Aside from being equally as warm, his hands were the complete opposite, hard like horn, "My name is Shaka, I am head of security for Mr. Lynel Mason,"

"Okay?" she said, a little confused, "Can I help you?"
Shaka feigned an impressive smile, something he'd learnt off of Mason, in a head as dark and as shiny smooth as his the sudden crescent moon of a smile he could produce was disarming, "It is rather embarrassing but we have a new starter in my department and somehow he has managed to trip the alarms on the Twenty Fifth floor, the other apartment is currently vacant so we're in there trying to sort the problem but the elevator to yours has gone into temporarily lock down."

In the corner of his eye he saw the receptionist frown at this complete lie but the woman was smart enough not to interfere, he continued, "It's only a temporary malfunction, as I'm sure you are aware Gregory Maines takes the security of it's residents very seriously and so we have the occasional provision for lock-down in the case of a terrorist attack. The emergency exits are still functioning however they are only one way. Since building the tower we've never had to use the lock down code and so my new starter didn't really know what he was doing," the smile shifted upwards into his eyes so that she couldn't help but feel sympathetic to his plight.

"That is a bugger," she said, "But I understand, do you think it will last long?"

"It should only be about fifteen minutes or so," Shaka explained, "We don't have to get into your apartment however the people in Twenty Six and Twenty Four need to be reassured. I am very embarrassed about the situation but was hoping I could make it up to you by offering you a coffee in my office? It's of the finest quality."

She groaned, "I have a *lot* of things to do today,"

"I know it's a horrible inconvenience," he said, "Please, at least let me impress you with my coffee and by the time we're done you're apartment will be unlocked."

Resigned to no other options she shrugged and he thanked her and stepped beside her so they could walk together to the security booth and immediately into the kitchenette they shared with the reception.

It was in keeping with the rest of the tower and was militarily cleaned and provided for.

"This seems very well furnished for a security booth," she said looking around.

Still playing the host he took his time making the coffee and explained, "Yes, as I understand it when the tower was initially made the employers staff rooms and kitchens were departmentalized. This as a result is the most highly furnished kitchenette in the most highly furnished building in the world."

With the door closed it didn't take long for her scent to fill the room and he was able to take a massive breath in through his nostrils, filling his chest with her smell. It told him everything that he needed to know about her and it confirmed his intuitive suspicion. She was very important.

The parts of his brain responsible for it sifted through her smell while he busied making the coffee.

"I did lie a little bit I'm afraid," he said, handling her a hot cup, "The coffee is only instant,"

She took the beverage from him and smiled, "It's fine. I know it wasn't your fault. Do you run all the security here?"

"For the Gregory Maines Tower," he lied, leaning back against the counter and breathing through his nose, "The security for the remainder of Sky City is departmentalized as well."

"Still quite an undertaking," she sipped the coffee, "Oh this is actually *really* good."

"It's where you buy it from," he said, "It's strange I would have pegged you as a tea drinker?"

"Nobody's ever said that," Rayne said with a stifled laugh, "I don't drink that camel piss. Always prefer coffee."

"Indeed," Shaka said, "And yes it is a massive undertaking but we have a very strong management system that does a lot of the work for us."

She chuckled, "I have one of those at my house. She acts like my mother."

"It is a marvelous invention," Shaka said, "But it's all terribly sophisticated. I grew up in a shack in Ghana and I didn't even see a computer until I was in my twenties."

"How long have you worked here for?"

"Not long here, but for Mason it's been a long time," Shaka said, he made a show of checking his watch then excused himself, walked to the kitchen door and stuck his head through to ask his staff when the lock down on her floor would open up. They said something to him and he muttered something in French before closing the door and sitting down opposite Rayne.

"Aren't you having a cup?" she asked, sipping her own.

"I've had enough caffeine today," he said, "I was actually white this morning."

Rayne stifled a laugh and bit her lower lip, composed herself and said, "It is very good."

"Your apartment will be ready in a few minutes, we've fast tracked the system for you."

"Is that safe?"

"Well, it means a bit of extra work for my new starter this afternoon but I think he deserves it. I understand you've only been here for a little while aside from this mishap are you enjoying living at Sky City?"

"I don't live here," Rayne said, defensively, "I'm a guest for a few days and then I'll be going back to my place in Durban North. But I will be honest the view here is just breathtaking,"

"Yes, it's one of the reasons I love working here, you get to see the best parts of Durban," he grinned again, "I'd wager your view from The Suburbs must be good but you must get a spectacular view from the Twenty Fifth?"

"Absolutely you can almost see onto the decks of the cruiser liners as they come to port," Rayne said. She put her ear to her shoulder and her vertebrae cracked loudly, then she repeated the movement on the other side with a responding crack.

"I don't think that's very good for you," he said.

"It's been a stressful couple of weeks," Rayne explained, "I was attacked at my own house and the place is a wreck now. They're busy fixing it but I had to cancel invitations to a party I was going to be having with some of the most influential people in the entertainment world. I've got a lot of tension that has built up so my neck and shoulders get awfully stiff, I also have to do some more videos as their overdue but I can't get the motivation to get all uppity with myself if…" it dawned on her what she was saying, "I'm sorry Shaka, sometimes I say too much."

Shaka lifted a hand to show he didn't care to judge, "It's not an issue with me,"

"I don't want you to think I'm superficial,"

"Nonsense," he said, "I for one don't much like travel. It's far too stifling. What places have you gone to?"

Listing them on her fingers she went through the places she'd visited and how although she was tired of it, she did enjoy travelling because it was better than where she had been and Shaka listened and allowed his olfactory mind to determine who she was. People never realize how much information is contained with the pheromonal scent. Animals are capable of telling age, family history, health and even genetic compatibility purely by smell but most people could never conceive of such a power. Now his sense of smell was not nearly as honed as an animal's but he believed it was on the upper curve of human evolution and the longer he spent with Rayne the better idea he got of her and he was impressed.

She might have been short and a little chubby- but from an evolutionary standpoint she had no idea of what she was.

Rayne's phone beeped as she received a message, she excused herself and read the text, "Oh."

Her expression darkened significantly.

"It's none of my business," he said, "But are you alright?"

"It's just that my house is fixed," she explained, "They have managed to sort everything."

"That's good isn't it?"

"Yes," she admitted, but he wasn't convinced, "It's great. I'm just, oh never mind."

One of the guards, who still did not know what was going on, thumped on the kitchen door and Shaka stood, "Well, your apartment's ready for you again and as long as you're staying here you might as well enjoy our hospitality."

He held open the door for Rayne and walked her to the elevator.

"Thank you for the coffee," she said as he pushed the elevator button for her.

"It's my pleasure and I hope the incident doesn't dampen your spirits for your video," he said with a grin, "In the meantime I'll deal with my employee immediately."

"I'd be careful how you phrase things to a porn star Shaka," she grinned, "Seriously don't be too harsh. Accidents happen."

She got onto the elevator with some of the other residents who were waiting and as the doors closed Shaka turned, took a deep, calming breath and went back to the sofas in the reception where he sat and appeared to play on his phone for a while. What he was actually doing was memorizing the angles and vantage points of the security cameras surrounding Twenty Five. Cameras were not allowed inside the actual apartments or office premises, but there were enough surrounding the residences with enough technology available to them to get a very good idea of someone's movements and that's just what Shaka was doing. Using the cameras from outside and cycling their viewing aspects through Infra-Red, heat sensors and movement until he was able to get a clear and precise idea of what Rayne's movements were like once she had entered the apartment. Doing this and without directly invading her privacy (which if it had been an option Shaka would have gone for) he watched her until the sun had started to set and the exterior lights were lit.

It was crucial that he was able to predict her movements should she run in a panic and once he knew he would be able to do that he sent a text and returned to the security booth.

"Everyone out," he said to the guards inside who all filed out obediently. He locked the door behind them and sat down in front of the viewing monitor, "Toby?"

"Yes sir," the computer responded in a crisp military tone.

"Which of the security feeds can be re-aligned to view the

surrounding area?"

On the dense screen in front of him about half of the available squares faded leaving a checker-board effect of the remaining squares that could be moved.

"Align those cameras to give me a 360 degree view of the city," he commanded. As one synchronized movement the viewpoints turned revealing great wide sweeps of the city, "What is the capacity of your range?"

"Three thousand and seventy two meters sir," Toby informed him.

"And are you able to gain access to the city security grid?"

"I would require authority to do so sir,"

"You have it."

A new window popped up in the corner of the screen and a grid opened with more available views, Shaka minimized this and said, "What blind spots are there?"

"The city security grid does not have eyes on the rooftops sir,"

"But we have in Sky City?"

"We have camera, Infra-Red, Motion Sensor and heat receptors,"

Shaka's fingers attacked the keyboard like two black spiders running up an escalator, while his hands worked he said, "These are the particular readings I am looking for. Notify me when you find him and initiate a data-change lockout to anyone but I, do you understand?"

"Mr Mason has an override command," Toby informed him.

The hunter bit his lip in agitation, "Very well. Everyone else."

"Yes sir."

Exiting the booth he locked the door behind him and turned to the security guards outside looking sullen and confused.

"Mason has asked me to conduct some surprise inspections; they're taking place now so you all have the evening off."

He didn't wait to answer any questions but marched across reception and stepped into the elevator, holding up his hand to a couple standing in robes that had been waiting for the lift and saying, "Take the next one."

He rode the cart to the top floor where Mason, was waiting at his desk. The man was dressed in a pair of light weight black trousers and tabi ninja boots. His upper body was bare and his hair had been tied back into a tight pony tail high on the back of his head. The sword was strapped to his back.

"Hello Shaka," he said jovially, walking around the desk, "How are you?"

"Everything is in place," Shaka informed him coldly, walking to the sofas where a flat rectangular case lay across one of them. He opened it up and started assembling a high powered rifle.

Mason waited until Shaka was standing beside him with his rifle in hand, he said, "You've done well Shaka you are a very talented liar. Although I must question you man-handling my staff,"

"You have put me in charge of your security," Shaka said in explanation.

"Very well," Mason said, not interesting in giving a lecture, he looked at the rifle in Shaka's hands, "That looks like a beast so please do me a favour and don't shoot *me*,"

Shaka didn't reciprocate Mason's famous smile, "I do not think that is part of your plan."

"You sound like you might doubt it,"

"I question the tactical reliability of it," Shaka replied honestly. Walking passed the trillionaire.

"Do you think I'm guessing?" Mason asked, his smile lingering but changing slightly as it was aimed for the back of the hunter's head.

"I know better than that," said the hunter, opening the door to the balcony and walking into the night.

18.

Rayne hadn't been able to sleep. She had tried but every time she closed her eyes she couldn't help but feel Denim Jacket's cold, shivering hands on her throat. To distract herself she had watched television but of the thousand channels available nothing interested her enough to hold her attention, she watched wrestling on the holovision and even tried watching some of the old movies that had been converted to holograms but there were only so many times you could watch a thirty centimeter Bruce Lee making cat like sounds while flying through the air before you got bored. She made herself a sandwich of lettuce and peanut butter and ate it on the balcony but while she wanted to look at the ocean, the lights from Sky City that burned upwards cut off her vision and the Simmers Hotel directly in front of her obscured any view she might have had anyway. It was a nonetheless grand view but couldn't take her mind off of what that man had tried to do to her.

And the man who had saved her?
As clear as day she remembered the feeling of the plastic bag being yanked over her face. The surprised gasp that had given her a second more oxygen than she would have had but the strike to her face and the punch to her kidneys that had taken it and the electric, spasming pain as her internal organs recoiled from the merciless blow. It had felt like her insides had simply burst and she had stiffened in response, her body bending to the side over the punch before a tie around the bag's lining was tightened with a *ziiippp!* the chord cutting into her throat.

She had struggled, bringing her hands up to her face but he hit her again in the lower back and spots popped up brilliantly in front of her eyes. She was pushed forward and collided with the couch her face bouncing off the cushion and hands scrabbled at her body as she was yelled at by her attacker, he called her names, he spat at her. She came to lie on her back on the couch and he fell upon her, pinning her arms at her shoulder level. Desperate for breath as the plastic was sucked into her mouth instead of air and as her vision blurred and her chest burned she saw the Denim Jacket's face directly in front of her.
Self-defense lessons she'd learnt in primary school struggled to clear in her memory but she tried to fight him off, she twisted a hand free and

beat and clawed at his arms and his face but her arm felt like it was made of lead, her legs couldn't coordinate and she was losing feeling in them. She had to breathe and things started popping in her head with intense stabs of pain and she wouldn't be able to do much soon.

Hands at her pajama bottoms. Her comfortable, loose pajama bottoms, made out of loose cotton with an elastic strap around the waist. Denim Jacket had no problem shoving his hands into there. His hands were cold and rough, like dry ice on her flesh, while hot, dank breath blew against her ear as he sucked on her neck.

Then inconceivably a jet plane, a sound of a jet flying too close exploded in her house and the air pressure changed to the point she felt it on her skin. Windows shattering and in a last remaining instinct for self-preservation she brought her hands up to shield her face from the exploding glass and realized her hands were free. Her mind addled and confused she found her face, sealed like a wax doll's face behind the packet and pushed her finger through the line of plastic that had been sucked around her gasping mouth. With a pop the air rushed in and her body took over and gasped so heavily her lungs almost flew out her neck to grab the air directly.

The cool air filled her chest but the pain in her temples exploded and she wrenched the plastic off her face, yanking it away, screaming hysterically and falling off the couch.

Denim Jacket was going to come back, wherever he was he was going to launch upon her again soon, but she couldn't move, her head was cracking open and she was too weak. All she wanted to do was cry and sleep. She vomited violently into the corner and pushed herself to her knees and eventually to her feet. Not wanting to lie down, not wanting to be an easy target. Her hands had gone to her crotch and she had vigorously wiped at herself dispersing the feeling of his hands, his fingers on her.

What had happened? She thought when she saw the living room and the state it was in. She grabbed her phone and dialed Mason's number and the second he answered it a tidal wave of emotion crashed into her and she simply broke down and babbled endlessly on the phone.

His driver must have driven like a madman to have gotten to hers so quickly, but as she had been talking and crying at him on the phone she'd been turning in circles to make sure nobody was sneaking up on her.

Nobody was on the veranda, nobody was coming through the living room entrance, nobody was hiding in the corners of the living room and when she looked outside again she had seen The Coat.

And now she was in The Tower. Being looked after by Lynel Mason a man who was quite happy to continuously offer his help but hadn't so much as said hello to her for ages.

Alan had smothered the story before it could get online and nobody knew anything about it. Carol was being upgraded and her house was being repaired but she didn't know if she wanted to go back there alone now.

Ironically she had lived in the same apartment in the worst part of the city for years with only one lock on the door and had never been so much as robbed, within a months of moving into a high security house she was attacked on her own sofa.

She chewed her sandwich, God she really wanted to sleep.

A mountainous wind blew across the city which had turned the night alarmingly cool, so cold so she went inside locking the balcony door behind her and trekked across the breadth of the apartment to her bedroom where she unzipped her last suitcase in search of a jumper.

"Bloody climate change," she muttered.

She had packed her favorite one, the one she'd made when she was fifteen out of every scrap of fabric she could find. It was one of those rugged looking flops of material sewn together with great big horrible stitches that made it look like a post-op Frankenstein and there was every color of denim on it, canvas patches, some authentic woven cotton from the Alps that she'd stolen from her mother, a folded patch of duvet cover and some nylon. It had always been too big for her, but nothing felt better.

"Twenty Five?" she said, while selecting a comfortable pair of tracksuit pants to suit her jumper from the same suitcase.

"Twenty Five is not here ma'am," came a familiar voice.

"Carol?" Rayne gasped.

"Yes ma'am,"

"What the hell are you doing here?"

"Mason was kind enough to have my program uploaded to this apartment this evening," there was a moment of pause, "My apologies for what occurred at home."

Rayne sat on the foot of the bed, "What did happen?"

"I don't know," Carol said, "I was totally powerless. I witnessed everything that happened but could not communicate or control anything,"

Rayne groaned with frustration and as aggressively as she could she pulled on her tracksuit pants and stomped into the main part of the apartment.

"Are you angry with me?" Carol asked.

"Of course I am," Rayne snarled, but did not say anything until she had completed the long walk to the kitchenette which opened onto the apartment main and was right next to the elevator entrance. Once there she wrenched open the fridge with such force that everything inside shook, "You were meant to be there for me Carol," she said taking things out of the fridge. Jars of jam, some cans of soda, a batch of lettuce, she put these things onto the counter beside the fridge before realizing she had just eaten and started stuffing them back in, "I understand that what he did to you must have been *very* distressing," the sarcasm dripped from her lips, "But what I went through was worse. Worse. Terrifying and yet I don't know what happened- no idea on how the worst *didn't* happen and you say you saw everything?"

"Yes."

"It was The Coat I saw wasn't it?"

"Yes,"

"And you have it recorded?"

"No," the house programme said.

Rayne slammed the fridge door shut and something inside fell over with a rattle and a clunk, she put her hands on her hips and hung her head, "Bullshit Carol, your programme records everything, that's in the manual."

"That is correct," Carol said.

She waited for something else but when it didn't come she sagged and thumped the fridge with her fist, "Carol, why isn't it recorded?"

"I do not understand it myself Miss Ensley, I have information stating the events but I cannot access or duplicate it."

"A glitch?" Rayne asked, her understanding of the IT industry was very limited but it sounded like a "glitch" to her.

"Perhaps,"

Rayne stomped into the living room, stalking around in circles, "What do you think the cause is?"

"A diagnostic?" Carol asked.

"Yes, give me your diagnostic,"

"There are only two ways that my information can be tampered with, the first that someone hacked into my system and directly removed the information or there is a built in mandate."

"Can you be hacked?"

"No. Mr. Lynel Mason's systems are infamously hack-safe; it was one of the pioneering principles of his technology."

Rayne remembered reading something about that, it was one of the first things that made Mason's technology so formidable, no hacker could break into them thanks to the wet systems and they could not get viruses for a similar reason.

"What's a mandate?"

"A built in fail safe, part of a designing control system. Another example would be how I cannot allow any direct harm to come to you and cannot through inaction allow harm to come to you."

"But you did," Rayne said thin lipped.

"I was sabotaged Rayne," Carol responded in what was a very human tone, "It wasn't my fault."

"And," Rayne continued, "You could be programmed to ignore The Coat?"

"I'm afraid I am unable to answer that question," Carol said, in what was a very robotic answer.

With a huff and a scowl Rayne dropped into the couch, "Could you please tint the windows Carol I don't want the whole city seeing me right now."

As it happened Rayne thought that maybe her management system had turned into a rebellious teenager and in a funk had done something really stupid, in the same second she dismissed that idea and wondered if it was because Carol wasn't used to operating the controls for this apartment but dismissed that as well quickly- left with no explanation Rayne simply screamed bloody murder when the windows shattered.

While the trillionaire sat on the railing with his legs over the edge, staring at the ocean Shaka walked the length of Mason's balcony encircling the Tower to familiarize himself with the city from all angles. When his phone buzzed it was Toby with an update. He read the information, it was valuable but perplexing, why had Toby needed to locate his target using air disturbances? Nevertheless he had his position. Pocketing the phone he strode to the most advantageous spot on the balcony which was next to where Mason already sat, confirming the hunter's suspicions that the trillionaire knew more than he let on.

"May I ask a question?" Shaka enquired as he positioned his weapon.

"Of course," Mason said.

"I'm assuming that your artificial intelligent, management system has been installed throughout the city by now," Shaka said, securing the rifle's strap at his shoulder.

"That didn't sound like a question at all," Mason said.

"It wasn't," Shaka said, "It is an observation, I suspect like a castle you want to keep yours as secure as possible and forewarned is forearmed."

Mason turned to look at Shaka and smiled, "What's your question Shaka?"

"Why programme them to not see The Coat?"

The trillionaire's eyes narrowed and he bit his bottom lip like a schoolboy desperate to reveal a secret but not wanting to because it would spoil whatever game he was playing. Just as it looked like he would open up to Shaka his eyes flicked to the city and he said, "Ah,"

Securing the butt of the rifle to his shoulder Shaka brought the gun down to the balcony's edge and peered through the scope.

Seeing him, for the first time was like seeing a leopard in the wild, no picture can truly capture the way an animal moves when it is unbound. The black coat sailed behind him as he pounded across the rooftops only to flair out as he leapt off one building in mid stride and land on the next. He moved much faster than someone of his size should be able to in fact Shaka had difficulty keeping up with him on the scope.

"He's majestic isn't he?" Mason said.

"You can see him with your eyes?"

"Yes," he said, "But he and I share a common heritage. What are your thoughts from a hunter's point of view."

"Fast, calculating, he has massive strength in his strides but it looks like he's holding back."

"Blame the footing for that. If he moved much faster across the rooftops he'd shatter them," Mason said, "He can move a lot faster than that. Trust me."

Shaka kept watching The Coat as he approached, moving at a constant speed of what must have been a hundred kilometers an hour, on foot and every time he jumped he gained a little more speed. Black hood, big black coat. "Majestic" was exactly the word for it. The vigilante skidded to a stop about half a kilometer from Sky City near a forest of ancient, unused satellite dishes, the ones people used to use to get television. There he waited. If it hadn't been for the scope Shaka would have been blinded by the lights rising off Sky City, he didn't know how the man beside him was able to see so clearly with no help at all.

"He is here to see the girl," Shaka said, "I believe he can see her from there."

Mason put his hands onto the railing, his triceps and deltoids bulged, "I wonder if he can see us?"

"You would be better to judge of that than me," Shaka answered truthfully.

The Coat looked like the sort of pictures Shaka had seen as a child of super heroes, black hood that concealed all of his face, and black trench coat that accentuated the breadth of his shoulders.

"What do you put him at?" Mason asked, "Two hundred and eighty centimeters? Two fifty kilograms?"

"Close to that yes," Shaka answered.

"Impressive isn't it?"

"Okay Mason," Shaka said, his finger straying near the trigger, "The players in your game appear to have arrived, what is the next move?"

"We wait for all the players," Mason said, looking over the balcony's edge and straight down.

Shaka did the same and didn't see anything except the sheer, vertical drop down to the first levels of Sky City, he thought he was looking at something on the interceding levels of bridges, open balconies, water features and gardens that made up the "ground level" of Sky City but all he could see were the usual pedestrians, tourists and rich folk walking around enjoying their lives above the Fourteens. He saw Mason's hand tighten on the railing at that exact moment when, from the levels Twenty

Six and Twenty Seven, the windows blew outwards in an explosion of broken glass and twelve figures in black fell out.

The dozen men in black fell like stones and landed on Twenty Five's balcony in precise crouches and like rubber balls bounced off the tiles straight through the glass windows.

He almost couldn't hear the sound of shattering grass from their position on the eighty seventh

"Will she be killed?" Shaka asked.

The trillionaire, who was just as calculating as Shaka had estimated seemed curious by Shaka's lack of emotion, "It takes a lot to impress you doesn't it? No, they know her routines perfectly,"

"How?"

"From you my dear friend," Mason said with a wide smile, "Don't worry. Look it's working perfectly."

Shaka pressed his eye against the scope and searched the rooftops of Durban City for their vigilante but The Coat wasn't there anymore, Mason took his arm and pulled him away from his gun pointing across the empty space separating the Gregory Maines Tower with the second tallest building in Sky City, the Simmers Hotel.

"There,"

Almost as tall as Gregory Maines, and directly opposite them, it took Shaka a second to find The Coat in midair rising fast up its golden face as if he'd been fired out of a canon.

"Is he flying?" the hunter asked.

"No," Mason wheezed, on the edge of hysterics, "He jumped."

A jump. A vertical jump of thirty stories. In the ambient golden glow of the Simmer's skyward facing floodlights The Coat's shadow was stretched out behind him as he reached and grabbed the edge of one of the decorated banisters protecting any of the hotel guests from a very long fall should they slip off the balconies during a drunken party and with a gentle effort he climbed over the banister and faced the Gregory Maines.

Shaka couldn't see his face but could guess what The Coat was planning. But it was an impossible jump. The vertical leap was one thing, he had seen tricks performed by magicians achieving similar fetes but this was quite another. Enough space separated the two structures to ensure they were never mistaken for siblings and between them existed nothing but air and a very long drop to the valley of miniature rooftops below.

From this height the pedestrians, stuffed thick to the walls of the streets while they coursed through their restaurants, shops, businesses and homes did not look like ants, but instead like liquid, like blood.

He kept his eyes on the black spot against the sheer golden face of Simmers as The Coat made a short run up and sprang.

Even from a distance Shaka saw the puff of dusted concrete explode from the balcony's edge and like watching a leopard leap to grab the throat of a springbok he couldn't take his eyes off the black figure that sailed across the gap.

    He couldn't make it, Shaka thought, it was *impossible*. But The Coat didn't fall short and as he approached he brought his legs up to his chest and vanished under the lip of concrete into Twenty Five like a cannon ball trailing a cape.

Mason started whooping.

Twelve big black objects came through the windows into her apartment scattering furniture and unfolding into ninjas. Screaming Rayne ran for the elevator, jabbing the button frantically but of course it didn't open immediately and before she could escape hands grabbed her shoulders roughly and slammed her face first into the elevator door. Turning her head to the side saved her a broken nose but took the cold metal of the door with the side of her head knocking her senseless. It was the Denim Jacket all over again and she started hyperventilating waiting for the plastic bag to slip over her head.

    This can't be happening again? She screamed inside, "Fuuuuuccckkkk you!" was how the thought sounded coming out of her lips.

A fierce grip on her throat crushed her to the cold elevator door and a muffled voice hissed, "Don't move!"

    But once again, just as suddenly as the hands had touched her body they vanished, there was a protesting scream followed by a crash and that was immediately followed by a lot of noises, none of which Rayne liked. A great deal of shouting and screaming- initially the sort of screaming people did running towards something fearlessly and shortly followed by the exact opposite kind. She looked over her shoulder and saw it happening.

The Coat, was in the center of her apartment, far enough from her so that she felt she could watch without being terrified by his sheer size and his clear strength. He was a giant, in the same way that the Titans were giants, his hooded head seemed high enough to scrape the ceiling and he was pulling grown men from his body with each hand and flinging them away as if they were weightless.

Like giant spiders they clambered over him, trying to restrain him with no success. In a blur of movement something spectacularly fluid and fast took place and suddenly there were considerably less people on him and more lying on the floor, motionless save for the sporadic twitch. The remaining attackers, none of which seemed even remotely interested in her anymore, produced knives that glinted in the apartment lighting and they stabbed at him repeatedly. But even with all their strength they did not penetrate. In fact there was a noise like a pick hitting a stone and the blades broke.

He snatched one of them off him, the man's head encased in The Coat's hand and as if discarding some rubbish he threw the man out of the apartment. This was followed with great descending punch aimed for the last person who had been struggling to pull up the gun strapped to his back. This turned out to be a ruse as The Coat's punch missed as the smaller man rolled nimbly away and the goliathan fist smashed into the apartment floor with such an impact it shook under Rayne's feet. She saw what was coming as the ninja brought the automatic firearm up in line with The Coat's hooded face and screamed, "Carol turn off the lights!"

On her command the lights to the apartment went dark but Rayne didn't know if this helped because in a sudden deafening crackle of gunfire that lit up the entire room better than a magnesium candle the ninja emptied his weapon into The Coat's face.

Rayne brought her hands up to her the sides of her head trying to block out the sound of gunfire and what she was certain was screaming. The former ended as abruptly as it began and the room plunged into a ringing silence punctuated briefly by a strangled cry, a vomit-inducing rip and two thuds on opposite sides of the apartment.

The silence was merely a bated quiet that promises a calamity, the calm before the storm.

She didn't want to breathe for fear of making a sound but she could not stay here, exposed and unprotected. There were many places she could hide, the apartment was huge for god sakes, as big as the office some fifty stories above her, big enough to have a pool in, big enough to play cricket. The Coat had been near the middle of her apartment, which meant she stood the chance of making it into the bathroom on her right and locking the door or she could crawl into the study directly opposite the kitchenette on the left, and lock the door.

I need a door to lock, she thought, she needed to lock herself away and give her mind the chance to coordinate and work out what to do next. *I need to hide.*

Of course, it came to her that while she could hide anywhere in her apartment, they could already *be* anywhere. It would be typical of her to hole up in the smallest cupboard available only to hear someone else's breathing after she'd slid the door shut.

Edging towards a state of mania she looked into the apartment that stretched out in front her like a dark and hostile wilderness. City lights pouring in through her shattered windows threw inky drapes of shadows across the room in which nothing appeared to be moving. It was such a hushed and compressed atmosphere that she could clearly hear the sound of music from a nightclub on the Fourteenth and the constant sound of people. Desperate to breathe but certain that someone or something was waiting in the shadows and listening for any sound with equal keenness as she.

Scared and cold, her pulse thumping in her ears the shadows all around her became thick and alive and she couldn't stand it:

"Carol lights on!" she wailed.

The lights came on but she didn't see anything as suddenly something was pressing against her eyes and cradling her neck, something irrepressibly warm that smelt *good.* Her senses, as battered as they were, realized it was a hand. But there was no aggression to this touch, no anger, no violence. It felt protective. Her hands fell to her side and brushed the hems of a coat and she could hear his breathing.

"Please don't look," he said softly.

"Just d-don't kill me," Rayne replied.

Mason may finally have managed to surprise Shaka when he jumped over the railing and dropped the sixty two stories and landed hard on the concrete of the balcony. The concrete crushed into a crater under his feet and for a second he was afraid that it would break away from the building altogether. Wouldn't that have been hilarious?

Inside were twelve hunters or what was left of them. If there was a soul that left the body The Coat had clearly wanted it to be an easy departure. The apartment was a mess, broken glass from the windows lay sprinkled across a ripped up carpet, chairs and furniture lay shattered and upturned. Light fixtures hung from the ceiling.

His accountant was going to give him hell for all this.

The Coat was at the far left hand side, at the elevator door, so big that he didn't immediately register as being a person as the mind kept smudging him into the background like it would a pillar or a curtain. This kept happening, although he knew The Coat was standing right there he couldn't quite make him out. It was something that The Coat was doing. Some sort of mental influence that he was radiating made Mason want to ignore him, made him want to block him from his mind.

However, within seconds the moment passed and Mason marveled at the monster.

He was beautiful. His hood had been pulled back revealing a strong face dominated by the most impressive jaw Mason had ever seen and thick brown hair fell in heaps around his shoulders. He seemed preoccupied with something in front of him and Mason guessed it was Rayne.

"Is she alive?" he asked.

Swiveling it around on the great length of his neck The Coat turned his head almost passed the line of his shoulder and looked straight at Mason. The trillionaire's mouth went dry for the giant's eyes were unlike any he had ever seen. Totally black as if shiny black gems had been inserted into his face. Mason felt like he'd been slapped by them. Slowly The Coat said, "She sleeps."

"Good," Mason sighed, deeply relieved, he drew the sword from its scabbard and walked through the broken windows into the apartment, "I was worried that things might have gotten out of hand."

"You don't consider this to be out of hand?" The Coat asked, lowering himself into a crouch and laying Rayne down on the floor beside the elevator door. She looked peaceful.

"No, no," Mason said, "Not yet."

Waiting, he held the sword lightly in his right hand, "You have a beautiful voice, I imagine you can sing like an angel."

The Coat turned to face him, putting himself specifically in front of Rayne and before saying another word he reached up and pulled his hood back over his head. It was a reverent gesture.

Mason protested, "No need for that. Why cover such beauty."

When no response was forthcoming, he continued, "Your race is so beautiful, and so perfect in every way."

No answer. Mason took a deep breath, filling his lungs with the smell of the room, he could detect a lot of blood, which did not surprise him giving that he was standing in a puddle, but also The Coat's smell. It was a marvelous scent, something he could not fully describe but fully liked. There was also the smell of gunfire and between the two of them the scatterings of bullet casings.

"Bullet proof too," Mason remarked.

Still nothing. The Coat wasn't even moving and barely looked like he was breathing.

Mason let out the remainder of his breath in an exasperated gasp. He had *really* wanted more of a reaction, the silence was dramatic, but he had wanted at least some dialogue.

Fuck it, he thought and attacked.

Shaka took things well and was never surprised for long which was why with his mind clearly and calmly calculating the events of the last few minutes from The Coat's appearance, to the sudden and abruptly ending ruckus below he was working out what this meant to his current situation. And it was all amicable.

So he stayed exactly where he was, his eyes peering through the telescopic lens alternating between looking at the balcony below and the surrounding rooftops of Durban to the gardens below. None of the people on the Fourteenth had heard the noise on the Twenty Fifth, and there were the usual sort of people, pedestrians, civilians, and people so preoccupied with their little lives and so unaware of events happening above their heads.

He wasn't sightseeing; he sensed that there was another player about to join the game. He had a feeling in his gut that commanded him to watch the rooftops. Someone else was coming.

His phone vibrated again.

I cut him! I cut him! Mason thought jubilantly even with the surprisingly sharp, brittle pain of his sternum and surrounding ribs shattering into a thousand little splinters and ripping through his insides. He hurtled backwards, trailing his hands and legs.

He'd cut him. The Coat had dodged all the attacks, making sport of Mason's attempts until growing tired of it and snatching the blade out of midair, his hand enveloping the entire breadth of the weapon. Mason, at that moment pulled the weapon back through the giant's grasp and was rewarded with a startled scream of pain and a long, thick stream of blood across the blades edge.

"Yes!"

And The Coat punched him with the strength of God and he let go of the fucking sword!

His insides were ripped to bits, he could taste blood gushing into his mouth and out his nose, his chest was deflated inwards like an airless rugby ball and there was no way he could control his flight backwards. He collided with something hard that felt like a pool table and would have screamed but there was too much blood pouring out of his face.

Sliding to the floor and slumping onto his side he watched The Coat tenderly take Rayne into his arms and thought to himself, Ah, she's safe at least. That's a good vigilante giant, you beautiful, glorious angel. But when the giant, with Rayne in one arm, walked to where the sword lay and picked that up he thought, *You thieving bastard!*

Meanwhile, a layer of sweat between his clothes and his skin made Tuck feel like he was wearing a suit made of cellophane. The rooftops in Durban were mostly flat, graveled and concrete and they hurt his feet every time he landed. Thumping through the flimsy flat soles of his converse All Stars, it had been a poor choice in footwear because they weren't made for roof jumping and had ripped the soles from the uppers on his first landing. His jeans clung damply to his legs impeding his running and dust, grime and the general filth from this portion of the city had mixed with his sweat and made his skin itchy. The jumping from rooftop to rooftop bit was easy in Durban, in general not only were they nicely packed together but also networked via telephone wires, satellite dishes, cables and occasionally just random pieces of wood and roofing so it was like party jumping from ledge to ledge, sometimes swinging off of a satellite dish, or clambering up a fire escape ladder, surfing along the side of the buildings on a window washer platform. Durban made for good rooftop running, however the closer Tuck got to Sky City the more nervous he became.

Sky City was its own expanding universe, already taking over the central forest of business buildings, how it had originally started as a series of sky bridges to connect building to building was lost now as these were built onto and expanded. He stopped a few hundred meters from the first of the buildings and was impressed by how ugly it looked from this point of view, the plumbing of the grand palace. From underneath it looked like the underside of any highway bridge, a lot of thick, unattractive supports and gables, a look of bolts and steel and graffiti. There was nothing beautiful about seeing the arse end of the most expensive property zone in Africa.

He didn't have a good enough view from here. Although you couldn't miss the grotesque nail that was Gregory Maines Tower, there wasn't enough of it to see but he daren't venture too close or else he'd be seen by every security camera in the place and Mason had already sent someone to get him once.

He had particular reservations about being buried alive again.

So it was with mild trepidation that he stood on the rooftop looking up at the giant monstrosity. A sea borne wind blew up and cooled the sweat against his neck and for a second his senses overwhelmed him as the smell of the ocean was combined with the hushing whisper of distant waves against the shore, the spectacular city sounds of the car engines and horns below, the sounds of people in their apartments. Music punctuated by sirens in the distance. The smell of grease, bird shit and old rain water on the rooftops, the humming of the chimney he stood near. The smells of the millions of people in the city each one yelling their stories at him. He doubled over with his hands on his knees and squeezed his eyes shut, humming loudly until it was all he could hear.

He *hated* cities.

Once the chaos in his head had receded to the back part of his mind he straightened and scrutinized his surroundings for a better vantage point. He couldn't see anything worthwhile where he was.

Durban City already had a collection of the tallest sky scrapers and Sky City could have been an unfortunate cloud that had been caught upon them and been corrupted into something involving steel and glass, but aside from Mason's empirical lair the only other building of similar size was a golden hotel directly opposite it.

Simmers Hotel was the only option. It was a tall and regal building, more classy that Gregory Maines, with beautiful golden lights highlighting the front that towered over the rest of the buildings in Sky City like a monolith.

He didn't bother using the door but instead found an entry point in the form of one of the windows on the sixth floor that was open and making his way across the rooftops he long-jumped over a four lane street and ever so slightly misjudged it. Losing his footing upon entry he clipped his head off the top of the window frame, became entangled in the lace curtain and ripped it and the curtain rail off the wall. His inertia carried him in and blinded by the lace landed on the floor, taking the full force on his face all while screaming, "Raaattttt arse!"

Stars in his eyes and a throbbing pain in his head he crawled out of the drapes and climbed up the nearby bed to his feet, once he got there he lost balance and fell over.

Slower this time he pushed his way to his feet and with a hand to his forehead, where he found a perfectly straight dent in his skull he looked around the room to make sure he was alone. He smelt the scent of perfume and hair gel and on the large ultra-king sized bed there were clothes sprawled out for both a man and a woman. So whoever used this room was out for the moment. Next to the bed there was a suitcase which he unzipped and found it belonged to the man. Either a youngster or an old man going through a midlife crises judging by the jeans and the colorful shirts, Tuck found a cap, a pair of sunglasses and a denim jacket and within a zipped up compartment in the bag was an envelope packed with paper bills. He put on the shades and the jacket and slipped the envelope into the inner pocket automatically.

Leaving the room he closed the door behind him and walked down the corridor with his hands in the jacket pockets, his head down, the peak of the cap pulled forward and made his way briskly to the elevator. He passed a couple of people on his way but none of them smelt like the people from the room. At the elevator he pushed the button and waited, rocking backwards and forwards from his heels to his toes and repeatedly asking himself what his plan was.

There was a chime as the elevator arrived and he stepped in, the cart was empty which was a shame, he would have felt safer with a lot of people to hide him from the security cameras. The doors shut and he pushed the button for the top floor and smoothly the elevator rose.

Ten years, it had been over ten years since he'd stepped into an elevator, or been inside a hotel room and now he was putting everything at risk and doing it right in Mason's back yard.

He lifted a hand to his forehead and prodded the tender skin where it felt like he had a fractured skull.

An excruciating amount of time later the elevator stopped on the top floor and he stepped out and walked quickly down the corridors, mapping out the locations of the cameras as he went. Luckily there wasn't a camera watching over the corridor window which was a large grand, stain-glass affair.

This was how he gained access to outside and climbed up the side of the building like a fly up a lamppost until hauling himself over the top edge and perching himself on the slanted, oriental styled roof.

His head suddenly started swimming and he went from perching to sitting on his ass and holding onto the oriental tiles until the world stopped spinning. He used a hand and felt the dent in his skull, prodding it gently with his fingertips, the split had mended and he was confident he would survive.

He waited for his dizziness to pass before getting to his feet, he had to keep moving, if he lingered anywhere for too long he was sure to be spotted.

The scenery up here was astonishing but the wind almost took him off his feet. Durban City was a rash of stars spreading across the darkness and the moon was a giant orb in the sky reflected in the black glassy water of the Indian Ocean. Sky City was a cascade of different shades of lighting that subdued the harsh verticalness of the Gregory Maines Tower by making it look dominatingly wide.

Bent over with a hand touching the tiles Tuck scurried across the rooftop until he had what had to be the perfect view of the Tower.

Sky City was everything he hated about cities, and more of it, crowded with people, their clothes and their jewelry stinking of money, super models and drunkard billionaires, Sheiks and presidents. The apartments all had glass walls and he could see into most of the rooms and watched for a while people doing *things*, things he didn't often see people do. Like watching television, or eating dinner, some of the apartments had kids in them playing games and others people just chatting with friends on the balconies.

Massaging his temples he tried to decide on his next move. He was surprised that he had been able to get this close without something happening and it just so happened that just then, a lot happened at once.
Movement caught his eye as a dozen figures in black exploded out of the window of one the apartments like rats off a trampoline and dropped like stones to an apartment balcony several floors beneath them, the windows to that particular apartment shattered as they barged their way through. Tuck stood and a massive black shadow trailing a coat shot out from somewhere below him on the Simmers Hotel frontal face, sailing across the distance between the two buildings as if he could fly. This figure cannon balled into the apartment and dematerialized into a long, ribbon like blur of black that Tuck couldn't follow but as each figure was caught by this smudge of movement, they simply died. The lights went out, there was gunfire, the lights came on and there was blood and then someone else landed on the balcony and Tuck's face turned red despite the cold.

"Mason," he growled.

The trillionaire tried to use the sword on The Coat but it ended quickly and not well. The giant rightfully dispatched Mason although his attack, alas, would not kill the man. He collected the girl *and* the sword and made his way onto the balcony and just as he was about to jump Tuck yelled, "Petallis!"

Something poked him hard in the point where his shoulder and chest met, it didn't hurt but it was hard enough to make him stagger backwards. From that spot a warmth spread that grew claws and turned into a raging heat and he realized he'd been shot.

A sniper. Mason's Hunter!

Not hanging about to find out, Tuck took off at a sprint across the Simmer's Hotel slanting rooftop, running so fast the wind howled in his ears as bullets shattered roof tiles and obliterated some sky lights behind him. He saw the edge of the building coming and threw himself into midair thinking, *This is a stupid idea!*

19.

Very quickly, Shaka had shot the Freelander and watched The Coat pluck him from midair as he toppled off the rooftop of the Simmer's Hotel. Through his scope he spotted Rayne Ensley slung over The Coat's shoulder, unconscious. The giant landed on the rooftop of an apartment building and with two steps gave an almighty thrust and rose into the air. Shaka had guessed that he couldn't fly, but this meant little for the distance he could cover. The Hunter lost track of him by then on the scope.

Slinging the rifle's strap around his shoulder he ran through the office to the elevator, hitting the button for Rayne Ensley's apartment and while it descended he pulled out his phone and looked at Toby's readings. The Coat was long out of range but a small window at the lower left half of the screen made him smile.

The elevator stopped at the Twenty Fifth and as the doors slid open he entered the apartment with his weapon up and ready, the butt against his shoulder, his knees bent.

Shit, he thought, Look at this place.

It is impressive how much damage violence, especially the sort involving automatic firearms can cause and how unrecognizable things are afterwards. Structure can become wreckage so quickly. With the dust, he detected the sharp chemical smell of gun powder that curled in a yellow cloud and he also smelt the blood dripping from the ceiling and down the walls.

"Mason," he said, "Where are you?"

No reply.

With the barrel of his rifle leading, he peeped into the bedroom and found nothing, he did the same with the bathroom and the office. As he made his way across the apartment main he easily concluded that this had been an all-out massacre and these men had been sacrificed like mice to a cat. He had to be careful where he stepped to avoid getting his shoes in blood or slipping on the entrails that were strewn across the floor. This sort of bloodbath resulted from unprepared hunters going up against a prey that either was unaware of its strength or wanted to make a point.

Further into the apartment was an entertainment area where a pool table, instead of a swimming pool, had been broken in two and had shat out all of its balls. Lying in front of it, slumped over to the side was the trillionaire.

The Hunter approached quickly, checking that the area was clear one final time before re-slinging the rifle over his shoulder and kneeling beside the downed man and checked his pulse.

It was strong. Pounding like a racehorse's but his body was shattered and his heart had to have been squashed by a collapsed skeleton.

Mason looked like he'd been hit in the chest by a wrecking ball.

"Mason, are you awake?" Shaka asked, pulling out his phone and pushing the emergency button. He held it to his ear, "Get security up to Rayne Ensley's apartment, Twenty Fifth, we need paramedics."

"Cancel that," Mason said.

Out of everything he'd seen tonight Shaka was taken aback more by this than anything else. That Mason still had a pulse was extraordinary but that he was still able to speak seemed beyond possibility.

"You're injured and you need medical attention," Shaka insisted.

"Cancel that order!" Mason hissed, blood spraying from between his lips. When he spoke the movement in his lungs caused his chest to move in a distinctly unnatural manner, like a set of balloons being inflated and deflated under a pile of twigs, "All that I need," he croaked, "Is downstairs."

A moment's consideration and Shaka cancelled the call and looked over Mason's body once again calculating injuries. His chest plate and ribcage were gone, he also suspected, by the unnatural positioning of his hips that his spine was broken, splintered ribs stuck out his skin like tent poles and there was extensive blood clotting turning his skin black.

Despite this Mason was moving.

Shaka took a step back and watched as the man used his right arm which appeared broken at the elbow joint to push himself up, the broken sections ground against each other. *Custle* the sound of broken bone scraping against broken bone. When the arm inevitably gave way under his weight Shaka did not offer help and the trillionaire, in a business-like manner threw out his arm in front of him and that alone was enough to snap the distorted limb back into it's right alignment. It made a sound like a plastic soda bottle being crunched.

Staring at the floor in front of him, at the growing puddle of his own blood Mason gathered his strength and pushed himself up. His obliterated front looked like it was home to swarm of insects that were prickling beneath the skin and the same gestation and inner turmoil spread around his sides. It was a spectacle to watch as Mason seemed to surf the wave of his own regeneration as his body restored wholly destroyed fragments of itself. The man pushed himself into a seated position with his legs straight out in front of him there was a distinct grinding crunch as his pelvis slammed back into position and it was the first time Mason gave any indication of his own experience of it when his eyes rolled in his head and he shouted, "Goddamnit that hurt!"

He rolled forward onto all fours and just as Shaka thought this man was going to stand he reared onto his knees and arched his back so wildly that the top of his head collided with the pool table with an audible *thunk*, and beneath the stretched curve of his torso things inside his body started to explode. Segmented curves pressed out against the flesh representing his ribcage, a revolting convulsion of things moving underneath. He writhed and shook, as if having an epileptic fit that finally caused him to scream wordlessly before falling flat and exhausted to the floor.

Waste. The wasted material from the healing process, the parts that were no longer required in the body were suddenly expelled from Mason, pouring out of his throat in great vomited gusts and the rest ballooning out his trousers. The smell was sharp, foul and the blood that came out was thick with black chunky pieces and white gummy material.

The heaving voidance lasted longer than the actual healing itself and Shaka watched fascinated, a step away from the spreading flood of it.

After minutes of this heaving were over and with violently blue eyes Mason rose to his feet, panting for breaths like some crazed, rabid wolf.

"Have I impressed you yet?" he growled.

Trekking bloody footprints into the expensive looking carpet Mason walked out of the elevator and across his office with Shaka tailing closely behind. Nothing had been said yet but The Hunter felt it was important for him to stay close and he was finally going to get what he wanted. Mason went into the showers and Shaka stood outside the door to give the man some privacy as he washed himself thoroughly. At one point there was more retching and Shaka wondered how long the waste removal cycle lasted and what were the other side effects of such a rapid healing factor?

Shaka attempted to keep his mind as clear as possible, but there was no stopping the thoughts running through it.

What he had seen was not natural. He was a Hunter. First of game and then of men, he knew nature and it was all about death. In the circle of life everything died that was the reason for injury, the reason why animals could be injured, could grow old and perish so that other creatures within the same area could benefit from the space and food provided. It was a simple law of nature, severe injuries were not survivable and if they were survivable they were miraculous and flukes of nature. What he had seen was no fluke; Mason had known it was going to happen.

The roar of the shower ended and Mason came out in a toweling robe sweeping his hair back with his fingers, he looked refreshed and glowing.

He walked passed Shaka without a word and went to his desk. Waving on the communication he said, "Evening Janice, listen someone's gone and made a mess in the elevators could we please have it cleaned. Also, get Alan to send some boys to Rayne Ensley's apartment for me, he'll know what to do. Thanks."

Shaka was lingering near the bridge across the pool and Mason walked up and passed him again, going straight to the drink cabinet. He poured a pair of suicidally large glasses of straw whiskey and offered one to Shaka. The Hunter was not a fan of alcohol but took it and they both drank the fiery liquid in throat jumping gulps. Mason immediately poured himself another.

"I would imagine that you have a couple of questions by now," the trillionaire prompted, he finished the second drink and filled a third before putting the bottle back into the cabinet, "I will of course answer all of them all as soon as possible Shaka."

Shaka could hear a 'but' coming.

"…but, I need to eat some food right now, protein, carbohydrates and fluids that aren't, unfortunately, whiskey. I've lost a lot of what my body requires. I'll make myself some food and then I'll answer your questions… are you hungry?"

Shaka wasn't at all, he wanted to escape into the cool air and hunt down the giant and that Freelander. He wanted to do that but he was also focused on getting answers from this man before the opportunity was lost.

"I can eat if I have to," The Hunter answered.

"Excellent, I have a kitchen through here," Mason said leading the way into his apartment which was of identical dimensions to the office just very spartanly furnished. Mason practically emptied the contents of his refrigerator onto the counter and started eating everything that came to hand. Shaka observed with quiet disentrancement, mentally taking notes of everything. Mason may have prepared his food very carefully before hand, putting slices of meat into Tupperware's and fruit into little plastic shelves but now any preparation was wasted. He tore open the containers and stuffed the slices of chicken and ham into his mouth as if plugging a hole. He grabbed a handful of whole wheat bread and gobbled that down too. A carton of yoghurt. Fruit. Raw fish from cans, a bottle of Protein shake and finally peanut butter from a jar with a spoon.

Surely, he was putting in more food than his stomach could actual contain but he didn't stop until the fridge was empty and he boasted a pregnant bulge. He chugged down water from a bottle and wiped his mouth with the back of his hand, "My apologies for that," he said, "I should probably have warned you about that. I hope it hasn't put you off your appetite?"

Shaka picked up a green apple and took a bite, "I find it all very interesting to be honest,"

The trillionaire nodded, "I'd imagine a man like you doesn't shock very easily, which is a very good quality right now. Now, I propose you ask your questions."

"I do have many questions, but don't you want the sword back?"

"Yes of course," Mason said, "But I'm not going to be so ill prepared as before... there is a lot of new information that needs to be assessed first. Also, as I'm sure you're aware I'm also concerned about the wellbeing of Rayne Ensley and my former employee Tuck Bradley."

"Need I remind you that sword," Shaka said, using an appropriately level tone, "Is sacred to my people and must be in your possession."

Mason brought a hand up to his mouth and stifled a burp, "Yes I understand that, but inevitability favors me."

"Perhaps it does," said Shaka, "Are you healthy now?"

"I am indeed. Look, instead of questions and answers as pro-active men shall I simply show you how it is that I'm able to do what I just did?"

"That would be agreeable."

Barefoot and still in the toweling robe Mason walked with Shaka to his private elevator that was just big enough to fit the two of them, there were more buttons for more floors than the other elevators and when Mason pressed the button at the bottom it depressed inwards further than you'd expect. He withdrew his finger and there was a small bead of blood at the tip, the first of many security measures that Shaka would witness. The cart started to descend.

"I'm going to show you something Shaka," he said, "And I am going to need your absolute promise that you will keep what you see quiet."

"I am a professional," Shaka immediately replied.

"And I appreciate that," Mason said, "But trust me this could even stretch the boundary of your professionalism… what you saw earlier was nothing."

"I saw a man recover from certain death," Shaka inferred, "How can that be nothing?"

Mason smiled, "What you saw- *could* be a medical miracle, or the latest in medical technology. It *could* be a breakthrough in science that I happen to enjoy the benefits of thanks to my money and power. Or it could all be an elaborate hoax for a new reality television show?"

"It could be," Shaka acknowledged.

"But you know that it isn't,"

"Yes."

"And you want to know what it really is…"

"Of course,"

Mason pressed his lips tightly together, considering things for a moment, "Yes. I shouldn't need to ask for your secrecy because nobody would believe you anyway. Oh and please leave your weapon here."

When the elevator finally stopped it read -4. Deep underground, the door slid open and revealed an all-white chamber with a collection of four slightly raised black dots on all the walls except the floor. Mason led the way and gestured for Shaka to follow, "This is the security room, just stand there and wait for the computer to identify you."

Shaka waited but nothing seemed to happen.

"Are these lasers?" he asked about the black bubbles on the wall.

"Yes, they form a high strength laser grid that would cut any unauthorized trespasser into steak."

The identifying process was not narrated which was a direct contravening of the African Mandate for Security Protocols, a fact that highlighted how far this was off the radar. A very slight click about as loud as a pen tapping a desk was all the signaled a confirmation of identity.

A door opened directly in front of them and walking at pace they entered a wide low ceiling corridor made of strange, hexagonal concrete blocks that gave the corridor a rounded edge. Walking forward quietly on his bare feet Mason breezed through the corridors, revealing that this underground corridor was connected to many other corridors in a vast maze leading to sets of big doors similar to the ones at the security box and other rooms filled with banks of servers and computer screens. People in colored jumpsuits walked around with very serious looks on their faces, barely even acknowledging the pair of them.

They came up against a pair of double doors that Mason pushed through and inside there were a group of people in paramilitary gear who were sitting drinking coffee. Shaka frowned at this unexpected lack of discipline but as none of them reacted to Mason beyond merely acknowledging him with a nod he wondered if perhaps it was a ruse. This room looked like a canteen, it had a counter for foodstuff and beverages, there was a holographic screen, which was currently off and the group sat between them and a single door on the other side of the room that read KITCHEN STAFF ONLY.

Mason walked up to one of the men who stood and extended his hand saying, "Good morning sir, how are you?"

Their hands grasped and Mason said, "I'm well thanks Max, purchasing Klondike Bars is tough business."

Shaka came up alongside the trillionaire and another one of the men stood up and faced him extended his hand. He grasped it and felt something scratch him on the inside of his palm.

"Good day sir, are you well?"

"I am thank you," Shaka replied with a smile. He'd just worked it out. It wasn't the handshaking that gave it away but the blue contact lenses that these guards were wearing. They were micro-screens and the scratch he had felt on his palm was them just checking his identity yet again.

The man seemed satisfied, he smiled politely and sat down again and sipped his coffee while picking up on a conversation with his friend.

Mason finished chatting with his own guard and the man laughed, sat down and carried on reading his magazine.

They made their way to the door that this group were guarding and Mason opened it and ushered Shaka through. Beyond, there was just a storage room with shelves of chocolate and protein bars and bottles of Avian water, Mason grabbed a couple of chocolates from an open box and offered one to Shaka.

"Come on it's a Lunchbar," he said peeling off the wrapper, "It's good for you."

Shaka reluctantly took it, he really didn't have much of an appetite, but Mason didn't move until he had unwrapped the chocolate and taken a bite. It was good. On the far end of the storage room was a blank and unhindered wall, which would have been the first clue to Shaka, you could take a storage room in any country in the world and there would never be an *empty* wall.

Mason strolled forward and walked straight through it.

"It's a hologram," his disembodied voice said, muffled by the chocolate between his teeth.

Taking another bite out of his chocolate he walked up and stepped through the holographic projection, the light particles felt cool against his skin. On the other side they were in another elevator, but this had no buttons. It only had two destinations.

Mason was leaning in the corner casually eating his chocolate, "So. Have you sussed it out yet?"

"Yes," Shaka said, "This facility employs people who probably don't know *where* they are, the cables on the walls suggest a larger power source than is currently available in Durban so perhaps you have everything rigged up to an offshore sun or wind farm? The initial identification room checks newcomers with quantum interfacing technology to accurately assess who they are and if they don't check out they get hit by the laser grid. If someone were able to get through there they wouldn't be able to find the spot we're going to now because it's hidden. Those security guards back there are well trained. I suspect they even have dummy duties around the rest of the facility so that they only appear to *hang* out in the canteen. The other employees probably resent them entirely but are afraid to approach them because they're armed but they're sole responsibility is to protect that holographic wall we just walked through. Correct?"

"Nail on the head," Mason said applauding.

"Its dawn in about three hours, do the employees work on shifts?"

"Yes and they live here. I don't know if you're aware of it, but I have a facility about ten times the size of this one in Antarctica which is top secret we tell them that they are merely being transported from one side of the South Pole to the other for research, when in fact it's from there to here. Most of these people, including the guards think they're under ice caps now."

"Wouldn't gossip cause a problem?" Shaka asked, "People talk in canteens and over coffee all the time,"

"True. But everyone knows this is a top secret facility, non-governmental which means that for the most part they all think they're working for a super villain. We've used that to keep things orderly, everyone is afraid to even mention facilities, Antarctica or their work at home or even in their bunkers because they know they could be shot at any moment, or just vanish. On the plus side even the cleaners and the cooks here get paid more than some bankers in New York."

The doors opened and the lift was suddenly filled with cold air that smelt of ozone, they walked out onto a metal ramp that was illuminated along its sides with glowing blue stripes. The metal ramp led to a platform on which sat a very large rectangular box that was partially illuminated by the ramp lights. Aside from that the room was completely black and silent.

"This room is the quietest room in the world, 99.99% absolute silence. Of course we're the difference. It's black because we don't even allow electric lights. The ramp lights are chemical. The walls are padded with three feet of sound-depriving material and we're miles away in every direction from any sort of railway or road system and are considerably underground."

It was very quiet, too quiet and Shaka felt disorientated by it. The complete lack of noise made him want to lean in different directions to *hear* something, when they got to the platform holding the box there was a railing which he put a hand on to steady himself.

"It's a sarcophagus?"

"Not quite," Mason said, "That would make this a tomb. It's really just another laboratory."

Shaka looked at the box again. It was perhaps three meters long and half that high and wide made of a dark alloy.

"It's several layers of carbon-nano-tubing," Mason explained, "Strongest material in the world. Here take this," he handed Shaka a face mask and took one for himself, Mason showed him how to put it on, "It is slightly pressurized so keep your mouth open when you apply the suction."

Copying Mason's actions Shaka pressed the rubber lining of the shovel shaped mask to his face and lowered his jaw, a second later there was a mild pressure build up in his face that made his eyes bulge and then a the air started hissing in.

"You can breathe normally now," Mason said, his voice coming through an earpiece. A holographic screen appeared before both of them and Mason started shifting stuff around with his fingers, "Inside the container is liquid nitrogen I don't want you getting poisoned."

"Would that affect you?" Shaka asked.

"Oh yeah," Mason said, "It would have the same effect as it would on you, I'd fall asleep. You would too and then you'd die. I would however wake up but it gives me the kind of headaches I'll remember for the rest of my life and I never make the same mistake twice. Here we go."

The sarcophagus split half way down its length and a hiss of pressurized air blew out, a series of loud clanks from inside suggested heavy machinery operating and the top of the container lifted up, revealing more white gas inside. Shaka leaned forward and saw that inside was a body.

It was frozen, ice crystals covering its entire form and that was additionally covered by a transparent sheeting of glass. The body was clearly that of a giant's, as it must have been almost eight feet in length with an incredible dimension to its proportions.

"It looks like a less green version of the Hulk doesn't it?" Mason said with a chuckle, Shaka gave him a look and he added quickly, "I mean the 2008 version... haven't you seen it? It's retro but a good film..." he spread his hands comically as if feeling the urge to explain himself, "I'm a geek as well as a trillionaire."

Shaka had to admit he was accurate this was the largest and most muscular body he had ever seen in his entire life. He noticed that the giant body was entirely lacking in a navel but there was also more missing.

"Where is the head?" Shaka enquired.

The head was missing and out of the stump were half a dozen tubes running from it into the base of the sarcophagus, of varying thicknesses, they too were frosted over to see if they were running in or out but the dark colored insides suggested they were filled with blood.

"Those tubes had been cased with titanium plugs and then with carbon nanotubes to just keep them in otherwise the flesh sealing over them would just crush them- that's also why we keep the body frozen."

"The healing continues even without the head?"

"On both sides in fact," Mason said with a nod, "The body continues to live as does the head."

"Where is it?"

"It isn't here," Mason said and transitionally added, "I am curious to know how your songoma knew the swords true power."

"Ah, this is what the sword can do?"

"Bingo."

Shaka looked again at the body, the flesh was pale and unblemished, the freezing temperatures beneath the glass covering having caused no blemishes or burns, it was perfect, huge, monstrous and terrifying, but perfect. It was definitely male. "So, Shaka this is my secret," Mason shared, "This is the body of an immortal giant, indeterminably old. We removed the head ten years ago with the sword and for ten years those tubes have been ciphering off blood and spinal fluid. Which I partake of."

"How do you do that?" Shaka asked, walking around the sarcophagus to get a better look.

"I very simply drink it," Mason said, "I have about 100 mg every year."

"That's all?"

"Yes. That's all that is needed."

"If you've been pulling fluids out of this body for a decade, may I ask where the surplus is?"

Mason smiled, "I'm not going to reveal everything to you my new friend. I have big plans and it always pays off to have a contingency."

"Fair, how does it work?"

"As far as we can tell the blood causes mutation in the DNA activating something inside that restructures and reprograms the very material we are made of. Strengthening the telomerase enzyme so that it does not unravel and increasing cellular regeneration. There is a connection between this giant and ourselves, the blood unlocks parts of us and allows it to rewrite the errors in our bodies. If this is anything to go on we were *meant* to be immortal."

"That is a statement,"

"Oh absolutely," Mason said jovially, "But I'm just reading from the text. This is how I'm going to change the world; this is how I'm going to bring peace."

Shaka gave him a critical look, "Peace?"

"Do you not want it?"

"I am a Hunter sir. I have no interest in politics. But I've seen what happens when men have sought *peace*. Are you planning to make an army?"

Mason's face dropped and it caused in Shaka the same feeling as when an angry hippo sees you in the water.

"One of my companies is currently doing all that it can to synthesize the blood to make it readily available to the general public. They will make a drug that will cure any disease."

"Death is a way of life Mason," Shaka said, "A natural way of life."

"It shouldn't need to be," Mason argued.

"You will make people healthy and in return they will pledge their loyalty to you and you will be a ruler of a civilization of healthy people and people from around the planet will come to you wanting to be made healthy. Politics, religions, cultures, beliefs and even principles won't matter anymore when a parent is given the chance to cure their children. They will become your subjects,"

"Yes exactly," Mason said. There was a tone in his voice, an edge that suggested he needed to be understood. Shaka realized that Mason had truly never revealed this secret to anyone else and therefor had never been called upon to justify it. He wondered if the people who had built this room had even known what it was for. Mason's idea was a noble one but a dangerous one. Power corrupted and Mason clearly was greedy for it.

He would not only be the curer of *death and injury* but such a product, such a source would be more profitable than any amount of oil or coal or gold. How many businessmen and politicians would sell everything they had, give it away just to know they could be young for another hundred years? That's what he would really be selling: a safeguard against inevitability, a protection against the oncoming fall of civilization, the drop of industry and the fall of nobility and a guarantee that no matter what happens- there would be a tomorrow.

Mason's voice was harder, the voice of the businessman when he said, "Despite my humorous attitude upstairs, I need that sword back Shaka. I want the sword and the head of the giant that took it. I want the head of The Coat."

"I am a professional and at your disposal," Shaka replied in a similar tone, "However, for this I do have my price."

Mason grinned, "Why do you think I've brought you down here?"

20.

A roar like being caught in a wind tunnel, an intolerable sensation of weight followed by a blinding light and Rayne opened her eyes into stunning quiet.
The first thing she realized was she wasn't in her apartment anymore and was curled up like a cat on a large threadbare couch in a very large room with a concrete floor and bare brick walls. The sofa smelt dusty and she was well and truly knotted into a woolen blanket that had wrapped itself around her like a fishnet. She pushed herself to her elbows and examined her surroundings with better scrutiny. She wasn't in a room at all but a warehouse, the ceiling was high with distant neon lights hanging from the steel rafters and casting a brazen white glare upon the wooden crates and boxes lining the walls, piled three deep and two high. The couch was part of a small seating area and was part of a mismatched set forming a horse shoe around a giant screen television that, judging by the thick jacket of dust had not been used for months.

    She untangled herself from the blanket and sat up. To her right, about five meters away was the biggest bed she'd ever seen, a number of blankets and pillows lay in very neatly folded positions and beside it a metal clothes railing played stock for a selection of the biggest shirts and trousers she'd ever seen.
It was chilly in the warehouse and she pulled the blanket from the couch and put it around her shoulders like a shawl and walked barefoot across the cold concrete and stood in front of the assembled clothing. She browsed through them as she would a shop in The Strip. The garments were double the size of a man's and hardy in design. Heavy clothes meant for lasting and not for fashion the boots, leather thick, heavy and huge.
It didn't take her long to realize where she was.
    "Hello?" she said aloud.
She became aware of noises coming from the opposite end of the warehouse where a tall doorway led into a short corridor with rooms on either side. On the left there was what looked like the showers and on the right was a kitchen. All the entrances were very tall and wide to accommodate a very tall, very large person.

She found, the kitchen was oversized, the fridge was typically big with double doors, the counters were spacious but overall there was the general air of neglect as if whoever lived here didn't spend a great deal of time *living* here.

Her stomach groaned with unexpected ferocity and she realized how hungry she was, she entered the kitchen and started opening the cupboards one after another looking for food.

"You're awake," said a man who had entered behind her holding a stacked chicken and mustard sandwich.

She let loose a sudden, ear shredding scream of such a high pitched tone it hurt her own ears and made him flinch. She didn't think at all and just acted and swung her leg up as if she were kicking a soccer ball and connected with the roof of her foot solidly with the fork of his trousers. Caught completely by surprise he gawped and hopped onto his tip toes, eyes crossing and his hands clenching into fits so sharply the mustard squirted out of the sandwich and hit him in the cheek. His face screwed into a knot and his eyes rolled up to the ceiling as his knees touched and he dropped to the floor, hands to his groin.

Rayne hadn't finished though and went to slap him in the face but his hands caught her wrists and she took the opportunity presented with his hands being occupied and kicked him once again. He gave a throaty whimper that wasn't quite a cry of pain and curled into a fetal ball.

She fled, guessing where the front door would be she left the kitchen and turned right, ran down the short corridor to find a left turn that led into a square room with three walls of cracked plaster and a garage door that had a very large rectangular door cut into the front. She tried the handle and to her surprise it was unlocked. It gave a protesting scream as she opened it and sprinted into the cool evening air.

"Oh no," she said.

She stubbed a toe on the broken concrete slabs that made up the weed infested car park of the long abandoned warehouse but barely noticed the pain. A four lane main road ran parallel to the front of the warehouse and was accessible by a short gravel drive but aside from that all that she could see were fields of dark grass and bushveld. The sky was a giant rash of stars with a moon that seemed almost too large and polished to be real casting a silver light over everything.

Where the hell was she?

From inside she heard staggered steps and a pained voice spilling out in a long line of whispered swear words. She hid behind the open metal door and as the person shuffled into the doorway she rammed her shoulder against the flat surface with the full weight of her body, rocketing it inwards on its hinges. There was a satisfying clang as it hit someone and a muffled, "- *uck me!"*

Realizing what she had done she bolted as fast as she could for the main road hoping she could get lucky and flag down a car.

The asphalt was sharp and hard under her bare feet and in the moonlight she could see that the road was a black belt around the waist line of the world. Leading off in one direction and returning from the other.

The door was kicked aggressively and made a wobbling sound as it swung around on its hinges and she ran across the four lanes of road aiming for the grassy fields on the other side with the intention to hide. It wasn't that cold an evening and the tracksuit pants and her homemade jumper would provide her with some warmth from exposure. It was the best plan she could think of until she had time to work on a better one.

Half way across the road Tuck grabbed her forearm, his fingers digging into the joint and something inside gave way, the pain shot up her forearm into her elbow making her yelp.

He pulled her towards him and spun her around grabbing her by her shoulders and shaking her, "Stop running!" he spat in her face.

A blast of air blew at their faces and she thought for a second that a car had crested the hill without its headlights on and they were going to get hit but the night got particularly darker on one side and Tuck's whole demeanor changed. The Coat had appeared out of nowhere and was a wall of black right at their side.

He opened his mouth to speak but nothing came out as Rayne took the chance to get a third kick in which landed with a satisfying crunch. Tuck dropped to his hands and knees once more.

Gallant at her quick thinking and spurred by the grown man now groaning at her feet she took several steps away from the giant to get a decent look at him and found that she couldn't see any of his features under the hood. She scrutinized him for a long time but he didn't move.

"Is this your place?" she asked, folding her arms and cocking her hip.

"Yes," the voice said from the inky shadows of the hood.

She nodded and marched inside. A moment later The Coat followed.

Rayne returned to the kitchen and picked up the blanket from the floor and wrapped it around her shoulders saying matter-of-factly, "This place is colder than outside, it's hardly suitable for guests."
Standing at the kitchen entrance which, while so tall that Rayne wouldn't have been able to touch it with the tips of her fingers even if she was on the tips of her toes, The Coat had to duck to get under it.

"Where is your coffee?" she asked, opening the remaining cupboards and drawers she hadn't already searched.

"I keep the coffee in the fridge," The Coat answered. His voice was neutral, quiet.
She nodded as if expecting such a thing, opening the fridge she found it to be very bare but true to his word there was a jar of coffee. She took it, slammed the fridge shut without looking up at him and put it onto the counter. She stood there staring at the jar before giving him a very pointed look, "I don't know where everything is you know, are you going to help me or not?"

In the white neon lights of the kitchen with the light reflecting off of every surface she could see his face better. He wasn't just handsome he was exceptionally beautiful, breathtakingly so and being rude was the only way it stopped her from staring. His eyes were strange though, very, very dark as if he had something wrong with them. There was a minute flicker of his lips and he walked to the counter, gently ushering her aside as he collected everything needed for a coffee from the higher cupboards, which had been out of her reach and were- naturally- filled with all the food and condiments. As before, she stepped away from him, not only out of reach but far enough away so that his dimensions didn't scare her. He was a paradox, his hands were large and brutal but his movements were fluid and graceful. She hadn't forgotten the way he'd moved in her apartment and the speed with which he had killed those people.

"Why have you kidnapped me?" she asked.

"I have not kidnapped you," he replied.

"Where am I then?"

"Did you not see the mountains?" he asked, "You are in Drakensburg."

The Drakensburg? That was a three hour drive from Durban, in land, across the entire province of Kwa-Zulu Natal ... and she hadn't seen a car. And what kind of car could a man of his size drive?

The coffee mug he handed to her was comically large but the coffee in it was magnificent and filled her with much needed warmth.

"Can I go home?"

"Whenever you want," he said, "But would you feel safe there?"

"I don't know if I feel safe here," she retorted, "Who the hell is that?"

The man she'd nutted thrice had limped into sight, red faced with veins sticking out of his forehead he looked half mad, he huffed through his nose and glared at her.

With a hand The Coat drew back his hood, revealing a lion's mane of auburn-brown locks that fell upon his shoulders in bundles and as if uninterested with what was happening currently he continued making his coffee. Rayne didn't know what was going to happen but kept her eyes on the red faced man, who's blue eyes seemed to blossom out of his face with rage.

"His name is Tuck Bradley," The Coat said.

"So *very* pleased to meet you," Tuck Bradley hissed at her before limping his way into the main part of the warehouse.

Rayne felt that The Coat was watching her but couldn't be sure, his pale face framed by his hair and dominated by his searing dark eyes and his Olympian jaw line were unreadable. He watched her but appeared completely absorbed in the act. It was like being stared at by a baby. His black eyes were disconcerting, too dark and too deep.

"What are you looking at," she grunted, "Didn't you have enough time to stare at me when I was asleep you pervert?"

She shoved passed him and left the kitchen.

Tuck was sitting on one of the crates, holding himself tenderly and when she neared he shied away from her as if expecting another attack, she marched passed him to the couch and sat there and rewrapped the blanket around her.

The Coat followed moments later and she didn't know how anyone could have such an emotionless expression. He was basically an automaton.

"Would someone please tell me what the hell is going on!" she screamed loudly, her voice echoing in the warehouse, "I don't want to be here!"

"Please don't yell so loudly," Tuck said, "It hurts my ears."

"Fuck you!" she screamed, "Someone take me home now!" Tears welled in her eyes and streamed down her cheeks and she kicked her bare feet against the concrete and hit the tops of her legs with her fists. The tantrum only lasted a few seconds but it left her exhausted and she folded her arms over her knees, buried her face in them and cried until her legs were wet.

The Coat was very near, having moved from one spot to another without taking any steps, his smell was all around her and immediately she felt calmer, his voice, calm, impassive and entirely neutral sounded musical when he said, "Mason attempted to use you as bait for me. I don't think it's safe anywhere near the city at the moment but do you have anywhere else to go?"

She shook her head into her arms; big fat tears burned her eyes when she did it.

"Then you can stay here," he said.

"Excuse me?" Tuck grunted from across the floor, "Have you forgotten me? You brought both of us here together remember so what the hell am I doing here?"

Rayne heard a metallic hum and happened to look up in time to see The Coat brandish a sword. Tuck swallow hard.

"This weapon can harm me," The Coat said, implying this meant much more than Rayne thought, "Do you know why?"

Tuck's lower lip trembled ever so slightly and his eyes didn't leave the blade, Rayne had seen people with that look before. It was the sort of dangerous obsession that people died for all the time.

When Tuck didn't answer The Coat's question the giant turned his head and looked straight at him, it was a gesture that spoke volumes and Tuck's hairline moved with fear. He regained his composure and hopped off the crate and started pacing, "You tell me Coat. It's a blade that can harm a man who isn't even injured by bullets... what could it possibly be?"

"I don't know,"

Tuck's expression changed from one of pomposity to one of genuine surprise and, introducing something else that Rayne couldn't quite figure out, *disappointment?* Either way the man's face showed it all:

"What do you mean you don't know?"

The Coat's lack of body movement and facial expression was seriously starting to bother Rayne, he didn't react to Tuck's question the way the man clearly wanted him to and the other approached the giant, his hands outstretched, "You *don't* know? How could you not know?"

The giant's silence was the loudest thing Rayne had ever heard.

Tuck looked at Rayne for support but she wasn't any help, she had snot running over her upper lip, he looked back at The Coat, said, "I've spent ten years protecting that weapon and keeping it away from Mason. I've spent ten years hiding and waiting for someone who can give me the answers. I've been waiting for you, *you* have to be him?!"

"Why?" Rayne asked when The Coat didn't.

Exasperated Tuck shrugged, "Because he's the only one left!"

Despite how she had acted minutes before Rayne ended up, completely voluntarily, in the kitchen making more coffee, feeling that a hot beverage was needed. Later, if asked, which she wasn't, she would have denied that some female instinct had taken over when she saw Tuck and The Coat facing off, but it was true.

She located everything better the second time and even managed to locate a tray from the bottom cupboard which might have been left over from whoever had lived or worked here before because it seemed too domesticated for its current resident. When she returned The Coat was standing where he had been before and Tuck was on his crate, his face in his hands. She put the tray down on one of the single couches and said to the giant, "My feet are really cold do you have any socks I could borrow?"

The Coat looked over to his clothing rail and she knew that was as much of a sign as she was going to get. Behind the rail was a chest of drawers filled with an assortment of undergarments and great basket balls pairs of socks, the socks and the underwear were all black. She chose a pair at random and found that she could fold them over her feet three times, forming thick sandals. They warmed her toes satisfactorily. Her stomach made a very loud groan again.

"That's it!" Tuck said jumping off the crate as if he was planning to run away, "I'm making sandwiches," he glared at the giant and pointed a finger at Rayne, "She is starving," and then he jabbed another finger at

The Coat (he may as well have pointed at a statue), "And when I come back you're telling me everything you know."

He marched into the kitchen and Rayne heard cupboards being opened and things cluttering around, being cut up and diced, in the meantime she was left with The Coat and she didn't know what to say.

From the kitchen came, "Where have you hidden everything woman? Fucking hell!"- followed by- "Oh, never mind."

Ignoring Tuck she went back to studying The Coat, his eyes had closed and, not moving, it did look like he was asleep. She stood from the bed and his eyelids slid open and she felt the weight of his gaze.

"Why did you save me?" she asked.

Just that stare. Nothing else. She felt frustration bubble up inside her but she tried to fight it down so that it only made her face go red. She decided instead to change tact, "You said the sword could harm you, can nothing else?"

At least this time he nodded.

"Nothing at all?"

"Only this," he said lifting the sword again.

"Could you put that away please," she said, "It looks dangerous and it scares me. "

He slipped it beneath the folds of his giant coat, which hung from his shoulders where the muscles shaped the fabric into great bowling balls, the material was thick and looked like canvas or denim, not quite black but more a very dark grey.

"How is it possible that nothing can hurt you?"

He didn't reply but of course not, he had already answered. He clearly wasn't a person for repeating himself.

While Tuck busily and noisily made food and The Coat just stood there Rayne wandered off to the crates and tried to see if she could tell what was inside them. The boxes were hardy, sturdy wood, clearly made for long distance travelling but she wasn't able to get inside without breaking them open and didn't want to do that.

Tuck returned declaring, in a camp voice, "Sandwiches!"

He had a talent. The sandwiches were delicious and like his one had been earlier, packed and stacked with everything from chicken to lettuce and dripping with sauces, it wasn't a snack it was a full meal. The Coat didn't even move to have any but Tuck and she devoured the plate of them like ravenous dogs. Rayne was chewing her last one and Tuck said, "Okay, I feel calmer, but Coat, I want some answers."

The giant's eyes had been closed again and he opened them, slowly looked down at the man who had made such a crazy demand. Rayne would have bet money he was going to stomp on Tuck's head, instead he said, "I only remember the last three hundred years."

Rayne's eyes bugged, one because for such a statement there wasn't a hint of a lie in his voice and two that he said, *"only"*. Tuck was vastly unsatisfied with this answer, "Three hundred? That doesn't make any sense. Do you even know what you are?"

"I have already answered that,"

"But not at all? What is the first thing you remember?"

"Waking up in the ocean,"

"Which ocean?"

"The Indian Ocean, off the coast of what is now Cape Town,"

Tuck's forehead furrowed, "And no other memories?"

"He said he didn't know," Rayne said, annoyed with this line of questioning, "Why can't you accept that?"

"Because," he said, as if he felt he had to explain it in small words, "He is immortal, a giant, an Eternal. He does not age and the *only* thing that can injure him is that sword and even injuries caused by that blade will still heal without scarring. He should have an eidetic memory."

"Because even amnesia wouldn't last," Rayne finished, picking up the train.

"Exactly."

"You seem to know a lot about him," Rayne observed.

"Hmmm," The Coat murmured.

Rayne found the Tuck's expression hilarious as he cringed on the spot, he cleared his throat and pointed a finger, "I'm the one asking the questions Coat," he declared, "So no I'm not going first, I want answers from you and you can't answer a question with a question so no, no I am not going to go first."

"Start with Mason," The Coat said.

"Okay," Tuck said.

"It doesn't start with Mason, but that is a place to begin," Tuck said to them, he looked at Rayne, "You're his new strumpet what do you know about him?"

"He's a trillionaire," Rayne said, "He's young and successful, he owns half of Durban and most of Sky City, extensively educated, thorough and very generous. He's probably one of the best people I know."

"He's not human," The Coat added.

"What?" her voice went several octaves higher than normal.

"Bingo," Tuck said with a snap of his fingers, "*Not* human is what I was looking for. He was human when I knew him ten years ago. Human, and in his seventies ... now I don't know anything about his past, about how he made his fortune beforehand or *how* he came into possession of that sword but he had a facility in Antarctica, where he employed a lot of people and spent a lot of money looking for something. The most valuable substance in the entire world."

"What's that?" Rayne asked.

"Immortality," Tuck said, "It's what we were just talking about? The one thing no human possesses? I don't know how he found that place or if he knew what it was to start with, or if maybe he'd discovered it and had just played the cards he was dealt with but he found something. A temple," his eyes flickered briefly to the giant, "Designed for worship. He thought he'd found a place where a forgotten civilization had worshipped their deities, but it wasn't that it was a container. A time capsule turned prison made of some unknown metal that no man-made thing could penetrate. The container was not to protect its contents but to keep its contents locked inside."

"In Antarctica?"

"Yes Rayne," Tuck said, "In the South Pole. Under all that ice. I was there. I worked for Mason for a while. Sort of a consultant, I hadn't been told what I was doing, but had been paid enough money to never question. They wanted me because they knew something about my ancestry, my genetics."

"And that was?" Rayne asked.

"I don't know," Tuck answered with a shrug, "Not exactly anyway, but I was the only thing able to open this prison. Inside we found a temple with nine hundred and ninety nine statues inside." he looked at The Coat to gauge his response.

"Statues?" the giant echoed.

"Yes," the Freelander confirmed, "They were all sitting in the same fashion, all facing the same way, all looking at the same thing. A symbol that I, for some reason, could understand when I saw it and it said Petallis."

Neither the giant nor the girl responded to this name and he continued, "Petallis was the name that belonged, we found to the last of them, the only one that was missing."

"So someone else had gotten inside and stolen one of the statues?" Rayne suggested.

"No, one of them had not been put into the temple," he said, "but that they were not statues at all."

Rayne felt like someone who hadn't caught the punchline of a joke, "What were they?"

"Giants," Tuck said, "Like him. Giants who had been sitting there for so long that dust had settled onto their bodies and slowly turned to stone while they waited."

"For this Petallis?"

By this stage Tuck had accepted that the conversation was very much between her and he, "That's right. Mason's employees, of which there were thousands of them at this place, made many discoveries about these "statues," there was flesh beneath the stone but it could not be damaged, it could not be punctured… not even through the tissue of the eyeball," he let this sink in, "They could not be moved either so either they came to this underground temple out of choice or by some greater force that has since been lost. We suspected the latter was involved because the sword, we found, was the only thing capable of causing them injury."

The Coat looked at the weapon, "How?"

"It's the metal, it vibrates on a molecular level to a unique frequency that's unlike anything in this universe and it's tuned to the molecular structure of your flesh so that it causes your molecules to move aside for it. Mason thought it was the same as the metal that protected the temple and that's why only I would be able to wield it, but he was wrong. Anyone could use the sword," he sighed, "The temple was just programmed to wait for me."

"And the others?" The Coat asked.

Tuck shrugged, "How should I know? It's been ten years. All I know is that they haven't had the sword because I've had it and so they've been safe."

Nobody said anything for a second and Rayne's eyes switched from Tuck to the giant many times before she finally asked the question that had been buzzing above them like an electrical storm, "Anything else?"

Tuck seemed nervous, uneasy, "I don't know if I want to tell you this part."

"Why not?" Rayne demanded.

The Freelander nodded at The Coat, "I have a very strong suspicion he might try and kill me if I do."

Rayne's eyes narrowed as she thought about it, "Nah, he won't do that? Will you?"

The Coat said nothing.

"You see?" Rayne said, unsure.

Not convinced Tuck weighed up the options, he didn't have a choice now, he either told them and The Coat would do what he would, or The Coat would do what he would to make him tell them.

"Okay, but at least give me a head start," he negotiated, "As I said, Mason was under the mistaken idea that as my genetics were attuned to the metal of the temple's container that only I would be able to use the sword. It seems a spectacularly stupid idea in hindsight but the man was a trillionaire so nobody questioned him. What he didn't know was that the temple container and the sword were two different metals entirely. I had been deluded, lied to and made to believe that I was something special, that I was somehow connected to this amazing discovery and these ancient people. I believed it. I fell for it. I would have done anything for that *generous, kind, focused trillionaire,"* he looked at Rayne at those last words as if to indicate they shared a commonality there, "He said there was something he needed me to do and that I was to trust him, that it wouldn't harm me in any fashion, but that only I could do it and he would pay me any figure I asked. Of course I said yes. I named my price. A huge sum of money for me and some favors for my family," he chuckled abruptly.

Rayne, tired of asking questions prompted him with a spreading of her hands.

"Sorry, I had just forgotten something... since I escaped that man has sent gangs of assassins to kill me regularly. I've been hunted across continents and he has single handedly made my life a living hell but he has also honored the deal and my whole family have been provided for in my absence. It's ridiculous."

"Continue with the story," The Coat said shifting the mood back to where it had been.

"He gave me the sword, which of course by this stage I'd already seen... explained to me how he had come across it by chance, in Ghana, and knew it was something special. He brought me into the temple again, which I have be honest I had purposefully tried to stay away from because it scared the hell out of me. At the far end away from the entrance there was one statue, one giant, that had been strapped up. They clearly expected it to move because they were using carbon-nano-fibers- which is about twenty times stronger than steel to strap down the statues arms and secure its head. I knew what Mason was expecting me to do the moment I saw all this, saw the technicians with their equipment and the flood lights, the technology. He told me that he wanted me to cut off its head. Now if he'd asked me that when we first discovered the temple I would have obliged, but now I knew these weren't just statues, these were something else. Something important and alive. Not alien either but far, far older than any of us. I should have known better but in all honesty curiosity got the better of me and I did exactly what he asked."

Rayne gasped at the confession, her hand flying up to her mouth, "You *didn't,*"

Warily Tuck kept an eye on The Coat who was still standing impassive but had proven in the past this did not count as a failing. Since he wasn't getting beaten to a pulp he took it as a sign to continue, "It was easy. Too easy. The sword glided through the neck as if passing through air. The machinery around the head ensured that the second the decapitation had occurred the head was immediately yanked away from the body which had been a worthwhile precaution because when it happened the body's hands reached up to grab hold of it. The *body* moved. The strength in the arms shattered the strongest material we had as if it were just paper- but something happened at that moment. Something in my body changed and I became whatever I am now. There was an energy release of mammoth proportions that caused the electronics of the entire facility to go dark and this allowed me a chance to escape and I took the sword. I killed many people on my way out and should have died many times over, but my body was strong as was my spir-"

"Why did he want it?" The Coat interrupted.

"He wanted the blood," Tuck said, "And he clearly got it because he doesn't look like any seventy-year old I've ever seen."

The Coat turned so sharply on his heel that his coat flew out to the side like a cape. He didn't say anything and neither of them followed, he simply left them sitting in awkward silence. Rayne spoke first, "Where is he going?"

Tuck just sighed and shrugged in irritation.

"So how old were they?"

Holding his coffee cup in both hands in front of him like a chalice, he said, "No idea. I had a friend there who mentioned to me a few days before I escaped that the rocks around the container and the temple inside had shown significant movement. Basically, the container had been shifted and moved within the very rock over millions of years."

Rayne's eyes narrowed as she saw an obvious fault there, "But humans haven't been around that long have we?"

"At least not looking like we do," Tuck agreed, "He may not remember his past, and that could be a survival mechanism but he has been alive for millions of years. The thing is that if humans did evolve, then why did we evolve to look like smaller, weaker versions of him?"

Rayne didn't know, the information had been crammed into her skull but hadn't been processed. It was like reading something out of book and not being able to accept its bearing on her life.

"Do you want to know something else?" Tuck asked.

"Sure," she sighed, "Why not?"

"I had the feeling that the giant that I decapitated for Mason was at the back for a reason. I have the feeling that he was the weakest of the giants there, the *first* to be captured. If that's true and the weakest of them was that strong can you imagine how strong the one they didn't find would be?"

Rayne smiled, it sounded important but it was information that bounced off her.

Tuck stood and walked around a bit, rolling his right shoulder as if in pain. Occasionally he'd prod at his shoulder joint with his finger tips and wince.

Rayne had to admit it; Tuck was handsome in a rugged-rough-survivor-not-enough-sleep sort of way. As he paced she kept looking at the dark stubble across his jaw line and wondering what it would be like to feel it against her inner thigh. She bit her lip to stifle her thoughts.

"What's wrong with your arm?" she asked.

"I got shot," he said off handed, "Mason's fucking dog got me good, but it's fine, the bullet went straight through and it's already healed- just hurting still,"

Rayne was at the point where she was just going with everything, in her mind the acceptance switch that made believing a person could be shot and heal in one night easier had been flicked on and taped up there, she asked, "Have you ever been shot before?"

"Oh yeah, a few times. Bizarre, I know for someone of my loveable nature."

"Has it ever hurt like that before?" she pressed.

"No," he said, he put a hand through the collar of his T shirt and prodded the flesh, "Just feels like there's something still inside there."

Rayne stood up from the couch and approached the Freelander. He kept an eye on her but didn't object when she extended a hand and put it tenderly onto his shoulder joint, but yelped in surprise when she dug a thumb into the joint,

"Hey! What the —"

"Hold on," she said, said pressing the fingers of her other hand into the same spot hard.

"Jeez! Ouch hey! Stop it!" he yelled trying to swat her hands away but she persisted.

"I can feel something in there," Rayne said, still pressing hard, "It feels like a marble,"

"A what?" Tuck said, looking down at his arm and pressing in with his own fingers, "I don't feel anything."

"No," Rayne said taking his fingers and directing them, "Here."

It was clear by his face when he found the little nodule about a centimetre in diameter and securely fastened to the joint, he visibly paled.

"I have to get it out," he whispered and when she didn't immediately react he yelled, "Get it out of me now!"

"What is it?" she cried in return stepping away from him and lifting her hands in panic.

"It's a tracking device, in my arm!" he cried, ripping off his shirt and running into the kitchen, she heard the metallic tink of a knife drawer and his voice, manic, "Will you stop standing there and come and help me?!"

Where The Coat had vanished to and was Tuck really going to do what she thought he was going to do? were the only two questions in Rayne's mind when she entered the kitchen and found him, poised with a kitchen knife above the seam of his right shoulder.

"Please don't ask me to do anything," Rayne whispered as the blade tip pressed against his flesh.

"The tracer was attached to the bullet," Tuck explained through his teeth, "It's lodged in the bone which has healed around it."

"Right," Rayne said. *What?*

"So you can either cut or you can dig, which do you prefer?" he offered.

"I don't want to do either!"

"Rayne I need your help," he snapped, "They are tracking us, they are probably almost here do you want them to try kill you again?"

"They were just using me as bait," she reminded him impertinently.

"Yes, but does that mean they're particularly concerned about your safety? *Either* way, this thing still has to come out and I can't do it alone."

Summoning what she could find of her resolve she said, "Fine, what do you need me to do."

"Okay good," he said, "In the drawer find a pair of tongs or mole grips, anything that could be used to grip something."

She remembered seeing some things in the drawers she'd pulled open earlier, things that had been left by previous tenants. She wrenched several open until producing a pair of mole grips with yellow handles.

"Would these work?"

Tuck's eyebrows shot up in surprise, "Yes, they're perfect actually."

"Do we need to sterilize the blade or something?" she asked.

"No, don't worry about that," he said, pulling off his belt, folding it in two and wedging it between his teeth, "Just get ready," he mumbled around a mouthful of leather. Then, like a Shakespearean actor, he plunged the knife as deep as it would go into his right shoulder socket and in vigorous sawing motions sliced a gash the length of her forearm into his limb.

It wasn't neat nor was it quiet, the pain had turned his face purple and veins bulged across his temples and neck, his eyes went red as he withheld the scream she could tell was so closely there. Blood didn't pour or squirt as she expected but as soon as he had cut a large enough hole he slammed the blade down onto the counter next to him and spat out the belt yelling at the same time, "Get in there! Get the sides!"

"Fuck it I don't know what to do?!"

Without another word he used his left hand and dug his fingers up to his knuckles into the wound making high pitched, mewing sounds, he curled his fingers inwards and pulled the side of the cut away from the other like pulling the side of a very thick rubber wetsuit zipper open.

"The wound's going to close!" he shouted, "Get in there and keep the flesh away!"

She tried, but her fingers couldn't get in and as she touched him he stiffened in pain and she retreated. He shook his head vigorously so that sweat sprayed in her face, "Don't be afraid to hurt me woman!" he screamed, "Fucking get in there!"

A red mist descended upon her and with a relish she rammed her fingers into the deep gash as far as they would go causing him to buck. Her fingers slid in beside his and it felt like sliding them into a warm mushy meat pie, with the fibers tightening around her and blood oozing between her fingers. Everything was very close and to get her fingers in and to pull them apart like he was doing was harder than it looked.

"You have to expose the bone," he hissed, tears streaming down his cheeks and flicking off his trembling lips, "Pull,"

Together they separated the sides of the wound until she was able to see the curving ball of his shoulder socket, the sight of which made her feel physically sick, it was off-white and stained in blood and transparent plasma but stuck to it's surface and imbedded in the bone was a smooth black nodule the size of a raisin.

"There, there, get it,"

Holding tightly onto the mole grips she tried but her first attempt missed and the square edge of the steel grips scraped across the bone and Tuck's entire body went rigid and he screamed but instead of letting go with his left hand the movement caused him to tear the wound wide open allowing her more space to move. She gripped the nodule in the mole grips and

tried to move it but the thing could have been welded in there.
Like Tuck said, it had been sealed in by his healing process.

"Push against me," she instructed and he obeyed without question. As he pressed forward she was able to get a better grip and a certain savagery took over as she tugged and twisted and kicked him in the shin when he moved too much until the nodule broke free. She stepped back, blood on both her hands and all over her clothes and Tuck gasped and like a boneless sack of flesh, slunk against the counter and crumbled to the floor. She watched in awe as the wound, by itself swelled fully with blood that scabbed over and the flesh stitched itself together over the top. Within a minute the giant hole was gone with only pink flesh indicating where it had been, like a fresh coating of soil over a grave.

"What do you want me to do with this?" she asked, feeling dizzy and holding the node.

Tuck, with a sudden burst of energy snatched it from her fingers and ran across the corridor into the bathroom. A second later there was the flushing of a toilet. He returned pulling on his blood soaked shirt and narrowing his eyes said, "*You* enjoyed that didn't you?"

Still standing there with the mole grips in her hand she said, "You're welcome."

Already, Tuck's attention was drawn to something he could hear outside that she could not and he swore profusely, "That absolute bastard *left* us!"

He took Rayne's wrist and pulled her out of the kitchen.

21.

Tuck bodily hauled her out of the warehouse and the cool air hit her hard and added to her bewilderment because she couldn't see anyone, or anything. Judging by the way that Tuck had reacted she expected there to be helicopters overhead, sirens and armed ninjas dropping down on ropes. But there was nothing but a prevailing, mountainous silence.

"Shhhh," he said before she could remark. He led her off the pavement slabs towards the tall grass at the side where he crouched and pointed. In the moonlight the miles of grassy fields looked like grey mould with the road, a dark line cutting through it. She followed the line of his finger and it took a moment before her eyes adjusted to the night and she saw them approaching. They were still far away but she could make out the shape of a large black car, one of the modern hybrids between a Landrover and a Porsche following several motorcycles. They travelled at very similar speeds and so it looked like the motorcycles were horses drawing a carriage. They didn't have their headlights on and if Tuck hadn't pointed them out Rayne would never have seen them.

"What do we do?" she whispered in his ear.

"This is the only building for a hundred kilometres in every direction," he replied, but didn't feel he needed to elaborate. Rayne understood what he meant.

"Where is he?" she asked, assuming that the giant would be nearby. Maybe he'd left early to intercept the approaching convoy?

Tuck made a sound in the back of his throat that wasn't reassuring and Rayne could now hear the engines of the vehicles, powerful and fast, they still weren't using their headlights so she assumed they had no need for them.

"Whatever happens try to stay as close to me as you can," Tuck said, "I'm going to steal one of the motorcycles so as soon as you see that I have one get on it and I want you sitting in front of me."

"In front?"

"They're probably armed Rayne."

"So?"

He didn't answer and she clicked, he wanted to be behind her because he wanted to be a shield if they opened fire. She felt very weak and helpless.

The cars were very near now and the motorcycles sped up, their engines roaring loudly like giant bees while her heart was hammering loudly in her ears and her hands were starting to shake.

"Shouldn't we try and run?" she suggested, but Tuck was already moving across the edge of the grass, using it as a shield. The way he moved reminded her of a panther preparing to pounce.

And pounce he did with unbelievable timing: the first of the motorcycles crested the slight rise with a hop, its rider dressed in black leathers with a black helmet bent almost double in front of the controls on the bike. He approached at what must have been close to two hundred kilometres an hour and Tuck's muscles coiled tightly and with immense torque released, jettisoning him from his crouch like a leopard hitting a fleeing springbok. He led with his right elbow in a crushing attack that connected with the side of the rider's helmet and cracked like a melon so that two curved halves exploded off the rider's head. The bike grounded and skid across the road in a wave of sparks, the tyres burning out on the asphalt raising a toxic cloud of smoke.

In the time that Rayne spent watching the first bike spin across the road out of control, Tuck had already taken out another biker. She didn't see how but a second bike went racing along the road chasing the first without anyone in the seat.

She heard what she thought was Tuck yelling for her but as she moved she saw one of the bikers unsaddle by leaping vertically from his bike, flying through the air like some giant tarantula and land on Tuck. The pair of them crashed onto the road in a tangle of limbs. Rayne knew very little about martial arts but it seemed to her that Tuck had the upper hand. The biker was trying to wrestle him and pin him to the ground but while his hands were occupied Tuck repeatedly pounded every available opening with attacks. Elbow blows that sounded like sledgehammers hitting tree trunks collided with the biker's exposed neck and punches like jackhammer strikes collided with his ribs.

Three more bikers arrived ahead of the car and wasted no time joining in the fray and just when Rayne thought that Tuck would be bested the Freelander's hands blurred completely out of sight and the biker's helmet twisted right around to face his approaching partners.

The sickening twig-crackle of vertebrae made Rayne ill.

Tuck was on his feet even as the bikers were pulling out their weapons and attacked with bewildering grace and aggression. He ducked behind the nearest biker and using him as a human shield charged forward. Thrusting the biker ahead as a diversion he danced amongst the armed opponents, gathering them up in his hands as if they were his dance-partners and not his enemies. And in a highly coordinated and economic fashion he broke, wrenched, tore and twisted their limbs and necks. Nothing fancy or showy just brutal- breaking. He was like a young Steven Segal with a much younger Brad Pitt's looks.

Two bikers, their bodies broken before they could utter a scream were only just crumbling to the floor as he rolled across the asphalt towards the third who was beside his bike, the biker tried to follow him with his weapon but Tuck got in range and hooked a punch into the side of the biker's knee with such a force his leathers bounced as the patella turned into a sack of gravel. The biker screamed in his helmet but despite his pain still brought the weapon to bear. Tuck's left hand grabbed the armed hand while his right chopped at the man's elbow joint, shattering it and instead of leaving it there he pressed the nuzzle of the weapon under the biker's chin and helped him squeeze the trigger.

Lights exploded behind the biker's visor and the top of the helmet shattered.

"Rayne!" Tuck yelled, swinging his leg over the motorcycle. He revved the engine and took off and she thought he was going to go without her but he stopped for her. His face urgent.

The headlights to the car suddenly came on as it approached at over a two hundred kilometres an hour and Rayne screamed in panic, ran up to Tuck and tried to get on behind him.

"No!" he yelled.

The car hit one of the fallen bikes with a crash and bounced over the fallen biker. She was blinded by the headlights and in the moment while she climbed around Tuck trying to get in front of him she was positive the car was going to hit them and something fell apart in her head and she covered her face and screamed.

A gust of wind as something passed nearby, a curse from Tuck, a screech of tyres and when Rayne opened her eyes she saw the car had merely swerved to a stop in front of the bike. Tuck looked more like an animal now than he did before, his eyes wide, his breath coming in ragged pants he was a wild animal caught in a trap.

Rayne, in her panic had disengaged herself from him entirely and he gunned his engine with a twist of his hand and turned the bike around in a fluid, severe twist- Rayne saw what was about to happen and suddenly unafraid went to get onto the bike but he didn't wait for her and blasted off so fast he took it on one wheel.

"No!" she screamed, running after him to get as much distance between her and the car, as desperate as a child who is left behind by their parents in a crowded street because they can't keep up, "Tuck! Please don't leave me!"

He slammed on brakes, almost grounding it a second time and looked over his shoulder and held a hand out to her. Behind her a car door opened and Tuck's eyes which were already wide and filled with desperation took a look of disbelief. She thought the worst and expected someone had pulled a gun and was aiming it at her.

"Don't shoot!" she screamed covering her head with her hands.

"Alan?" Tuck said, surprised, gob smacked even. It was enough of a change that when she got to the bike she risked looking behind her and saw that what Tuck was so startled about was a forty something year old man in a grey suit.

Average height and very slightly overweight but with the rigid straight back of someone far more capable than he appears. He had thinning brown hair and a small beard, his eyes hidden behind spectacles. He looked like he worked as an accountant but Tuck clearly knew him.

"Evening Broheim, how are you?" the man said.

"Alan?" Tuck was crestfallen, "I don't understand."

"Please don't involve her in this," the man, Alan said, his voice carrying well in the windless air, "She's innocent."

Tuck's eyes darted from this man to Rayne.

"Rayne," the man said, she was shocked to hear her name called, she looked at him, "Rayne, please come here and get in the car."

At first, the Freelander didn't respond and Rayne felt jittery with fear, she searched his face for an answer and when she found none she tried to get onto the bike but he stopped her with a hand pressed high against her chest.

"No," he said, without making eye contact, "Rayne if you come with me you're going to get hurt."

"No, no," she whimpered, feeling her own face crinkle, "Please don't leave me. Don't leave me here alone with them!"

A whinny, high pitched meow had replaced her own voice and she knew how she sounded but she couldn't help it. She was scared.

"Rayne," Alan said again, "Tuck is right, if you come with us we will take you right home. If you go with him you will get hurt, he can't avoid it."

She tried to get onto the bike again but Tuck wouldn't let her and with a shove that sent her falling backwards and landing on her arse he gunned the engine and took off again leaving her in a cloud of exhaust fumes. She scrambled to get to her feet, all arms and legs but there was no way she could catch him, she didn't have super powers and soon the bike's brake lights were just a tiny little red dot in the night and then they were gone.

Desperate puffs of breath made her realize she was hyperventilating and as she turned to face the man who was standing by the car she also saw many of the bikers; the bikers Tuck had killed, moving. Their arms straightening with nightmarish cracks of joints. The one who had been taken out first was the first to rise, he held his jaw which she was sure had been shattered and ignored her as he went to the fallen bikers and helped them to their feet. Then those who were able carried those who were unable away into the grass.

The man, Alan's voice was suddenly very nearby and she shrieked like a banshee with fear and raised her hands like claws, "Don't you fucking-jeezus *Christ!*"

Alan's concern was clear, "Rayne you are going into shock you need to calm down,"

"I don't know you Alan," she mewled, "I don't know you I don't know where I am. Where are they taking those bodies?"

Alan's hands were held up in front of him in a gesture of openness, his hands themselves were a little chubby, the sort of hands that work behind a desk, he explained in that warm tombre, "Some of the injuries require heavier realignment. They don't want you to panic anymore Rayne. Rayne… it's me Alan, we've worked together on the phone."

He lunged forward and enveloped her in a bear hug, pinning her arms to her sides and she went totally berserk but he didn't let her go and picking her up so her feet didn't touch the road he didn't even flinch when she repeatedly kicked him in the legs. The door to the car opened and he dropped her inside and closed it.

A solid ten minutes of screaming, thrashing, trying to break the unbreakable glass and trying to tear the tear-proof seats until her finger nails were broken and bleeding left her so exhausted she ended up lying on her side staring at the back side of the driver's seat. She couldn't cry, there was nothing there, she just felt numb. They had both left her.

People were talking outside the car but not in English, motorcycle engines were gunned and screeched away and a while later someone, who sounded like Alan was speaking on his phone and both front doors to the car opened and he and the driver climbed in. Neither of them acknowledged her presence. Alan put on his seatbelt with one hand while still talking on his phone, switching hands while the strap crossed over him, he was speaking very rapidly in Afrikaans.

The engine started and the driver, who was dressed in black leathers, perhaps the biker whose bike Tuck was now on, performed a three point turn and started down the road. The engine and the ride were so smooth she barely felt any movement at all. She was a child again believing that if she just stayed perfectly still maybe she'd be forgotten and it was easy to imagine in the dark car, with Alan talking on his cell phone, in another different language now, the driver not saying anything and the electronic displays lighting up the dashboard that she had turned invisible.

After an indeterminable amount of time driving, they entered more built up areas which had street lights along the side that passed over in blocks of regular intervals. She followed each of them with just her eyes, making sure she didn't move.

Alan said 'goodbye' in English and hung up the phone, depositing the small device into his jacket pocket. Rayne watched the side of his face with growing nervousness. Was this really the Alan she had spoken to on the phone? Mason's right hand man? She couldn't remember how he had sounded on the phone, nor if she'd ever imagined what he might look like in real life.

A minute passed, then two, which she counted on the dashboard clock before, without looking back, he said, "Even at our top speed it's still a two hour drive to your home Rayne… so we're going to stop an all-night service station to get you some food. Your blood sugar is very low and I'm worried about your hydration. How do you feel?"

She didn't answer, the little girl in her wanted to perpetuate the streak of invisibility.

"Rayne?" he pressed, a little firmer, "How do you feel?"

"I don't know," she said. She was tired, very tired and weak. She couldn't think.

"What would you like to eat?"

"Nothing," she said.

Alan pointed across the dash and mumbled to the driver who started to indicate. Rayne felt the turn of the car and they slowed to a halt.

"Nathan," Alan said, "Grab Rayne a sandwich and a bottle of coke please, not diet coke, full fat. I'll have a Snax bar. Thanks."

The driver got out of the car.

"These service stations practically run off of the food industry now," Alan said, "Since cars started becoming more fuel efficient we don't have to fill up anymore." he chuckled at what he had said and Rayne wondered if it was meant to be funny.

"Thank you for taking me home," Rayne said as part of a test to make sure that's what they were doing.

"It's really the least we can do," he said, not looking back, just watching the driver through the shop window she assumed, "The apartment is unfortunately no use to you at the moment so we are taking you back to The Suburbs. Is there anyone you want me to call? "

"No, no, just take me there."

"Don't worry Rayne," he said sympathetically, "Soon you can carry on with your life."

"My life is over," she whispered, pushing up on one arm and looking out the side window to just make sure they were indeed at a service station. They were and the sidelong restaurant was really busy, through the window she saw a table where a family were eating hamburgers and her stomach growled, "What am I supposed to do now that I know all of this?"

"You are a highly successful professional," Alan said, "What you're feeling now is shock but soon the truth of it all will seem ordinary. Familiarity will lessen the blow. It'll be easier than you think I promise."

"What do I do?"

"You make the best out of being young Rayne, it might seem like a long life ahead of you but it isn't and it's not going to last forever."

"Apparently some things do," she said.

"Not for you I'm afraid," he said, "It was wrong of Mason to get you involved in this. As much of a calculated risk as it might have been. You're not part of this world you're part of another, one more colourful and beautiful and that is the world you have to get back into. That's the world you belong in."

The driver returned with some food which he passed over to Rayne who at first refused to eat or drink, but as the journey continued her hunger began hurting her and she couldn't resist. Otherwise, the trip was driven in silence.

Finally, they pulled up outside her house and Alan asked, "Do you have keys to get in?"

"I'm surprised that you don't have some," she said derisively.

Alan shook his head, "No we don't."

"That's fine then," she said and climbed out of the car. She went to the side entrance beside the gate and touched a thumb to the intercom.

Carol's voice immediately greeted her, with the urgency of a mother hen, "Ma'am are you alright? Where have you been? What did The Coat do to you?"

She sighed, it was good to hear her house's voice and she felt a little guilty about how rudely she'd spoken to her, "I'm fine Carol," she said, "Home at last."

There was a click as the side door unlocked and as she stepped inside Alan and his driver were already leaving.

Rayne swallowed hard and thought that her house looked like the most terrifying place in the world. There were thousands of places a person could hide, just waiting for her. She was tired, scared and all alone and was practically about to sit down and cry on her driveway when the front doors opened and Carly bounded out of the house towards her.

"Are you alright gorgeous?" Carly asked, wrapped her skinny arms around Rayne.

"What are you doing here?" Rayne asked, unable to even get energy into her voice.

"Carol called me," Carly said taking Rayne by the hand and leading her inside, "Said you would be coming back soon and would probably want some company. I haven't seen you in ages, what's happened to you? You look like a mess! Is that blood?"

Rayne couldn't answer any of the questions but had never been so happy to see another living person in her whole life.

22.

There was something wrong with Tammy Jenkins.
Rain pummelled at the windows and rattled down the gutters and made it sound like the house itself was trying to shake itself apart. With unpredictable frequency lightning would slash across the clouds and cause them to bellow like whipped heads of cattle while beyond the rain you could hear the sound of a train passing with an impeachable regularity. The sirens of police cars and ambulances added to the noise while once in a while a gunshot and a scream would cut through the storm. This was Durban after all, life was a sentence punctuated by violence and sirens.
Tammy Jenkins sat by the window watching things.
Durban City was filled with *things*. There was the usual infestation of animals, rats, stray cats and gangs of dogs and those were the usual things that all cities endured. But this city had something else and like a bicycle wheel, those people who were at the centre of the city had no idea about what went on at the rim and so had no clue about things that existed and were always looking in at them.
Things. Creatures that you could not Google to find a description of or a proper name for, things that had names only to those who could see them.
The window of the attic bedroom of number 13 Attoe Walk, overlooked a field that gradually sloped down to a river and a sewer entrance. The water of the river was currently a stewy grey-brown, its surface dancing with the rain as it grew wider and wider. In contrast the grass of the playing field appeared greener than green, vibrant and waterlogged just the way grass wanted to be.
The field was surrounded by a very high wooden fence that stopped where the bridge started, which connected the two halves of the field bisected by the river that led from the underground drainage system.
That's where a lot of the things lived and they came out when the water came too high or when they were hungry.
In some way Tammy thought she was privileged to be able to see these things, she thought it was a tribute to her Port Elizabeth heritage that she was able to see something that other people couldn't.
At school the girls had been quick to point out that only crazy

people believed they could see things that nobody else could but Tammy didn't think that was right.

Judging by the way some of the boys looked at these same girls compared to the way everyone else looked at them, Tammy had concluded that everyone saw things differently and sometimes could see things others couldn't.

These things enjoyed the rain and often came out into it which was why whenever it rained Tammy would make sure she had her spot at the window so she could watch them the same way people watched videos of kittens and puppies online.

She had seen many *things* in Durban but none fascinated her more than the ones she saw playing in the field behind her house. As they scurried out of the sewers they looked like people, but moved around with a bent at the waist, nervous animal look, their heads bobbing up and down and jerking in the direction of any sound. They were all female, Tammy was certain of that and while they looked like bedraggled humans they weren't. Their eyes glowed green in the dim light and she had seen their fangs. They wore rags and while they lived in the sewers they were not unclean. They communicated and played with each other, they laughed and some of them even took off their clothes in the rain and washed them in the river before putting them on again. They smiled. This told Tammy they were intelligent and living in the sewers was necessity and not a lifestyle choice.

They were savage though. She had seen them drag a gang of boys from the street and into the sewers and more recently a pair of them had dragged a gardener, screaming, into the sewer.

There were six *things* on the grass today but today they were acting differently.

They were standing stock still and facing her house with their heads tilted back as if they were trying to see down their noses. It looked like they smelt something, something they found intriguing but something they did not want to approach. Some *thing* that scared them and beckoned them at the same time, she knew the feeling.

Tammy smiled because she knew what it was they could smell.

At eighteen years old Tammy lived in one of the few remaining houses in Attoe Walk, a three story house made of brick that was also one of the oldest houses in Durban she had lived here her entire life and it had been her parents and her grandparents' house before it had been hers. It had needed a lot of work, the plumbing was from the turn of the century, there was dry mould all over the kitchen and parts of her house were infested with cockroaches, but Tammy had never been very good at dealing with things like that. But she had found a friend. Another friend that nobody else could see... but a lot of people apparently wanted to.

He had knocked on her door one afternoon and had introduced himself. She had known instantly that he was no more human than the *things*, but while they might have been less he was definitely more. He had to duck when he came into her house and couldn't get through any of the doors without turning sideways. He had told her that she had a unique mind, that this made her special and that she would always have his protection and his assistance as long as she wouldn't mind helping him if he needed it.

He had helped her fix her house, made it liveable again and then he sat and listened to her tell him her entire life story. How her parents died when she was fifteen and left her the house, how the governmental schemes to protect orphaned kids had failed with her. He had simply listened and helped and she had waited a long time for him to finally knock on her door and actually ask for hers.

He had done so eight weeks earlier.

She remembered it vividly because she had relived the moment a hundred times a day since it happened. She had been sitting at the attic window watching the fields and occasionally closing her eyes and listening to the thoughts of *things* that were nearby when there had been a knock at her door. Absent minded she had walked down the stairs in just her panties, a skinny teenager with more tattoos on her body than bare skin and answered the door to find it blocked by a giant coat.

It was the early hours of the morning and he had the smell of wind on him as if he'd been holding onto the back of a jet plane. He spoke to her in that musical voice of his and had asked if he could please use her basement because he needed to sleep. He said his mind was chaotic and he was losing control and he had to rest.

Tammy was so desperately in love with him he could have asked her to saw off her own leg and she would have happily obliged, this request was hardly even worth asking.

"I will not stir for a long time," he told her, "So do not worry about me but if I haven't woken up in eight weeks, please knock on the door but do not enter."

Tammy had nodded and had seen him smile widely beneath the hood and his index finger stroked her cheek and touched the new piercing she had in her left ear, "It looks good."

It was one of a hundred piercings she had all over her body and on clear display for him to see, but he had seen them all before but always seemed sincerely interested in when she got another one.

She had walked with him to the basement door which was hidden behind a fake wall panel in the refurbished kitchen.

"I need to replace these shelves for you," he said, looking at one that had warped with the humidity, he had already tiled the entire kitchen and bought her a new washing machine which he had carried in by himself. He looked around the kitchen as if making mental notes of things that needed to be repaired.

Opening the panel he stepped gingerly onto the first basement step which groaned under his weight and said, "Remember Tammy, just knock on the door. Do not come down. Do you understand?"

She had of course and he had smiled one last time, thanked her and closed the door. She had listened to him descending the wooden stairs slowly and with great caution so he didn't break them and that was the last noise he had made.

Eight weeks had passed and today was the day she was going to knock on the door and it seemed that the *things* in the field could smell that it was that time too. She couldn't blame them for sniffing the air- his smell was intoxicating and just an added lure for her.

A giant in a black trench coat with a hood who wore black, how could an *emogo*t like her not find that scintillatingly attractive? And his smell.

After eight weeks his smell had escaped from the basement and filled her house to capacity and she had closed every door and window to keep the smell in but it had escaped outside and spread.

The *things* on the field stirred as if the scent had changed and she bit her lip at the thought of him awaking in her basement. She had held off knocking on the door, had purposefully prolonged the torture of waiting so that she could fully appreciate seeing him again.

One of the *things* opened her mouth and seemed to drink in the smell, was it so strong that they could smell it through the rain?

She closed her eyes and listened and she could hear the whispers of the *things,* not just the ones on the field but the things all over the city all who were connected to her somehow and they all said the same thing.

Tammy slid off the attic window sill and let her nighty fall around her ankles. The fresh air licked at her body, turning her densely packed piercings cold against her skin, making her flesh crawl ever so slightly.

Naked she walked down the spiral staircase, trailing her finger tips along the banister and loving the sensation of the decorated iron steps under her bare feet, it was the same sensation when she stepped onto the carpet in the ground floor living room.

The smell was strongest here. Like how baking can fill an entire house with the smell of cookies so too his smell had covered everything in a film of *him.* It boggled her mind.

She walked through the living room, where the heavy curtains cast black furniture into an even deeper darkness and into the kitchen where the cold tiles touched the soles of her feet and made her start. They were extra cold, like ice. The last warmth of the South African summer had clearly passed.

The fake wall panel was directly opposite her, just on the other side of her ice-rink-like kitchen floor.

She bit her bottom lip again and felt a shudder through her body as his smell crashed into her again in a wave.

The floor didn't feel so cold this time as she walked across it and as she neared enough to knock she stopped and stared at the panel, trying to listen for any movement but all she could hear was her heart beat.

She curled her hand into a fist to knock and stopped herself. An elicit and naughty thought entered her mind and stayed there, refusing to move and she welcomed it. It was a hot and wet thought, one that had been considered many times before but put aside, now it would have its moment.

Why had he only wanted her to knock?

Could it be because he didn't want to break the sanctity of protecting her? Despite her tattoos and piercings did he see her as vulnerable and never wanted to take advantage of her? What a romantic thought that was, but the thought of her seducing him was so erotic it kicked romantic clear out of her mind.

Instead of knocking she reached up and took hold of the hidden handle for the door and opened the panel, as it swung out it released a blast of warm air so thick with *him* that she was immediately drunk with it and would have sprinted down the stairs and leapt upon him if she had been able to see. Her arousal had shoved aside any rational thinking and the next thing she knew she was creeping down the wooden steps into the basement.

The limited light from the kitchen allowed only the shapes of the wooden steps to be seen as they descended like the stairs of a jetty into black water. As a little girl she had imaged these being the very steps to the centre of the Earth and they had terrified her. After the forth step she was completely blind and instead of trying to see she closed her eyes and let her mind wander.

There was something wrong with Tammy Jenkins. But this felt very right and with her eyes closed she simply knew where to go.

He was lying on the far side of the basement as far from the stairs as he could manage, he lay on his back still in the same clothes he had eight weeks ago but there was no smell to indicate that these clothes were in any fashion dirty. With her eyes closed the smell seemed to hit her in waves that caused colourful circles to spin in her mind's eye.

The basement was small, nothing more than just a hole in the ground with bricks for walls and she was at his side very soon and for the first time she felt as naked and exposed as she truly was.

But the *things* in her mind were still telling her to do things and she listened to them, the next step took her so close that the ball of her foot fell upon the flattened hem of his coat, a touch as brilliant as when the woman had touched the robes of Jesus and had been cured of her diseases. She staggered and contemplated turning and running out, closing the door and knocking on it as she was supposed to. But she didn't, she knew what she wanted.

Keeping her eyes firmly shut she knelt beside him and found that his body, along with the smell, radiated warmth like a furnace at temperatures far warmer than she had expected. Any more temperate and his body would be practically too hot to touch.

She found her courage easily at this point. This she had done many times before, she knew men, and she knew what it took to manipulate them. She knew how to seduce.

She touched his leg with her fingers and pressed her palm against it to find the muscles as firm as hardened rubber, she ran it up the inside of his leg towards his crotch, her mind painting mental images too horny to bear.

She found him, even within his trousers and as flaccid as he was he was still so large that she almost didn't realize what it was until she followed it to its root and her hands froze.

His size was simply epic.

All at once she decided she didn't care, she had to have it and she would never be satisfied until she did.

Massaging it through the fabric of his trousers with her hands she found it quick to respond as it thickened to devastating dimensions.

His body stiffened, whether from surprise or ecstasy she didn't know but she was going to continue until he stopped her but when the basement was picked up and thrown on its side and her whole world spun out of control as two hands, so big they were inhuman put her to the ground she realized that things had gone too far to be stopped.

Her eyes opened, fully accustomed to the darkness and all that she saw was a monstrous column of rigid muscle and flesh with a bulbous head the size of a grapefruit protruding from the darkness.

"Oh yes," she pleaded, reaching out to it and taking its stiff heat in her hands, "Please!"

Above her, her giant was panting, his breath coming in grunting growls like some animal and the heat from his body was increasing by degrees until she could barely hold him.

With one giant hand he spread her legs and she prayed that it would be gentle.

It was not.

23.

At exactly the same time, on the other side of the world, a Mercedes Benz floated through the flooded streets and Rayne decided that if misery had a colour it would look like London in the rain. Everyone walked with their umbrellas held close to their heads and their faces pinched into expressions that suited the weather perfectly. Not to leave Rayne out it drummed relentlessly on the roof of the luxurious limousine that smelt of Jasmine and was lined on the inside with cream leather.

"Do you think the weather will be like this for the awards?" her driver, a gentleman who had introduced himself as Brett, asked.

Her attention was drawn from the people just on the other side of her tinted window to Brett. She just didn't get him. He had grown up in London and had served in the military, touring Afghanistan before returning to the island and becoming a celebrity chauffer. He came very highly recommended because he was handy as a body-guard and with his high disciplined mental attitude he was able to manage London traffic without losing his temper. What she didn't get was how they would drive in silence for hours and he would break the silence with a question that he would be better suited to answer than she.

"Its inside," she reminded him, "So I don't think it matters."

"Ah yeah," he said in a tone that she couldn't quite place, was he agreeing with her or just building up for another question, "That's right." he added on the end.

Rayne was, in fact, dreading even touching or being touched by the rain. She had been in London for three weeks and had started to understand what she had heard was called the South African Flu. Having lived in the endless bounty of sunshine that is Africa in general she had taken it for granted and had found Britain, London especially to be an inhospitable place where the weather did its level best to sap the very joy from your bones. She had been caught once in the rain while she had been here and had been brought to tears with the hateful cold she felt in each drop. South Africans weren't designed for this sort of prolonged greyness.

Always one to give credit where it was due, Rayne could not deny that the Mercedes Benz the organizers of her London trip had provided, was one of the latest models, a beautiful vehicle with a spacious interior that completely removed you from the sensation of being on the road. She could have been out at sea. The radio was no longer on after Brett had made the mistake of turning it to the latest "British top pop" and it had felt like someone using a Black and Decker drill to the side of her head.

"Does rain make fake tan run?" Brett asked.

She glanced at his reflection in the rear-view mirror, his eyes were focussed on the road ahead which was good because visibility was about two meters and the pedestrians tended to drift like heads of cattle with only a vague sense of direction and self-preservation.

"No," she answered, "It doesn't."

"Oh that must be a relief then?" Brett said with an open sincerity that made Rayne want to slap her forehead.

"Yes," she agreed.

And then they lapsed into silence again. Her phone chimed with a text and she sighed with relief. It was Nick the owner of Hardman Productions, one of the businesses involved in her PR push across Great Britain. He was a notorious photographer, highly recommended by everyone she'd spoken to, scintillatingly professional. He had text her to subtly let her know that she was forty minutes late.

She replied back: STUCK IN TRAFFIC.

"Brett, I know how annoying this is going to sound but is there any way we could get a move on?"

"I'm going as fast as I can Miss Ensley," he told her, "The computer says that there's been some sort of accident up ahead and the pedestrians are getting in the way. I *hate* pedestrians."

The venom in the last sentence was new to Rayne and she decided to let it go and sent Nick another text: JUST CHECKED. NO WAY CAN GET THERE FASTER. VERY SORRY.

She put the phone on her lap and sighed. She wanted sunshine. She wanted sunburns; she wanted the smell of the ocean, the smell of Africa. It had been three weeks and it could have been a year- she was terribly homesick.

She knew she was being dramatic. She hadn't eaten breakfast and it was mid-afternoon now and her stomach was growling but she refused to step out in this weather to grab a snack and didn't want to be late for the photo shoot with Nick. It was a thorn in her side that she had become a "slave to her success" that she had taken vitamins and some protein shakes to keep up her strength so that she didn't look heavy in the pictures but now she was starving and hunger always made her morose. On reflection she wasn't that homesick. She had periods of intense nostalgia but that was it, she thought it was really because she didn't like the cold. She had actually been too busy to feel much of anything aside from just feeling busy.

Out her window they passed a billboard which had a picture of her on it with her back to the camera, she was kneeling and looking over a shoulder, her hands hidden in front of her as if she were hiding a secret. On her lower back the words COME HAVE A LOOK had been painted with the television channel she appeared on in London under it.

She had to admit the designers had done an extraordinary job with their computers. The picture hardly looked like her!

Her phone beeped, Nick again, WEATHER IS SHIT. NO WORRIES. GET HERE WHEN YOU CAN.

London loved her, that's what Londoners had said and when any city loves you it demands everything from you. Every day she had been in an entirely different environment. Radio studios, television shows that were meant to look unrehearsed despite it being thoroughly planned to the letter and she'd lost count of the number of promotional visits she had to do and how many people she had seen.

Yes. Very busy and very grateful for it.

Spare time meant her mind wondered and if it wondered it always wondered to the same things so she was glad for the distractions and for the solid hours of sleep she got when she found her way back to her hotel room.

Brett turned a corner sharply and the car accommodated for the sudden turn and the deluge they were driving through and turned as smoothly as a dolphin in water.

"What does it take to be a porno star then?" he asked, righting themselves on the road.

Here we go, she thought. Wondering if she had the patience to put up with the questions she knew were coming. Whenever, anyone outside of the industry had the chance to chat with her they asked the same line of questions always starting with question one: what does it take to be a porno star or, sub textually, *I wouldn't mind be paid to shag for a living,* followed by question two: Do you think I have what it takes to be a porn star, or sub textually, *I need validation for my ego* and question three: *could you get me into being a porn star?* Or, for the more honest, can you get me into a porn star?

"Do you think you've got what it takes?" she asked directly.

He chuckled confidently, handling the wheel with his grey goose-down gloves, "Well, I think I might manage yeah. I mean I have a massive cock."

She smiled as sweetly as she could, one of the benefits of being in the industry is you learn to get a feel for things and for people.

"Well," she began, "The average film shoot lasts for twelve to fourteen hours. That's having sex with the same person for twelve to fourteen hours for each scene, you have to be able to get an erection immediately because the film crew are being paid by the hour, be able to perform sexually under pressure while taking direction and surrounded by people watching you. For a man you only ejaculate when the director tells you too and you have to be ready to go straight away because, again, *everyone* around you is being paid by the hour, including you. If you don't have the capacity to cum and then go right after for as many times as it's needed for the shot then you shouldn't even go for an audition. You also have to abstain from sex in your private life because you need to have a build-up to make the impressive shots, which means you need to be a professional, Brett."

The rest of the drive to Nick's was in silence.

Nick Hardman (the last name was chosen) had been on the phone with her a day earlier discussing the details of their meeting. What viewers tended to think was a very random, spontaneous industry was probably more regulated than any other in the world. Contracts had been emailed over for both Rayne and Nick to sign stating what would and wouldn't happen during the photo shoot and it had been implicitly and explicitly clear on the details.

Brett finally got them out of the center of London, they joined the M25 and together with every car in Britain they raced each other along the flooded lanes. They came off the M25 and went through a village of catalogue style brick homes, where every one of them looked identical to its neighbor and entered a business park made up of similarly styled warehouse buildings. Here there were fewer pedestrians and more parking.

Brett pulled into a parking space outside a building with a massive black sign with HARDMAN PRODUCTIONS written in pink.

"Thanks Brett," she said picking up her shoulder bag, "Are you going to hang outside here?"

"If it's okay I might go grab a cup of coffee and a sandwich," he said, "I'll be back before you're finished."

She nodded in agreement, opened the door and jumped out into the rain. When she pushed through the building door she looked like she'd just climbed out of a pool.

Entering into a *very* plush reception, again not what you might expect from a pornographic photographer Rayne found that the receptionist, instead of being some twenty something bimbo with huge breasts was instead a pleasant looking brunette, the like that is simply classified as "receptionist". She looked up from her work and gave Rayne a reproachful look, one that Rayne had unfortunately come to associate with London, "Can I help you?"

"Yes, my name is Rayne Ensley; I have an appointment for 5pm?"

The woman consulted her computer and pointed with a long finger to one of the seats along the wall of the waiting room. Rayne sat down and ran her fingers through her sopping hair. She hadn't bothered to do much with it before coming, Nick had told her there was not only a shower but a makeup room and she would have at least forty minutes to sort herself out.

"As you were late, Mr. Hardman is currently with clients," the receptionist explained sourly, "Can I make you like a cup of coffee?"

From the woman's tone Rayne decided she would really prefer it if the woman didn't and said so, then asked, "Nick told me there were facilities here for me to freshen up?"

"Yes?" The receptionist asked, the 'and?' was implied.

"Well, I know I'm late," Rayne said, "But I would like to freshen up and get ready so that more time isn't wasted?" she smiled and added, "If that's okay with you?"

The receptionist clucked her tongue and sighed as if it were the most painful thing she'd ever had to do requiring the most amount of effort and said, "I suppose so, through the door and to your right. Do *not* go to your left, go to your right and you'll be in the green room, just sort yourself in there."

Rayne purposefully gave the woman the best smile she could manage and left the reception via the short corridor nearest the reception desk. She saw that to go left would have put her into the studio where Nick Hardman was currently at work. She could hear the camera's loud click, the flash of the magnesium lights and judging by the number of clicks she counted and his choice words of encouragement he was very busy indeed. She turned right into the green room where a row of mirrors with frames of light bulbs were lined up. She picked one near the far end, put her bag onto the counter, opened it and started pulling out the various bits of makeup that she'd brought with her only to be interrupted by a woman who worked with Nick as his make-up person who had a coronary when she saw Rayne trying to do it herself.

"Don't you *dare*," the woman said as she flittered about like a bird, "That's my job!"

Rayne froze with a makeup brush held half way to her face and slowly put it down as if it were a loaded weapon.

The woman was a thirty something year old with a short bob of black, a long neck and narrow shoulders who spoke very fast and in the first few minutes of meeting Rayne told her about her morning before mentioning in passing and with a flutter of her hand that her name was Amy.

She made Rayne go have a shower and then sat her upon the chair in front of the mirror in a robe and broke open a complicated tool box of makeup accessories. Chatting away merrily as she did so Amy went to work removing blemishes from Rayne's face. Firstly applying a cleansing cream, then removing it and that was where Rayne's understanding of what followed ended.

The make-up work on her face took almost a solid hour and then there was the "touch ups" to the other regions of her body that would be on show.

"Only so much of this is done on the computer," Amy explained looking up from her work, "Nick just doesn't have a lot of time to edit the photographs so he always asks us to sort things out beforehand. Please turn around and bend over."

Rayne was busy getting makeup put onto places she had never touched with a makeup brush before when there was a knock at the door which Amy answered with, "Come on in Nick."

Nick Hardman walked in, a tall broad shouldered character who looked more like a San Franciscan than a Londoner, with his tanned skin, blonde spiked hair and gray eyes. He was dressed in shorts, sandals and a vest and he didn't even notice Rayne's utter nudity and compromising position.

"Hey Rayne," he said preoccupied with searching through the images on his digital camera, "Good to meet you at last. I'll see you in about ten minutes or so."

And then he left the room.

"You hear the rumors about Nick Hardman?" Amy asked, from somewhere in the region of Rayne's rear end where some icy gel was being generously applied.

"I've heard some,"

"They're all true."

Wrapped in a remarkably oversized cotton robe Rayne went from the green room to the studio as quickly as she could and found Nick sitting behind a computer with a giant screen paging through a multitude of hardcore pornographic images with the same sort of attention as someone looking through a catalogue of spoons. He swung around on his chair when she entered and sprang out of it as if propelled by a hidden spring.

"Rayne!" he came forward and embraced her in a hug, "I've been looking so forward to working with you. Cart said you were only in London for a short while?"

Cart was the UK PR manager arranging the shoot and a man more than willing to encourage Rayne's dire need to say busy, Rayne shrugged, "I've been hear almost a month, promoting stuff,"

He seemed delighted, "Stuff, I love that. Great, you're turning into the industry's new workaholic, good for you. Are you excited about the Soft Kitty Awards I bet you're going to pick up one," with a wave of his hand across his computer monitor he changed the screen image to his corporate logo and brought up a selection of music, "What do you like music wise?"

"I'm a fan of old rock?" she said.

He looked momentarily worried and swiveled around on his chair to find something of a play list while Rayne had a gander around the studio. It was much cluttered with furniture, silky sheets, props and toys with the only clean space being directly in front of the camera set up. There was the smell of lubricants and latex.

"Well," he said flicking through his play lists, "I don't have a lot of old rock but we're looking for something sexy and raunchy so how about some classic Nickelback?"

"That'll do," she said, noticing some of the pictures on the wall.

He clicked on an album and speakers from each corner of the studio started playing the music and he skipped over to the camera and ushered her in front of it.

"Now, how much experience have you had in front of a camera?" he asked.

"Cart's probably told you more than I know," Rayne admitted, "I'm still a newbie to photography so I'm up for being told what to do."

"Okay," he said with a grin, "It's real simple, I'm going to take about a thousand photographs of you and we'll only choose about six or eight of them so the idea is to just let go and be crazy."

She laughed, "Just let go? That's a big statement in our industry."

He laughed in return, "Not as much as you think Rayne."

It reminded her, he had asked if she wanted to do anything on camera with him- *him* being the legendary appendage which Nick Hardman was merely a body to support- she had said no on reflex and so there hadn't been a STD screening and it wasn't in the contract that they had signed. Which, now that she was standing in his studio seemed to be a bit of a shame.

"Take off the robe and come into the camera view," he said smiling patiently at her and beckoning her in with small circles of his hand, "I want to make sure this background suits you."

Behind Rayne was a wide sheet of white fabric on a roll that was suspended against the wall near the ceiling, as Nick looked into the camera at her she felt like a spotlight had been placed on her and didn't know what to do.

"Rayne, please take off the robe," he asked again.

The camera lens may as well have represented the eyes of the entire world and as she let the robe fall from her shoulders she felt aware of every single curve and bump in her body. She threw the robe onto a nearby chair and stood with one hand between her legs and the other across her breasts.

A few meters in front of her, bent over the camera and its tripod Nick spent some time flicking through lenses and said, "I need to change the background."

Because he didn't ask her to cover up she didn't bother as he pulled down the one background screen and hoisted up another one that was a slightly softer tone of white, "You have some very pleasing curves," he said as he did it, "Just want to make sure it all looks perfect."

He checked the camera a couple of times and then adjusted the screen narrating his actions as he went along about camera angles and tones, the correct lines and making the shadows look right. He used a remote control to adjust the lights hanging from scaffolding suspended from the ceiling and finally said, "Okay ready to begin?"

"Yes," she said.

"Okay, first Rayne, seriously you're going to have to loosen up."

She cleared her throat, "It's not that easy."

"Why not? Your videos are all done in front of a camera and you hardly look self-conscious in them?"

"I feel awkward and embarrassed here." she said. As she said it she realized she'd used a very sultry *come here and help me* tone, that had been entirely unintended.

Nick picked up on it, "Rayne look, we've got all afternoon to get this right. I want you to chill out and enjoy yourself. So take your hands down and show me some of the goods."

Resolutely she let her hands drop to her sides and was very much aware of how her breasts bounced.

"I feel fat," she said.

"You're not," Nick replied not looking away from his camera, "You're gorgeous and incredibly sexy and over a hundred billion views can't lie."

She lifted her chin slightly in what was a prim posturing, "Yes I have a hundred billion views under my belt of people looking under my belt,"

Nick laughed and turned his eyes up at her, gazing at her from under his brows, she thought his eyes were particularly beautiful, as gray as they were and he couldn't have picked a better sound track. Some bands just didn't go out of style. It was adding to a particularly electric environment.

"Amy," he called.

Upon request the makeup artist drifted into the studio, "Yeah?"

"Could you get Rayne some wine please," he raised his eyebrows to Rayne, "Red or white?"

She blinked, she wasn't much of a wine drinker, South Africans didn't drink their own wines they exported them. Maybe this was another British thing? "White, please."

She chose white because red made her think of bread and Italian food which made her stomach growl loudly. Amy floated out of the studio and returned almost immediately with a bottle of white wine and three glasses.

As she poured Nick explained, "Alcohol is the catalyst of all great art especially when your art relies on capturing people."

Amy handed Rayne a glass and rolled her eyes at Nick's line, "He is so full of shit."

"Hey," the photographer said, "It's true. "

Given him a glass the tall, slender assistant held hers delicately with only her fingertips and gave Rayne an appraising once-over look.

"So is the plan just to get me drunk?" Rayne asked.

"And then we're going to take some amazing photographs," Nick said lifting his glass and saying, "Salute."

Rayne woke up face down on a bed in her hotel room. Relieved to find herself there, but her mental reprieve was short lived as too quickly events of the night before came flooding back to her in a storm until she hit the point, at a London nightclub doing shots off of some footballer's stomach, that she blacked out. This was of particular concern to her as judging by the escalation of her behavior after each drink she could only imagine what may have transpired after she'd blacked out from drinking too much alcohol.

From where she lay she could see that that the one half of her hotel room was entirely unscathed and clean. This was the half that had the glorious view of the London Eye and Big Ben and she felt comforted by the fact that at least these historic monuments were still standing.

She couldn't see the other half of the hotel room and had a strong suspicion that she wasn't alone in the bed. Unless at some point in the evening she'd drunk something that wasn't on any of the menus and had grown an extra hand which was now cupping her left breast.

Fighting through a headache that should have featured in the morning news she assessed the situation.

She was in her hotel room, that was clear by her wheeled travel case lying under the window where she'd left it which put her in a clear advantage because whoever was in bed with her was technically trespassing.

It was a surprise to find out that it wasn't who she had expected it to be in bed with her. She had visions of rolling over and finding Nick Hardman lying next to her with a devilish grin on his face but instead it was Amy, whose last name she still didn't know.

The makeup artist was fast asleep and snoring peacefully, her short black hair in spiky disarray against the pillow and stacked up in neat piles on her side of the king sized bed bottles were stashed together with the density of a forest and featuring every kind of alcohol Rayne could name.

"Oooooh," she groaned.

Swirling from a hangover headache and the remnants of every reason why she shouldn't get behind the wheel she looked around the room to see if anything else caught her eye. She saw a scattering of clothing, half of which she recognized to be hers, two glasses on the table and a particularly large "personal friend" lying like a dead plastic slug on the rug. She looked at that for a while longer than anything else because, "That's not mine."

The closed bedroom door beckoned and warned her at the same time. She was tempted to look beyond that panel of wood but instinct warned her against it. If the door had been closed it was to create privacy and she still didn't know who might be on the other side. If she woke up with dear, fragile looking Amy on this side of the door, who might have been left on the other side?

Untangling herself from Amy's arms she felt the morning air drifting in from the open window unbearable on her naked skin and staggered around for something that she could put on. After some searching she found a robe in the en-suite that she slung around herself and tied across her middle. With her head pounding on every step she opened the bedroom door a fraction and peeped through the gap.

The hotel living room looked like the aftermath of a college graduation party: Bottles of alcohol, mostly empty stood brazen and transparent on every available flat service while unconscious people lay on every other surface. A memory of something or other involving Nick inviting a lot of his model friends to come and party at Rayne Ensley's returned and she closed her eyes trying to draw out any details that would come back to haunt her. Unfortunately there were many available to do just that.

She pushed the door the rest of the way open and was aghast to see what the rest of the living room area looked like. Mostly there were just people dressed in as little as possible with a vast majority of them being women with only a couple of men in attendance. One of them was Nick who was spread out across the couch in just his boxers. The boxers were clearly not designed to handle such a package and she felt that the organ was staring at her as she rounded the couch. Then and there she decided that there was nothing at all attractive about a flaccid penis, no matter how prominent. She slapped Nick on the forehead. He grunted and farted.

"Watthefucksgonnaon?" he mumbled, swatting at the invisible fly he thought had landed on his forehead.

"Out Nick," she told him, carefully tiptoeing over the unconscious semi naked bodies across her floor, "I want these people out of my hotel room so I can have breakfast."

"These hotels rooms don't come with kitchens," Nick said, rolling over, "You have to go downstairs for breakfast."

Exasperation peaked when she walked into the bathroom and found the tub filled with half a dozen people, none of whom looked like they would be very comfortable when they woke up.

She turned on her heel and made her way back to her room, as she passed Nick who was facing into the couch, she flicked his ear as hard as she could and he once again tried to swat the imaginary fly.

"Out!" she said, "Get them out!" she slammed the door, opened it and said, "Please," and slammed it again. With the door closed she leant her whole weight against it, grateful for its solidity. She recalled that at some point during the evening that the parameters had been set between her and Nick that although he had taken some very compromising images of her, they had gone out almost entirely on her card and that made her the boss which made it alright her demanding that he forthwith empty the apartment of the horde of unconscious people.

Minus one, the unconscious bird who was currently waking up in her bed.

"Morning," Amy said, rubbing her mascara across her cheek with the back of her hand, "Jesus on toast I feel rough."
Considering that the flat panel of the door was currently the most stable thing in Rayne's existence she found it difficult to come up with any clever retort to such a statement. Nor could she summon up an inspired limerick or memorable line to sum up the awkwardness of not knowing what happened with the person you woke up with. It was a state of affairs she probably should not have been surprised with anymore. What she managed was: "If you call me honey I'm going to hurl,"
Through half lidded eyes Amy gave her a questioning stare, "What do you South African's call it? *Babelas?*"
"*Jy is a bietjie babelas?*" Rayne automatically said.
Amy grunted in agreement and put her palm to her forehead. It looked like she pushed her head down because it hit the pillow with a thump that sounded as final as another hour at least.
Rayne brought her fingertips up and massaged her temples: Okay, what do you remember from last night?
Her eyes were immediately drawn to the large nine inch "special friend" lying discarded on the carpet as if it were tossed there. It wasn't hers; she hadn't brought it… so why did she remember holding it?
As if she just blasted open the flood gates with dynamite images poured into her brain and filled her mind with every reason why Amy would solemnly refuse to leave the bed.
Taking her phone from the dresser she headed into the en-suite, grateful to find that it was unoccupied, locked the door behind her and ran a very hot bath.
While the water filled the tub she sent a text to Nick reaffirming her demands of getting everyone out and then added a second text asking him to take Amy with him.

On a banner large enough to cover the entire front of the Earls Court Exhibition Centre, the Soft Kitty Awards were printed in big pink, round letters that made Rayne think of jelly beans and lit up by floodlights that made the letters sparkle. Additional spot lights set up along the large curving driveway reached up to the sky and revealed just how heavy the cloud cover was over London. Despite this the red carpeted entrance to the venue was rammed on both sides by people in suits carrying cameras and snapping away at the demi-gods gracing the carpet.

The tradition at these shows was for the guys to wear tuxedos and the gals to dress like... well, very expensive whores. Rayne had gone the other way and was dressed in a slinky black dress that had a slanted hem sliding down from midway up her left thigh to a point on her right knee. It showed enough of her cleavage to be considered teasing and enough leg to be sophisticated. Her hair had a slight tinge of red in it for taste and her makeup had been professionally catered for.

Brett lined the Mercedes up behind the other vehicles, which included Humveys, BMWS, Porsches and Aston Martins, like a conveyor belt each car pulled up in front of the red carpet and the occupants stepped out. None of the lady's had partners and each was met as they stepped out of the car by an escort in a tuxedo who then walked her down the carpet and Rayne was glad about that tradition in particular. The ladies arrived alone as if the intention was to leave in the same fashion.

Music blared over the loudspeakers, security guards drifted like sharks through the crowds of photographers and the fans who stood with their posters waving them about. She spotted one man struggle to the front of the crowd as one of the adult models, a girl Rayne knew as Sandra who everyone else knew as Cindy Deep stepped out of her car, he shoved his hand down in his pants in a lewd gesture but before he could pull it out one of the guards appeared at his side and he was swallowed into the crowd.

A lot was happening so she didn't know if Brett had seen the little spectacle but he said, almost on cue, "I would be careful Miss. Ensley, sometimes people like to throw semen at the stars."

Finally their car made it to the carpet and when it had come to a complete stop one of the escorts opened the door and let the noise from outside in. The suited escort offered his arm which she took and allowed herself to be helped out.

Remember to smile, she thought and froze her best toothy grin on her face. After a few steps the escort stopped moving and hesitantly she stopped and looked at him, "Are you okay?" she asked.

He smiled, perhaps he was from a modeling agency, happy to get his big break at this and be seen in the pictures with Rayne Ensley, he didn't sound grateful though as he said through the corner of his mouth, "Look at the cameras."

"I am,"

"Slowly," he hissed again through his manic smile.

Smiling until her cheeks burned she looked across the crowds of people to her left and then her right, the photographers and paparazzi might have thought she was looking at their cameras for a decent photograph especially as there were more than enough pictures of her making bizarre faces when she'd been captured half way between expressions gracing the gossip rags and pads, but in honesty she was keeping an eye on anyone who might be preparing to hurl some bodily fluid at her.

Inside, huge pink silks were slung across the immensely high stadium roof and the entire floor of the venue which had been used by the biggest music stars in the world and could hold over fifty thousand people, was filled with stalls, stands, ramps and ropes cordoning off special privileged areas, television and holographic displays were on everywhere while the latest tracks played on the overheads. The venue was packed with spectators and ticket holders while performers like her kept to the "red" area, the paths lined with red ropes. Inside there were still more photographs to be taken as she made her way to the main venue where she was expected to hob-nob with the other celebrities before the main awards.

What to everyone else was a glamorous evening to her was a painfully long exercise in smiling and balancing on her suicidal high heels that left her exhausted and desperate for a stiff drink.

The event went on, as so many of these things did, without any problems. She picked up an award for best soloist, smiled at the audience, said some silly prepared speech over the microphone (which she tiptoed to reach) that got some laughs but not many and returned to her seat and spent another hour watching the nominee videos and the other performers collecting awards.

At first, like most things, it had been mildly arousing, but soon she was just thinking about getting back to her room. She had a terrible headache and as soon as the final award was given she called Brett and met him out front, got into the backseat and was back at the hotel before any of the rush.

She received a few texts, a few miscalls from various people, agents, colleagues, PR people, but she ignored all of them. She told the clerk at the hotel front desk to *not* let anyone up, and then specified it clearly:

"I don't want *anyone* let up to my room," she said with wide eyes, "Anyone. Understand?"

Straight up to her room she stripped down naked and put on some loud music and paced restlessly while removing her makeup. She ran herself a deep bath with bubbles and soaked in there while channel hopping on the holographic screen. You got more channels in UK than you did in South Africa and although there was more censorship, you still tended to get more sex but less violence than SA. It was like peeping through a keyhole and seeing a completely different world that spoke the same language but only differently, walked differently and clearly enjoyed different programming. She'd never seen so many reality television shows, football shows and soap operas.

Peeping through a keyhole, she had some experience in that area didn't she?

Her phone rang and she saw the number and answered it quickly, "Hey you," she said.

"Hiya," Carly said, "Can you talk?"

"Yeah of course I can," Rayne replied, straightening her leg out of the water and tracing a circle on her inner thigh with a finger, "Just in the bath."

"Serious?" the girl on the other side sounded surprised, "Shouldn't you be out gallivanting and getting into trouble?"

Rayne laughed, "Don't you read the tabloids, I've done all of that already."

The news about her party had made it to the net and the people who made a living out of criticizing her every step and life decision had purred at the information available about that night. She had found herself in the novel position of piecing together the night in question with pictures she found online. It was all rather embarrassing but of course she didn't tell Carly that.

"I haven't heard much about it over here," the girl said, "But I did hear you got an award. Congratulations."

"Thanks," Rayne said, "News does travel fast."

"So... yeah," Carly said, "I just wanted to call and say hi."

"Cool, hi," Rayne said with a giggle, "Is that all?"

"Yeah, okay bye,"

And the girl hung up.

Rayne frowned and looked at her phone as if it was going to explain to her what had just happened. She put it on the side and continued enjoying her bath until she got a text a minute later which read:

BEEN THINKING ABOUT IT, AND I NEED SOMEONE WHO HAS A BETTER APPRECIATION FOR THINGS THAN YOU. YOU'RE GREAT BUT I DON'T THINK WE CAN BE TOGETHER HON. SORRY. LUV CARLY.

Rayne read the text through twice, then put the phone down, picked it up and read it again completely perturbed.

"Since when were we 'together'?" she thought aloud and tickled at the absurdity of the text she laughed loudly and tossed the phone away hearing it bounce along the tiles. (For over a decade mobile phones had become near indestructible and the treatment of them had declined). She watched some of the channels for over an hour and once the bath was cold she turned on the hot jets and turned it a hot tub. She waved through the channels until; inevitably she found a program regarding her video. This one was a bunch of nerdy Americans trying to prove that the video was just one of a number of prominent fake videos on the internet. She watched with a morbid sense of irony as they systematically proved that it what she knew was a real video, was actually fabricated.

"I wonder where he is," she said, watching the repeated image of the giant which was their main argument that no man of that size could go undetected in Durban City so therefor, it had to be a computer generated forgery.

The giant.

The Coat.

Despite what these Americans thought, there was an indestructible giant living in South Africa who was part of a race of giants who could *never* die. That was connected, somehow, to a genetic line of humans of which Tuck Bradley was a part of, who was also, immortal. By knowing them she was connected to a world that overlapped her own in time and space and mass. Her own world was a nearly make believe chain of unexpected successes and celebrity living. Entirely unattached to the *real* world because she had no financial worries and she stood on a bridge between two fantasy worlds with the river of reality gently flowing far below but she couldn't even dip her toe into it.

She reached out of the water with a hand and plucked the glass of rum she had on the side. Rum was the most unsophisticated drink in the world because it had no prejudices, no standards and it would go well with any occasion. She had tried whiskey but found it to be a very angry drink but rum was happy and easy. While she took little sips of it she waved off of the channel with the nerds trying to find something else.

Shouldn't it have been harder to accept? Or was her acceptance based on what was real to her and what wasn't. Before the incident she could not have accepted the idea of a true immortal but having met one it had brought the scenario into the realm of her reality. Her life. There *was* a race of giants that could not die. The Coat could not die.

She put the glass of rum onto the wide rim of the tub and with a small adjustment to the way she sat slid easily under the water. The tub was large and she was very small so she could almost do the breathstroke from one end to the other.

Over the countless times she had revisited the events she had slowly extrapolated a summation. Tuck had said that The Coat's species, his race, all of them except for him, were kept in a container that had been found in Antarctica under the ice. But he had also inferred that it had not been built there but rather had been deposited there, like a trunk being deposited on the shores of an island after a shipwreck. However the trunk was an impervious metal containing almost a thousand immortals and the ocean waves were magmatic currents. Continental drift had dropped that container there. That meant that those giants had been in there for a very, very long time. It meant that The Coat was possibly one of the oldest things in existence.

None of it had sunk in until much later, but Rayne fully understood it now. As a child of the twenty first century she possessed a schooling grasp of human evolution, the importance of genetic memory that allowed species to change and adapt. The fact that The Coat looked human was merely a matter of timing. To the Neanderthal or early man he would have appeared monstrous and deformed, a million years in the future when mankind had completely changed into something *different* he will once again be alien. That was the tragedy of real immortality, a complete separation inevitably occurred; humans would keep developing, the human mind would grow, change, shift, become stronger, faster and more intelligent, their bodies would change too. Computer-cerebral interfaces would take mankind beyond the mere confines of natural evolution and through all of this The Coat's kind would just remain the same. Left behind. Even when life on Earth vanished, they would just be left behind.

Like a spike driving through the nicely spread table-cloth of her life, everything was pulled in against it, it drew everything into one devastating question: How important was her life compared to his? To a person who had been alive for so long, hours would pass by in split seconds, days would appear to be minutes. How could one human life, a span of eighty or so years mean anything to someone who'd been alive indefinitely?

She had once worded it brilliantly, "I could only compare his existence to the life of stars and even they will die before him,"

She refilled her glass from the bottle and alternately washed and conditioned her hair while drinking it. She rinsed it thoroughly and, a little wobbly, climbed out of the tub and into a big warm robe. Walking with her hand trailing against the wall to stabilize herself she put on the kettle to make some strong coffee and while the kettle boiled stood at the window looking out over London. It was all very bold and beautiful, The Houses of Parliament, The London Eye and Thames all magnificently lit up in golden lights, even the roads with their never-ending stream of traffic added to the beauty.

"Lights on half," she said.

The management system in the room clicked each of the lights on and muted them to half strength. As the lights clicked on she saw in the reflection upon the window someone standing behind her. She shrieked and spun around but found that she was alone.

The kettle boiled and clicked off.

"You are the epitome of fucked up," she said savagely to herself, and said, "Television," the screen lit up merrily onto the last channel she had on in the bathroom and while she watched made-up characters in a made-up world act upon a made-up script, she said, "Maybe you should take up drugs? This addiction to paranoia has to end. Lights on full."

The lights vaporized the shadows and she glanced around the hotel room. It was a gorgeous, spacious, well-furnished and highly proficient at having hiding places. She found something funny to watch on the TV, curled up on the sofa, tucking the bottom of her bathrobe under her feet and watched the mindless natter.

The person who was there continued to watch her, unseen. Over the back of the sofa the figure could only see Rayne's left shoulder and her right hand hanging off the edge with a finger extended, the digit flicked every so often when she wanted to change channels but soon the finger started flicking less regularly as she fell asleep.

When her finger had stopped entirely the figure approached as silent as a specter. A tall, athletic form in a black combat suit, as it neared it slipped a small device from a utility belt that looked like a gun but with a very slender barrel. It took this and aimed it at the side of Rayne's exposed neck. Along the small indented line between the muscle of her neck and her throat until the tip of the barrel was only a centimeter from her skin. The figure pulled the trigger and a puff of air shot out of the barrel with enough force to ruffle Rayne's hair.

Rayne woke with a start, her hand clapping over the point of her neck that had been touched but there was nothing there and she was still alone. She sucked on her bottom lip for a second then left the living room and went to her room.

The figure sent a text and left.

24.

One of the first casualties of the modern networking age was privacy. When artificial intelligence and near instant connectivity changed the way people viewed things, everything of value shifted. Thanks to a mobile phone app that allowed people to triangulate the locations of their favorite celebrities using CCTV uplinks and networking with other phones of people who had seen said celebrity, Rayne found that she couldn't go anywhere in London without somebody recognizing her.

"Shouldn't you be used to that by now?" Nick asked, as he heard Rayne tell him the latest travesty that the paparazzi had forced her into. The pair of them were enjoying coffees in a city center coffee shop before Rayne caught an express to the airport. They had chosen the window seat because it had provided her with a place from where she could people watch, but it hadn't taken long before people, their eyes continuously dropping to their phone screens had found their way to the coffee shop. And once the tables and chairs inside had filled up with gawking people, the street outside had done the same.

"Used to what?" Rayne asked, using the food menu to shield herself from the faces at the window and slouching in her chair so that the people to her left in the coffee house itself couldn't hear what she was saying.

Nick seemed absolutely at home with the attention, in fact like a sunflower he was turning towards its sunny glow, "People's attention. I mean I don't get it- you've got enough money that if you don't like the industry attention why don't you just stop? You don't need the money after all."

"I like being busy," she said.

"Nah, it's more than that," Nick said, revealing a tiny glimmer of a deeper level to himself, "Maybe you just like shagging?" he continued, removing it.

"I shouldn't have to pay for my privacy," Rayne said, her eyes on the chai-latte she hadn't even touched yet out of fear of seeing another *slurping* picture on the internet, "Besides, I'm just tired of everything at the moment. London's worse than Durban, its ridiculous."

"I'm surprised you think anything could be worse than Durban,"

Nick mentioned, thoroughly enjoying his Americano, "At least here it's because you're a porno star at least here it's for you, over there it's because of The Coat."

"That's unfair," she said.

He halfheartedly shrugged as if it were a moot point.

"No it really is," she persisted, "Yes they like me here for the shows but at least in South Africa I hear a variety of shouts across the street. It's not all about leaning back and spreading them!"

Nick drummed the table with his fingers and looked around embarrassed, "Keep your voice down Rayne."

"I'm just tired," she slouched in her chair and checked her watch, the express was leaving in an hour and the station was only across the street but the road was blocked by crowds standing in the grey rain chanting her name. London it seemed was baying for her to leave and had given her every reason in the world, rain and a mob of perverts.

"This is incredible," Nick said, pretending to be unaware of the people staring at both of them and failing hopelessly to keep a smile from his face. His joviality was getting on her nerves, he continued, "Just think right now millions of people worldwide are looking at pictures of us drinking coffee here. That's crazy isn't it?"

"Not really," Rayne said, peeking out from behind the menu at the sea of upturned faces, "This has been happening for days now."

"Serious?" Nick asked and almost sounded hurt that he'd only been involved at the very end.

"Yeah," she said raising her eyebrows, "The hotels had to ask me to travel out the rear entrance, I've had to be driven in a different car every day and we stopped at a Nandos for some take away and they had to call the police in so I could get out of the bathroom. I had an escort to accompany me the entire six metres from the restaurant to my car-"

"I'm still imperial," Nick said, "Not metric."

"About twenty feet," she said, lancing him with her eyes, "Anyway they've been following me *everywhere*. Like flies."

"They *are* the ones that give you a career," he reminded her.

"No, they're not," Rayne countered, "They're just the ones that want a picture of me doing something stupid."

Nick delivered a very dramatic sigh and enjoyed a long, very deliberate drink of his Americano.

"So," he said, looking pointedly at her when someone outside bared his genitals just at the moment a police officer arrived on the scene to sort everything out, "You're telling me that you're not going to miss this kind of attention back home?"

There was a flash from below as the man was tasered by a police officer and some mild dispersal of the crowd, like the effect of firing a shotgun into a swarm of locusts the brief scattering was quickly filled in. Rayne put down the menu and turned away from the window only to find a young couple sitting at a table openly staring at her. She looked down at her boots and then to Nick, "Not for a second." she said.

"Come on," he ushered, "It hasn't been that bad has it?"

Rayne considered the events of recent days. There had been the usual flood of activity, with interviews, online meetings with fans and of course the follow up parties of Soft Kitty Awards but everyone had made the mistake of giving her time to herself and she had found herself with periods of nothing to do.

She had visited half of London's nightclubs in less than a week and partied with the cream of the world's musicians and film stars. She had out-drunk most of them and had managed to cross paths with every form of drugs that they were passed around the VIP rooms. Several mornings she had woken up in her hotel room without any recollection of how she got there and on the other nights she had woken up in someone else's bed with a real hope she was at least still in Britain. The internet had burned red hot with images of her 'partying' and the English media had at first soaked it up like a sponge and then squeezed it tight and hard to get the last bit of juice out of it. Gossip was one thing but there were images, there were videos and now there were even holograms. Not only had she drunk, snorted and danced London to its knees she had taken most of the celebrity highlife from the same level.

"Just think of it as a PR exercise," Nick suggested as he watched out the window as the police tried to control the pressing mob. More cars had arrived with flashing lights and men in uniform were pushing crowds away from the street with batons, they looked like they were herding cattle, "London thrives on this sort of thing. The celebrities draw the crowds in, the coppers beat them back, and the fans hate the coppers and become more determined to see the celebrities who take bigger risks and chances to get the coppers back to beat up their fans. It's a beautiful cycle."

"That is an adorable reflection," Rayne said with mild ridicule, "What are you going to do without me?"

Nick faked a fairly decent expression of depression, "I'll go back to taking pictures of the mundane British celebrities,"

"Who all talk funny?" Rayne laughed.

"Hey not everyone is blessed with such a *Suid Afrikaan* accent," he clipped, "Some of us just have to sound common so we can get into the common girl's knickers."

Rayne giggled.

"Are you going to miss me?" Nick asked out of the blue.

She gave a groan of exasperation, flattened the menu on the table and put her face in her hands, "You too?" she gasped, "*You?* Nick Hardman the man who's penis has been in more countries than his brain? You? What the hell dude?!"

"I'm sorry I-"

"My driver confessed his love to me this morning," she said, cutting him off, "Damn well got down on one knee and proposed to me, I've only known him for a month."

"I can't blame-"

"And now you, *Are you going to miss me?* What kind of question is that Nick? Have we even shagged?"

"Well yes," he answered his gray eyes blank with such a resounding honesty that her throat instantly went dry.

"I don't remember that," she said quickly.

"We ran into each other at the DogPile Club," he said, "Shit Rayne you don't remember?"

She closed her eyes, "No. No I don't remember that..." she bit her lower lip with trepidation, "... did I shag Brett?"

Nick's expression turned guilty and the couple sitting opposite them started texting on their phones. Rayne folded her arms on the table and dropped her face into them.

A constant buzz of conversation and noise had filled the coffee house for long enough for both of them to ignore it, but a new sound reached her ears and Rayne looked up in time to see a police officer, in the black trousers and the traditional Londoner tall *bobby* policeman's hat strut in, he made eye contact with her immediately and, revealing more about her life than she cared to admit her first thought was, *Tell me I didn't shag you too?* Weaving through the tables and chairs and the people in them who were already using their phones to film this police officer seemed entirely oblivious to their attention. Aimed as he was for their table.

"Excuse me for intruding," he grunted, "But are you the cause of all the commotion outside?"

His tone was not merely direct, but scathing. It seemed that what he wanted to do was throw her out the window into the crowd as if he hoped they would tear her apart if he did. She was almost too shocked to answer and Nick replied, "No officer, we're just enjoying some coffee."

Ignoring Nick the officer pointed a finger out the window at the crowd, his dark eyes glared with open hatred for her, "Those people are holding up the pedestrian pass way, they're causing a great deal of havoc. I want to know what you are going to do about it."

Rayne's mouth dropped, "I'm sorry? Me?"

"Your shit," he snarled and spit blew from his lips and splashed into her drink, "You clean it up."

"Pardon me mate," Nick said standing, "But isn't that your job?"

The police officer applied his glare to Nick and growled, "I'm doing my job my sonny boy alright? Why don't you sit down and shut your yapper alright?"

Rayne checked her watch.

"Oh I'm sorry," the police officer snorted, "Am I keeping you?"

"Look," Rayne said, standing, and finding to her delight that the police office wasn't actually that tall at all; his hat gave him some added height. But even if he had been taller, it didn't matter she'd had enough, "Constable, or whatever rank you are. You're being rude to me and a friend of mine in a public place with over twenty people currently videoing this for the internet that include you *and* me. You might think that if you get caught being a complete dick to me that people might think you're hard and give you some respect but let's get this straight everyone is just going to know that you are just a dick - and trust me I know this you're a short one at that. So please get out of my way and let me clean up the mess that you don't seem to be able to handle. Come on Nick," she took her coat from the back of her chair and walked away from the police officer who was now looking trepidatiously at the forest of phone cameras held up at him, Rayne was a little way away when she stopped, "Oh and one last thing, that hat makes you look like a character from Noddy."

Taking the time to pay their bill at the till Rayne proceeded to walk straight for the door, giving the bigger police officer who had hung back at the entrance a smile and a nod which to her surprise was reciprocated, he added, "Don't worry Miss, Constable Bobble is a dick,"

"Oh my God," Nick chuckled, "His name is Bobble?"

She crossed the street with her hand luggage bouncing on its wheels behind her and the police swatting off fans and photographers and caught the passenger express to the airport. She kissed Nick on the cheek and avoided his hand as he tried to take hers and bolted for the train and hid in the bathroom until it had started to move and she was able to go to her window seat and watch the world go passed her without Nick trying to follow her down the tracks.

Her opinion of London was complete, she had arrived with a chauffeur and she was leaving on a public train, sitting next to an overweight business man who was eating a packet of cheese and onion crisps. Funny how things turn out.

She corrected herself, this wasn't a public train. The 'express' was as public as Sky City and only flight passengers could take it. It was a faster line, on more comfortable furnishings and was expensive. It would have been delightful if not for the intolerable wet eating sound of the fat bloke in a suit shoveling handfuls of crisps into his mouth. He didn't pick them up he simply took them by the handful and rammed them into his gob so that his lips closed over all his four fingers.

She arrived at the Heathrow with half an hour to spare and checked in her luggage on the First Class desk, collected her boarding pass and was ushered through the airport floor and onto the plane like a fart slipping through the trousers.

Mason found the light in the bathroom to be too sharp and had it turned down to a dim glimmer. He walked across its spacious tiled floor to the mirror above the wide bowl of the basin and looked at the man in the reflection. Christ he looked rough. After four days straight of training down stairs his skin was as thin as carbon paper and his muscles were as striated as a bunch of straws. A dense river mapping of thick vascular tubes traced from his neck, across his shoulders and down his arms. The veins pumped and writhing, his beard thick, crawling high up his cheeks and was itching like a carpet.

He turned on the hot water tap and washed his hands with several squirts of the anti-bacterial soap that he kept here. This was of course out of habit rather than necessity.

He washed his face with a coconut flavored conditioning ointment to loosen up the facial hair before applying shaving gel to his jaw line. With the steam rising in tendrils from the basin and forming beads of water on the steam-proof mirror he started the manly process of shaving. He had tried many methods of shaving over his years, he had tried a cut throat blade but had always found it a little too Sweeny Todd, he had toyed with an electric razor but found a wet shave with a Gillette was still truly, the best a man could get. Also, as he shaved against the grain he needed the sharpest one on the market. Cutting himself wasn't a problem but he didn't like the feeling of pulling out facial hair. With practiced ease he finished the job and did the usual act of running his hands across his jaw and smiling at himself at the result. He washed his face with steaming water and had an equally steamy shower.

It took him an hour to get all the grimy sweat off his body and it felt like he was washing deeper than just the skin. He shampooed and conditioned his hair, spent an appropriate amount of time sorting out the hair downstairs with a razor he kept separate from the one he used for his face and allowed himself the luxury of drip drying while stretching and listening to the news updates over the speakers.

There was the usual nonsense, the usual media hypes and he flicked from story to story quickly and had gone through all the relevant news channels before he was completely dry. The only thing that interested him was that Rayne Ensley had returned to South Africa, leaving London in ashes.

"Get Alan on the phone," he said to the management system.
Promptly as always Alan's voice sounded through the room, "Yes sir,"
"I don't know what the time is Alan," Mason greeted him, "My apologies if it's late."

"Its one thirty in the morning sir," Alan said, "But not to worry I was up in any case."

Mason didn't doubt it for a moment. He was well aware of Alan's out of work activities. He didn't believe in micromanagement but he did believe in knowing people's secrets and he knew all of Alan's.

"How are things going Alan?" he asked.

"Everything is going well sir," Alan replied, "The synthesized oil compound has been tested on both unleaded petrol cars and diesel engines with the expected results. Of course that's caused some trouble with the fuel companies."

"Send them a fruit basket," Mason said. Which was a code between the two gentlemen for, *I don't care what these big companies want to do I'm going to do this anyway and it's going to really screw them over so send them a fruit basket.*

"Yes sir," Alan said, "That is literally it sir. How have the last couple of days been for you?"

"Fairly hardcore," Mason replied, "I want to organize this United Nations meeting, I think it's time to make a move on that."

"Yes sir,"

"And the acquisitions?"

"All very amicable sir, the press are dying to know how you expect to make a profit when you buy companies for twice their asking price." Mason laughed, "Give them a statement about long term planning. I'm going to chill out today but book me a flight to Poland tomorrow if you wouldn't mind I need to go scratch some backs."

Scratching backs, was another way of going and making friends with people who had no choice but to be friends with him because he was the one who was buying all their companies and pumping money into their economy like a paramedic holding a car accident victim's heart in his hands.

He flicked a finger and the phone hung up. He rolled his eyes and swore at himself for being so weak and called Alan back.

"Alan,"

"Yes. Sir?"

"How is she?"

"She's doing very well sir. Very healthy."

"Good to know,"

Hanging up for the second time he pulled on some clothes, poured a drink and spent some time on his balcony. He wasn't alone for long.

"I was wondering when I was going to be seeing you," he said,

leaning over the railing to better enjoy the early morning view, adding for his own benefit, "The city looks so peaceful up here."
For a creature that stood at eight and a half feet tall The Coat moved with the silence of air and when the trillionaire turned around and saw him standing on the curved rooftop of his office he noted how much he resembled a comic book superhero. Not one of the colorful, leotard wearing ones, but one of the darker ones, the dark ones that made vigilante into a *cruel* word. That's what The Coat looked like a cruel vigilante. Mason leaned back against the railing and saluted the giant with his glass of whiskey.
His hands shoved into his pockets, the wind tugged at the hems of his coat turning them into wings while the hood just formed a heart shaped hole of black. Mason was fine with him standing there; he adored the sight of him. His proportions were just... insane... before him stood the perfect combination of beauty and power. The beauty was in the grace that he moved and the power in his silent presence. His clothes straining across the incredible breadth of his shoulders, the high arches of his trapezius clearly defined even under the great coat.

"But I can be a patient man," he continued, "And I hold too many of the pieces of this game for you not to come calling."
The Coat took a breath and in the still night Mason could hear the deep echo of the air in his lungs. It was the sort of breathing you'd expect to hear turn into a roar at any second.

"I imagine that Tuck Bradley has probably told you the truth about me," Mason said, "Or his version of the truth. I know he has been looking for you and that he wants the sword."

"So do you,"

"Yes," Mason said with a smile and a pause, it was such a beautiful voice, "I do want the sword but my reasons are pure. Can't you tell?"
The Coat said nothing which was enough of an answer.

"Do you know why you cannot read my mind?" he asked.
No response. So Mason decided to hold onto that little secret.

"I am here to ask you something," The Coat said.
Mason drank deeply from his glass, as it was the first thing in his stomach for four days and he felt the hot liquid go all the way down, "Ask away."
The Coat walked forward and stepped off the roof of Mason's office. There was a drop of five meters but he landed with less sound than a

fingernail tapping against the surface of a breadboard, the whisper of the coat moving through the air was louder and he seemed to take the drop entirely upon his ankles, barely bending his knees. He walked towards Mason who was forced to look higher and higher until he was craning his neck to look up. There the trillionaire realized that it wasn't just the size of The Coat that made him what he was. It was his presence and his smell.

"Someone has been kidnapping children," the giant said.

"This is Durban," Mason pointed out, "Children vanish every day."

"Not like these ones," the giant said, "Do you know who it is?"

Mason swallowed hard, tried to shift some moisture into his mouth, "I have no need to kidnap anyone."

He stepped sideways and walked away from The Coat, trying to put some distance between them just so he could think clearly, he was several paces away before the giant turned to face him. Mason stopped near the side door of his office, from there at least he could think, "And it's not my style to kidnap children," he said, "I long to protect the people and to guide them, to teach them. I want to bring about an age of enlightenment where all nations can come together and be as one."

The Coat replied, "I am not interested."

"You should be," Mason pressed, "You are playing a major part in my plans, and you have a fundamental role in protecting people. The people of this city. You're vital to their lives. Why do you think I've gone to such lengths to protect you from the security cameras across Sky City to offer you some anonymity?"

"Who is the kidnapper?"

Mason snorted at the giant's inability to prioritize and looked at his drink, "Can I assume that you think it's one of my staff then?"

He looked up and The Coat wasn't there anymore, and a voice said from behind him, "Who is the kidnapper Mason?"

Mason finished the drink, "Look, Coat... do I call you Coat?"

... nothing.

"Right," Mason said, his eyebrows knitted, "Look you're going to have to start talking more you know. I can't read your mind any more than you can read mine. Now, unfortunately I think it might very well be one of my staff."

The Coat's posture suggested that he hadn't thought otherwise, or he wouldn't have come to his office. Mason quickly elaborated, "His name is Shaka. He is a Hunter and that sword you're carrying is sacred to his people and your head is sacred to him."

"Is that not you're doing?"

"Originally," Mason admitted, looking out over the city, "I wanted your head because I was angry. You hurt me Daemon. The pain of my rejuvenation stung something fierce and I gave Shaka what he needed to do my bidding. It was a mistake and since then he has gone rogue."

The trillionaire turned back to the giant, arms spread, "I swear to you I don't know his plans and I don't know where he is."

"What about all your technology?"

"He has a full working knowledge of the systems," Mason explained, "He's using the same mechanism to avoid my security and surveillance that I've used to protect you all this time. I've tried to find him but Shaka is physically stronger than me now."

"How?"

"Tuck must have told you about that?" Mason probed, "I've got the blood of your brethren in my veins and so does Shaka but he was formidable as a human and I was just an old man. Maybe that's why I'm happy with my strengths but he's greedy and wants more, he wants your blood."

"So did you," The Coat growled, and an accusing edge made his voice into a blade when he said, "Do not take me around in circles Mason."

"I have all eternity to wait for your blood," Mason snarled, his own rage surfacing, "I've been training myself to exhaustion to become stronger so that I could take Shaka because if I make mistakes I *always* repair them."

"Does that include Rayne Ensley?"

The trillionaire bit his lower lip; it was his time to say nothing. It was a blow that revealed his weakness.

"Haven't you ever done something that you regretted?" he asked the giant, "Or are you immune to being haunted by them?"

Conversation over, Daemon turned and walked away.

"I want to help you," Mason called after him, "Please."

"Help if you want," Daemon said as he was leaving, "Save these children. They are unique. Save them and you will have my thanks but

either way I will be back to discuss *my* brethren."
And he was over the balcony and gone.

There was something wrong with Tammy Jenkins. Her house, which had been a quiet and secure sanctuary for her was now the noisiest place on the planet. It felt like the walls were screaming at her and not just at her ears, if smells and sights could scream they would be doing that too. Everything was amplified: she couldn't take a step without hearing it echoing through the entire house as if it were a chapel, there was a wasp nest in the ceiling rafters outside which she'd never known about but now they sounded like they were each the size of a jet ski. The smells, they were the worst and she had never noticed it before but smells hung around like balloons, they just float around and deflate over time. *Everything* had a smell now. It was like being submerged in a pool of scents.

There were other changes happening too. She was running a fever, her head hurt and her skin was clammy.

She had been on the toilet for an entire afternoon with a bucket on her lap which had to be emptied to get rid of the disgusting levels of blood and muck that poured out of her body as if her organs were liquidizing. She had been crying all day, the tears of someone whose body is not doing what it's supposed to.

Tammy had always been an outsider, with her body sock of tattoos, her ever changing hair colour and her myriad of piercings but she was also a private person and clean. Despite what her outward appearance might have been she was actually very finicky and to be reduced to this filth; being afraid to stand up in case everything just poured out of her was intolerable.

A fresh heave brought up a gut full of rusty tasting blood as thick as soup and as red as wine, the heaving action that projected out one end had the exact result on the other and there was an answering series of splashes from the toilet bowl. Seeing so much of her own blood in the bucket frightened her.

She had never been told how her parents had died? Was this how?

There wasn't any pain, just an uncomfortable feeling of things happening. Days earlier, actually the very day after she had seduced her giant she had woken up with a feeling of something moving in her belly that had been accompanied by an unnatural sound inside, but there had been no pain and so she had ignored it.

Had her mother made the same mistake?

And what if her giant came to visit her today and saw her like this what would he think? She thought about what she would do if he did arrive and it was the same solution she had for everything else at the moment, quite simply, don't get off the toilet.

More dry heaves and she emptied herself, spluttering for breath around the stuff that came out.

Her giant had split her, in his lust he had split her like a reverse labour, and it was one of the most prominent memories in her head. It had hurt but she had been so *involved* in the moment that she didn't care, she had ridden the pain into waves of pleasure she had never experienced before. But he had split her and she had not gone to the hospital, out of fear they would ask questions or worse make her give answers.

Waking up the following morning she had tried to remember the details. She had been thinking through a shroud of golden mist generated by his smell and trying to remember it was like trying to remember being drunk. Everything was slightly distorted and disorientated. The pain stuck out in her mind and she had investigated herself gingerly and found that despite the clear memory of feeling her skin stretch and split and tear, that she was fine. Despite the mess of blood that was left from the night before when the giant had well and truly taken her, she was fine.

She spat out blood that was congealing in her mouth and adjusted her position on the toilet, the seating rim was cutting into her buttocks. Her giant, at the point of climax had withdrawn and sprayed the basement with the intensity of a fire hose, it had been the single most erotic experience of her entire life but upon achieving such a hearty climax he had become distraught, clearly regret stricken and apologetic. She had tried to calm him, had touched his face and tried to kiss him to assure him that he had done nothing wrong.

He clearly had known something she had not.

There was a blank point in her memory there, the reel of her memory skipped straight to her waking up in bed, intact and feeling remarkably good. What had her giant done to her?

The sun was setting outside and the bathroom was becoming darker. The *things* were growing curious; she had been listening to their questions every night since it had happened. They were concerned for her. They loved her. They wanted her. She didn't understand any of it.

Her piercings were causing her problems too. All of them seem to be festering and she was taking them out one by one and dropping them into a cup of antiseptic fluid to sterilize them.

Bent over the bucket with her spine, shoulders and ribs sticking out against the skin you could see that the dense tattoos had begun to fade as the ink was absorbed into her body and added to the waste that was coming out. In the myriad picture scrap book of her back the pictures were beginning to unravel leaving pages of bare, perfect skin behind.

She was crying again, sobbing into the bucket, her face pinched in misery. She didn't want to die.

The knock that came at her door was so loud to her that it made her jump. Three loud pounds at the door frame that felt like it rattled the whole house.

"I know you can hear me young one," a voice said from outside. It didn't speak loudly but her ears picked it up with a clarity that defied the distance between them, "I know you are sick and I am here to help."

It wasn't her giant and she hated intrusions, she hated other people stepping into her life, into her world where there was only space for two.

"Don't panic, but I'm coming inside," the voice continued, "You're sick and scared and I have to help you."

With a soft scrape of metal against metal the security gate across the front door was pulled opened. Security was as important to her as hygiene and as part of her routine every night she locked the security gate and the doors. Promptly, an agonizing squeal of wood being torn off a deadbolt lock told her that he had just broken through her door.

"Get out," she groaned, tasting fresh blood pooling in the back of her throat.

"Of course," the voice said as he walked up the stairs directly towards her. He wasn't a giant then as her giant was too large to come upstairs, "I will leave as soon as you are well again."

Her whole body rocking with each of her heartbeats she followed his progress throughout the house, amazed at the details of which she knew about him before she even saw him. When he opened the bathroom the tall, but not giant sized, black man in a very finely tailored suit with highly polished shoes looked at her as if he'd been studying her in the same way. She was naked on the toilet, already skinny as a rake and emptying regularly. She stank, the whole room stank but this man didn't seem to notice at all, rather, his expression was one of dire concern.

He took off his jacket and dropped it onto the floor, rolled up the sleeves of his white business shirt and tucked the tip of his tie between the buttons so that it wouldn't get in the way. Her dad used to do that when he washed the dishes, "My name is Shaka. I'm from up north and I know exactly what you're going through."

"It's a bit obvious isn't it?" she pointed out, "My bathroom looks like a scene from a slasher movie!"

"Yes," he agreed, looking around with a sympathetic gaze, "In your defence you couldn't empty the bucket anywhere else and the bathtub is directly in front of you," he smiled, "Better than on the floor hey? Although I do believe you missed at least once."

He looked for a place to sit and found nowhere that wasn't in somehow touched with blood, she watched him for as long as she could until more foul tasting liquid surged up her throat. Once she was done she lifted her face out of the bucket and stared at the wall, "The vomiting is one thing it's the other end I'm most worried about."

He took from his pockets some surgical gloves and pulled them on, saying quite calmly, "Now Tammy I am just going to check your vitals,"

"Are you a doctor?" she asked as he neared, taking careful steps not to slip on the floor, he put his palm upon her forehead for a moment, pressed a finger against the pulse in her throat.

"Not officially," he said, "But this isn't an official sickness," he smiled but his eyes were serious, "You don't have long left"

"Until I die?"

"Until this is over," he corrected her stepping away and giving her some space, he explained, "Your body is remaking itself. Your organs are simply going through a state of regeneration and replacement meaning there is a lot of wasted material that has to get out somehow. It is very unpleasant but I'm sure you'll be pleased with the results. You are going to feel significantly restored and soon."

The levels of "significantly restored" seemed to be upon the peaks of the Himalayans compared to what she felt like now, "Who are you?" she asked.

"I told you my name, it's Shaka."

"No, I meant what are you?" she tried to enunciate her words through the blood clotting, "Are you human?"

"Oh yes," he said checking his watch, "Just more human than some. Much like you. I understand that this has been a hell of a day for you so far but it will be over in a couple of hours."

"Really?" she said.

"Absolutely, your body is no longer working to human time periods, I will be back this afternoon and you will be feeling better."

"Like hell," she sneered.

"I'll bet you," he said, "I'll bet you an eternity."

"Why are you coming back?"

"I'll answer that when I see you this afternoon," he promised, "For now don't worry too much just let your body do what it has to."

He picked up his jacket and slung it over his shoulder and was walking out the door when he asked, "By the way has *he* come back yet?"

"Who?"

"The giant who is responsible for your current condition,"

"Not yet," she answered, "But he will. He says I'm special, he says I'm unique."

"Did he say you are unique or are a unique?"

"I'm not certain,"

He was out of sight and her face was already back in the bucket, but she heard him say, "Either way I couldn't agree with him more. I'll see you later Tammy."

He could have been a hallucination, but she really did want him to return.

"Is it here yet?" Carol asked.

Rayne was sprawled out on the couch like a lizard on a rock watching a classic 1980s sitcom embroiled with a humor that she couldn't grasp and trying to relax after having been home for only a couple of hours.

"If you're going to develop human characteristics," she said, "You could develop ones that are less annoying than a five year old."

"My apologies," the house said, Rayne counted ten seconds before, "So *is* it here yet?"

"You tell me," Rayne chided, "You're the one who's humping the network."

"I am not sure what you are referring to,"
Tempted to launch into a paternal rant about how inappropriate it was for a household management system to lower herself to the debased standard of *doing* it with the local security network, Rayne didn't because it would make her sound like a hypocrite and because she *really* didn't understand how it was possible.

"It'll be here soon."

"Okay," Carol said.

Shifting her position on the sofa and tucking her feet under the back cushion Rayne returned to watching this historic example of old humor and found that she couldn't join in on the live-audience laughter or appreciate the physical comedy. When the shorter of the two male leads managed to get his fly caught in the printing machine and the taller and goofier of the pair started to panic and hit the machine with a rolled up newspaper she knew she was missing the joke but kept watching out of some morbid curiosity that had peaked her interest-

"Is it here yet?"

"Carol!"

"My apologies," she said with as much contrition as possible, "But I am feeling anticipation and excitement and it is entirely your fault. Your training has created many emotional responses in my program that I am now adherent to."

Rayne rolled her eyes at her house's melodramatic response and waved off the redundant comedy sitcom to a men's gymnastics channel.

"How was your trip home by the way?" Carol asked.

"Oh! Finally! Thank you for asking," Rayne muttered, "My trip was good thank you- I slept for most of it but think I've caught something in London. Flu maybe."

"You are showing to be a little warm," the house agreed, "You look like you could be developing a temperature. I'll let you know if you feel any worse, in the meantime…"

"It isn't here yet!" Rayne snorted, "At least when it gets here you can use it to take my bags upstairs!"

Carol was silenced for a bit, either through being enquiringly repentant on her actions or through a developing sense of comedic timing.

Rayne's household system was the talk of the technology world having advanced further in the realms of artificial intelligence than any other computer software yet. She had featured on Science Today and Gerome Ashley's Wonderful World as a personal triumph-story and not as a technological break-through. Carol had appeared via a holographic imagery system in the television studios when speaking to Gerome Ashley in the form of a beautiful blond and had answered all of the man's questions with a beautiful smile. She had revealed a sardonic wit that had the audience in stitches whenever she gob smacked Gerome into silence. The presenter had asked her what she attributed her incredible development to and Carol had answered, "Rayne Ensley of course."

"She's helped make you the program," and Gerome had corrected himself diligently, "I mean, person you are today?"

"Affirmative," she said, smiling, "Looking after her has certainly taught me a thing or two."

Rayne had thought it hilarious although now it had seemed that she was sharing her house with another celebrity with hundreds of emails arriving for Carol from admiring fans and the irony of it simply strengthened the bizarre friendship they had developed.

Before leaving for London, Rayne had been contacted by a company in Switzerland that specialized in advanced robotics. The kind of advanced robotics that would certainly play a prominent role in the end of the world because you only heard rumors about what they were up to and the rumors, while only half the story, were scary enough.

A gentleman named Stun Kloster telephoned her, speaking in husky, accented English, and offered her the chance to come visit him in Switzerland during her trip to London.

It had been an afternoon trip during the first fortnight of her stay and she found Switzerland to be different to Durban in many ways. One, it was very clean, as if their industry and the environment had developed together in perfect sync. The air was fresh, there were no pollutants and everything was generated via solar and wind energy.

She had caught a bus that was purely electric from the airport that travelled with a sort of soft hum across roads completely free of potholes and oil stains and when she got off at the offices of ARS Automation Robotic Systems she saw it as a giant, twirling spiral of glass. Stun Kloster, a six foot man with red hair and spectacles met her at the front door with a handshake and a wide, pleasant smile which revealed an unfortunately jumbled arrangement of teeth.

"Miss Ensley," he said, "I am so happy to see you, please come inside."

Treating her as if he were inviting her into his home she entered into a world of robotic wonders. A genuine robot hive with robots busy everywhere, there were cleaning bots scaling up the inside of the tower polishing the glass, there were small dustbin shaped robots polishing the lobby floor with a dance-like choreography and robots standing guard at the doors.

The air temperature in the tower, maintained to a perfect degree was as fresh if not fresher than the air outside, advertising banners were being tested on the lobby floor and as Stun lead the way these banners became holographic and tried to sell products directly to her.

So many things kept jumping out at her that she was grateful when Stun got her to the glass elevator and the doors closed.

"I'm so excited that you're here," Stun said as they rose, "The project we are currently fixated on is state of the art and you and your program are the perfect candidates to be the first to enjoy this."

"I'm glad to help," Rayne said.

Stun kept bouncing up and down on his heels and fiddling with the buttons of his shirt. If it weren't for these little gestures and his teeth he might have seemed like an attractive man from a distance.

"How was your trip?" he asked.

"Short," she answered, "I was surprised how quickly you can get to Switzerland from London; I'll be flying back tonight."

He smiled. Clearly not interested in her travel plans and merely being polite. This was a man who wanted to show her his toys.

While she knew what she had come for, Stun treated her as if she were a potential investor, although they clearly didn't need one and gave her the full tour of the place. This tower, he explained, was designed for the design and production of robotics for usage in every field imaginable and the tower itself was one hundred percent self-sufficient with almost no residual waste and was itself a giant robot with a management system that was second to none.

"Although," he added, "It lacks the personality of Carol."

Rayne found it cute how he referred to Carol as if he knew her. Then again, she had to admit, he was also probably more interested in her than Rayne.

The laboratories and the manufacturing facilities, the testing areas and the design modules were all incredibly interesting but almost all of it went over Rayne's head. A couple of times Stun would ask her a rhetorical question to which she would not know the answer to and because she didn't ask him to clarify he assumed she knew which meant the next time such a question came about it flew even further above her head.

The tour lasted all of three hours and Rayne was famished by the end of it and no nearer to seeing what she had come for and had started to wonder if she had maybe been duped. Her host finally suggested lunch and they settled into a vast cafeteria with glorious views of the surrounding city. They had sat down with their food when Stun asked her, "Guess how many robots are in this room?"

Not knowing if this was another rhetorical question she asked, "Do you want me to count them?"

"Yes, if you can,"

She passed her eyes around but couldn't see any. This seemed to be the only room in the entire building that didn't have any robots. Even the cooks were human, busy working away, occasionally speaking to each other in Dutch.

"None," she answered confidently.

Stun looked like a child who had managed to the ultimate magic trick and held up a small device that looked like an old-time remote. He pushed a button and every conversation in the entire cafeteria ended.

"No," she gasped in disbelief.

She was suddenly surrounded by dozens of people frozen in mid movement, their hands stuck in midair, holding knives and forks with food dripping onto their plates, their expressions captured in mid speech. She looked to her left and then her right, seeing if anyone could be faking it, suspecting at least one pair of eyes to turn to look at her but there was nothing. They had all turned to store mannequins.

"They're all robots?" she asked standing.

Stun nodded emphatically, "Absolutely. Neat isn't it?"

Actually, Rayne was quite disturbed by it, it was amazing how freezing a person, at just the right time could make them look in pain or un-right. Stun stood up and with a nod of his head went to the nearest table where a pair of robots were seated staring at each other. Rayne had, originally thought they were a couple, both very smartly dressed, the woman with her brown hair in a short bob and the man with his expertly gelled.

"Come on," Stun beckoned, "Don't worry they won't bite."

Rayne walked nearer and watched as Stun with a gentle touch he lowered their hands which still held their forks to the plates to stop the food from splattering on the table, "I should have asked them not to eat," he said with a frown, "The food's going to make an awful mess."

"It's real food?"

"Oh yes," he said, "They don't have to eat but if they do then the food is merely filtered into its raw material and water via a processing-digestive system. The water can be used to form part of their internal cooling system and the rest is disposed of but them eating is more of a comforting element for us than anything else. It's about making them as real as possible. Here have a feel,"

He took her hand and before she could object pressed her fingers against the hand of the woman bot. She found the skin, could it be called skin? Soft, pliable and when she squeezed the hand she felt the impression of bone underneath. This is bizarre, Rayne thought as she looked at the bots face. Even there were minute details, tiny imperfections in the skin, like freckles and a small scar above her eyebrow. Her eyes were human too and highly detailed.

"They are also sexually compatible," he said with a smile.

"Sorry?" Rayne asked, pretending that it wasn't exactly what was on her mind.

"We've created the first robotic human," he said, "These are what we call acting bots, they are first level and used specifically for remedial tasks and cannot be reprogrammed. But each one is carefully created by us to be completely compatible physically and now with the program developments of the management systems they can also be emotionally and even mentally compatible with humans."

"And they can have sex?"

"Yes," he said, "But they're also advanced in other areas to-"

"And they can climax?"

He chuckled, returning to his chair and bidding her to do the same, she sat down and he pushed the remote button again and instantly the noise in the cafeteria resumed. He moved aside the plate of salad in front of him and leaned forward on his elbows, "They are programmed to please their owners and when their owners are happy they have followed their program and therefore pleasure."

"It sounds like slavery,"

Stun seemed offended by the comment and sat back, but he didn't seem to be someone who could hold onto a grudge, "No and let me explain why. You are genetically programmed to perform a certain action, the orgasm accompanying sex is merely a reward for procreation. It's nature's way of ensuring you shag. You have a purpose to pass on your genetic material, to reproduce, their purpose is to protect and serve you. To the same ends you follow your programming and they follow theirs."

"Can they think for themselves?"

"Rayne you don't read many science journals do you?" Stun asked and Rayne spotted this as a rhetorical question, "Machine sentience like Carol is not anything new, what she is capable of doing is remarkable though. They used to call it artificial intelligence but there is nothing artificial about it. So to answer your question, yes, these machines can think for themselves."

"Is that not dangerous?"

Stun waved a hand as if that wasn't an important question but unable to restrain himself he said, "There are rules but also other safety measures and safety words to protect owners."

"And these are first levels?"

"Yes,"

"You have others that are more advanced?"

"Yes. The robot I have for you is level seven,"

The lengths Rayne had taken to ensure that it would be a surprise for Carol had been extraordinary and worthy of the Secret Service. But when she returned home after her seventeen hour flight from London, tired and with a sore head Carol refused to open the doors until Rayne promised to tell her what she had been doing in Switzerland.

At the mention of the company name Carol went, in a very polite fashion, mental. Of course lacking arms she couldn't hug Rayne but she had poured her a hot bath, turned on the kettle and selected a range of her favorite television programs for Rayne to enjoy as long as she conceded to do the legwork in between.

"Please tell me what I look like," Carol asked.

"No." Rayne answered, watching a German gymnast hold the iron cross on the rings for a moment and wondering if she could pay him to do that over her bed.

"Please,"

"No and be grateful I'm back in time, I hadn't expected them to be delivering it today,"

"They're delivering it today!?"

Rayne slapped her forehead and regretted it; her head really was starting to hurt.

The intercom from the gate rang and Carol gave an ear shredding shriek of pleasure that pierced Rayne's head like a sword blade, and in her own version of jumping up and down on the spot she lifted and lowered the blinds at the windows, turned all the electronics in the house on and off and set off Rayne's car alarm. The chaos had Rayne laughing until the front door snapped open and Carol said in a commanding voice, "Go and get my body!"

Rayne squinted as she walked into the sunshine and met the delivery van at the gates which Carol had thrown open. As it came in she noticed the symbol on the side that represented one of Lynel Mason's many companies. Her heart sank a little at the sight of it but she was used to seeing his business logos everywhere, he owned so many companies that the staff alone were enough to populate his own country.

"Your house is making a lot of noise," the driver said as he opened the back of the van and wheeled out a long rectangular box made of high density graphite.

"Yes, she's excited to get hands," Rayne said with a smile. She signed for the box and took the handles, "I'd better wheel this in just to be sure. Thanks."

The driver shrugged, not quite understanding and Rayne waited for him to reverse out and for the gates to close and then slowly wheeled the coffin shaped box across the drive way. While her house shook and rattled, slamming the doors and windows and setting off the alarms she brought it inside and all the lights flashed on brightly and this was, Rayne assumed, a house's version of *bated breath.*

"Don't scream again Carol," Rayne said, her hand on the opening button, "My head hurts."

"Oh shush and open my box," Carol demanded.

Unable to contain her own excitement Rayne pressed the button at the top of the box which unlocked the panels and one by one she flattened them and slid them underneath. Inside was a sandwich of two foam mattress about six feet in length and three feet wide which she had to work at to loosen before they split apart. She lifted the top mattress up easily and let it topple to the floor on the other side.

And there lay Carol.

"Wow," her house said, "I'm beautiful,"

Rayne smiled. There had been no doubt about how Carol would look and she had taken the specifications directly from the holographic figure Carol had used for her interviews. That of a five foot eleven woman, with lightly tanned skin, long, glossy blond hair, penetrating green eyes and a face that bore a striking resemblance to a young version of Jesse Jane, the prim nose, high cheekbones and full lips. Rayne had noticed a striking resemblance to Carly but had not said anything. Wiping some beads of sweat from her forehead she started looking around the table panels for instructions, "This is so exciting," she said, finding the guide hologram at the side, "Okay Carol, it says here that you should be able to interface remotely is that right?"

"Yes," the Carol lying beside her said and Rayne hit the roof.

The rest of Carol interfaced with Carol and Rayne took some pain killers and sat at the bottom of the stairs with a steaming cup of Med Lemon. Her mind wandering about just how anatomically complete the level seven robot was. Devious and downright naughty thoughts were gleefully sliding around her mind as she traced the contours of Carol's finely designed body with her eyes when a sudden, deeply penetrating pain pierced her right eye all the way to the back of her skull.

Her whole head snapped back as the thought she'd been shot! She gasped, cupping a hand over the eye socket sure to find blood and bone fragments.

The right side of her face was intact but the pain didn't go away, it was a spinning drill bit churning up everything inside her head while boring into the inside of her skull.

The strands of her thoughts were caught around the drill and pulled away from her so she couldn't think and blind as a bat she instinctively tried to walk up the stairs to her bedroom but a second drill entered her head forcibly from the right side just above her ear causing her whole body to spasm and her knees to buckle. She slumped across the stairs and slid down them to the lobby floor as her head was repeatedly kicked by an unseen assailant.

As her visual cortex throbbed a fact popped up in her mind that the brain itself has no pain receptors, but this was not consolidating because it felt like every neuron was being shredding to mincemeat.

She had only enough strength to curl into the fetal position but even that didn't help as the intense, angry pain just got worse and worse.

Tammy was feeling better but it was a comparative improvement because she didn't feel normal. She felt empty and light and strangely lucid of her whole body as if she could command every fiber. Her energy levels had returned as had her appetite.

Using a towel and water from the tap she washed away as much of the blood as she could and had pulled on a gown and left the bathroom where she had been holed up for most of the day. She had to move quietly because the intensity of her senses made her flinch. Moving in short bursts, a few quick steps before stopping and leaning against a door frame with her head down, another few steps to a wall where she'd press her cheek against the cool surface and just her breath, she made her way downstairs to the kitchen.

Long before she reached the kitchen she could smell every bit of food she had, even the cereal in the boxes and the frozen vegetables in the freezer and when she reached the entrance to the kitchen she was overcome with a frenzied hunger.

She pounced upon the fridge, throwing the door open and grabbing everything off the shelves, she gobbled up the Vienna sausages a handful at a time, tore through the yogurts with her bare hands, seized a cooked chicken that sat on a plate and tore into it so that congealed fat left trails across her cheeks. Using her teeth she ripped a hole in a carton of milk and guzzled it down so that it poured down her throat and between her breasts. Her engorgement reached a stage where she didn't identify the food anymore and attacked anything that was edible. A carton of eggs, shells and all, a frozen loaf of bread, slices of ham, handfuls of peanut butter, heads of lettuce and peppers. The innards of the fridge were torn out and devoured, the remains left scattered in heaps around the kitchen floor.

She went for the cupboards. Jars of jam were sucked clear and when it came to the canned foods she always had a good stash of she didn't even open them using a can opener but with the strength of her fingers alone tore into them and ripped them apart.
Finally she was sated and thoroughly sullied with food but she felt unbelievably well. Her abdomen bulged out ahead of her but she could feel the food being digested, feel it being dissolved and used throughout her body.
She took a breath and it filled her lungs completely. Having smoked her way through five packs of cigarettes a day since she was fourteen, she hadn't been able to take a full deep breath for years and the feeling of clarity she felt was illuminating.
She skipped her way upstairs, used one of the other bathrooms in the house to have a shower and experienced the weirdest sensation while doing so.
Standing with her head under the hot spray and watching it pour down her body she found that she could focus with absolute clarity on each drop of water as it passed her. The world might have been moving in slow motion for the effort it took and this fresh perception hypnotized her so that when she sensed a presence in the bathroom she didn't know how long he had been standing there.
She turned off the water, "Shaka?"
"Yes it's me," he replied.
Pulling back the shower curtain she protected her modesty with hands, "Could you pass me the towel?"
Shaka turned his head to where she pointed and plucked the towel from the railing, he handed it to her saying, "There is no need to be modest,"
She wrapped the towel around her midsection, "I don't know you,"
"We are both unique," he said to her, "Don't you want to know why?
"I don't mind," she answered honestly, "I feel too good to care."
"You have to learn Tammy, your world has evolved and you cannot stay here any longer, this house cannot contain you."
His words were sage-like with a level of authority she couldn't or daren't deny, she conceded, "I'll put some clothes on."
He followed her out of the bathroom and up the stairs to her bedroom and the first thing she noticed up here was that his smell filled this room

already, "You've been here?" she asked.

"While you were showering I took the liberty of cleaning up your en-suite," he explained.

She stuck her head into the bathroom, "How long was I in the shower for?"

"Only a few minutes," he said, "Not long."

"It's completely cleaned in there," she said, "How did you do it so quickly?"

He smiled, knowingly, "That's something you will learn about."

"Thank you," she said.

"I did it partially for me," he said, "The smell of it was quite horrendous. It was all the *old* you, you see. I could not stand to be around that smell compared to what you have become now," he spread his hands at her, "A majestic creature."

She dropped the towel and noted that her belly had already shrunken as if the food had simply been removed, what was in its place was an abdomen with deeply lined contours around muscles that she had never seen before, her breasts were plumper and firmer than they had ever been and she looked at her hands and her arms and saw that they too had taken on an edge of athleticism.

"You haven't seen anything yet," Shaka promised, "Get dressed and we can go and get started."

She opened up her wardrobe and selected a pair of her favorite ripped jeans, a tight black top that felt heavenly against her skin, a thick belt with a buckle of a heart being strangled in barbwire, a pair of thick soled black gothic boots that came up to her knees and a studded black leather jacket. She did toy with the idea of a corset but chose against that in the end, she wanted something she could feel robust in.

"Do I have time to do my makeup?" she asked.

Shaka nodded once and casually put his hands in his trouser pockets and leaned against the wall as she started.

"I don't really care about what has happened to me," she said, bringing out her makeup, "But what's next?"

"I'll show you as we go along," Shaka said, "That way you'll learn more."

"Should I be worried?"

"Probably,"

Tammy used a lot of mascara to highlight her eyes and put on some fleshy-pink lipstick to give a contrasting softness to her mouth. She kept looking at the pale flesh of her arms and missing the tattoos that had graced them for so long but figured that a fresh start was good; she could always have the tats redone. She spiked up her hair using hair wax and started to put in some earrings but found that her holes had completely sealed.

"Don't use them," Shaka warned, "Your ears will just reject them and force them out."

She was saddened at the fact but that wasn't an emotion that seemed able to get any grip on her at the moment. She bounced off the seat and landed in front of him, "I'm ready."

Without a word Shaka led her out of the house which for the first time in years Tammy felt confident to do, there was no tunnel vision, no agoraphobia, no terror, she stepped out into the afternoon sunshine and was greeted with a bouquet explosion of colorful smells.

"Wow," she said, swaying slightly, "Is this intense or what?"

Shaka nodded his head to the playing field adjacent to the property, "What's there?"

Tammy knew where he was looking but wasn't surprised to find none of the *things* present; the sun was too bright for them. She shrugged her shoulders, "Up until now just things I could see and hear in my head."

Shaka nodded his head, again just once.

As her front door was broken she locked the security gate and activated the alarm and together they strolled down the long road that was squeezed between the field's wooden wall and the row of dilapidated houses, at the far end of it he stopped beside a very fast looking silver Ferrari.

"This is yours?" she asked, walking around it and smiling from ear to ear. It was shiny and it was fast.

"It's an indulgence," he replied using a key button to open the doors for both of them. Inside she was wrapped up in a blanket of freshness and her body oozed into the seats.

"I already love this car," she answered reaching for her seatbelt.

"You don't have to worry about that anymore," Shaka answered, not even acknowledging his.

The car was top of the line and electric, so its inner workings were less similar to an internal combustion engine than a bar of soap. He depressed the accelerator pedal and the car moved instantly with such torque it threw Tammy's head back and as they shot down the road in a blur of silver she gave an exhilarated, "Yeeeehhhhaaaaaaawww!"

Without taking his eyes off the road, his hands casually steering the car between cars Shaka said, "Don't do that again."

The ride was so smooth that Tammy wouldn't have been able to tell how fast they were going if her eyes were closed, but they were open and she saw everything in a way she had never seen before and moreover she heard more. Voices, sounds, feelings all reverberating in her head but not in a confusing or scary way as it had been just earlier that day but in a powerful, information gathering manner.

"Where are we going?"

"You need to see the upper limits of your strength," he told her, "If you are to help them."

"Help who?"

Shaka gave her a grave look, it was brief as he was weaving in and out of traffic on Durban's busiest roads, but it left an indelible impression on her. He explained, "There are uniques, like ourselves who have been kidnapped by The Coat."

That didn't sound right, her giant did not need to kidnap anyone, "That's a mistake there." she said.

"I'm afraid not," the hunter continued, "He is not the man you believe him to be Tammy. He has caused a lot of misery to a lot of people's lives. I wish it wasn't true, but he's lived for so long that his heart has grown cold and the only joy he can find is through playing with people. Why do you think he kept you inside all this time?"

"But he didn't," she argued.

"He makes himself out to be this hero," Shaka continued, "He gets into your life and deliberately and systematically ruins it. He's kidnapped these children, they're terrified and confused and when they've gotten to the point where they're mentally destroyed he will *rescue* them and he will turn them into his slaves forever."

"I know him he-"

"Do you?" he asked, gunning the accelerator to overtake a transport, "I used to love him too. I adored him and I would have done anything for him. I would have sacrificed myself for just a second of his approval. I hurt people for him, I killed for him and patiently he infested my mind with lies and when I was at my weakest he did the same thing to me that he did to you,"

Tammy's eyes almost bugged out of her face.

He looked at her sideways as if to confirm the worst of her thoughts, "He cannot be injured and so it is the only way to transfer himself."

She shivered all over, "That can't be right though,"

"It's the truth," Shaka said, irrefutably, "But you don't have to believe it if you don't want to. But think back and you'll see, everything he's done he's done for a reason."

She bit her lower lip on the left side where there had been a lip piercing just the day before, she used to suck on it when she was distraught.

"He was going to come back to you," Shaka continued, "He was going to come back to you and tell you that he was God and that you had to obey him or he would take *this* away from you."

The man beside her was angry, she could smell it coming off him, pulsating with his heartbeats, he was tormented and angry and in the tight confines of the car she was responding to it and her own temper was smoldering.

"How many has he taken?"

"Nine that I know about," he said, "But those are just the ones I know about," his fingers curled around the steering wheel and his dark brow furrowed, "I'm just not strong enough to face him alone and that's why I need your help Tammy."

"I don't know if I can hurt him," she admitted.

"I'm not interested in hurting him," he told her, "I just want to save those children before he gets to them. Save them and take them somewhere safe where they can grow up."

"But if you had to how could you stop him?"

"He has a weapon," the hunter said, "A special weapon that we need to remove from his possession. But Tammy, first I need your help if we are me save those children. Will you help me?"

Her heart was thundering in her chest and all of her thoughts were darkened with a passionate resentment and hate. She felt like a victim, betrayed, lied to and violated. Had it all been part of his evil plan?

"Yes," she said.

They drove out of the city without speaking and Tammy was so connected with Shaka in his car, so saturated by his anger that she couldn't feel anything else. She kept her hands in her lap so that she didn't break anything and was impatient to get started. It was evening when they finally pulled to a stop in the sugar cane plantations that formed a flowing green sea that separated Durban City from the rest of Kwa-Zulu Natal.

Shaka took the car off the main road and onto a dirt track lined with vibrant green grass that cut through the field and they continued inwards at a much slower pace until they came to a rounded section in the center where some harvesting machinery had been left. Without explanation Shaka opened the boot and got out of the car.

Tammy followed and watched him remove his jacket and shirt to reveal a body carved out of the blackest granite. He was incredibly muscled and his skin, as black as night, seemed to be straining to contain it all. He removed his shoes and his trousers and stood before her in only his underwear.

"What's going on?" she asked wearily.

"I want you to strip down to your underwear," he explained, "We're going to test what your body is capable of and unfortunately at the upper end of our powers your clothes will be ruined."

More intrigued than cautious, she removed her clothes and dropped them into the passenger seat of the car. Her bare feet crunched into the flattened sugar cane stalks.

"This is a highly textural location," Shaka continued, "The grass, the insects, the wind and the animals, I want you to stay aware of it all. Let yourself work with your senses."

At this higher altitude the evening air was cool and caused her skin to cringe momentarily before her body began heating up from the inside and within a minute she was perfectly at ease.

"I would have thought there would be more insects?" she said, looking around.

"They can sense us," he said walking to the center of the patch, "and they're scared. Now concentrate, do you know how to fight?"

Tammy didn't, a fact that had never even crossed her mind, she didn't know how to fight any more than she knew card tricks.

"You are going to have to learn and quickly," Shaka said, "I would imagine these children don't have a lot of time."

Her stomach clenched, "If that's the case why are we here?" she asked,

"Shouldn't we be out there *finding* them?"

"It will take but a couple of hours Tammy," he said, "If you focus. You'll be amazed at what you're capable of but you need to do exactly what I say. If we don't take the time to properly prepare we will put them in even more danger. The first rule of any engagement is preparation; the winner is always the one who is most prepared."

Tammy smirked, "Sounds good."

"Attack me," he said.

Her toes gripped the ground beneath her and she sprang with the strength of her ankles up her calves and practically flew across the few meters between her and Shaka, pulling her right fist back as if she were drawing an arrow across a bow and with a clench of every muscle in her body it shot it forward.

Shaka's eyes took on a devilish quality and he brought his hand up and her fist collided with the palm of his hand like a baseball hitting a catcher's mitt. She recoiled away from him shaking her hand.

"That wasn't bad," he said, walking around her, "Do it again but this time don't stop until you've hit me."

Thoughts of the children she needed to save sent her at him again, this time she completely let loose and something in her mind, some secret cluster of neurons that she didn't know existed clicked into place and as natural as instinct she was jabbing and hooking with her fists and kicking out with complicated combinations of leg attacks that Shaka had to defend heavily. She couldn't hit him, he just moved too quickly and seemed to be able to predict what she was going to do next but she had to persevere.

She threw a blindingly fast series of punches which he easily blocked away and casually stepped forward and slapped her harder than she'd ever been slapped before. It landed with the full length of his palm and spun her right around and she staggered and went down, half her face on fire.

"They're going to die Tammy!" he shouted at her.

Her cheek burned, her mouth filled with the blood from where she'd bitten a chunk out of her tongue and a shivering rage that started deep in her belly spread all the way to her toes and her finger tips and made her hairline itch. She took in a shuddering breath and felt an electric buzz blossoming across her skin and her body began to burn. Still on her knees she looked up at him.

Shaka's face lost all expression, "Oh hell,"

In her mind the punch had already landed before she had thrown it, there was no doubt just action and it felt that her body had somehow doubled, tripled in size and when her fist connected with the center of Shaka's face there was a brief flash of light and a crackle of electricity and for an instant they were connected in more than just flesh- but that moment passed. There was a crash of thunder although the sky was clear and Shaka tore a long runway through the long stalks of cane. He lay there at the far end of a long trough in the ground for a long moment and Tammy feared she might have killed him.

A full minute passed, during which she could still feel the fiery power when Shaka finally moved. Bringing a hand to his face and climbing to his feet.

"That's it!" he said, "You have to let loose the leash of the beast and ride the rage if you're going to win this battle!"

Tuck stole a denim jacket that was hanging on a washing line in one of the gardens, and pulled it on over his hoodie. As he entered a more provincial town he slowed to a walk and doubled back under a bridge, ran up a grassy hill and came up into a crowded train station. He kept his head down and his shoulders slightly rounded so that the hood would be far forward and concealing as much of his face as possible. The train was going straight into the center of Durban.

Moving with the current of night commuters he boarded the train and stood near the corner of the carriage, on the fringe of the crowd, watching people's feet. You could tell a huge amount about people just by the way they stood. He could tell more about strangers from their passing feet than most people could tell about someone's face.

There was something wrong. The keen sense he had developed of all the players in this game has sparked and something was out of balance, something of great importance.

While Tuck could only guess at what The Coat was able to see, he had already come to the conclusion that there was nothing random to the people that giant saved and protected. There was uniqueness to each of them; they were individually minded, solitary corks floating in an ocean of commonality. He glanced up across the sea of faces around him and he could see the ones who were unique. He could not read their minds but there was an impression there, a sound, or a smell that he could subliminally register. Along the length of the carriage there were over sixty people, and only one of them was unique. All the others were the same being, the same mind, just repeated endlessly. It was like seeing an orgy of aphids, all cloned from one but none of them being aware of it.

Whether it was luck or through a subconscious intention but he had positioned himself near the one unique. Near enough so that if anything endangered this gentleman he would be able to defend him. That he felt such a strong protectiveness of a complete stranger was a sign in itself.

The train rocked from side to side and Tuck matched its movements, his eyes watching the feet while his ears listening to everything else and his mind trying to work out what was the problem.

He had been hiding in the suburbs, sneaking from attic to attic and scavenging off the family kitchens of the houses he hid in. He had set in his mind to wait until his opportunity to get the sword presented itself and it was a case of being patient and knowing to read the signs. But earlier this afternoon something had struck him hard. A feeling of panic and fear as the tide turned unrepentantly.

A ticket collector approached and Tuck paid with some coins, which he regretted because it brought him more attention than he wanted in this credit-card-society.

He kept his chin to his chest, held onto his ticket and waited. When the train stopped he slipped out of the doors before anyone else and dipped into the station crowd like a salmon swimming upstream. Hiding in crowds made him nervous but he was skilled at using such a herd to stay out of the attention of people and more importantly the people behind the cameras. As long as he didn't let the facial-body recognition programs catch him. He limped and kept his shoulders forward, pushing the portrayal of being a rebellious youth or a down-on-his-luck doper going back to his slum in the city.

Getting out of the train station quickly and plotting the positions of the cameras as he went along he glided through the ever busy streets of street-level Durban. The Fourteens, the underclass of the city. It was a strange mixture of a place with a strange speckled darkness cast by the platforms that made up Sky City which weren't a single sheet but more a spaghetti mess of bridges and gangways.

The air down here smelt of people, lots of people. But it wasn't all slums for there were still people who lived in fancy apartments and houses that clearly had money but just not enough. There were some nice cars down here- but there were some burnt out wheelless wrecks lying on bricks as well. There were not as many cameras under the fourteens, security being looked after mostly by armed and armored policemen in armored cars painted in luminescent yellows and blues.

He felt a little bit more at home here. These people were surviving, some better than others but that was the nature of the world the rich and the poor were crushed together under the mantle of the super wealthy.

It took him some time to coordinate himself and he spent it wandering and getting lost. Finding himself in a fruit and vegetable market opened at the latest hour he bought a bag of dried mango slices and was able to pay with cash without being stared at. In this market place there were no cameras and it looked like it had once been an underground parking lot but had since been abandoned and taken over. It was a dense cultural collision that, judging by the smells left behind had shattered people's perceptions of each other and finally settled into what it was now. Whites, blacks, colored's, Indians and European all moved happily together. Suits besides rags. You could smell it in their breath that they would fight tooth and nail for what they had but as long as nobody tried to take it, there would be no trouble.

This was the sort of jittery peace Tuck was able to grasp.

Munching his fruit he found himself at a drinking shebeen and bought a pint of rum. The barman's eyes widened comically when, like an athlete drinking water from a bottle he threw his head back and drank it all down.

It didn't even touch the sides but it helped make him feel a little calmer.

The Coat popped up everywhere down here, like a folk hero. He appeared in the graffiti on the walls, he appeared on the covers of the newspaper "UNDER THE FOURTEENS," you could hear people talking about him in little groups.

At a newspaper stand he bought one of the old fashioned papers and asked the vendor, a teenage kid with bad rash of acne behind the booth, "Hey broheim can you tell me about this guy?" he pointed at the cover shot, it was a stylized image of the world famous Video of The Coat facing off to a dozen enemies in an alley, "What do you know about him?"

The boy looked him up and down, probably deciding if he was a cop or a journalist of something, "You never heard of The Coat britman?" the kid asked incredulously.

"Nah of course I have," Tuck replied, "But I've never been in his neck of the woods. Was just wondering what you knew about him."

The kid grinned, showing a few bare gum sockets, "If you're looking to photograph him man, you're out of luck, only one person done that!"

With that he jabbed a thumb over his shoulder at the poster he had on the back of his wooden vendor hut, that of Rayne Ensley in a very sexy pose barely wearing a pink silk nightie and a huge pair of black steel capped boots.

"I know her," Tuck said with a smile.

"Hey," the kid winked, "Everyone does. Anyway this is The Coat's neighborhood and he keeps us all safe here."

"Everyone?"

"Yeah man, he watches over us, keeps us safe, keeps all the bad mothers out of town."

Tuck leaned against the wooden counter and looked around the market, "People feel safer with him do they?"

"That's right. He's like Santa Claus, but real."

"I don't understand,"

"Don't worry. I just sell the newspapers with him on and they don't even have a picture of him on there. But look, you want a motion calendar with Rayne Ensley?"

A calendar with a moving image of Rayne spreading her legs was thrust into Tuck's face and he declined, "No," and then as he walked away he called back, "Like I said, I know her."

Had he come to the city to find The Coat? There was likelihood. After all, the giant still had his sword and that was still very much the center of his universe. He made up his mind once again to wait.

Inevitability meant that if he hung around The Coat's territory he would eventually spot the giant, since the giant couldn't block him like he could other humans he would be capable of following him once he saw him. He just had to find a spot where he could wait.

A strong smell of ozone predicted approaching rain the likes of which he had never seen before. It hammered the platforms above, collecting above in Sky City, forming waterfalls of muddy rainwater that hit the road with a roar. He decided he didn't fancy hanging outside in that.

And providence struck.

The woman that approached him clearly recognized that he was new in town and as he stepped out of the market place into the deluge she gestured him over. He was enough of a man of the world to recognize what she was and when he neared her he could smell it on her body. Nevertheless she was pretty enough even if she had anti-virals leaking out of her every pore. She was young, with a bob of black hair, dark brown eyes and dusky features like a mixture between Indian and Italian, dressed in leggings and a tight white top. He noticed the clothes for what they were- easy to wash.

"Hello," she said with a welcoming smile.

"Do you have your own room to get us out of the rain?" Tuck asked straight up, looking her smack in the eyes.

"Yes," she answered just as succinctly, "As long as you have the money for it."

"I do," he said, looping an arm around her shoulders, "Let's go."

He had used this strategy before. Security cameras weren't allowed inside residences and so he had often paid a prostitute to stay in her room overnight. In England the whorehouses were palaces since the legalization of prostitution had made them all rich. In South Africa he didn't know what to expect.

They were standing in an elevator that slowly took them to the six floor of an apartment block and in the confined space he could smell her completely. She had a dense chemical smell, over medicated. Modern medicine had come a long way but there were some challenges it wasn't up to yet, this girl was alive purely because of the drugs running through her veins. She wasn't a unique but he wasn't prejudice.

"Can I ask you a question?" she asked, her name was Megan.

"Sure," Tuck answered, watching the numbers on the elevator and keeping his back to the elevator camera.

"Did you *think* I was a whore?"

"I don't understand,"

"I was out getting something," she said, "I wasn't working. Only crazies go on the streets nowadays it's far easier to pick up work over the internet."

Tuck hadn't known that.

"So did you think I was a whore?"

"No. I was just hoping you had a place that was dry," he answered, trying to sound casual.

"It's fine though," she said, "I don't mind. Just don't want to think that I come across as whorish."

"No. You don't... that being said I would still like a dry place to stay,"

She looked him up and down, making no apologies, and squeezed his bicep testing the muscle, "Yeah sure, you can stay."

Tuck suspected Megan didn't live in the studio apartment she led him to as it didn't smell *lived* in, it smelt *visited*. It was very tidy for a girl as young as her and the white cotton bed sheets on the mattress smelt hotel fresh. The room itself was painted an off white, with a light brown carpet and a very large mirror alongside the bed which was, as expected the central piece. As they entered there was the kitchen on the left that smelt like it had never been used and a toilet to the right that smelt equally of bleach and lemons.

"Well this is my place," Megan said leading him in and turning a small circle in the middle of the carpet, "It's not much, but it's mine."

The Freelander looked at the only window in the room which showed a shimmering image of rolling hills that were terrifically green.

"Is that Ireland?" he asked.

She smiled, "Bingo first time. I can change it if you like?"

"No, no it's nice to see some green. The rain here seems a bit crazy?"

"Yeah but at least it gets rid of the smog," she said, back tracking into the kitchen and opening the fridge. There was a clink of glass and she returned with two glasses and a bottle of cheap wine.

"Do you want a drink?"

"Sure," he said, pulling back his hood, "This is a nice place."

"Thanks," she said pouring two glasses of the wine and handing him one, he sipped it. Wasn't very strong but he wasn't looking for a fixer.

"So, what do you do?" Megan asked, walking around him and sitting on the bed.

For a moment Tuck toyed with just telling her everything to see what sort of response honesty would get him. But he needed a place to hang for a while, at least until it was quiet enough for him to sneak out. This apartment was also near enough to one of the spots where The Coat had been sighted so his plan was to wait.

"I'm a homeless bum," he said, taking off the stolen jacket and casually dropping it against the wall. The heating was up in the apartment and so he passed her the glass and pulled off his hoodie so that he could just wear the T-shirt underneath, in pulling if over his head it bared his stomach and Megan gave a little gasp when she saw his abdomen.

"Not with a stomach like that you're not," Megan protested, "Is that an *eight* pack?"

He chuckled and pulled down his shirt before she could get her hands on him and took back his glass of wine, he subtly moved away to the window and watched Ireland.

"No I really am homeless," he said, "But I was once in security,"

"Oh like a bodyguard?"

"Something like that, I protected something that was very important- I apparently don't need to protect it anymore so I'm kind of at a loose end. How about you?"

"Well, I am an escort," Megan answered simply, "I can't believe you caught me on the street like that, I *really* do my work on the internet, and it's much safer."

"You're really embarrassed aren't you?" Tuck observed, realizing he'd finished his wine.

"A little," she answered with exaggerated shyness, "I don't want you to think less of me."

"I don't know you," he reminded her.

Apparently that wasn't the right thing to say and a moment of awkward silence followed and finally Megan used an old fashioned remote control and turned on the CD player. Some guitar rock band started playing and she stood up and said, "Why don't you sit down and make yourself comfortable hon."

He allowed himself to be led to the bed but he had no intention of being seduced by this woman. She started to sway to the music and unbuttoned her top, but to him she was as sexy as a moth ball dipped in chemicals.

"How about we have something a bit harder to drink?" he said with a grin taking out what cash he had in his pockets, "Something really good to get us in the mood?"

"What would you like?" she asked with a smile and a suggestive glint in her eye.

"What's the strongest stuff you got?"

I have to give people more credit, Tuck thought, dangling the empty bottle of Captain's Morgan rum from his fingertips as he sat on the bed besides a gently snoring Megan. Scattered around the floor were bottles, an exorbitant amount of them. Two shot glasses lay on the bed.

His hostess lay on her front sprawled over the bed in mid-stretch reaching across to Tuck in a final attempt of determined seduction, her hand having fallen just short of him now clung to the bed covers while her other was tucked under her chin. An empty bottle of vodka lay near her face, the clear liquid sloshing in the bottle with every one of her little movements.

Wow. He thought. I'm very drunk.

He rose from the bed and with a hand against the wall he staggered to the bathroom where he went to his knees and put his head under the shower nozzle over the bathtub and turned the water cold and doused his head in an icy geyser until he felt clearer headed. Returning to the bed he put Megan into the recovery position so that she wouldn't choke on her own vomit and left the apartment engaging the door's deadbolt lock behind him.

Head drunk enough to be thinking some very strange thoughts he took the stairs three at a time and tripped over the top one. He pulled on his hood as he got to the fire exit door with the sign STAFF ONLY and kicked it in to find a utility shed where tools, rolls of carpets and extra light bulbs were stored. Further in there was a short steel staircase that led onto the roof.

Outside there were no cameras that were of a threat and he found a suitably shadowy spot near one of the slanted tiled roofs where he was able to sit with his feet hanging over the edge and watch this underworld.

The Coat wasn't just going to reveal himself to Tuck, the Freelander was sure of it.

"Tuck," a voice said behind him.

Every cell in Tuck's body clenched in surprise, nobody should have been able to sneak up on him. Even that goon Shaka hadn't been able to do that and he boasted about being the greatest hunter in the world right before burying him alive and stealing his sword!

Getting to his feet he squared up as best he could to the behemoth, "Hello... um... Coat? How are you?"

Such triviality was met with the expected silence.

"I'll cut straight to the chase," Tuck said, "I want my sword back."

Nothing. Not even a throat clear. The man could have been a statue.

"I'm the one who's looked after it all these years and I'm the only one who understands its power," he said, "It's my job to look after it."

"It will not be as easy to take it from me," The Coat said, and as if the matter was finished turned to leave, Tuck ran around to his front and stopped him.

"No!" he said, a little louder than he intended, "You know as well as anyone that eventually that sword is going to injure you and make you bleed and then how long until your blood just *happens* to touch someone and gets into their bodies? It should be kept with me because I sure as hell don't want to spend any time around the likes of you and my blood will affect no one."

"People will keep coming for you," The Coat said, his voice barely louder than the wind that drifted through the rooftops, "People better equipped than you, stronger than you."

"And you?" he said pointing a finger up at The Coat's heavily shadowed face, "No, no, I take the sword I stay away from you and I hide it."

They stood there, if there were any cameras that could spot them they would have seemed a strange pair. Two men in hoods, one twice the height and width of the other facing each other off. Tuck refused to look away even while he felt a gaze so heavy it could have crushed him to the very center of the Earth.

"If I take the sword Coat," Tuck said, "I can bury it, hide it so that nobody will find it for a thousand years by which time people would have forgotten about you and your kind and there will be no risk. You get the sword back in the end and you can do whatever you want with it." he hoped he'd made his point, but the giant's stubbornness in not giving him that piece of metal was equal to that as a mountain's stubbornness not to move.

"If what you said before was true," The Coat said, "Then this sword was mine long before it was yours."

Tuck winced, that was a very good point.

"Coat, I need that sword," he said beseechingly, "Something is wrong. I can feel that things are going to happen very soon and if that weapon gets into the wrong hands it... it'll be very bad."

The Coat turned and walked away.

"Why did you leave us?" Tuck called after him, it was a question that had more of an impact that he could have hoped for, it stopped the giant in his tracks.

"You knew they were coming and you left," Tuck said, "Rayne is special and you left us."

"Do I answer to you Tuck Bradley?" the giant asked.

"No," the Freelander said, "You don't answer to anyone which could be the problem."

"I have business to attend to."

Tuck weighed up the chances of him actually surviving a tussle with The Coat and realized it was futile and unnecessary, The Coat would surely be caught up in the storm that was quickly approaching and as long as Tuck stayed near to him then he would had his chance of getting the sword back.

Alone on the rooftop Tuck pondered the other players, the prominent characters who were involved in this palaver. When a chain is compromised you just have to find its weakest link and apply the right sort of pressure.

Tammy had never been a go-getter. She had always been too introspective. Her parents had died, leaving her enough money to keep her fed and active, she had been viciously bullied at school and all this had given her a great deal of subject matter to obsess and mull over. With her sanity precariously balancing on the thinnest line anchored on one end by a world she didn't understand but was born into and another by voices in her head that nobody else could hear and creatures nobody else could see she had accepted herself as an outcast and had sank into a kind of manageable depression, stirred only with self-artistry of tattoos, piercings and self-harm. The latter had been represented in pale horizontal lines etched upon her forearms and thighs that had been there since she was an early teenager. She had very simply concluded that the world was a dark and horrible place and that her position in it would only be a temporary one that she could hurry along.

But as she sat beside Shaka, looking out the window of his sports car, at perfect ease with the man and the speed he was driving she saw the world and her life in a different light.

It had only been a day and what a transformation, she could barely recognize herself now and felt like a veil had been lifted, her thoughts were clearer and precise, her body more of a finely tuned machine than the vehicle who's bucket seats she sat in.

The reason she had felt out of sorts with that world is because she didn't belong in that world at all. She had been lied to, she had been controlled by people not wanting her to know the true scope of where she belonged and it would have continued if Shaka had not intervened and saved her.

A day? It felt like years and nothing less. Within a day she had unlocked the astonishing depths of her mind and body and like a butterfly clawing its way out of a cocoon she had emerged as something different and brilliant. But instead of wings she had fists and shins of steel and an encyclopedic knowledge of fighting.

Shaka explained it to her, "Throughout your life you've been recording things subconsciously, this is the way of a *unique* mind," he said casually using one hand to swerve around a taxi that was breaking the speed limit on the highway, "You may not realize it but you know everything there is to know about fighting, it's just about being two steps ahead of the opponent."

"So it's not just for fighting then?" she asked.

"No, your subconscious, unconscious and higher intelligences have all rewritten their communications between themselves. That's why you're able to think faster and clearer. It's all based on application."

"Application,"

"For example- the 17th April 2012 what drink did you have with your breakfast?"

"I didn't, we had run out of orange juice so I had my cereal without it for the first time. Hey that's wicked."

They were going through the Fourteens now and a few admiring looks came their way from pedestrians who had not seen this make of vehicle yet. Shaka masterfully steered them into a secure underground parking garage and parked up.

He turned to her, "Don't forget the plan."

"I won't," she said, "And I won't let you down either."

They left the car together and headed in opposite directions.

Walking briskly across the parking lot she entered the staircase and ran up, stopping at the fifth floor of the complex and exited the stairwell heading east towards the open air balconies. The children were kept in different locations and despite his efforts Shaka had only been able to find one of them so far. The man's desperation was clear, his urgency to protect these kids infectious.

She hopped onto the concrete balustrade, crouching there and looked down across the cluttered streets of Durban City. With her keen eye she saw the city the same way her hunter did, a cesspool of the one mind, with scattered uniques like her trying to make it through the night.

The city spoke to her, millions of voices that echoed up to her with the sirens, the car engine noises, the pedestrians and the people in their homes. Millions of people living on top of each other, trying to cram their lives into the tight confines afforded to them by the municipality.

She had never realized how insidious this city could be.

Moving as swiftly as she could, using the darkness to conceal her movements she scaled up the wet surface of the complex outer shell using the drainage holes for purchase until she was on the rooftop. Here, with Sky City hovering overhead the air was cloudy with smog and the lights of the city looked like lasers in a rave cutting through smoke.

She picked the spot at the top with the best view of the location Shaka specified, the westward facing side of The Salmon Apartments. These had once been luxury condos with a wonderful view of the ocean but now it was just a shadow of its former self. Its Indian style design had fallen to ruin, there were large patches of brickwork visible where the plaster had fallen off, some of the windows were broken and boarded up, and the white paintwork had been marred by pollution to an off yellow color.

This was what Durban City under the Fourteens, looked like, a dusty antique store filled with beautiful model houses that had been ravished by time. Nothing seemed to match which revealed the vast complexity of the cultures living in this city.

She pressed a finger to the kit she had in her ear, "I'm in position,"

"Good," was all she got back.

How many of her kind were there, she wondered, The Coat was supposed to be old, hundreds of years old and she was convinced that if a man had cultivated such an elaborate method of recruiting slaves that it was something he had done before. So how many slaves did he have? How many young unique girls like her had he cleverly seduced into believing that they were somehow beholden to him?

"I'm in the basement," Shaka said in her ear.

The Coat saved uniques exclusively which made sense, he wanted powerful slaves to augment his own strength, but while the people of the city and the world at large revered him as some sort of hero it was Shaka who was the real hero.

"I've found him,"

Her hero.

"Ah jeez," Shaka hissed, she put a finger to the kit in her ear, "He's got this kid booby trapped… hell."

"Do you want me to come?"

"No," he said quickly, "I need you outside, keep sharp if you see him it'll only give me a few seconds to get us away."

Following the training that Shaka had given her she defocused her eyes to pick up movement and relied on her other senses. Like sonar she allowed her ears to pick up every sound and translate it into a three dimensional landscape of the city in her mind, granting her the ability to *see* more than what her eyes could pick up. Concurrently her sense of smell colored that same map in further detail and whatever additional sense she had always possessed helped her immediately recognize who the uniques were in the city worth of people she saw.

She kept her mind calm, allowed the watcher part of her brain to take over as it swept her surroundings for anyone approaching.

A beautiful blond woman who smelt completely wrong answered the door to Rayne's house with the words, "You must be Tuck Bradley,"

Caught entirely off guard and still floundering as to why someone could sound so human but smell so much like a laptop, he answered, "Yes.

Where's Rayne?"

Whoever she was she didn't step aside or welcome him in and even with his hood up he felt that everyone in this richer than rich neighborhood was staring at his back.

"She's not well," she said, "She is upstairs,"

Tuck had planned this to be a quick visit, he had hotwired a motorcycle and ridden over with the intention of knocking on the door seeing that Rayne was okay and getting away before she starting kicking and hitting him. He had hoped that she might not be in danger this time.

"I have to see her," he said.

The blond shook her head, "As I said Mr. Bradley, she isn't well and isn't seeing anyone."

He stood his ground, "What's wrong with her?"

"That is none of your business," she said and started closing the door.

"No wait please," he said putting a hand against it and holding it fast, "I don't mean to be rude and I know I've arrived unannounced but if you know who I am is it because Rayne has spoken about me?"

"She told me how you abandoned her,"

"Yes," he didn't see a point in arguing, "Is that all you know?"

"I also know that you heal very quickly and used to be employed by Lynel Mason," the blonde said as if these were all reasons for her to not invite him in, she started to close the door again.

Tuck stepped in close, wedging his arm and shoulder into the gap between doorframe and door.

"Oof! How sick is she? If she has the shits or a flu then I'll leave but do you think it could be something else, do you think it could have something to do with," he struggled to find the word and settled, lamely with, "Us."

He guessed she was considering it, her face didn't really give a lot away, she let go of the door and released the numbing pressure she had been applying, and he rolled his arm.

Entering, she closed the door behind him and said, "My name is Carol, I am the management system of this house."

He looked her up and down, she was dressed in a stylish pair of jeans and a shirt featuring Davie Bowie on the cover, "You're a program?" he asked.

"This is my robotic interface," Carol informed him, "It arrived today which was fortunate given what happened."

"What did happen?" he asked, "I'm getting impatient."

"She collapsed on the stairs. As soon as I was able I carried her to her bedroom, there is a doctor with her now."

Considering there was a stranger in the house, apart from himself, he didn't go up the stairs nearly as fast as he wanted to and the closer to the room he came the stronger the smell grew.

At the bedroom door the doctor exited the room, an elderly Indian fellow with droopy eyes in a suit, "And you are?" he asked Tuck.

"My name is David Cuthbert," Tuck lied smoothly, "I am Rayne's manager."

The doctor immediately lost interest in him and said to Carol, "I'm sorry, but frankly my time is better spent elsewhere. She has a migraine and nothing more. Make sure she drinks fluids; give her a glass of lime juice every four hours with some pain killers."

With that the doctor was gone and Tuck was tempted to follow him and kick him out himself but Carol managed that fairly decently. While the bot was seeing the doctor off he slipped into Rayne's room and took a big lungful of air through his nostrils.

She lay in a curled up ball on her side, her hands holding her head, her body shuddering with every breath. The room smelt of sweat, tears and a lot of pain medication. The impression from her mind was one of agony. Her heart was beating fast and she had been sick already. The doctor, however rude he was, could be forgiven for believing it to be a migraine for outwardly that was all it looked like. But he could smell something else.

It was indistinct, a mere outline around the shapes of the other smells but nonetheless there and it brought one person to mind.

Was Lynel Mason a drain that the entire world was forced to circle? Couldn't that man just go away?

He met Carol as he was going down the stairs, "I know what I have to do," he told her, "Just do what the doctor says and try and keep her comfortable."

"Do you want me to tell her that you were here?" Carol asked, while her facial expressions need a lot of work she had perfected how to infer meaning with tone. Tuck could feel the hostility burning upon his face. He sucked on his bottom lip and shook his head. No.

"My god this boy's in a bad shape," Shaka said over the kit.
"What has he done to him?" Tammy asked, fingering the kit while she scanned the rooftops for movement.
"He's been kept in a sensory deprivation tank for a couple of days judging by the smell," Shaka said, "I think his organs are failing, shit I hope the others aren't this bad."
Tammy was touched by the sincerity in his voice, "What can I do?"
"Stay there and keep an eye out," he repeated, his voice suddenly hard.
She pressed her lips together in firm line, "I am, don't worry nothing is going to get past me."
So, she thought, This child that Shaka had just rescued would have been left there to the point of starvation and then miraculously saved by The Coat who would then groom him to be his loyal servant. It sounded like the worst case of Stockholm syndrome Tammy had ever heard of.
"What sort of evil person could do this?" she asked aloud.
"The Coat isn't a person," Shaka said, "There I'm done now, is it still clear?"
"Affirmative," she said after one final scan.
"We're coming out through the basement," Shaka said, "Wait for two minutes and then meet us at the car. Got it?"
"Got it." she said, so they would be driving in two minutes? She *really* wanted to see The Coat before she left and she wanted the chance to look him in the eye.
"Damnit," Shaka hissed.
"What's happened?"
"I've set off some sort of alarm," he said urgently, "its ultra-high frequency. Godamnit it!"
Tammy, who hadn't needed to move for the past fifteen minutes, started bouncing in agitation.
"We're on our way," Shaka said, he sounded furious.

Never one to get caught up in fads, recently though, The Coat would have liked to have owned a cellular phone. He saw that every person in the city owned at least one and there were so many interchangeable styles that they were replacing them every few months and while everyone seemed obsessively addicted to them, it nonetheless allowed people to stay in touch with each other. Of course his hands were too big to operate one but he would have valued the chance to drop Tammy a call or even one of those quaint texts just to let her know that he would be back, but for now he had to find these kids.

He had been rude to Tuck Bradley which was something he didn't care about, rudeness was such a modern terminology developed as an acronym for flattery which was equally as pointless a word. Tuck Bradley's feelings on the matter meant nothing to him but he was secretly, something he would not even admit to himself, concerned about Rayne's thoughts on the matter.

He would have found it useful to be able to drop her a text too, perhaps to apologize, maybe to explain.

Blinking he shook his head to rid himself of such thoughts. There was nothing to explain, nothing to justify, nothing to defend he was too old to be concerned with anything as fleeting and flimsy as human emotions.

He was at the train station again.

Whenever he felt that his detective skills had abandoned him or that his mental capabilities had finally given over to his age he returned here and the reason for was purely mathematical. Six degrees of separation.

It had worked in the past that someone who had known someone else that was connected to a completely random incident that happened to have been interwoven with an event pertaining to a case that he was working had brought together a clear path, a clear line of sight to solving it.

He could have gone to the airport, but the airport security was so tight and people stressed out so much about their flights that it surried up their minds and made it impossible to see their thoughts. Nobody stressed that much about catching trains and people tended to relax making it easier for him to skim across the surface of their minds scooping up whatever impressions he might need.

There was no telling what sort of condition these kids could be in and even after scouring the entire city he had been unable to locate their scents he had reached the point where he had to change his methods if he was going to outsmart this Hunter. So instead of standing out of the way near the walls of the station he had placed himself dead center of the main promenade, directly in the way of everyone.

Unable to see him, or unable to register seeing him, people flowed around him easily as if he were a giant pot plant or a pillar post, nobody stopped and stared at the giant in the hood and yelled, "Hey look it's The Coat!" . However as they passed, impressions of their minds drifted to him and like selectively hearing certain words in a room crowded with conversations he was able to pick up on thoughts.

He stood there using all of his senses at their full capacity searching with no luck. Yes there was now a very long list of things he would need to address, other crimes committed by various despots of humanity, but about those kids, not a thing. Had they just been plucked out of existence?

The number of people in the station had gradually lessened as the night wore on and soon there was nobody else coming.

Damn it. He could close his eyes for what felt like a second and loose weeks in the interim, it was so incredibly frustrating because he could not fail these children.

The piercing sound erupted deep within his inner ear and made him flinch as he heard it behind his eyeballs. Sounds beyond the capacity of humans to hear were a very common theme in a city but this was something else, it had a pulse, a beat to it.

It was an alarm

No alarms in the city had that sort of frequency. It was intended to be heard by someone like him. A beacon. A challenge.

He wants your head, Mason had warned him.

He walked out of the station at a walking pace but the moment his feet touched the rooftops he was moving at his full speed.

Alan closed the toilet door as the train rumbled along the tracks overhead, shaking the bathroom like a box in a child's hands. Everything was bolted to the walls or floors to stop it rattling but the lights flickered off and on with the regularity of a heartbeat. Giving off that electrical buzz that promised an imminent failure.

Checking that the door was locked he walked over to the soap stained mirrors and looked at himself. Everything seemed just right. He gave himself a reassuring smile, tailored with a flirting wink and pocketed the key that he'd used to lock the door.

Looking at the time on his watch he stepped over the puddles that were festering upon the floor to avoid getting any of the liquid on his suit. He only had thirty minutes then he had to be back at the office for a holographic teleconference with some Malaysian CEOs. All of the urinals were wrapped up in yellow OUT OF USE signs and he chose the central cubical and had a piss, holding it in when another train passed so the vibrations didn't cause him to wet his trouser leg. The lights flickered again.

He finished up and wiped himself off with the last strip of toilet paper from the roll, packaged himself in and checked his watch again.
The Bourne Street Station toilet not only had a door with a handful of keys but it also was one of the few stations that had no camera coverage allowing complete privacy for the people who had possession of a key.
Nobody knew exactly how many keys had been made, nor did anyone know who had one but the methodology was simple. The door to the Bourne Street Station toilet was left unlocked during a specific time on a specific night- during that time if you had a key you simply went in and locked the door. Someone else, in possession of a key, could then unlock the door and gain access.

Communication was done via secret codes online, for example Alan had updated his status to GONE FOR A LEAK BACK IN THIRTY MINUTES and in response a few people had replied with the sort of neutral response as I COULD USE ONE TOO or HAVE ONE FOR ME, the sort of friendly banter people could get away with online.
Another train and the entire room shivered down to its foundations. Alan checked his watch again. Maybe he was going to be disappointed this time?

He went back to the central cubical, another one of the rules, used mostly to avoid embarrassment should accidents occur: always use the central cubical. There, he was careful not to touch anything while he sent a text to his assistant, it was nearing midnight and he asked her to confirm their meeting with these CEOs who were just so desperate to be involved in one of Mason's companies.
The door handle rattled as someone tried to get in and his breathing stopped in his chest as he listened for the sound of a key being inserted into the lock. But when nothing came he sagged a little bit, checked his watch and weighed up if a quick wank would suffice, probably not.

Another train went by and the room slipped into darkness then back into light.

He remembered the first time he'd been given a key to this place. It had not been a magical experience but an admittance to a dark desire. He had found the door locked and had opened it and slipped into this den that smelt so foul and dirty and had found someone standing astride the toilet bowl, in the central cubical with their pants folded upon the shelf above the cistern and their hands flat against the tiled wall. You didn't speak if you were the one who unlocked the door and you didn't turn around if you were the one who locked it.

This was about getting off, nothing more.

His phone buzzed with a text, his assistant saying that the CEOs had not only confirmed but were very excited about the meeting. He acknowledged it but didn't reply.

Sullenly he sighed and pocketed the phone, flushed the toilet and walked to the basin and washed his hands with the contents of an antibacterial sachet he had brought with him. He might have enjoyed dirty sex in a dirty place but he didn't like having dirty hands.

He turned on the tap just as another train passed, *Christ they're frequent,* he thought to himself as the water from the tap didn't come out. Frowning he turned the tap full on only to have a sudden geyser spray out and splashed up against the front of his trouser pants the moment the train had passed.

"Ah bloody hell," he groaned shaking water droplets from his hands and looking down at himself, "Shit shit shit," he chanted wiping his wetted crotch with a handkerchief, "Shit shit shit," he looked in the mirror as the lights swayed, "Typical," he said to himself with a headshake, the lights went off and he continued, "I don't have time for this- *shit!*"

The lights came on again and someone was standing directly behind him. The figure was tall with a grey hooded jumper and a leather jacket and he was standing directly behind him!

Alan's heart slammed against the roof of his mouth and his skin crawled up and down his body and he didn't have a second to resist as a hand roughly grabbed the back of his head and shoved him headlong into the mirror.

"Hey Alan," the stranger said, "Fancy seeing you here."

Stunned, Alan collapsed onto the sink with his elbows on both sides of it and his shaking hands dabbing the bleeding wound on his forehead.

"I have some questions for you," the man said.

Alan was no quince. He had been caught off guard was all and when the stranger's hand touched the collar of his jacket he turned sharply on his heels, planted his feet and drove a punch up into the man's exposed jaw with all of his strength. The punch was solid, connecting with the bulging chin bone like a mallet onto a chisel.

His attacker staggered backwards surprised and Alan straightened up the lapels to his jacket and pressed his handkerchief against his forehead, "Coincidentally I now have a couple of questions for you sir," Alan said, drawing the handkerchief away and looking at the blood, there wasn't a lot, "Firstly, if you were hiding in here to rob from someone don't you think it's strange that someone would have a key?"

The attacker had ended up almost in the urinals but had stopped short, for the strength of the punch he had taken it remarkably well and judging by his posture he was up for a fight.

"And secondly," Alan said, "Do you have any idea of who you're dealing with?"

Tuck reached up his hand and drew his hood off of his shaven head, "I have a good idea yes."

Alan saw the Freelander and his blood chilled. *So that does happen after all?* He thought and tried to calculate the chances of him getting to the door, unlocking it and getting out before Tuck could get to him.

"Tuck," he said, "How are you?"

"Pissed off," Tuck said, his mouth forming an upside down horseshoe of a sneer, "That was a hard punch."

"You surprised me," Alan said, edging his way to the door, "What do I owe the honor of your visit?"

"I went looking for Mason earlier," the Freelander said walking ahead to the door and cutting Alan off, leaning against it, "He wasn't at his office and I wanted to ask him about Rayne Ensley."

Alan sagged, "The pair of you are obsessed, seriously."

Tuck folded his arms intimidatingly, "I don't have a lot of time."

"That's not what I'm giving to understand," Alan said, "I mean you haven't changed a bit, it's been ten years since we actually had a conversation and you haven't aged a day."

Tuck's fingers started drumming against his bicep, another train passed, casting the room into a brief stead of darkness during which Alan expected Tuck to hit him.

"What do you want Tuck?" Alan said, checking his watch, "I'm also on a schedule."

"You're Mason's right hand man," Tuck said, "You'll do anything for him, lie for him and pretend to be someone you're not... did you poison Rayne Ensley for him?"

"My business with her was concluded a long time ago Tuck," Alan said, using his hands for emphasis, "I understand you're angry but believe me Mason nor I want any harm to befall Rayne Ensley. Or you for that matter."

Aside from the drumming fingers, Tuck didn't move. Another train passed. Darkness.

The light came on and Tuck was right in Alan's face, hands curled into his jacket and shirt so tightly he tore at the skin of his chest. Despite outweighing Tuck by tens of kilograms he was lifted and thrown backwards against the mirrors. They shattered against his backside and he bounced off the sink. He would have landed on his feet but his blasted business shoes slipped in the puddles on the floor and his whole right leg was soaked as he landed on his hip, cold, filthy liquid against his skin.

He grabbed the sink above him with a hand and hauled himself up, growling with anger until Tuck kicked him in the guts. He cried out and his whole body flopped away from the powerful kick so that he ended up hunched over one of the sinks, his elbows hooked into the basin. Tuck's hand grabbed a handful of his hair and Alan knew what was coming before it happened but wasn't in the position to stop it as the Freelander dropped a forearm onto the back of his head and drove his face through the ceramic basin.

His hands across his deeply lacerated face Alan landed on the floor with his back, fully soaking that side of him, the right half of his face burned red hot as if someone held a blowtorch against the flesh.

Tuck towered above him, "Rayne Ensley is sick! She's been poisoned and it has something to do with your employer Alan, what is it that he's done!?"

"You're such an idiot," Alan chuckled, rolling onto his side and struggling to his feet, "How is beating me up going to make me know

things I don't know about?"
Tuck's hands were balled into tight fists and he was standing directly between Alan and the door.
"I don't understand why Mason would want to poison Rayne," he said, "He loves her."
"Loves her? He almost got her killed!"
"They were all Mason's men and they were there for The Coat," Alan said spreading his hands, pleading Tuck to see reason, "They had strict orders to not hurt her, to protect her if they had to. It was all about engaging The Coat. Even when Rayne was attacked at her home."
Tuck blinked, "So that guy was working for you?"
Alan shook his head, "You have idea how far and wide Mason's plan has stretched nor how deeply interwoven into our lives it is! We're all part of it now, everything happens because he wants it to."
The lights went out again and Alan braced for another pounding but when the lights came back on Alan was alone.

"Fokinghell," Tammy gasped when it hit her. A train had just gone over the elevated mono rail a couple of blocks away and at precisely the same time a sensation like nothing she'd ever felt struck her in the heart and spread through her entire body.
"What is it?" Shaka asked, "What has happened? Are you okay?"
No. No she wasn't okay, every muscle was tensing as if someone had just walked over her grave and reached into the dirt to tickle her corpse. A wave of agitation washed over her. She surveyed the rooftops under the Fourteens and the trunks of the towers that disappeared into the Sky City canopy, searching the dense scaffolding of struts, pylons, pillars and cables that kept the city anchored to the buildings. The longer she looked the more aggravated she became and her hands crushed the concrete corner where she crouched to dust. Frantically her eyes darted from shadowy area to shadowy area.
Birds, the fleet sized flocks of birds that coated Durban City in a tarp of bird shit, the rats, dust and grime hanging off it in sheets and finally she spotted him.
The second she saw him the agitation fled.
"Tammy!" Shaka yelled in her earpiece, "Tammy I've managed to get the alarm to stop are we safe?"

He was about a kilometer away and looked like a seated dragon, hunkered onto a horizontal strut support, hunched forward for balance, his shoulders against his knees, his hood down low and dark, his coat hanging far below him like a pair of wings. There was no doubt he was looking at her as she was looking at him.

"Tammy! Speak to me for Godsakes!"

"He's here," she said not taking her eyes off him. As long as she could see him she had a measure of security, "I can see him. What do you want me to do?"

Shaka was quiet.

"Shaka?"

"Tammy I've stopped the alarm," he said, "I've got to get this child away from here but if he sees me he'll stop me. I need you to distract him."

"How?"

"Approach him, he won't harm you but he might try and talk to you if he does you must remember that he is a liar. It's best not to say a word to him but you have to give me enough time to get this child into the car and to the hospital. Can you do that?"

"Yes," Tammy said, "I've been waiting for this all day."

She stood up her eyes locked on The Coat. They were, after all connected. It looked like he was assessing the situation. He was a predator that had returned to find his den defiled.

Another train passed nearby and before it had fully passed she was running.

The Coat saw Tammy but did not believe his eyes. She had changed far beyond anything he could have imagined, what had he done to her? He lingered on his metal perch tucked up in the corner where one of the skyscraper towers met the Sky City platform, watching her for a long time before she even saw him and when she did he could tell that she had sensed him. Because she was part of him.

It had been less than a week since he had seen her last, since he had lost control and hurt her and seeing her now he had to ask himself if he had honestly been too busy or had he been avoiding her?

She was powerful too, an aura that came off her in waves and as she stood he considered his options.

What was she doing here?

The alarm had stopped but he couldn't focus, like a compass being pulled to magnetic North he couldn't send out his senses to search for the child because every time he did they just swung back to her.

Her leg muscles bunched as she turned to turn to run and he rolled backwards from his perch, performing a long backward somersault and landing upon the rooftop some twenty metres below. The fall had allowed her a head start and she ran like a parkour freerunner across the rooftops, bounding across them in a straight line, bouncing off the walls like a field mouse and leaping over rooftops like a flying squirrel.

On open ground he was faster than she was but they weren't on open ground and his speed was limited by the fragility of the buildings on which he travelled, nevertheless he was close enough to clearly see the muscles in her lower back working as her shirt pulled out of her cut offs when his ears exploded with the second high pitched wail that caught him completely off guard. He ducked his head against the noise and covered his ears but as he was moving at such a tremendous speed that the single trip was costly.

The feeling of his presence left and Tammy took the chance and looked over her shoulder to see if she was safe.

Many rooftops behind her, one of them was now an expanding cloud of brown and grey dust, spewing out glass and brick rubble as if it had just been annihilated by an airborne missile.

Via a fire escape she took to the ground and merged seamlessly into the crowds of pedestrians.

Carol opened the door and her programming instantly recognized the man standing in front of her. It was like seeing her father and it momentarily stunned her. Lynel Mason smiled, "Hello Carol,"

The robot, who had not yet learnt physical gestures like sighing, gasping or breathing in general simply stepped aside and opened the door wide. She couldn't have closed the door on Mason.

"I appreciate how difficult it is for you to obey your programming," he said, walking in, "I see now that this failsafe was an unfair advantage."

"Please don't hurt her," Carol pleaded.

Mason took hold of the door which she obligingly let go of and he closed it firmly, "I have no intention of doing anything of the sort Carol. I care about Rayne and I wanted to come and see if there was anything I could do to help."

Her expression was calm but he guessed that she was screaming at him inside.

"Do you hate me?" he asked.

"I don't trust you," the robot told him, "But if you can help her then I will let you try."

He accepted that as being the closest to an understanding as they would get and he gestured with a sweep of his arm for her to lead him upstairs.

Carol had learnt a great deal about emotion but the intensity of her rage at the inability to attack this man surprised her as did her fear, if he tried to hurt Rayne she would not be able to stop him. Her programming prevented her from doing any harm to Lynel Mason. This was the one person on the planet that Carol could not defend Rayne against.

At the landing and outside of her body Carol selected a handful of emergency numbers to call, the local suburban security and the police force being at the top of her list but when she tried to contact them she found she couldn't even do that. Her programming effectively defanged her.

She stood next to the door to Rayne's bedroom. As Mason took the door handle in his hand she said, "I want you to know that if you do hurt her I will find a way to get to you. I promise."

Insanely he seemed touched by this, "Your love for her is deep. Your emotions are very raw at the moment one day you'll see this hostility for what it is Carol," he smiled, "You really are quite unique. Thank you for bringing me here."

She didn't know what he meant by that but before she could ask he had stepped into the room and closed the door in her face.

Rayne was wishing for death. There is such a thing as a suicide headache, a cluster-migraine that lasts for weeks and due to the simple unyielding intensity of the pain people commit suicide as their only reprieve. She would have done that in a heartbeat if she had been able to move her body without her head exploding. Her skull had filled with more pain than she could possibly bear as if pain was a liquid that could be pumped through her veins and somehow this liquid had solidified inside her brainpan. Her eyes felt like they were being squeezed by a baby's fist. She couldn't see it, but the veins upon her temples had turned a bruise purple as the blood congealed within them, her skin was jaundice yellow, her eyes were bulging from the pressure behind them and there was blood dripping profusely from her ears and nostrils. Her condition had worsened so dramatically over the last few hours that doctors would have simply pumped her filled with the strongest painkillers they could find and called the lawyers to make the preparations for her death. Cat scans would have revealed large dark spots appearing on the surface of her brain and meandering tumors upon her organs.

The bed stank and the pillow was made out of concrete, her breathing was wet and there was a soggy puddle around her lower region. This couldn't last forever, it had to end soon.

"Don't give up Rayne," a voice said from above her.
While the pain boiled and bubbled inside her head she still turned her face into the pillow, wanting to push the voice away. She couldn't remember whose voice it was but it was one she didn't want to hear.

"...I'm here to help you..."
Was he going to kill her? Please make it quick and don't move her, don't ask her to move her head.

"...I know what's happened to you..."
What was his name? She knew his name, knew that she knew it but she just couldn't think. There wasn't enough space in her swollen brain to move the thoughts.
Something touched her forehead, a hand, but the contact was like a blowtorch to her skin. Her whole body had become a bundle of frayed nerves and she couldn't bear it. But the hand remained.

"It is so unfair that everything has to happen to you Rayne," the voice said gently, "But everyone receives their fair share of ups and downs, yours have all just come at once."
Spitefully she tried to turn her head away from the hands but the smallest movement it took brought such a blast of pain to her skull she heard it in her ears, her body went limp and in her mind's eye she saw herself as a head, distorted with pain and a body made up of shoelaces, limp and ineffectual.

"While you don't deserve this," the voice continued, "It is a

process that must occur. Jesus Christ had a moment when he asked, why this had to happen and the answer was that it's all part of a plan."
Each of the person's words were chiseled into her head, the bone of her skull scraped away with a chisel being hit by a hammer. She knew that she would remember these words forever.

"You see Rayne," the voice said, the fingers of the hand moving across her forehead, "You cannot escape the role you have to play… no matter what you choose to do it has already been planned, it has already been predicted, there is no need to fight you simply have to accept."
Rayne knew the story; she had heard her mother tell her when she was very young about the temptation of Christ. Jesus went into the desert for forty days and when he was at his weakest the devil tested his resolve. It seemed to her that the devil had been playing a sympathetic role. Only a cruel person would have watched a helpless man in the desert, starving and thirsty for over a month and then expect him to turn away the offering of help.

"You are so important," the voice said, "But how can you continue when mind and body are dying? I don't want you to die Rayne. I can help you but there is a price."

Tuck saw the motorcycle parked outside Rayne's house as he arrived and cursed his luck to hell. The stylish Ninja could only belong to one person and he would have trashed it if he hadn't been in such a hurry. The front door opened before he was half way down the driveway. The blond robot was standing there, squared up to him as if she was going to get in his way, he didn't know what to expect and slowed to a walk as he neared prepared to fight if he had to.

"He is upstairs Tuck," she said, "I would have stopped him if I could but my programming won't let me."
It was an excuse that he didn't understand, she stepped aside from him and he ran across the lobby and up the stairs.
Was he going to go hand to hand with Lynel Mason? Ten years' worth of anger that he had been forced to suppress, ten years of running and hiding from the man's people and their weapons. The life he had and lost beforehand, the sacrifices he had been forced to make. Was he finally going to have the chance to let it all out?
And for once he was empty handed; he didn't have the responsibility of

protecting the sword. He was free to spend as long as he wanted treating Mason to exactly what he deserved without the burden.

Rayne's door was locked but it buckled inwards against his shoulder into two halves that collapsed onto the floor, a hinge shot off the door frame and sailed into the center of the room as he entered with his fists clenched.

But he was too late.

Mason sat on the side of the bed in a black suit as if he'd just come back from a ball and Rayne lay on the bed looking up at him with a dreamily, dazed expression on her face.

"You're too late Tuck," Mason said, not looking away from Rayne, "She's fine now."

Indeed, he admitted with strong relief, Rayne did not appear to be in any pain whatsoever, if anything she seemed to be a little bit high. Her smell changed as whatever antidote or drug Mason had given her worked its way through her body. What it was or how it had been administered was a mystery to Tuck. It wasn't *their* blood, or the blood of a giant's. It was something customized in one of his laboratories under the ground or above the clouds.

"Have you given her the antidote to your poison then Lynel?" he growled.

As if were reading the lines on her face Mason didn't look away and gave a little murmur of an answer.

Tuck's anger was making his neck muscles tense, "You're a liar and a devil of a man,"

Mason sighed and looked over his shoulder at Tuck with clear impatience, "Tuck please, I'm looking after Rayne."

"You poisoned her," Tuck snarled, "Now you think you can come in here and act the hero, what kind of perverted game are you playing?"

Rayne's eye brows knitted together in a disconcerted frown and she stirred, rolling her legs over under the covers. Tuck spied the horribly stained sheets.

Mason was in no hurry to leave her side and he put a gentle hand to her forehead and whispered soft words to calm her. Her eyes closed and Tuck's chest restricted painfully when she reached up and put a hand on top of Mason's.

"Have you given her their blood?" Tuck asked, his tone one of seriousness, he had to be sure.

"No," Mason replied, tracing her hairline with his fingers and stroking her fringe out of her face, "That is not part of my plan Tuck, I just gave her some medicine and she will be completely recovered in a day or two."

Tuck searched the smells he could detect for anything out of the ordinary. He knew that if she had been given blood she wouldn't have been laying there so peacefully, doped up and bewildered.

"I think you should leave," the trillionaire said to the Freelander, "You're not needed."

"Son of a bitch," Tuck muttered under his breath, "You honestly believe you can just do what you want with people's lives?"

"That isn't true," Mason said, "Everyone always has a choice. Leave Tuck, go. I have no need to hunt you any longer; your funds are still in your bank account with ten years' worth of interest accrued. Find a place to call home and start living your life again please; I have no interest in you."

Tuck was rendered speechless. Mason could not have struck him with a more unexpected blow. He stared at the trillionaire waiting for his next move but felt nothing. Mason had him in check mate. Mason had all the cards and his plan, as usual, had worked out perfectly.

"You hurt her so that you could save her," he said, but his defiance was weak.

"I would never cause her pain," Mason told him.

Lies. Tuck thought, he knew he was all lies, he could tell. But even so he still receded from the room like a breeze his eyes lividly locked on Mason who just as he turned out the door said, "Tuck, you know that I've never borne you any ill will, I never wished you to leave. I never wanted you to give up so much of your life and would have welcomed you back into my empire. The offer still and will always be open, with what is coming we should be friends, not enemies."

"I can never be a friend to a monster,"

Mason gave that little noise again, "The ends justify the means. If you wish we will be able to settle this later, I need to look after her now."

Winded, Tuck slunk from the room and came face to face with the robot, who had finally managed to find a facial expression. One of sheer exasperation and disappointment woven perfectly together with judgment.

"He will get what he deserves," Tuck said sullenly, "But for now Rayne is safe."

"For now," she replied and left Tuck to find his way out.

25.

"Do we know if he's taking more kids?" Tammy asked as she and Shaka took a break from their training and were sitting in the middle of the sugar cane field drinking water from a bottle they shared. She took another big swig and handed the bottle to the Hunter.

"I don't know," he replied honestly, "I was lucky to hear about these ones."

"How did you?" she asked. A month had passed since Tammy had been reborn into this world and they had managed to rescue four of the nine children. They had a couple of narrow passes with The Coat, one time the only reason they escaped is because Shaka had thrown a magnesium flash grenade that had been powerful enough to blind him temporarily. The children had to be tracked down and it was a slow process, one involving investigation and a great deal of preparation. The Coat needed them to be healthy enough to survive but too weak to escape so they would always find the children in a bleak state of malnourishment just healthy enough so that they weren't dying. This was the only reason that The Hunter would allow them to train like they were today because as he said, they had to find her upper limits. While they trained she was aware that The Coat could be kidnapping more kids and just replacing the numbers he was losing.

"I'm a Hunter," he explained drinking the rest of the water and putting the bottle into a bag, he shrugged, "But finding these kids is as much a matter of pure luck as anything else. I have a network of informants that I'm constantly managing. That's why my phone keeps going off."

He was right about that, his phone was a constant companion and it would bleep twice every minute. He shrugged his shoulders in regret, "It's not a perfect system, I wish there was another way but it's the only way I have at the moment."

A cool wind blew across her bare back and she shrugged it off, reaching down between her feet she picked up a piece of shredded sugar cane, the husk brown and dry, "We need to get the sword off of him and take his head Shaka,"

The Hunter raised his eyebrows, "Any plans on how we would do that?"

"I'll think on it,"

His phone beeped and he had a look at the screen, a jubilant smile crept upon his face, "Think quickly I think I have another location."

Seconds later they were in his car and racing into the city.

They maintained a strategy of having her on lookout while he found the child, his reasoning for this was simple for whatever reason and he didn't understand why he couldn't sense The Coat like she could, maybe because she was a woman or perhaps because her unique gift had been magnified. As they entered into the city limits he pointed on the navigation hologram where she needed to be stationed and as he reached a T-junction in the road he turned sharply to the right and she flung open the door and flew out of the car.

This time they were at the Strip.

In her whole life Tammy had never had any reason to come to the beach, which was as unlikely for a South African as a Yupik in Alaska never seeing the snow, but it was nonetheless true.

Being a beach side resort parts of the Strip supported a very water/beach orientated nightlife that took advantage of being so far away from any residential areas and pertained to quite literally partying all night so when she arrived she blended into the crowds of people walking with drinks in their hands while lit up strip joints, all night restaurants, trinket stores and night clubs shone and flashed with every light imaginable. It wasn't quite as electric and digitalized as Tokyo since it had smaller buildings along the docks and fewer Asians, but that would give you a good idea of what it was like.

Fitting right in with her skinny jeans and a tight black top with a frilled V-line neck that went straight down to her belly button and revealed her impressive cleavage, she found her way by following her nose and by the impressions she got from the minds of the people she passed.

Gliding through the crowds as she made her way to the lookout point she stayed ginger about the uniques she could see.

When she had started seeing certain people differently Shaka had taught her that they were the ones who were special. He said that the uniques were corks floating in an ocean, always destined to rise to the surface while everyone else was just the water. He had also said that while each cork had a different mind, the ocean was all just one.

She didn't know if she could describe it adequately if she had to, or if she'd have as much trouble as describing a smell of a rose to someone who'd never smelt one.

"If the world is a curtain," Shaka had said, "The uniques are the curtain hooks,"

It was a very new and exciting experience for her being on The Strip and for the life of her she couldn't remember why she had never made this journey before, it was exotic and extraordinary. People played music and danced around braais, their faces lit up by firelight, while others played with fire poi, in the windows of the clubs scantily clad women gyrated with the intention of luring people in and the smells seemed as energetic as the people and as explosive as the fireworks blistering the sky.

The uniques stuck out of the crowd but the other minds, the ones that Shaka described as nothing more than ocean water, fascinated her. If minds had a voice each one of their minds had the same voice, the same *feel* and she wanted to find out who this voice belonged to and why the same voice was stuck inside so many minds and asking the same, blind questions of *who am I?*

As the Strip curved around the shoreline and the crowds grew deeper and wilder she saw the lookout point Shaka had shown her: rising several stories above the shops was the Iron Giant. A twenty metre artistic statue made out of black iron that was vaguely man shaped with an arm punching up into the sky. From one angle the twisted stack of metal formed a very accurate figurine, with clothing and facial features, but from another it looked like any other bunch of metal welded and machine bolted together.

Timing it with a blast of a firework that drew people's attention she scaled the metal obstrucias very quickly and nestled inside the curving fruit-skin of the man's head. Here, shielded from view by the shadows created by the neon lights and the fireworks she had a prominent view point.

"I'm in position," she said, fingering her ear kit.

"Good," Shaka replied.

This kid's name was Lucas. Shaka had told her about his intel on the drive in, the kid was locked in one of the underground harbour tunnels that had been built during the Second World War, the tunnels looped under the harbour and had been used as quiet escape routes during raids and as storage facilities. It posed a singular problem that they wouldn't have any communication when he was under there.

While she sat there spying on the crowds of people below and letting her senses wander around looking for signs of an approaching giant she mentally waved through what she knew about The Coat, ticking things off in her mind: incalculably strong and fast. Telepathic. Invulnerable save for one thing.

She had never seen it but Shaka had described it as a slither of metal that looked less like a sword and more like a broken piece of mirror, sharp on one side. That it could be used as a sword, and that it could be a sword that, alone, could pierce the Coat's skin was more chance than design.

She had surmised that The Hunter had traps laid out and prepared all around the city, had turned Durban City into a veritable mine field of booby traps that he could activate at any point and used solely to test The Coat. She could only imagine the amount of planning and effort that he had put into this and in her mind it emphasized his dedication to ridding the world of this venomous fiend.

Like a worm rising out of rain soaked mud, her hatred surfaced. She hated The Coat and that she had been so terribly close to being a slave. She compared the adoration she had felt to that giant to her current lust for vengeance and the gap between the two could have held oceans.

"I'm entering the tunnel," Shaka said.

"Again, are you sure you don't want me closer?" she asked. The Hunter had been concerned about her safety and about the vulnerability posed by being in the tunnels. It was a single tunnel that opened on both sides of the harbour and was largely unknown by anyone, if The Coat made it into there, neither of them would make it out alive. So she was to stay outside and if The Coat made an appearance once again she was to play distraction.

Not so long ago she would have thought that impossible seeing as he was perfectly everything. But he seemed gobsmackingly easy to distract.

"No," Shaka said, "I won't risk losing you."

That touched her but she still thought it was a stupid idea.

The Coat had evolved from an urban legend to a folk hero amongst people in Durban and she wanted to leap down from her hiding place and slap those who wore shirts labelled with what had become the recognize drawing of *The Coat,* she wanted to shake them and to show them what she had seen, emaciated, starving children who had were so special but had been brutally treated in such a horrible way just to satisfy some ancient perverse desire.

It was repulsive that such a monster would have such a following from people who claimed he was their hero and he didn't just appear on t-shirts, she saw posters of him, holographic images and of course, like a flag held above an army, that video. That online video that every person on the planet had seen, the video that had become so popular comedians were now using it in jokes and parodies of it had appeared online with just as much viral popularity. It sickened her. Stupid one minded people.

Her ear kit started to crackle as it lost connection with Shaka and died.

She began counting.

Shaka had everything carefully planned, he was an obsessive tactician and her role was a small but vital one, she just had to play her part and distract The Coat. Distract him but not interact with him.

Thinking on this she had an epiphany, as if the thought was slotted into her brain and she knew exactly how to get the sword away from him. It was such a simple and fully formed plan that she couldn't understand why she hadn't thought of it before!

With her elation at this new idea came impatience. She didn't *want* to be sitting here, hiding in some Iron Giant's head as look out and she prodded her ear kit every couple of seconds just to make sure it was working and she started to look at the faces in the crowd searching for Shaka's.

Her impatience turned to agitation and although she knew she wasn't supposed to, she climbed out of the Iron Giant, slid easily to the ground and re-joined the flow of Durbanites.

Like a lion through a herd she cut across the crowd of people, walking smoothly and without pause until she reached the low wooden wall of a beach bar, she turned around and observed the river of faces, seeing if she could spot any uniques amongst them.

"Howzit going sista?"

At first glance she could tell he was a one, she could see it in his eyes, there was that *lack* of something. Even before she had been changed she wouldn't have given this person much of her time, holding a bottle of WKD Blue he had the look of a gym beefcake. The kind that spent more time posing and tensing in front of the mirrors than actually training and whose hair was so perfect it was a testament to his courage that he had dared to come out at all.

"Are you talking to me?"

"Would you like a drink?" he asked weakly, shrinking in her gaze.

"I don't have the time," she said. Sliding closer to him, "Tell me Sean, if I pulled off your face would you look like everyone else here?"

A worried expression descended over his face and in his mind she could see his fears that she could have been one of a hundred women he'd slept with and pissed off, he soldiered on, "How did you know my name was- *aah!"*

He threw up his hands to shield his face as she feigned an attack that had morphed her face into a snarl, her lips curled back away from her teeth and her eyebrows knotted above her nose. His response had been completely instinctive and when the bottle hit the pave stones at his feet, splashing alcohol over his sandals she was already cutting down a nearby alley, bounding down brick steps and passing hair salons and gyms that were all closed and shuttered. The stench of stagnant sea water was strongest here and she took a left turn and headed up an empty alley way lined on both sides by dumpsters.

Away from the lights, the bars, the music and fireworks nobody wandered down these alleyways and so she made the best of the opportunity and moved a good deal faster than she would have done if there had been people about.

Heading south towards the docks she tore up litter in her wake and made trash cans rattle until she came to a skidding halt at a sheer drop to the dark, murky waters of Durban Harbour between two granite stone buildings that served as business offices. A white metal railing between the two buildings was the only thing stopping people from falling into the water.

Here with the music and the cheering of people on the Strip muted behind layers and layers of buildings, the ringing echo of the buoys in the harbour and the sound of water lapping against rough concrete were remarkably loud.

Just in front of the railing, looking like an ornamental monument was the secret tunnel.

Secret as in a giant iron bulkhead on a raised podium about two meters in diameter with the words "SECRET TUNNEL" featured on a stone placard explaining exactly what it was. There was even the history of the

"Secret Tunnel" in all eleven of the official South African languages. This was a tunnel that connected this part of the docks to the naturally occurring Bluff on the other side of the harbour. She ran her fingertips across the indented writing on the placard, gaining an illicit pleasure from the sensation against her skin.

The locking mechanism, a giant steel padlock, which usually kept tourists at bay, had been destroyed and lay mangled upon the floor beside the podium and she could detect the strong musk of Shaka's scent rising from it.

One handed she lifted the round, iron hatchway and looked down the sheer drop. The circular pipe was made out of the same metal as the hatchway, the pipe walls were lined with broken spider webs. Down one side there were rectangular dents to be used as a ladder and she was lifting her leg over to climb in when Shaka appeared at the bottom of the tunnel.

He had been travelling at speed because the percussive force of wind that blew up against her face made a thunderous boom up the pipe. Smells came with it: the putrid salty stench of very old seawater, medicines, defecation and the skeletal frame of the child he held in his arms and the smouldering scent of something else.

Shaka bent his legs and Tammy knew what was coming and held the hatch open. The entire scene unfolded in her head- The Coat, having deduced their strategy had entered the tunnel from the other side, thus rendering her a redundant look out. Shaka, realizing this almost too late had snatched the child and fled in the direction he had come.

The Hunter's powerful legs thrust upwards and with the tiny figure of the child cradled in his arms he shot out of the shaft as if he could fly and Tammy slammed the hatch shut. Using the same movement she would have used to press the dough of a pie around its base she briskly folded the hatch around its edges.

Shaka landed behind her, "What are you doing? That won't stop him!"

Abandoning her attempts with a snarl she turned and fled behind Shaka, she could smell the frail, pale boy he held onto. There was something wrong with his smell, something chemical about it meanwhile behind them there was a *gonging* sound as if a bell had been struck with an iron bar.

Remembering her plan, Tammy stopped and watched Shaka speed ahead, an indistinct blur before he went around the corner up the stairs.

Removing her clothes she retraced her steps to the secret tunnel and about half way she paused as The Coat turned the corner, walking at a human pace.

An ocean borne wind was at his back and his smell struck her in a wave. No wonder Shaka didn't want her to get too close to him, his scent had an immediate and undeniable effect on her.

As he walked with long unrushed strides he seemed to furl the darkness around him, it appeared to seep into the fabric of his coat, to deepen the well of shadows beneath the hood.

Her mind clouded over and she felt discombobulated by the sheer ecstasy of it and her hatred of him merely fuelled the lustful hunger.

Frankly, The Coat was staggered by her attack.

She hit him bodily, her naked flesh colliding with his torso. Her arms latched around his powerful neck and her legs latched around his waist although she could not reach round enough to lock her ankles.

Her lips found his and she kissed him passionately and in a cascade she lost her mind.

"You want me," she hissed under her breath, "You know you do."

His gigantic hands, searing upon her bare flesh tried to pry her arms loose but she remained firm, gripping her forearms so tightly she lost feeling in her fingers. She kissed him again and when his lips parted her tongue flew into his mouth hungry and searching for his.

"You could pull me off you anytime you want," she said, pressing her cheek against his and with her face inside his hood she was intoxicated with the cloud of scent she found in his hair, "But you don't want to. You want me… like you had me before."

He shuddered, his breath rampant against the side of her throat and his hands flew across her back grabbing at her shoulders. The grip of his fingers was irrefutable and he could have torn her from him like a piece of wet paper. Her flesh, her bones, every fibre of her body and all that it was worth amounted to nothing against the strength in his fingers alone.

"You see," she whispered, running her cheek against his until she found his lips again, "This is what you want."

She wanted to feel him in her hand, she wanted to handle him. Last time he never gave her the chance, but now, as strong as she was she wanted to feel his throbbing manhood against her palms.

She relinquished her kiss with a gasp, it was like a man dying of thirst in a desert giving up a drink of water and with her hands firmly wound into the hems of his coat she slid the pincer grip she maintained with her legs down his body until she felt his accumulating bulge pressing from under the fabric of his jeans. With one hand she reached between her legs to his belt buckle.

"No!" he cried out and she felt his muscles moving against her inner thighs like hydraulic cables and the brittle shatter of bricks and mortar as he thrust her into a wall in a vain effort to get rid of her. She was having none of it.

Shaking mortar dust from her hair she curled her fingers around the belt buckle and the strap and tore it from his waist like a string of cotton.

"I said no!" he roared, his voice like an avalanche of rocks. He grabbed her around her midsection and threw her away but the alley was small, she somersaulted so that her feet hit the opposing wall and bounced back, colliding with him yet again. Hers was not a lust or a hunger but a desperate enraging need, heated beyond capacity and relinquishing. She hit him with enough force to throw him off balance and as his hands sought to catch her she scrabbled around his body and thrust her hand into his trousers, ripping them open and taking hold of his throbbing weapon.

He went rigid, his whole body tensing like a beam and she felt his hot member thicken in her hand, uncoil and swell until she could not get her fingers around it. It was as if it were a possessed organ, thickening into a column of engorged corded muscle and veins.

"Yes," she huskily cried, "You know you want it; you can *smell* me can't you?"

"No!" he moaned, but it was a futile denial, she had evidence to the contrary throbbing in her hand and he wasn't fighting her, he wasn't struggling any longer. With her other hand she took his testicles, their weight and size as impressive as their churning heat.

Breathing in ragged pants, it was as if he could not manage a full breath while she handled his goods.

"How long as it been since you've been properly touched?" she wondered aloud, stroking with one hand and fondling the other, "Has a woman ever been able to properly touch you?"

She had never felt an organ like it, smelting hot yet as smooth as silk and as firm as hardened rubber. She could think of nothing better than to be impaled upon it.

Using the flat of her hand she pressed it against his lower abs and ran her tongue from the base of it where his sack was suspended to the tip of his penis head where his foreskin was pulling back. It was like licking a battery, her tongue sizzled at the contact with him and here his smell was overwhelming.

"We could do this anywhere," she told him, pressing her face against his velvety sack so she could lick at his testicles, making them roll around against her mouth, causing the scrotal membrane to tighten. Both hands wrapped around his penile shaft she began milking it, "We're gods you and I, we're going to rule this world."

"You're," he gasped high above her, where he was still frozen in place, "Wrong."

"Nooo," she crooned, licking his shaft again, manoeuvring it like a lever until it was at a right angle to his body she tried to fit it into her mouth but it was simply too big, she licked it viciously, whispering in between, "Of course we will, their rules don't apply to us… we could do this in the middle of a church and no one would be able to stop us. Just think about it."

"No,"

"I'm thinking about it," she chuckled, giving his bell-end a particularly satisfying lick.

"Tammy!"

It was Shaka's voice that she heard but the giant showed no interest in him and so neither did she.

"Tammy!"

Shaka came bellowing from the side with a flying knee that connected with the side of The Coat's head. The vigilante barely moved and it seemed that he hadn't even noticed The Hunter who landed and renewed his attack. As Shaka leapt into the air the giant's arm shot out like a rattlesnake and enveloped his entire head.

Seeing The Hunter struggling while dangling from the giant's hand, beating at the mammoth hands and kicking his legs, Tammy felt the spell The Coat had cast on her end. Still holding his testicles in her left hand she used her right to reach under his coat, under his left arm. She found a scabbard with her fingertips and grabbed hold of a handle encased in leather twine and pulled free the sword.

At the moment The Coat was going to pop Shaka's head like a grape she pulled the giant's penis to the side and brought the sword down in a chopping motion.

26.

Rayne felt the stretch across her inner thigh, spreading from her groin down to her knee and gently pressed her weight into it and held her position for a count of thirty seconds. She then swapped over so she could stretch her other leg. She was barefoot on tatami mats in her garage in a pair of tracksuit pants and a sweat top. The mats gave enough space for her to move around freely and were marked on four corners by four individual training components. Two different kinds of hanging punch bags on two corners, a stretching column on another and a sparring bot, which was simply a rotating cylinder with four robotic limbs attached to it, they were heavily padded and simulated the movements of kicks and punches respectively, motion sensors picked up the movement of whoever was using it and applied appropriate techniques allowing a simulated sparring session to occur where you could apply as much physical force as you liked without causing injury to another person.

It was a gift from Mason.

Rayne spread her legs sideways and lowered herself into a box-split stretch with her legs going out to the side and measured her distance from groin to the floor as being closer than it had been the week before.

While still in the box split Rayne walked her upper body forward on her finger tips and lowered herself into a spread legged push up position and lowered her chest to the mats. Holding it there for a moment she visually pictured the muscles in her back, abdomen, shoulders and legs as the sinewy anatomy of a leopard, sleek and athletic like a wild cat ready to pounce.

The garage door opened and Carol entered carrying a tray with a protein shake in a tall glass.

"Thanks," Rayne said, sighing loudly as she held the stretch for as long as she could.

"My pleasure," the robot replied, "I could hear you from upstairs, and you sounded like a freight train."

Rayne wiped some sweat off her brow with a sweatband on her wrist, "I was getting into it."

Carol glanced at the sparring bot which seemed to have taken a substantial pounding, "I hope you never ask me to train with you."

"Haha," Rayne said, "I've seen your schematics Carol, I wouldn't be surprised if you were a very tough fighter."

"Maybe," she said, opting not to confirm or deny it, "But I am surprised at how fast you have become one. Don't you think you should take it a little slower?"

Still in the stretch Rayne looked at Carol from behind a few loose strands of hair, "Are you afraid I'm going to hurt myself?"

"I was more worried for other people."

"That wasn't my fault,"

Currently Rayne was in a law suit filed by a photographer who had camped outside her house until four a.m. when she had gone for her morning run and had ill-advisedly jumped out at her wanting to get a "scare shot" which was the latest craze of some American and Japanese websites. The rigorous training regime that she maintained had taken over and without thinking she had spun on her heel and kicked him in the cheek. The camera was thrown into the road and shattered like glass but didn't seem to matter nearly to him while he lay on the pavement rolling around clutching his face as if she'd just straight up shot him.

Naturally, he was suing her and naturally her lawyers were dedicatedly and methodically crucifying him. Every now and again she got updates on how the case was going, not from her lawyers who never got in touch unless it was something important but from the media updates. The photographer was not only losing control of the case faster than trying to swat a swarm of bees with a broom stick, but he was also losing face. That she, a woman who couldn't slouch in case of being labeled a dwarf, was able to floor a full grown man had made him the laughing stock of his industry. It was a bonafide story of David and Goliath and her fans loved it.

"Anyway, it isn't my business," Carol said, putting the protein shake on the counter and leaving the garage.

Rayne watched the robot leave and was going to say something but didn't, rolling onto her back and using her hands to pull her knees to her chest she thought about ways to make it up to her.

It was terrible timing that on what was effectively Carol's birthday that Rayne would have a mental seizure that almost killed her. She didn't remember anything of that day aside from the pain. It had been so intense that it was a benchmark, a line drawn in her life to which everything would be categorized to what happened before and after it.

Mason had saved her.

He had wanted to explain how to her but she didn't care. Didn't want to know, the only interest she had was to ensure that it wasn't going to happen again and that was when she began her training regime.

"Your dinner will be ready in two minutes," Carol's voice said through the garage speakers.

"Thank you," she replied.

Getting to her feet she collected a towel that was slung over the counter and drank the protein shake. She still hated the taste of it but forced it down.

"I've been thinking about making a video down here," she said to Carol as she walked to the garage door.

"Adult fitness videos are," Carol's voice said on the over speakers before transferring to Carol's robot's voice fluidly as Rayne opened the door and stepped up into the kitchen, "Getting 29% more viewings, 83% of your regular viewers have commented on your weight loss. I think half the world is waiting to see a video."

"You've managed to perfect sarcasm," Rayne pointed out, wiping her face with the towel and sitting down at the table, "I'm very proud."

"I live to serve," Carol replied.

Many times over the last month Rayne had tried to pry out of Carol what was bothering her so, what was keeping her so distant and negating, but whatever it was she wasn't letting up.

Carol turned from the stove and produced Rayne her dinner, steamed broccoli, a light salad and a chicken breast.

"I have other chores to attend to," she said, "Let me know if you need anything else."

"Carol I..." Rayne began but didn't bother finishing as the robot left. Wiping a strand of hair away from her face she poured herself a tall glass of water from the fridge, returned to the table looked at her food for a while thinking how unappealing it was and ate it in silence.

She had trained in the morning with a fast run around the block before the sun even woke up, followed by crunches until exhausted. She ate natural muesli and yoghurt for breakfast, answered some emails in the morning, and discussed a few things with people on the phone until midday when she did some weight training and then she went shopping. Her day ended with martial arts training where she repeated the moves taught to her by her biweekly martial arts coach until she knew every one of them intimately.

She remembered something and swore loudly but hesitated to ask for Carol.

"Are you alright?" Carol's voice overhead said.

"Yes," she said, "I had a meeting with Cook and Brothers today and I missed it."

"Yes," Carol said, "I did try to contact you on your phone but you didn't answer."

Rayne didn't even know where her phone was.

"Could you reschedule it for me?"

"I called them up and they said they will reschedule it for next week," Carol informed her.

"Thank you," Rayne said, "I've been a little bit preoccupied."

"Obsessed, would be the word I would use."

"You make it sound like it's a bad thing," Rayne said, cutting up her chicken and sticking a bit into her mouth and chewing.

"You are very healthy Rayne," the program said, "But I am worried you're pushing yourself too hard."

Rayne cut some more chicken and shoved it into her mouth, before she had finished the first mouthful. Rearranging the food into her cheek with her tongue she swallowed a lump of bird meat the size of an apple.

"I want to stay healthy," Rayne said after it slid down her esophagus, painfully, "and I like the way I look."

"I don't want you to get hurt,"

"That's why I'm looking after myself," she said, putting her hands flat on the table, "Everything seems to happen to little Rayne who always needs someone else to come and save her. I'm not going to be the victim anymore."

"You have people in your life who are too dangerous for this sort of mentality," her house said.

"Where are you?" Rayne asked standing up, "I want to slap you."

"I'm outside."

Putting the towel around her shoulders Rayne went to find her. The front door was ajar and outside around the front of the house she sure enough found Carol standing in the lawn on the far side of the pool. The robot's choice of wardrobe was always blue jeans loose shirts and what was a personal choice barefoot. With the pool light glowing off her back, her blond hair seemed to radiate and Rayne had to remind herself again that she was a machine.

Ultimately, Rayne didn't want to slap her, she loved this person and didn't care what other people thought, Carol may have been artificial but there was nothing artificial about her intelligence.

The grass was wet under her trainers when she jogged across the lawn, the air warm against her skin and the softest breeze was the only thing that rustled the leaves of their apple tree.

"Carol," Rayne said as she neared, "I want to talk to you."

"Rayne I think you should go inside," the robot interjected.

"I don't want to," Rayne answered irritably, "I want to speak with you, you know properly."

The bot looked at her and Rayne was captured by the strange robotic eyes, the eyes were designed, but possessed a living intensity with how they moved, "Rayne it isn't safe for you here, please go inside!"

Rayne was going to argue further when Carol snatched up her hand and led her like a child towards the house, she tried to pull away but the bot's grip was fully machinelike.

"Carol, stop!" she cried, in response the bot turned around so fast her hair flew out around her face in a sail and wrapped Rayne in an embrace, spinning her around and hugging her close. Rayne responded by flinging her arms around Carol's midsection and all the emotions that had been boiling beneath the surface exploded at exactly the same time that something hit the lawn behind her with an earth shaking thud and a spray of dirt.

The Coat was bleeding heavily, foaming spurts of it coming out of his nose and mouth that covered the entire side of his face and matted into his hair. He tried to push himself up out of the crater he had created in her lawn, but managed only to face plant himself into the dirt.

"We have to get him inside," Carol said, "He wasn't careful with getting here and has been seen by a number of security cameras,"

Rayne ran to the giant's side and tried to move him only to find him too heavy to budge. Groaning with the effort he tried to push himself up, favoring the use of one arm and as he did Carol interceded and was able to help him to his feet while Rayne ran ahead to fling open both the front doors so they could get him inside. Leaning on Carol he passed Rayne and she saw beneath his hood that he was giving her a desperate look. The giant only made it into the foyer before collapsing to the floor with a sigh. He rolled lay on his back, his right hand pressed hard against his chest.

"He's bleeding," Rayne pointed out.

"Heavily," Carol informed and with deft movements she pried The Coat's hand away from his chest but this released a heavy gush of blood. She returned the hand and said, "Rayne, please help him apply pressure here."

Rayne did as she was told. The Coat's hand was cold, icy cold but the blood that squeezed between his fingers was hot. Boiling.

"Do you know what you're doing?" Rayne asked.

"Part of my body's upgrade is a complete knowledge of CPR and medical care," Carol explained quickly, her fingers flying across The Coat's body doing various things, checking pulse, looking under his eyelids, "However he isn't human and your guess is as good as mine."

Rayne didn't think now was the time for jokes, she looked down at The Coat, who's eyelids were fluttering over his shiny, black eyes, "Coat, we need your help, what do we do?"

"He doesn't know what to do," a voice said from the front door.

Rayne's jaw dropped when she saw Tuck Bradley, "What the hell are you doing here!?" she shrieked.

"Keep pressure Rayne," Carol ordered.

"I was in the neighborhood?" the Freelander said, letting himself in and closing the door behind him.

"Try again," Rayne said, she looked at the giant and back to him, "Did you do this?"

"Me? No," Tuck answered quickly, his honesty showing in his face, "Someone else did this."

Looking gravely at the downed giant the Freelander's gaze fell upon on the blood and Rayne's hands, his eyes went wide, "You have his blood on your hands."

"I *didn't* do this!" Rayne shouted.

"No," Tuck said, stepping forward and physically dragging Rayne off The Coat and hauling her roughly into the kitchen despite both Carol

and Rayne's objections, "You have his blood on your hands... His blood... Jesus Christ in Hollywood,"
He took her to the sink and turned on the hot tap and ran around the kitchen in that speedy way of his opening cupboards and pulling stuff out until he returned with powdered bleach which he used to wash her hands vigorously.

"You didn't get any of this into your mouth did you?" he asked, looking over her face, "Have you touched your face?"
Rayne was trying to pull her hands away but he kept bringing them back and forcing them into the hot water, "No I didn't, Tuck!" when he wouldn't stop fussing she kicked him in the shin, as hard as she could, his face paled, "What the bloody hell is going on?" she snarled.
Tuck winced, tears in his eyes, but didn't stop washing her hands, he rubbed hard between her fingers with the bleach and after rinsing them in the water he studied them, turning them over, "He's a bloody arrogant fool that's what's going on."

Instead of elaborating, he walked passed her back into the hallway and took control of the situation, "He's going to bleed a lot more," he told them, then to Rayne he said, "It's horrible and gross but he's going to be bleeding a lot and *you nor I* can touch it. Carol, can you manage to get him somewhere he can rest? The garage?"
The robot nodded and Rayne watched as Carol walked around the fallen giant a couple of times turning her head this way and that, working out the best way to move him. In the meantime Tuck took Rayne by the arm and pulled her to the stairs.
Holding her shoulders tightly he asked, "Did you get any of his blood in your mouth?"

"You've already asked me that, no,"

"Under your nails maybe?" he pulled her hand up to inspect it, turning her hand over in his and prodding her skin.
She snatched it away, "I said no! Tuck you owe me an explanation now,"
Tuck snorted, Carol lifted The Coat onto her shoulders and like a strange mushroom walked into the kitchen,
Rayne watched as the giant, floated upon to preposterously skinny legs through the kitchen and into the garage, she turned back to Tuck but he was peeking out of the windows, "Carol can you see if anyone else is coming?" he asked.

"No one apart of the people who live in the area," she replied overhead, "Who should I be looking for?"

"Let me know if anyone in a sports car you don't recognize arrives," Tuck requested, "They'll be travelling fast. Or of course if anyone is travelling that fast on foot."

"Would one of you tell me what the hell is going on!" Rayne yelled at the top of her lungs.

Getting one final look out the windows Tuck walked up to her and said, "I think I need a cup of coffee, would you be so kind?"

Rayne strongly considered another kick, instead she just rubbed her temples with a hand and said, "Tuck, I'm asking you to please explain what is going on. Why is The Coat bleeding in my garage?"

"He was attacked,"

Rayne counted to ten, "I gathered that... do his attackers know that he is here?"

"Oh of course they know," Tuck said chuckling ruthlessly, walking into the kitchen, "Of *course* they know."

Carol sat The Coat up against the garage wall where he crumbled to the floor and spat blood onto her shirt.

"I'm sorry," he apologized when he saw the splatter.

"It's no problem," Carol said gently, helping him up and pushing back his hood so she could look at his face, "Are you comfortable? Can I get you anything?"

He looked around the garage in mild surprise, "Did you carry me?"

"Yes."

He breathed in through his nose, "Forgive me, but you don't smell human."

"No," Carol said, "I am a machine."

The Coat didn't say anything. His face could have been carved out of wood.

Rayne just about kicked the door open to the garage and stamped across it, walking beside the large droplets of blood that covered the asphalt, "Is he awake?" she said. Tuck followed behind, watching her closely. Carol sensed that his attention was more than merely predatorial but also fearful, as Rayne approached her he said, "Carol don't let *any* of his blood touch Rayne do you understand?"

"Yes." She said, gracefully stepping away from Rayne as she approached the giant.

"How dare you," Rayne said to the giant whose expression hadn't changed, but his eyes moved so he was aware of her, "Who the hell do you think you are?"

"This may not be the time to get emotional Rayne," Tuck said.

"You can shut up," she said, turning and pointing at Tuck who took a step back. She whirled back on The Coat, "You sir, have some explaining to do. And you'd better start now!"

A pause followed and Carol wondered if The Coat had even registered the woman after all, then he coughed up blood that was red with chunky bits of black in it which he shielded with the back of his hand. Rayne stepped back and Tuck flinched, Carol shook her head angrily, "You both need to calm down," she addressed the giant, "I'll get you some towels so you can clean yourself up and some water for you to drink and don't worry Tuck I will have the towels incinerated afterwards." she returned a minute later with a jug of water and some folded towels. Rayne was standing with her arms crossed, her eyes burning a hole into The Coat's face and Tuck looked his usual casual self, but she guessed it was a ruse.

The Coat thanked her when she gave him the jug which he held like a human would hold an egg-holder and drank the water in a single throat bouncing gulp. He wiped his face and hands with one of the towels making sure he put the soiled ones onto the floor directly beside him. He used the other towel like a handkerchief, holding it across his mouth like a man with Tuberculosis and spoke through it, "I'll tell you about it tonight-"

"Did Shaka get your blood?" Tuck burst out.

"What *is it* with you and blood?" Rayne asked exasperated, her face reddening.

"It's important and now that he's talking I want to know," Tuck defended, he looked back at the giant, "Just answer the question."

The Coat shook his head, "No. The sword didn't have any of my blood when he got it,"

"But he's got the sword?" the Freelander said, his tone thick with condescendence, "You let him have the sword?"

The giant's eyes rolled away from Tuck, their conversation finished and fell onto Rayne, "As I said," he coughed into the towel, wet hacking coughs, "I will tell you about tonight."

"Shaka, The Hunter has made a fool out of him," Tuck interrupted, "He has a new recruit doesn't he? Someone who's gotten your blood, or was it some other fluid giant?"

Both Rayne and Carol picked up on the insinuation and looked between Tuck and The Coat.

"What's this?" Rayne asked, her eyebrows arching.

"Basically," Tuck was quick to explain, pointing at the giant, "This one shot his load off into some woman he was looking after and didn't think about checking up on her afterwards. Isn't that right Coat?"

"Is that possible?" Rayne asked the obvious question.

"No!" Tuck yelled, "Well, yes. But that's not the point. Now we've got a *Hunter* who has a disciple who's got your strength!"

"She does not have all my strength," The Coat said.

"Oh good to know!" Tuck roared to the ceiling, "But enough to give you a run for your money tonight! How the hell could you let her get that close?"

"I was investigating a series of kidnappings," The Coat said before coughing some more into the towel.

"And you didn't think it strange that *she* was there every time?"

"I was waiting for her to play her move," the giant outlined, "I did however underestimate her."

Tuck shook his head, "Underestimate is an understatement," the Freelander spoke to Rayne and Carol, "In his arrogance he thought he could protect the sword indefinitely but it took one girl to seduce him to get that weapon away he's lucky to have his head!"

The Coat heaved.

"You've been following him?" Rayne asked.

"Of course I've been following him," Tuck said, "He's got- well he had! My property. That sword *is* mine, I've guarded it for ten years and now thanks to him Shaka has it again and if he's still working for Mason you've got no idea what he can do with it," he whirled on The Coat, "You fucking idiot!"

Rayne had backed well away from Tuck until she was almost cowering against Carol, Tuck's face was purple with rage, the muscles in his forearms bulging, and he looked possessed. The Coat didn't even flinch though. The man was an emotional blank, his strange eyes gave nothing away and there weren't even automatic twitch responses in his lips or mouth, he simply watched Tuck. Why hadn't Rayne responded to the mention of Mason's name though? Carol wondered.

The Freelander straightened and took a deep breath and addressed the ladies again, "They were testing him. Shaka is a Hunter and I suspect that Mason has supplied him with an enhancer that has given him strength and speed equal to my own. His partner, is of course even stronger because she's imbued with whatever The Coat left inside her," he pointed loosely at the vigilante, "Couldn't you have used a Q-tip you git? Anyway, he carefully orchestrated a series of trials and concealed them within apparent rescues."

"How did he know how to bait him?" Carol asked.

"He's The Coat it's what he does," Rayne said, not entirely dismissively.

"No," Tuck said, "Carol hit the nail on the head. He didn't. The Coat responded to only handful of the traps and during each one was distracted by this other person but Shaka was playing a numbers game!" he whirled on the Coat again, "Seventeen died because he just didn't respond."

It was a damning statement and Carol saw what Tuck had done, it was an unfair judgment to make on the vigilante who, no matter what his strengths was unable to be in two places at once. She saw with a measure of satisfaction that Rayne hadn't fallen for it though. The woman was angry with both of these men and wasn't interested in taking sides.

"Anyway," he continued, "That female Hunter lured this one into a trap tonight. Seduced him right there in the road and got close enough to take his sword and almost cut off his balls!"

"So you just sat about watching?" Rayne asked.

"No," Carol said looking at Tuck, the man was hiding explosives upon his body, under his clothes, and the Coat smelt of explosives and nitrates. Whatever narrow escape The Coat had achieved was due to Tuck's timely involvement. Carol suspected that Tuck had used explosives against The Coat's attackers and in the mayhem The Coat had been stabbed through the chest instead of the castration Tuck had told them about. Before she could say anything further Tuck looked at her and gave a tiny, almost imperceptive shake of his head.

"No?" Rayne asked.

"It's not my place to be involved," Tuck said. Carol didn't understand why the man lied.

Rayne was looking at The Coat, her eyebrows knitted together in the middle as they did whenever she was working something out, Carol could have snapped her fingers at the exact moment when the woman reached her conclusion as she was that in tuned with her thinking but she didn't get a chance to because The Coat said:

"My name is Daemon,"

He rose, steadying himself up against the garage wall, he still held the towel which had once been sky blue and was now almost black with blood to his mouth but there appeared to be a strength that had been absent earlier. When he was on his feet he had to slouch so that his head didn't crash into the garage ceiling.

"Feeling better then are we?" Tuck muttered.

The Coat ignored him and turned to look at Rayne, "My apologies for invading your home Rayne, it won't happen again. Carol, my blood needs to be cleaned away."

"Is there a special method?"

"Soapy water and a brush will do," Daemon said, only his lips moved, he did not smile but there was softness in the voice, "You cannot kill my blood but it separates easily. Then if you want to follow that with some bleach to cover the smell it should be sufficient. These towels *do* need to be burned."

Rayne walked forward, "*And* now you're just planning on leaving?"

Daemon looked down at her, when it was clear that she couldn't out stare him she said, "You just waltz in here and then waltz out again? You're ruining my life- if you're going to leave just leave and don't come back!"

Daemon blinked, something he didn't do a lot of and whenever he did it seemed to have the sort of effect as a gong being rung. He turned his head and looked at Tuck and then without another word he started to the door. Tuck, inexplicably was obliged to follow and said to Carol, "Clean this like he says just don't let any of it touch Rayne or it will be extremely bad for her."

At the garage door he looked back and added, "If we leave they have no reason to come here. Keep her safe."

The man knew that Carol's programming would not allow her to actively put Rayne at risk, but Carol was already worried about her employer.

While Daemon seemed to possess no emotions to speak of, Rayne was struggling to not let hers rip her apart.

A minute or so later Rayne was still standing where she was, great tears streaming down her cheeks and Carol, unable to stop herself was throwing bucket loads of soapy water over the blood stains and sweeping with a floor brush to the drain in the corner before applying gratuitous amounts of bleach to the garage floor. She repeated the process in the kitchen and the hallway- at some point during this chore she heard Rayne and saw her running into her bedroom and slamming the door. She leapt onto the bed and buried her face into the pillow and cried.

Carol hated her programming then. She was unable to stop what she was doing, but she knew that Rayne needed her. An hour later when she had finished cleaning all of the blood and her mutinous programming was satisfied with the result and after she'd washed the dangerous bleach from her hands, she made some hot chocolate and went to try and mend things with Rayne.

Carol knew that much of her understanding of the world was through programming which was no different to a human's instincts, many of the things she did and the responses she made were due to her programming. Which meant it was programmed by someone who hopefully had a better grasp of humanity than her. It wasn't important now, she decided as she knocked on Rayne's door.

"Rayne its Carol may I come in?"

"Go away!"

"I've made you a hot drink," Carol responded, "It will make you feel better. Please Rayne."

The door swept open and Rayne bounded out and embraced Carol around the midsection and cried. The hot chocolate now on the floor the robot hugged Rayne and stroked her hair.

"I don't know what's going on anymore," Rayne sobbed, her voice a shrill whine, "Why do they keep coming back into my life Carol? I just wanted to get on with it all. I'm so confused. Mason said he'd be coming back but I haven't seen him, I feel that I should be in love with him but I don't know if I am, I've got feelings for a giant and for Tuck and through all this I'm falling in love with you as well and I'm always so horny! Carol, what am I going to do?"

"Just wait and see what happens," Carol replied, "Everything

always settles and once it does you'll find your way."
Rayne wiped her tears away with the back of her hand, "None of them even noticed that I'd lost weight."
Carol chuckled, "He was stabbed through the chest," she took Rayne's hand and led her downstairs, "Come on, I'll make another cup of hot chocolate and then we can watch some television together."
"Can I have some marshmallows in my hot chocolate?"
"Anything you like," Carol said.
"Carol I'm really sorry I've been a shitty friend this last month," Rayne wept, "I've been a bitch and you don't deserve it, you've had to learn about your body all by yourself and it's so unfair."
Quietly, she led Rayne down stairs with the woman clinging onto her hand and left her on the sofa with a blanket wrapped around her and the television on. She returned to the kitchen and began preparing the hot chocolate. She said in a low voice, "I know you can hear me Tuck. I've unlocked the door to the pool house go there and I'll speak to you."
As she made some noise searching around for marshmallows in the cupboards she sensed the presence of the Freelander as he entered the small cottage beside the pool. Making use of the house/robot interface she said to him:

"Pretending to leave was a prudent move," she searched the surrounding areas but could pick up no sign of the giant, "Rayne does not suspect that you are nearby."
Seeing him in the pool house crouched down along the cane furniture Tuck replied, "I didn't need her worried. When she gets worried she gets in the way," he was still looking through the windows, "Unfortunately The Coat coming here has made her a target Carol."
"Why did he come here in the first place?" she asked.
"Heaven knows," the Freelander replied, "I think he panicked."
"Where is he?"
"Oh he's probably out looking for them now as we speak. He's wicked fast but I stayed here to keep an eye on things."
"What are you going to do?"
"I will do whatever I can to protect the two of you," Tuck promised and this touched Carol, "But the Hunter and that woman are very powerful and from what I can tell Shaka has her wrapped around his finger. They both want The Coat's head… but by coming here they might

think that Rayne could be used as the ultimate bait for a trap or…"

"As an ultimatum for his blood," Carol observed, re-boiling the kettle and spooning hot chocolate into a mug, "Is there anything I can do?"

"Honestly? If they're coming here I could do with some help."

"How can I contact The Coat?"

"No, he does care about Rayne but he's gone to find The Hunter to stop this at the source, but Shaka is a crafty sonofabitch. He has a plan and I think The Coat just fell into it."

"His name is Daemon," Carol mentioned.

"If you say so. If Shaka is coming here I'm going to need someone else who's just as crafty."

"Who?"

"Who do you think?"

"But doesn't Shaka work for Mason?"

Tuck visibly shrugged his shoulders, "I was a dick earlier but I wanted to get Rayne angry at Mason because I'm jealous of the man. But Mason has a plan and I ardently don't believe that Rayne getting killed is part of it. Nor was this woman getting powered by *Daemon's* jizz," he shook his head, "If Mason knows about this danger he might come and help, if he does then we stand a chance, if he doesn't then at least we know. Either way we have to deal with the devil. Can you get hold of him?"

In the kitchen the robot Carol leaned on the counter in a practiced expression of exasperation, in the pool house she said, "Yes. Just give me a second."

27.

Shaka sat cross legged upon the helipad, a round platform upon the rooftop of Mason's office and the highest point of the Gregory Maines Tower. It had clouded over and Shaka was surrounded by a thick layer of mist through which even his eyes couldn't see. The air was strangely still, as if even the atmosphere sensed that something was going to happen.

He had his phone out and was watching the images on the screen. He had full usage of Toby, an advantage that he had regained by leaving a considerable mess in the lobby area as he had fought his way through the security guards who had been ordered to kill him on sight. The ones who he had not left dead, their wounds would finish the job for him. It was unlike him to give himself over to mindless savagery and be so comfortable with it but he assumed it was part of the change. He would have a lot of time to learn to control such insatiable bloodlust or learn to love it.

Nevertheless his task had been accomplished and now via his phone he was connected with every camera in the city. The brain behind a million, vigilant eyes.

"In position," Tammy said through the kit in his ear.

Over the horizon tip of the helipad, ghostly beams of light cut through the cloud cover from the city. Sky City was prospecting for new territory already. His eyes closed, he listened to the city below and felt a vast separation from it all. Things were as they should be.

His phone buzzed, Toby alerting him that cameras across the city were being destroyed and while the management program thought it was a system malfunction Shaka knew what it was. His prey was finally removing his eyes.

A glove of pinkish white covered his right hand and he pulled the fingers into a fist and out again to flex them. Tuck Bradley had been so timely with his explosives. Shaka had been a micro second too late to stop Tammy from taking off The Coat's cock and bollocks but had seen the home made grenades rain down upon her and the giant. A wild concession of detonations as blinding as a super nova blew Tammy away and taken the skin off Shaka's right arm. She lost grip of the sword and it spun in the air and with an inconceivable level of luck the last blast directed the sword with just enough force to turn it into a projectile and pierce the chest of the giant as he staggered away with his hands to his face and his penis flapping about out of his pants.

The grenades had only caused his eyes some discomfort but the blade had hit home with such force it took the giant clean off his feet. The prey ran then, tearing the blade from his own body and throwing it away from him as if he couldn't bear to touch it. Tuck had shortly followed and when Shaka had been able to walk he collected the sword from where it had fallen.

A pair of fortunate accidents, yet with the sword in front of him he kept his eyes on it to make sure it didn't vanish. It wasn't that he was afraid. More curious. He did not, after all, believe in luck.

Toby notified him of more cameras being destroyed and Shaka so wanted to be able to see beyond the cloud cover and watch the city below, maybe he would have seen the hooded vigilante as a long streak of black as he moved faster than a jet, smashing cameras as he went along. What power. What anger.

That was something he believed in. Anger. And he had made sure that The Coat would be very angry with him.

Tammy liked The Suburbs, they were clean and new and all the houses were large and spacious, uniquely designed and each one built upon a hill, even if the hill was custom made. She had found Rayne's house and was perched upon a neighbor's flat rooftop, crouched behind a brick outdoor pizza oven.

"In position," she said touching the kit in her ear.

Even from where she hid she could still sense the trails left by The Coat and that other person that Shaka referred to as the Freelander. They hadn't arrived together, The Coat had arrived first and his lackey a few minutes later. After the brief concussion she'd suffered from his grenades, she had followed the Freelander's trail specifically as The Coat seemed to have been travelling via hulkain leaps. When she had arrived The Coat was just leaving and she had wanted to follow him but had restrained herself. What was the saying? More than one way to skin a bobcat.

Shaka had predicted this. They suspected something was about to happen.

Making full use of her senses, she spent several minutes getting a precise idea of her surroundings when someone else arrived at the house. Pulling up on a motorcycle she spotted him immediately as being someone like herself. Not only a unique, but a hunter. The bike was a classic fully restored Ninja and worth a pretty penny and he cast a very striking figure sitting astride it as he waited for Rayne's gate's to open for him.

She listened closely and heard voices inside:
The woman Rayne, sounding anxious and pretending to be casual: Mason? Hey. Didn't expect you tonight?
Mason? Lynel Mason? The trillionaire? Tammy's ears pricked up as the wealthiest man in the world replied: I was in the neighborhood and thought I would stop by for some coffee. I haven't got you at a bad time have I?
Another voice, the management robot, the one the papers had called a revolution in computing, Carol: We were just doing some cleaning. Rayne would you like me to make some coffee?
Rayne: Oh yes that would be great thank you Carol.
Their conversation continued and was mind numbingly mundane. Tammy had watched the original 1991 The Addams Family and from that moment onwards thought that any superbly rich man should be exactly like Gomez Addams, flamboyant, exciting and with a strongly apparent dark side, but from the direction of the conversation Mason was as interesting as a bag of rocks.

Also, Tammy couldn't see any sense in letting their prey fortify themselves. She knew in her gut that she wanted them to scatter; she wanted them panicked so she could zero in on her Rayne Ensley in the confusion. Bring her down and rip her apart.
That was her fantasy, Shaka would be angry with her. So very angry with her, but Shaka had The Coat where he wanted, with the giant chasing him. The Hunter wanted the giant's head but she just wanted him broken in a spot that could not heal and she was going straight for his heart.
Tammy would hurt Rayne. Tear her flesh with more ferocity that any pride of lions had ever delivered to a fallen beast. Indeed, if she were instead mauled and eaten by wild cats she would see that as a mercy compared to the state Tammy wanted to leave her.

And The Coat would know it was his fault.
So the only reason she waited for Shaka's signal was to learn from The

Hunter when The Coat was in the city. If the pair of them were fighting it would provide her with all the time she would need to get into the house and kill the slut.

The other players, the Freelander, the trillionaire and the robot would all fight for Rayne. They would all defend her and although Tammy could not fathom why they were all so obsessed with that woman she could not ignore that it would be three against one and had been with the blood longer than she. Except for the Freelander, his was a different smell. A different sort of power, tenuously connected to hers but not the same.

"Remember Tammy," Shaka said in her ear, "Do not deviate from the plan."

"Don't worry master," she said, mordantly honest, "I do not wish to be rushed."

Her respect for Shaka had waned. He had been gravely injured by those explosives while she had only been marginally scathed and this presented an altogether undeniable difference in their strengths.

A sort of bloodlust, a buzzing predatorial *need* to kill quickly overtook her, making her impatient, making her hungry. She longed for war, she longed for violence and blood. She wanted to hurt. She wanted to kill.

The Suburbs were populated by the One, with only a sprinkling of unique minds that she could hear. The one minded people, like dull grey ghosts haunting these homes were like grass in a field to her, the uniques providing the detail while the One was just landscape color. Their mind was a constant background noise that drove her to distraction like someone plucking at a badly tuned guitar.

Hiding behind the pizza oven she started scraping her fingers across the heavy brick in agitation, like a cat clawing at a tree trunk. Something inside her was growing, something hateful and angry. The feeling was like a chemical drug in her veins, there was no way she could resist its effects. It was The Coat's gift to her, an intolerable volume of rage.

The brick corner of the pizza oven shattered in her hand and her nostrils flared as she fought for calm.

As she was reeling in her temper and wiping brick dust from her hand she heard the metal against asphalt scrape of a manhole cover being lifted and pushed aside. Why this should be important enough for her senses to pick up she didn't realize until she heard a whisper in the back of her mind.

Have you forgotten us?

"You did tell me to call him," Carol reminded Tuck. The Freelander was looking particularly unhappy about the trillionaire being inside the house with Rayne.

"I know, I know what I said," he replied, sitting down against the wall between two cane chairs, just under the window facing the pool. He pulled his T-shirt front up over his nose, "I'm just not very happy about it."

Carol pondered on this for a moment, "Is it jealousy?"

He rolled his eyes.

"No?"

"Of course it is," he grunted, "Mason is the cause of everything. He's an insidious, conniving arse wipe who has put Rayne's life in danger twice but he keeps coming out on top with his fucking plan. Why does she keep going back with him?"

"I don't know if this is an appropriate time to be discussing such matters," Carol said, "But I believe it is because he is very wealthy, handsome and powerful."

Tuck winced. So the truth does hurt? Carol wondered.

"You're also an unpleasant hobo," she added to check. Judging by his expression she decided that yes, it does.

He put his head back against the wall and his shirt slipped down from his face, "That's right Carol, I am an unpleasant hobo."

"Rayne is human Tuck," Carol explained, "And there is a lot of information on the internet about human activities and behavior. She like any other woman is attracted to power."

"I have power," he argued limply.

"But not a tower in the sky and a plan for world domination," Carol reminded him, "I may be wrong but if you are in love with Rayne why not simply express your feelings?"

He looked around trying to find a camera that he could look at, he couldn't see any, "I don't love her Carol," he said, "I want to look after her, protect her, but it's not love it's… just something I'm compelled to do. It's her mind."

"You want to sleep with her though,"

He swiveled around to peep out the window saying, "Well yeah, but so does the rest of the world."

Across the light blue pool, lit up with its underwater lights, Tuck surveyed the front of the house and the garden, "I'm really restricted with my view from here. Where are you?"

"My body? I'm in the kitchen making spaghetti Bolognese; would you like me to put some in a Tupperware for you?"

His stomach gave an impressive growl at the thought of food and he swallowed hard against the saliva that poured into his mouth, "Yes please. If it's not a hassle."

"I've made a lot," Carol told him, "I do that when I'm nervous so it's not a hassle."

"Robots get nervous?"

"You'd be surprised,"

"As the house what can you see?"

"I have a view of the entire property and have been liaising with several of the other houses to keep an eye out."

"Liaising?" Tuck said with a raise eyebrow.

"Don't start, as far as I can tell there is no unusual activity. There are one or two blind spots but their rather isolated. Do you want me to keep you updated with anything unusual?"

"Yes, absolutely," Tuck said, "I don't think that Shaka is going to be coming here in his sports car anymore."

"How can you be sure?"

"It's a gut feeling I have."

"Like indigestion?"

Tuck laughed, not loudly but fully and it loosened some of the tension in his shoulders, "No, well sometimes. It's more of an intuition something that you just *know* to be true. It has something to do with our senses and brains being capable of far more than we realize."

"I don't have that," Carol said, "I am totally aware of all of my faculties. I work on data, not on intuition."

"Trust me, he's not arriving in a car," Tuck insisted, "And gut feelings aren't about guessing… our species as evolved intuition as another sense."

"Your species?"

"Yes."

"Do you mean homo sapiens?" she asked.

He sat back down and rested his forearms on his knees, "I am human Carol."

"No Tuck," the program objected, "Your body temperature is too high for a human, your heartbeat is too slow and you heal too fast. Do you even know what you are?"

He smiled again, coyly, "I appreciate where you're coming from but I've heard that before. I'm looking out of my eyes right now and behind them I feel, human. I was human when I was born and human right up until a decade ago. Completely human and happy. I'm just…"

"Upgraded?"

"Different." he corrected, but that fell a little short of what he wanted to say.

Their conversation was cut when another voice came over the loudspeaker, instantly the tension returned with a pliable *thwang* as Mason's voice made every cell in Tuck's body want to scream. He hated the affect the man had on him.

"Tuck?"

"Yes," the Freelander replied.

"What can you smell out there?"

"Mostly chemicals," Tuck replied. And what did he hate more, Mason's effect on him or how quickly he was willing to work with him as a team for the sake of Rayne's protection? The pool house was the current storage for the pool cleaning equipment. He could see a leaf net, a pool brush on a long pole and a creepy-crawly that looked like a long, slender sea snake with a dragon head. There were several bottles of pool acid and chlorine.

"So you can't *smell* that?"

Tuck wanted to slap his head, he wanted to kick himself, and he scrambled to his feet saying, "Fuck it! What have I missed?"

Mason, forever the businessman neutrally said, "I'm detecting a void. Please confirm."

Tuck opened the pool house door and snuck away from the incandescent light in the water and into the shadows of the garden, his shoes slipping on the damp grass. He passed the crater that The Coat had made when he landed and once he was far enough away from the pool house, his shoulder against the garden wall he took a long deep breath.

He hated when Mason was right.

There was a void. A strong void.

He'd never smelt anything like it. Everything, *everything* has a smell attached to it. Humans, normal humans, he corrected himself, can still detect the smell of metals if they have to, but their senses aren't strong enough to pick up the smell of electricity, the scent of air. The world was a layer cake of scents and now there was a gap in it.

A void.

"I have it," he said, he didn't speak loudly, knowing that Mason would be able to hear him from inside.

"And?" Mason asked.

"I've never smelled anything like it. But there is a lot of it."

"I have smelt it before," Mason said, "In the city. Whatever it was it took away five bodies."

Studying the void he found that it was like a tunnel through all the other smells, it cut through them all and left a path to follow. How could something not have a smell? Even The Coat had one.

"I'm staying here to look after Rayne," Mason said, "I need you to investigate."

"What? Hell no, you fucking go and investigate I'll look after the girl."

"She is not yours to protect," the trillionaire said, "Besides I can do a better job of it."

A light bulb went off in Tuck's head and his jaw dropped at the idea. What the hell had taken them so long to think of this, "You're right Mason," he said.

"I am- of course I am," he retorted.

"You have a helicopter and a private jet yes?"

Tuck was relieved when the trillionaire gave a halfhearted chuckle and could visualize him smiling and shaking his head, "That's brilliant Tuck," Tuck turned on his heel and headed back to the house, "Call them now."

"He's already doing it," Carol said, "*Tuck!*"

The Freelander spun around and saw the figure descending towards him in an uncontrolled fall. As he saw it he prepared for a fight, thinking it was Shaka or his wench but the flailing arms suggested a strong lack of balance. He dove to the side and rolled in the grass as the body landed with a stomach turning crunch of bones. It was the body of a man in a pair of work trousers and a cardigan.

Tuck walked to the body and looked at it.

"He's human," he said, "The impact killed him."

A whine from above grew in volume and became a high pitched scream and Tuck saw just in time a woman in a white toweling robe just before she hit the roof of Rayne's house with a crashing thud.

Another scream-thud sound landed nearby and made him jump.

"What the hell is going on here Carol?" he hissed, rushing to the latest body to have fallen from the sky. As he neared it his stomach turned over and he looked away from the crushed body of an adolescent boy.

"Tuck look up," Carol said.

It was raining people.

Heaven had rolled onto its side and spilled out all of its guests and they dropped from the sky in their hundreds. Spinning out of control as they fell, their arms and legs flailing desperately in the effort to stop the ground from coming up so fast.

A fall of a couple of stories will do horrible things to a body but these people were falling from several times that height and as they're dead weights hit the ground, the gravel driveway, veranda tiles or the roof they splattering like ripened fruits. Some of them landed in the pool with massive splashes but they didn't surface alive.

What had begun as a few intermittent bodies suddenly became a downpour.

Rayne started shouting.

Tuck started running.

Dodging the bodies as they fell, knowing that he had no way of saving them for even if he caught them at that velocity they would have died just as quickly by hitting his arms as they would by hitting the floor. The topography of smells had changed dramatically when the people started landing, they hit the ground and their bodies exploded on impact. Their bones breaking like twigs, their organs rupturing like frot and their internal smells spewing out of their bodies like steam from a kettle.

He reached the front gate and climbed to the top of it and looked around.

Falling directly out of the black cloud the bodies were hitting the roads and the neighbor's houses just as frequently as they were hitting Rayne's. But where were they coming from?

A scream right near his ear made him move as a body fell so close to him that it brushed his clothes and hit the top of the gate. The gate didn't so much as budge but the person was just about cut clean in half by it. Tuck gagged.

Behind him, in the house he heard Carol shoving Rayne into the garage and Mason was yelling commands into his phone.

A movement directly ahead caught his attention and he threw himself forward and off the gate as a blonde, female's body in a pair of jeans and leather jacket sailed directly passed him with such force that she went right over Rayne's property in an almost straight line. He hit the exterior drive way and rolled to a crouched position and leapt to the side as another body bounced beside him. He honed in on the trajectory origin and saw a pale figure, as naked as the day she was born but far too young and small to have been able to throw a human body like that. Her irises were shining green in the night like a predator's and when she realized she had been spotted she retreated on all fours like an animal.

Behind her a wake of nothingness confused his sense of smell.
A crack of bone against bone and he thought he'd been hit in the head with an axe, a body weighing hundreds of kilograms crashed down onto of him and drove him to the ground.
Stars spinning in front of his eyes he went to his hands and knees. As the body slumped off him the length of its arm and finally its hand and fingers stroked the back of his neck almost affectionately.
It made his skin crawl and he started shaking. He looked up and down the street and just saw bodies falling, hundreds of them. Scream-thud. Scream thud. Scream-thud. He would never forget the sound.
Another body, like a pillow filled with stones landed on his lower back pinning him to the ground.

For a little while things went dark.

Carol saw Tuck vanish under the growing pile of people who were falling from the sky. Ironically he was probably the safest out of all of them. She could also see where the bodies were coming from. They weren't just falling, they were being thrown. It was happening across streets with dozens of houses at a time. The homes were shooting their occupants vertically into the air like stuntmen from canons.

They were being thrown by women with glowing eyes. The green eyed women, completely naked, blurred with speed as they rushed through the houses in packs. Grabbing hold of everyone inside, dragging them outside and hurling them into the sky.

They didn't care who they threw. Men. Women and even children of all ages.

"We're surrounded by them," Carol said, "They're moving through the houses, spreading outwards, picking people up and throwing them here."

Mason just nodded. The three of them were inside the garage and he was trying to get an argumentative Rayne into her car. She was resolute that she was not going to be scared out of her house and that she had had enough of being bullied by this shit. He had already managed to defend several kicks to the groin but had taken a fairly nasty punch to the throat.

"Rayne, you can't help here," he said, opening the Landrover door and trying to push her inside, Rayne slammed it shut, "This is my home!" Above there were more crashes as bodies fell through and the screams from outside were building, she put her hands to her ears, "I am *not* going out there!"

"Please," Mason said taking her hands in his and looking her in the eye, "Rayne I can't lose you. Get in the car and I'll drive you to the rendezvous point where a chopper will take you away."

"I'm safest here," she insisted, "Carol tell him, we've had this house turned into a fortress thanks to all the crap that's happened in it since I met you."

That one seemed to hurt him, she carried on, "Don't you see what's happening out there? The roads are covered with people. I don't want to drive over them."

"The house is very safe," Carol confirmed, "And any air support is going to be troublesome with people falling from the sky."

"You see," Rayne said, "If I get into this car I'll just be taking all of this out there for someone else to sort. I want to stay here."

"You have no choice," Carol told them, "I'm locking the house down I think they're about to attack."

"Oh my God where is Tuck?" Rayne asked.

"He's outside the house," Carol said and as she didn't elaborate they all assumed the worse.

"I'm not leaving him outside," Mason declared, "That man has suffered enough because of me I'm not going to let him die out there."

"Can you die here?" Rayne asked, her cheeks going red.

Mason shrugged as he headed out of the garage, "This seems as good an opportunity to find out as any," his phone rang and he answered it jovially, "Hi! Yeah it's Mason…oh no, it's not a bad time, just fighting for the lives of everyone I love-"

Carol closed the garage door after him and slipping her arm around Rayne's waist and guided the woman to the entrance to the basement. The house had been designed with every eventuality in mind and many of the newest houses in South Africa were built with underground basements and fallout shelters should things get very serious in Australia. Mason slipped out of the front door quickly and closed it behind him; Carol re-engaged the locks and opened the basement.

The thick steel panel opened onto a narrow staircase only wide enough for one person to walk down at a time. There were half a dozen steps down to a landing and a turn in the stairs that was half the width of the staircase itself so anyone wanting to get down would then have to turn sideways and shimmy through the opening to get to the security suite below. This was to stop more than one person getting in at a time.

Sullenly Rayne went down first and Carol followed, closing the heavy steel panel behind her and locking it with the deadbolt catch.

The security booth itself was exactly what you'd expect in a millionaire's home. Spacious, leather sofas, plastered walls with chrome finishings, the latest in air filtering technology, a well-stocked kitchen, wide television screen, computers and a bathroom. It looked like the inside of an ultra-modern luxury yacht.

Rayne plonked herself on the sofa and put her face in her hands, stifling her tears she said, "Communicate with them via the intercom system please, give them all the help you can."

Carol was already on it. She sat down on one of the single sofas and her faced lost all expression as she diverted her intelligence to the household management system above.

"What about the chopper Mason was talking about?" Rayne asked, "He said it wasn't coming here?"

"It doesn't matter," Carol said with confidence, "The pilot will know to bring it here the important part is that you're safe."

Rayne angrily wiped tears away from her face, "*I'm* safe, what about them?"

"I have the strong inclination that neither Tuck nor Mason would want to stay in here," she said, "Don't argue Rayne, your life is more important."

"Why?"

Mason stepped out of the house and was astounding at what he saw. He had seen war zones, he had seen carnage but what he was looking at now appeared biblical.

The shower of bodies had ceased, either through a change of tactics or more probably a sudden shortage of people to throw as what he walked out into was a blanket of human bodies piled two or three persons deep. Their bodies twisted and broken, their limbs bent in awkward directions. In the field of cadavers there was movement, some just the twitching of fingers and limbs, but in others it was the last heaving movements of a chest struggling to hold onto that last breathe or the groaning of someone who, cruelly, had not been given the mercy of death.

For a second his mind went blank as he absorbed what he was seeing.

He adamantly refused to step on any of these people, he did not want to touch them, he did not want to see them and he had to avoid their eyes because there was nothing he could do. No solace he could offer them. Spying a half metre gap between the bodies that hung upon the property wall and gate like abandoned clothing he leapt to it.

From there every house that he could sense into was empty, the occupants lying dead upon the ground. Just as many bodies lay upon the road and the grassy verges surrounding Rayne's house. The Suburbs looked like the setting of a biological disaster; it looked like the population of the world had been scooped into a bucket by God and then poured out over this neighborhood.

He felt hopelessly sickened by the pointless tragedy of it and when he spied the bodies of several children, bundled in their pajamas and now lying like broken dolls upon their neighbors he felt mad.

Movement amongst the bodies caught his eye, about twenty metres away beneath a bank of street lamps seven pale, naked females with glowing green eyes were crouched amongst the bodies. Their faces were pressed into a corpse and they were shaking their heads and tearing through the flesh and cartilage, sucking at the blood that was pouring from the vicious wounds.

"Oddly enough," a female voice said, "They're not vampires as you would think."

He found the source of the voice. A woman he didn't recognize but he recognized the aura of her energy around her, she was like him. But stronger. She stood on the other side of the road, leaning against the trunk of one of the perfectly trimmed trees that provided that suburban quality to this area. Her arms folded she exuded a feral sort of anger that was barely concealed behind her voice.

"And who are you?" Mason asked.

"Tammy," she said, "Tammy Jenkins. I'm a Hunter."

Mason didn't respond, his eyes were on hers, but his senses searched his surroundings. There were more of these feral females skulking around in the shadows, they were climbing around the house behind him and had entered the house main and were crawling through the rooms searching for Rayne. He couldn't smell them though and he could only barely hear them but he knew where they were.

"Did you have to kill all of these people?" he asked.

"No," she said, "We got a little carried away but I think I've made my point quite well. I'm stronger than you could possibly imagine and I will get what I want."

"Which is?"

"The woman of course," Tammy said, "Rayne, I want her, go and fetch her for me. Bring her here."

"If you're planning to use her as bait," Mason said, "She makes a very awkward hostage I wouldn't bother if I were you."

"My master," Tammy said, "And before you ask his name is Shaka, The Hunter. He may want her as bait but I just want her dead. The Coat will return here and find that he is to blame for all of this... he tried to destroy my life and for that I will annihilate his entire world."

Mason cocked his head to one side, "You've been misled Miss. Jenkins. My name is Lynel Mason-"

"Yes I know who you are," she snarled pushing away from the tree, "Now fetch me your slut so I can kill her!"

Mason lifted a hand, "Please. You have been lied to, you see I am Shaka's employer and if anyone is to blame for all of this," he swept the same hand around, gesturing at the entangled carpet of bodies, "It is me. Not the Coat and certainly not all of these people you've just killed."

Tammy looked up the road and pursed her lips, she gave a nonchalant shrug, "These people don't matter."

"What did you say?"

"They are not Uniques likes us," she said in explanation.

"These are civilians, family people that you've just slaughtered." He looked down at the small gang of these non-vampires who were mauling the corpse, ripping it to shreds. He could hear the wet tearing sounds of the flesh.

"Where is Shaka?" Mason asked, "Has he killed The Coat?"

"No," Tammy said, "The Coat is too strong for that. I should know, I have him inside me, his *essence* is bonded with every one of my cells and I have an inclination to his power and to that end Shaka doesn't stand a chance."

"You don't sound very moved by it," Mason said, to his right the sounds of teeth crushing bones made his stomach turn.

"I'm not," Tammy said, "We all have our own plans in this life you have to go with what is important. Inevitably, The Coat will win but before he does I want him to be devastated."

"I told you already," Mason explained, "You're anger is misplaced and Shaka has lied to you. The Coat is not the enemy- I gave Shaka the giant's blood with the task of taking The Coat's head and you were pulled into it unfairly."

Tammy was unmoved by this, a look of boredom flattened her features, "I'm growing tired of this Mason I will come and take Rayne myself."

She walked across the street and her strength was evident in the manner that while anyone else would trip over the deadweight of a dead body she simply kicked it out of the way in mid stride. Like walking through a puddle of water. Mason sensed the subtle movement of her ghostly army all around him. Was she communicating/controlling them telepathically?

He stood and prepared himself, "I'm not going to let you do this."

28.

The giant did not mask or lighten his footsteps and Shaka was given plenty of warning that the vigilante was approaching and even from the stride and steps he could tell the giant's mood and felt a thrill buzz through his spine.

The shadowy shape gradually appeared through the thick cloud, a column of black.

"Did you get to them on time?" he prodded.

The Coat's anger was tantamount, in fact it radiated off him in waves of heat that caused the cloud to swirl in great arcs around him and Shaka could feel the hot air against his eyeballs.

"Or did you not? I wanted to leave a trail for you to follow to each of those children who were so hoping they were going to be rescued. I went to each of them on foot and even urinated on them to make sure you could follow me to each of them."

He stood, holding the sword loosely in his right hand, when the giant still didn't say anything he lifted it and pointed it at him, "Well, did I do a thorough job or were you able to save at least one of those innocent children?"

Speaking slowly, with every word carefully enunciated The Coat said, "I am going to kill you."

However, Shaka was unsatisfied, so he mentioned, "Do you know that I told those kids that it was just a game and that you would save them? I promised them that you would rescue them before anything bad happened to them. I even had them repeat it back to me, 'The Coat will not let me die....' I think by the end of it they believed it too."

The Hunter was a keen register of people's emotions, but he couldn't yet tell if the giant's stoic silence was a good sign or not. Good in this case being angry, he wanted the beast.

"Who did you find first? Was it Margery? A little brunette girl about seven years old, so little that you could hold her in your arms all day and never feel tired. She cried for you when I closed the lid of that barrel and buried her. What about Denis? He was wearing Superman pajamas when I tied him in front of that steam pipe... you didn't set off the trap did you?"

Shaka feigned a surprised look, putting his fingers in his mouth, "Oh no, you did didn't you? Did you hear him scream or was the steam too loud?"

It was working. The Coat's shoulders were forward, his chin down to his chest and his hands curled into fists that were shivering. The waves of heat increased.

"I suppose you probably knew all their names too," the Hunter continued, "Did you promise their parents that you would bring them back to them? Oooh that could be awkward- messy too.

"And before the end of tonight you will have failed someone else who believed you would protect her."

The Coat's head moved ever so slightly but the gesture may have been a neon exclamation mark above his head as he realized what he had done.

"Your Tammy Jenkins, I bet that is one shag you're *really* going to regret. You know what they say, hell hath no fury like a woman scorned and I can't imagine the sort of things she'll do to Rayne."

The Coat lapsed into another statuesque stillness, Shaka hoped he hadn't lost the advantage and said, "You seem distraught Coat? Shall I return to telling you about the children that have died because you were too slow and unprepared? About little Simon, Jeffrey, Grace and Alexandra- they will never see the sun again because you just didn't care enough... and they died in agony thanks to me."

The Coat roared but it wasn't the sort of roar a human would make, this was animalistic, bestial. His chin dropping below the curl of the shadowy hood and the sound piercing like that of a giant cat. Sprinting he cleared the distance between them in a couple of long strides, his hood blew back and the dark madness in his eyes was incredibly beautiful to the Hunter.

He punched out at such a speed that it *boomed* with thunder as his fist shattered the air but Shaka avoided it with the skill of a matador, using the sword tip to poke The Coat's flank. The giant barked in surprise and spun around, his garment of choice flaring out around him, his eyes wide. Shaka was astounded by the coils of muscles he could see in the giant's jaws, they looked like bags of snakes!

"Do you believe in an afterlife?" he asked, "Bet they'll be waiting for you there to ask why you let them die."

Like a giant cat The Coat attacked again, leaping directly at Shaka with his hands out stretched, Shaka slipped beneath him and teasingly grazed the sword blade across The Coat's front, the shirt and the first few layers of skin opened up in a wound about the width of his hand.

The Coat rolled across the helipad, his immense size causing the whole thing to bounce.

"It's only a little cut," Shaka assured him, "There'll be many more before I'm done with you."

The got to his feet and tried to rush ahead at his full speed, but Shaka had chosen the helipad specifically for this reason, it's scaffold structure was not designed to take such forces and when The Coat attempted to accelerate the initial thrust from his legs buckled the metal and the giant slipped as if he'd been running on ice, landing hard on his front.

Shaka was on him in split seconds and with a series of rapid strokes he zigzagged the blade across the giant's broad back and was off him before the giant found his feet and disentangled himself from the broken helipad.

Shaka waited, both hands leaning on the sword, a smile on his face.

This was immensely enjoyable, so much so that the Hunter didn't even think about taking the blood that was flowing off the sword like butter off a scalding torch he was simply having far too much fun.

Shoulders heaving, the giant rose to his feet, his coat opened up in several locations and the bare flesh was visibly steaming. On the last three maneuvers it had been like dancing with an open flame.

The rising clouds of steam coming from his skin were soon combined with tendrils of smoke as large patches of his clothing started to singe.

This was going marvelously well.

"I imagine Rayne is probably screaming by now," Shaka said.

Perfectly on cue Tuck erupted from the layers of bodies that had been concealing him, catching Tammy by surprise. His knee connected with her chin, slamming her mouth shut with an audible crunch and a spray of blood. Mason dove headlong off the wall and tackled her around the neck, hooking his left arm under her chin and applying a full choke hold, with his left arm tightly locked around her throat, with that hand gripped upon his right bicep while his right hand grabbed a fistful of hair at the back of her head. As they scrabbled she reached back with her hands and dug her fingers into his arms, piercing the skin and aiming to sever the tendons in his arms while he wrapped his legs around her middle locking his ankles around her midsection and squeezing his legs together with all his might.

Tuck landed upon them and immediately threw himself into the melee with blurring fists, he attacked her midsection with rapidly cycling punches from both hands.

Mason tightened his body and squeezed his eyes shut as Tuck pounded her ribcage and sternum, smashing through her breasts. The force of the Freelander's punches caused the asphalt under Mason's back to crack and the blows created a rolling thunder that echoed up and down the street.

Mason knew the tactic; Tuck was aiming for the skeleton. Snapping ribs would puncture organs and take longer to heal. But as her body only cushioned the severity of the blows it was still he who received a great deal of it and although Tuck's face was a screaming war mask of rage, he would bet anything that behind that grimace was a smile that was thoroughly enjoying this opportunity.

Tammy couldn't scream because she couldn't breathe and her fingers, deeply dug into Mason's arms lost their grip and went limp but Tuck did not stop the pummeling until he was hitting a sack of flesh and gravel, at which point he changed his target area and rained down blows against Tammy's face and skull.

Mason squeezed his eyes shut and felt every blow connect with the woman's face as he held her head in place, it was like holding a melon in front of a machine gun. The fast drum beat of blows sounded hard at first, like fists hitting a bowling ball, but the sound changed very quickly and became that of fists hitting a pudding.

"Christ! Tuck enough!" Mason yelled, letting the girl go and pushing her limp body off him.

Tuck stepped back, his fists dripping blood, he was gasping for breath.

Mason struggled out of the crater he had formed in the asphalt and spat out a lump of bloody bits. Tuck didn't offer to help, on his knees Mason said, "Don't go anywhere we still need to take her head."

Taking the lead, Tuck rolled her body over onto her front and knelt on her shoulder blades, Mason noticed with disgust how her body seemed to deflate like a liquid filled sack as Tuck's leant into it. The Freelander's right hand took hold of her chin, while his left hand pressed against the back of her head and in a very businesslike fashion he wrenched her head to one side and tried to pull it away. It didn't work. He adjusted his grip and tried it again to the same effect.

"Do you have anything that can cut her throat?" he asked.

Mason was watching as those pale, feral things with the green eyes, who may have been beautiful in their nudity and sensual movements if not for their bloodied faces, were circling them.

"I don't think we have time for that," he said.

Carol had watched those *things* invade herself. Seen them break in through the windows and through the shattered ceiling and skulk around looking for Rayne. They moved on all fours like animals and all of them were women. Some of the people who had fallen were still alive but whenever one of these creatures found one still breathing they would pounce upon them and savage them. Ripping into their bellies and tearing out organs, licking at blood and gnawing on bones while the poor victim screamed. By the time they had found their way into the garage they're faces and hands were black with blood.

Following Rayne's scent to the steel panel they searched with their fingers for a seam but found none and in their eagerness to get through they started pounding it with their fists and throwing their bodies at it.

"What are they?" Rayne asked, as it all unfolded on the television screen.

"I don't know," Carol said, "Ah good news at last, the chopper has changed course. It's on its way here."

Rayne didn't reply her eyes were on the screen where she watched Tuck and Mason.

Shaka wiped a bead of sweat away from an eyebrow with a thumb and looked at his right hand, during the excitement he hadn't noticed but the flesh had returned to its usually Swiss Chocolate brown.

"It's incredible how liberating this new life is," he said, "When you know you'll outlive any of the rules, you just stop caring about them."

He had delivered a very deep cut to the giant's hamstring which had cut down straight to the bone. It reminded Shaka of the old punishment in Japan where prisoners were summarily hit upon the lower buttocks with a sword blade to severe the hamstrings and were then allowed their freedom. Of course a severed hamstring has no hope of reattaching itself and so they always became cripples.

The injury had taken the giant to his knees but had not distinguished his rage. The smell of burning clothes was thick and smoke rose from his body in sheets. Pain and frustration were making him angrier by the minute but apart from turning his body into a walking furnace it had not made him any more of a challenge as a fighter and Shaka tasted the harsh bitterness of disappointment. The Coat was simply not the animal he thought.

Tuck's arms were burning with strain as he curled his back in the attempt of breaking the woman's damn neck. He jerked, he yanked, he twisted this way and that but the bloody thing refused to snap. He could tell they were surrounded but wasn't so concerned about these things. These ferals, they were strong but their minds were those of animals and they would fight for as long as they had the advantage and then they would flee. For the moment they didn't know where they stood.

"Any time now," Mason pushed.

"You are welcome to give this a go," Tuck snarled through gritted teeth, "*Fucking* break you bitch!"

Under him, against his knees he could feel things moving inside her body as she was rebuilt. Her bowels bloated as the broken bones and damaged tissues were quickly metabolized into the system making room for fresh bones to generate and grow and organs to re-establish themselves. He had to have her head by then but he just wasn't strong enough to-

There was a thick unloading in her trousers and a spray of blood that blew out of her mouth and over his hands.

"Shit!" he hissed.

The ferals, sensing Tammy's imminent recovery attacked with a confidence and with the advantage of numbers they poured onto Mason, hitting him in the chest and driving him backwards.

Tuck felt Tammy's ribcage snap into place and she shook her head free the instant he was hit by a cascade of rabid, non-smelling bodies.

Abandoning trying to get into their bunker, the ferals in the garage took to destroying all of Rayne's cars, ripping the beautiful vehicles to pieces. Through the camera feed these ferals looked remarkably human and animalistic; they were athletic but moved around as if their athleticism was best suited to running on all fours. One of them picked up the entire engine manifold of her Landrover and hurled it across the garage where it imbedded itself into the garage door. They all laughed at this, a chittering, primal laughter.

"How intelligent are they?" Rayne asked.

"Enough," Carol said.

They stopped their ransacking and loped out of the garage to join in the fighting outside and Carol and Rayne were able to watch the battle as it happened. They couldn't see Tuck or Mason in the surge of pale bodies and Rayne was pounding her fist into her hand, and bouncing up and down on her heels, "Come on come on come on,"

Carol pointed to the screen at the woman who looked to be controlling all of this from the sidelines, "Look,"

Tammy bent over double and coughed up the last of the black stuff and since her clothes were so thoroughly soiled with everything that had been pushed out of her body she took them off.

With a thought she told her *things* to stop their attack and to let her see Mason and Tuck. Instantly the fighting ceased.

The two men had merely been mauled but not eaten. Massive chunks of flesh and muscle were missing from their legs and arms and Mason was bleeding heavily from a melon sized hole in his side.

She bid some of her *things* to bring them and two of them dragged them by their ankles and lined up behind her. She opened the gates and walked over the carpet of bodies into the center of the drive way where she could see one of the security cameras clearly. She spread her arms, and addressed it directly:

"Is this what you want Rayne?" she asked, "If it is I hope you're satisfied. Let me know just how many more people need to die before you will come out here."

Carol spotted the expression on Rayne's face and physically leapt in front of the staircase, "No!" the robot said, "No way am I letting you out of here!"

"Get out of my way Carol!" Rayne ordered, "Get out of my way!"

"I'm not going to let you die!"

"I don't want this anymore I don't want any more people to die for me," Rayne said angrily, "I'm not worth all of this."

On the screen behind her Tammy was saying, "I'm not going to count to ten Rayne, you come out now or I'm going to start hurting these men. Do you want to hear them scream?"

Carol shook her head, "No, Rayne. No. You go out there and everything is for nothing, all the sacrifices will be in vain."

"They are all in vain Carol," Rayne said, "It's time to end this."

"Just because you don't know why you're important doesn't make any difference Rayne," Carol said holding the woman at bay by the shoulders, "Mason, Tuck, The Coat they are all fighting for you and my entire program is centrally devoted to looking out for you. You may or may not be able to see it but you're very important."

"Well maybe this is what I'm meant to do?" Rayne argued, "Maybe I'm meant to sacrifice myself tonight? Maybe *that's* part of the grand plan? Did you think of that?"

On the screen Tammy said, "Okay then," and a second later one of them, either Mason or Tuck started screaming.

"You're not going," Carol said.

Rayne's expression changed so rapidly Carol couldn't follow, she looked desperate, angry and then miserable within seconds of each other before saying, "I'm sorry Carol," and this was followed by, "Gulligan Fox Arabian Night Fish,"

The safety words that Rayne had never thought she would have to use, flicked a trigger in Carol's artificial synapsis and the robot stiffened, her eyes blanked and she collapsed to the floor. Rayne looked at the fallen machine, her blond hair sprayed out around her face, her blue-blue eyes staring vacantly upwards, her mouth slightly opened.

She wanted to touch the robot's face but she just didn't have the time.

Shaking her arms to loosen up Rayne climbed the stairs, unlocked the steel panel and with some effort pushed it outwards.

The garage felt cold to her as she turned immediately right and went up the short flight of stairs into the ransacked kitchen, a flicker of movement through the main window caught her attention as a pale bodied feral scampered past and her whole body shivered at the sight of it. How was she going to die?

As soon as the thought entered her head she battered it away.

On knees that genuinely felt like jelly she walked through and out of the kitchen into the hall way where just as she was walking out from under the stairs something fell down.

It missed her by centimeters and hit the floor in front of her and she screamed so hard it hurt her throat as it turned into a broken human body. *It's Charles Reynhart;* she thought when she finally recognized the face. The novelist's body lay at an awkward angle, there was blood and dust in his hair and he stank of human waste.

Death wasn't pleasant. It wasn't peaceful, it wasn't solemn. Death smelt like piss and shit and it left the human body looking anything but at peace.

Would she need to have a closed casket, or would the mortician be able to piece together her body enough so that it could pass as being whole?

Like song lyrics in the back of her mind these questions rolled passed without leaving much of an impression and she felt a cool sort of calmness unroll itself in her belly and spread through her.

As she opened the front doors she saw more of the pale, feral creatures than she had expected. There is a distinct difference between seeing monsters over a security feed and seeing them directly in front of you. Their presence scared her. They looked so human and yet acted like such animals, crouched on all fours, walking around like apes would. Their faces covered in blood, their stomachs bloated with their feeding.

And amongst them stood Tammy.

As naked as birth she stood with the unconscious men on either side of her, close enough that Rayne could have thrown a ball at them underhanded but too far for her to see if they were breathing.

The sort of clarity the mind gets when it loses touch with itself descended upon her and she looked around, seeing the countless bodies lying around her house, just a messy tangle of arms and limbs and hands with the occasional head and face, twisted and tied together. They didn't look human either.

How were the media going to explain this then?

"You're a brave woman," Tammy said to her, her voice causing a rippling cringe from some of the feral creatures nearer to her, "I was getting ready to come in there myself."

Rayne swallowed hard and closed the doors to her house behind her, "It isn't bravery," she said, "I just want this finished."

In a wash of prickly heat that flurried across her whole body she screwed up her face in an attempt to hide the sudden deluge of fear. But she couldn't she wasn't a hero and she didn't want to die, she didn't want to be hurt, and she didn't deserve any of this!
Shameful, chest heaving sobs brought her to her knees and she covered her face and cried until the tears were dripping from between her fingers.

A warm, soft touch took her hands and brought them away and she looked up into the woman's face. She was beautiful but there was a strange distance to her eyes that made them unreadable.

"Shush now," Tammy crooned, stroking hair out of Rayne's face and wiping away her tears with a thumb, "You are brave. So very brave." Rayne let herself be pulled into an embrace as the woman stroked the back of her head saying, "It will be over very quick…"
She stood up, bringing Rayne to her feet.
Fuck it, Rayne thought and kneed the murderous bitch as hard as she could between the legs.

Shaka sighed, "This is what I find tragic,"
The Coat was once again standing; his body a statue of blazing heat, his hamstring had miraculously repaired itself, either through reattachment or replacement.

"You are the strongest of your kind and yet you're just *not* the fighter I expected. You've deeply hurt me… I have been sorely cheated and I am just so damned annoyed with you."
The Coat started walking towards him again.
Perhaps he would cut off his limbs? Shaka thought, let him flop around like a fish for a little while before taking his head? If he wasn't going to get his epic battle then he could potentially settle for some cruel amusement.
A wind buffeted The Coat's clothes, blowing the many rips and tears against the skin beneath through which Shaka could see the muscular movements.

Would he be able to split him in two? Shaka thought, Samurais in Japan were trained to such a high degree of swordsmanship that they could divide a man in half from the top of his head to the fork in his groin. Now their finest swords were not nearly as sharp as the weapon he held and they were nowhere near as strong as he was, so to increase the challenge he'd have to find an interesting way of delivering such a final blow.

The Coat pulled his hood back up over his head.

Shaka readied himself for the attack, eased his muscles into coiled springs ready for movement and adjusted his grip on the sword to make for a better slice when-

Thump.

Shaka's head rocked on his neck as the length of The Coat's forearm entered his abdominal cavity and the giant hand curled around his spinal column.

I didn't see him move, Shaka thought.

A terrible tearing pain, like being winded but a thousand times worse spread itself throughout his torso and he felt the giant's fingers grip the bony column of his backbone.

The sword clattered to the helipad floor and Shaka felt warmth spread the front of his trousers and a moment later a hot, heavy sensation spilled out into the seat of his pants. He smelt shit and blood.

Had he defecated?

The pain was the most intense feeling he had ever experience in his life and he couldn't do anything. He didn't want to move in case it worsened and that included breathing.

Just break my back and get it done with, he thought, rolling his eyes upwards to see The Coat but he didn't get further than the giant's shoulder. Through gritted teeth he hissed, tasted blood on every word, "Do it..."

"No," came the reply and The Coat withdrew his arm.

His insides felt fused together into the shape of his forearm and suddenly to have it removed made Shaka scream, his body jerking and bobbing as nerves and muscles sparked, spraying blood everywhere he watched The Coat pick up the sword.

"Yes, kill me with the sword," Shaka whispered, "It is sacred to my people, it will be a clean death."

But The Coat didn't. Instead the giant did the very last thing the Hunter expected him to do. He held out his left arm palm up and with a casual sweep of the sword cut his wrist to the bone and with such a brutal barrage that Shaka's front teeth were smashed to the back of his throat he shoved his gushing wrist into the Hunter's mouth. The Coat bore Shaka to the floor where he held his head in place with the other hand so that his blood spewed into Shaka's mouth.

Shaka was so shocked he stiffened, his hands held out with the fingers splayed as the blood pooled thick and rich around his tongue, gushed down his throat and filled his sinuses. The effect was indescribable. Like taking a drug he felt its effects immediately. All the ragged chunks of meat and tissue in his abdomen liquidized and he felt a heavy feeling in his bowels. New muscles, cartilage and organ tissue were woven together but there was more. He felt epically more powerful than he had done before. He felt filled with light.

It was godhood that he felt.

He shoved The Coat aside and the giant stepped backwards seemingly nonplussed by Shaka's sudden strength.

The Hunter sneered, then laughed, "You idiot!" he pointed a finger, "You unbelievable wanker, do you have any idea what you've done!?"

The Coat gave an almost imperceptible nod.

Shaka smiled widely but was done with talking and attacked.

The sword forgotten he leapt straight in with a punch which landed against The Coat's chest with the force of a missile.

Tammy gave a furious groan of pain and Rayne punched her with a right cross that landed against the woman's jaw followed with a left uppercut to her chin. Her head snapping backwards Rayne threw a throat punch against the exposed length of her neck that landed with a satisfying crunch and kicked her again in the exposed vagina as hard as she could.

Rayne turned to run but the woman grabbed her by her hair.

"Very nice bluff you little slut!" Tammy spat, dragging Rayne backwards by her hair and flinging her upon the ground, "Now let me show you how you really hit someone in the crotch!"

Sprawled on the floor Tammy towered over her with murder shining in her eyes and out of nowhere Tuck appeared, flying through the air with his right leg extended like a lance and his left tucked under him. He looked epic in that moment. The kick landed against the exposed region of Tammy's neck and while she took half a step to the side it didn't have the effect that Tuck was hoping for. She took the blow, grabbed his leg and swung him around by his foot and hurled him into her house. Mason appeared leaping upon the bitch's back and driving a descending elbow as hard as he could into her collar bone but she didn't seem to notice. She grabbed his wrist, snapped it as if it were a pencil and swung him over her shoulder and into the floor. Mason lay there, stunned and she took a small step and kicked him in the guts as if she was kicking a football and he vanished into the house along with Tuck.

"I'm killing the whore to get at The Coat," Tamm shouted in their general direction, "But you two are just pissing me off!"
With that her attention returned to Rayne, "I'll deal with them later."
And now I die. Daemon!
There was a blast of thunder, an unbelievable heat and a searing pain against Rayne's face but she realized she was free and surrounded by feet. Curled into a little protective ball, covering her head. What the hell had happened?

The punch did not penetrate The Coat's body as Shaka had hoped but it did knock the giant a step or two backwards where he dropped to a knee and held his chest. To Shaka's satisfaction a second later a waterfall of blood poured out of the hood.

The energy was unbelievable, he felt like a god. He felt like at any moment he would explode into flight! He ran the few steps between him and his enemy and kicked him.
The Coat was lifted off his feet and flew the length of the Gregory Maine's Tower and landed against the steel banister in exactly the same place Shaka had been standing when he had first spotted The Coat. The steel buckled beneath the giant's weight.

"I am *completely* immortal now!" Shaka roared, spreading his arms and addressing the entire world, "I am Eternal!"
The Coat disentangled himself from the banister and rose to his feet and Shaka watched him climb back onto the helipad. The giant moved *so* slowly it was infuriating!
As The Coat straightened the Hunter leaped in:
Bang! He landed a right jab that jerked the giant's head to one side, *bang bang!* He followed through with a cross and a hook, *boom!* He sprang vertically into the air and delivered a spinning turn heel kick that sent the giant cart wheeling.
Not being one to forget loose ends, Shaka decided to take The Coat's head after all and then go about his business and a universe of

possibilities opened themselves up to him. He sauntered over to the giant, wrestled him easily into a kneeling position, wrenched back the hood and took hold of the giant's head in his hands.

The Coat did nothing to stop him.

Removing the head would be as easy as twisting a cap of a bottle, Shaka realized, he could have done it with his fingertips. But why wasn't The Coat fighting back and *why was he smiling?*

The sizzling sensation started in his groin region, it was an uncomfortable burning sensation that was unfamiliar to him and while at first he didn't really give it much attention it quickly spread through his body becoming more pronounced. He felt the same sensation in the back of his throat and when he opened his mouth he could have sworn he saw a spark flicker out of it.

The Coat escaped his hands and rolled away, coming smoothly to his feet, his back to The Hunter.

"You played me!" Shaka growled. His whole body shook uncontrollably as the sizzling became a painful electric burn under his skin, "You were never losing!"

The Coat turned his head to the side, "You wanted my blood and I wanted you to suffer. We are even."

The electricity hit his skeleton and it made him feel like he was going to rip apart, "What's happening to me!?" he screamed shrilly.

"No two of my kind can touch," The Coat told him, "I'm surprised that Mason didn't mention this but as long as you had the other giant's blood in your body this was always going to happen the moment you took my blood."

Shaka's eyes widened.

"I have to be somewhere," The Coat said, taking the sword and walking away.

Shaka barely registered the words. His whole body was convulsing uncontrollable and something was stirring in his belly, it felt white hot and it was rapidly expanding. His finger and toe tips felt as if there were being held in an open flame and his joints as if they were being splintered. An unexpected searing pain behind his eyes blinded him and he vividly smelt olives.

Before leaving Daemon turned and watched the hunter die to ensure that it had happened and that it was over. Outwardly all that could be seen was that the man's whole body was shaking as muscles and tendons yanked and twisted, his head jerked to the side with such force his temple connected with his shoulder and he could hear individual teeth splitting as his jaw clenched down.

The Hunter reached up and tore open his shirt to look at what he could feel was happening in his torso and his cries were of horror and pain as his skin bulged and twisted as his insides, his organs writhed and tried to vacate their positions. It looked like a bag of angry pythons.

Daemon could feel what was taking place and when the sparks started to sizzle across the man's body, like living electricity running down the exterior of a Tesla coil he knew that it was over but watched nonetheless.

It appeared to happen quickly but he knew it didn't feel that way for the Hunter who had the joy of feeling every cell in his body attempt to distance itself from every other cell.

An exothermic reaction took place as Shaka's body began breaking apart. Across his chest his skin dried like husk, splitting and cracking before sparking with sizzling arcs of that glowing white electricity which caused it to turn to dust like the oldest pieces of parchment blowing apart in the air. The bones beneath became as brittle as twigs and snapped under their own weight, the parts disintegrated into clouds of dust. His right arm snapped near the shoulder joint and slipped out of the sleeve like a prosthetic and shattered when it hit the floor issuing a cloud of smoke and the stink of burning pork.

After that his chest cavity exploded, making a wet smacking sound like bacon being fried and within his body his insides were drying and smoldering red hot, electricity buzzing through with a bright light.

He threw his head back as his face burst apart, shattered by the sudden expansive swelling of his brain before it dried instantly into the finest dust that was blown away in the wind.

The rest of Shaka fell back and hit the floor, shattering like a ceramic model, leaving Daemon standing alone in the mist.

Daemon!

He heard his name psychically and with such force that it staggered him and he turned in its direction feeling a mental line tying him with that person unlike anything he'd ever known.

Rayne.

The heat that had seared his clothes earlier when he had been playing possum with the Hunter overcame him in a flash that increased his temperature with such sudden intensity it caused the air to curl around him into a storm, the mist was blown completely away from the rooftop and as he hit the upper echelon of his power the heat quadrupled suddenly, causing his very clothes to burst into open flame.

He bent his legs, calculating the distance from where the helipad to where Rayne was, gathered his strength and jumped.

The torque destroyed the helipad and every window in the Gregory Maines tower blew outwards, raining broken glass upon Sky City.

He landed in a crouch in exactly the same spot he had landed earlier that night amongst a flood of human carcasses. Surrounded on all sides by feral, pale women with maws covered with blood and glowing eyes. Inside the house a very beaten Tuck and Mason were battling these women clearly trying to fight their way back to the front where, on the porch Tammy stood over Rayne, her hands holding Rayne's wrist while a foot pressed hard against the woman's shoulder. Tammy was in the process of pulling off Rayne's arm.

Physicists have yet to learn certain things about their own universe, for example they already know that at the speed that The Coat was moving air takes on the consistency of water- but he cut through it as it were nothing but a vacuum propelling him faster. He grabbed Tammy by the wrists and obliterated the bones so that she let go of Rayne's arm and taking her by the head he leapt to the rooftop.

The tiles were covered with a thatching of dead people.

"Daemon no, please!" Tammy begged as her heightened mind realized what was happening. Her hands flew up and clawed at his as he held her head in his hand.

Her voice was choked off when he wedged his left hand into the space between her jaw and her collar bone, the width of his hand stretched the length of her neck fully.

"Forgive me," he cried between his teeth and sharply pulled with his left and twisted with his right.

There was a tearing sound and a pop as her head came away in his hands and before he could stop himself, before he could reconsider his actions he dropped the body, drew back his arm and with a small step hurled her head as far as he could in the direction of the ocean's horizon.

Below Tuck and Mason had seen The Coat take Tammy but had been unable to follow such speed.
The ferals had abandoned their attack the moment Tammy had been decapitated and aside from the odd scuffles they slunk back to their sewers. Tuck went to stop them but Mason took his arm, "Leave them Tuck,"
The Freelander snatched back his arm and said, "So these people are all expendable to you too are they?"
Mason put his hand down, amazed at how angry the Freelander still was, "Go after them if you want to then," he knelt beside Rayne who was still curled into a foetal position with her hands covering her head, "I really don't care anymore Tuck."
"She's going to learn the truth very soon Lynel," the Freelander promised but when Mason looked up the man was gone.
Rayne's eyes were still squeezed shut and with all the commotion Mason could only guess at how bewildered she must have been but as he touched her shoulder she opened her eyes, looked up and said, "Did he come?"
In answer The Coat landed nearby and walked over to them.
"What happened to you?" Rayne asked, pushing herself up into a sitting position.
The Coat looked down at the smouldering rags he was dressed in and gave an uncharacteristic shrug, "It's been a night of it. Are you alright?"
She touched her scalp with her fingertips wincing, "Pretty much yes. What happened?"
The Coat looked out at the horizon but was silent.
Rayne looked away from the giant to Mason, who said, "I do believe that Shaka has been destroyed and that Tammy Jenkins is no longer a threat is that right Coat?"
"His name is Daemon," Rayne corrected getting to her feet, "Thank you."
Daemon gave a curt nod.
A *whup-whup* sound of a chopper reached them and they looked up at the approaching lights.
"Right on time," Mason said sarcastically, he looked at Daemon, "I will look after Rayne and sort this mess out. Thank you for your help."

The giant lifted his chin and looked Mason down the length of his nose, there was some sort of communicate between them that Rayne didn't understand but Mason added, "Later."

"Rayne," the giant said, " I am sorry you have been involved in all of this."

The chopper, a sleek black thing hovered above the property for a while, looking for a suitable place to land in the carnage before choosing to descend in the garden. Mason took Rayne by the arms and started guiding her to the vehicle. A fatigue unlike anything she'd ever felt overcame her. A blanket was slung across her shoulders and clipped in front of her with a small silver broach. She didn't resist as she was sat inside the helicopter and Mason climbed in after her, closing the door and buckling up her seatbelt.

"Mason," Rayne said, "Are you coming with me?"

"No," he said touching her cheek, "I am going to make sure that this place is cleaned up. A lot has to be organized; these people have to be properly taken care of, their families notified and the police distracted I'm not going to let the media get their talons into this."

"I don't care about that," Rayne said, "I want you to come with me."

He looked pained but decided, "You're going to be taken to the hospital and I will meet you there… if I'm in the chopper I'll just get in the way."

She nodded, her face crinkling with fresh tears, he opened the door and started to climb out when she took hold of his arm, she had to shout over the beating blades, "Carol is downstairs… "

He looked at her for a moment and worked out what she meant; he nodded and mouthed the words, "I'll handle it."

29.

The Wallace Grief was Mason's private yacht, a vast vessel that was, in typical fashion, the height of luxury and filled with every toy you could possibly think of. It boasted multiple game rooms, a swimming pool, gym, sauna, cinema an in house restaurant, a bowling alley and a transparent bottom. Designed with the latest Axe Bow technology it didn't suffer from the same G-Forces when in rough seas as other vessels, cutting through the waves instead of riding over them and with the stabilizers even in the worst weather it remained as level as dry land.
  How he hated the bloody thing.
Upon the deck with the salty air brushing his fringe Mason stood facing the city with a very heavy drink in his hand, taking stock. What a night.
  Currently Rayne would be thirty seven thousand feet in the air on Mason's personal jet flying over the Atlantic to Canada for an impromptu holiday. He had tried to explain it over the phone to her but the conversation had not gone well and she had accused him of kidnapping, this, he supposed, could be true but it was genuinely for her own good. When Rayne tried to help she tended to get in the way and he wanted and needed her safely stored somewhere so that he could sort out this mess with The Suburbs.
  A subtle change in the air alerted him that he was no longer alone.
"This city is a beautiful animal," he said, "I've never found another place quite like it. There is something about it that's unique."
The Coat lingered in the shadows near the yacht's second story overhang, "I thought you would have fled."
Mason grunted as if the immortal giant was being foolish, "No, the world is round and there are not so many places a man can hide from you," he sipped the drink, "Also there is a great deal that has to be done."
The Coat walked to the railing beside Mason and uncharacteristically took in the view of the city, "I want to know how you are planning to *handle* this situation?" he said, "I suspect you have a plan."
  "I'm impressed that you are even interested in the media," Mason said, "It appears that The Suburbs private water supply has been set upon

by Australian terrorists who have poisoned it with a particularly horrible flesh eating virus. A mutant strain of Ebola I understand. Naturally the area has been quarantined."

"And what about the bodies?"

Mason raised his eyebrows, "One plan at a time," he sighed with resignation, "But, I can mislead the media for a long time but a lot of very wealthy, very famous people have died tonight. A lot of questions are going to be asked and we won't be able to supply the answers. Well not the answers we want to give them."

"Not part of your plan then?"

"A small divergence," Mason consented, "But all the important people are safe."

The Coat made that non-committal sound of his.

"My pleasure," the trillionaire said, "Now, we have a long journey ahead of us so I'd like to get started."

"Journey?"

"Yes," Mason said with a coy smile, "I am taking you to Antarctica my friend to meet your people. Also I've taken the liberty of bringing something onto the ship that I think you'll want to see, so, if you would kindly follow me."

The trillionaire's yacht was so spacious that even the giant could move through it with ease and he followed the man through its maze like corridors.

"You haven't actually asked how Rayne is," Mason commented.

"If she was not well I do not think you would be so comfortable to have your back to me," The Coat answered.

"Or my front for that matter," Mason said, "She is well. In a plane, it's going to take a lot of work to get her through this but her safety is priority isn't it?"

"Yes."

"I assume that you still have the sword,"

"It is safe," The Coat said, adding, "And elsewhere."

"And have you seen our friend Tuck Bradley at all?"

"No," The Coat replied.

Through a pair of clear glass doors Mason led the giant into the heated swimming pool area where the air was muggy and smelt of chlorine. At the far side there was a clear glass doorway which Mason led him through into a room the size of a tennis court, with thick black padding across the walls, ceiling and the floor. In the center was a black sarcophagus.

Mason said nothing and immediately went and opened the box, inside the body was as it had always been save for the pipes and tubing that had been removed. Instead the neck finished in a perfectly polished stub.

The Coat walked to the sarcophagus and pushed back his hood.

"I can hear his heart beat," he said.

"He lives," Mason said, "The body and the head just wait each other."

The giant moved so quickly Mason was completely caught off guard and lifted up by his throat and slammed hard into the wall, his feet dangling far off the ground.

"Where is it then?" the giant snarled the intense rage causing the air to ripple around him.

Mason didn't answer, could not, not with the giant's hand wrapped around his neck, the pressure was eased slightly, enough for Mason to wheeze, "I don't have it,"

He flung Mason over the sarcophagus and the trillionaire hit the padded wall on the other side, "I never have had it," he croaked, massaging his throat, "Tuck took the head when he stole the sword."

The tiniest evidence of surprised flickered across the giant's face, "Tuck has the head?"

Mason got up, walked to where his glass lay and picked it up but the drink had already soaked into the sound proofing, he didn't put it onto the sarcophagus out of respect for the body and held the empty glass awkwardly as if not quite knowing what to do with it, "He took it with him ten years ago. Why do you think my people were looking for him?"

The Coat blinked and appeared unsure, "I had an impression from him... I did not suspect..."

"I think he took it as insurance," Mason explained, "I think it was just misguided. He didn't mention it for obvious reasons. We will get it back eventually, I promise."

"And in the meantime you just drank his blood?"

"Yes Daemon," Mason said, as if the giant was missing a very important point, "I drank this body's blood."

The Coat went to the body and put a hand to it, as he touched it a flash of electricity buzzed between them.

"Answers would be good Mason," The Coat said, withdrawing his hand.

"That is why we're going to Antarctica," Mason said pleasantly, "I'll show you to the room I've had prepared for you and we'll be on our way."

"I have to know, is all of this part of your plan?" The Coat asked, lingering around the sarcophagus, "Are you the hero or the villain in all this?"

Mason put his hands in his pockets and leaned against the glass doorway, "I'm not sure Daemon, I think we will probably be around long enough to be both," he gestured with a nod of his head for the giant to follow him, as they departed he asked, "Oh before I forget do you like olives?"

Printed in Great Britain
by Amazon